P₁

a

CE𝖭

PALLAS
and the
CENTAUR

A novel set in Italy
in the time of
Lorenzo de' Medici
1478-1480

LINDA PROUD

Linda Proud

GODSTOW PRESS

First published 2004 by
The Godstow Press
60 Godstow Road, Oxford OX2 8NY
Tel 01865-556215
www.godstowpress.co.uk

ISBN 0-9547367-0-2

Set in Centaur and typeset by Alacrity, Banwell Castle, Weston-super-Mare
Cover design by Joanna Turner

Produced in Great Britain by Bookchase (UK) Ltd

We would like to thank the many subscribers
who have made this publication possible

Dedicated to the memory and inspiration of
Sheila Rosenberg.

Map of Italy in the 15th Century

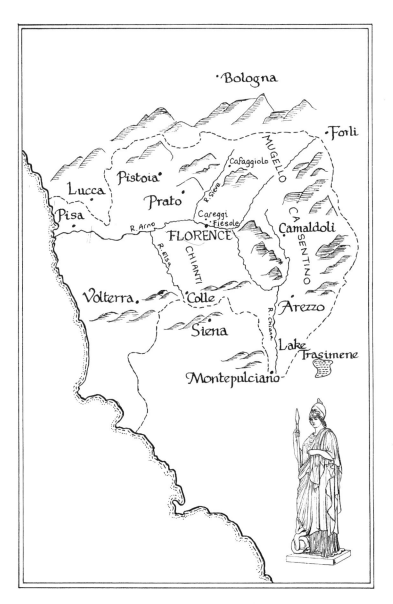

Map of Tuscany in the 15th Century

CONTENTS

We have made thee neither of heaven nor of earth, neither mortal nor immortal, so that with freedom of choice and with honour, as though the maker and moulder of thyself, thou mayest fashion thyself in whatever shape thou shalt prefer.

PICO DELLA MIRANDOLA

PREFACE

EVERY LIFE has a meaning but not all lives are remembered by history. Some merit mention in a book; some merit a whole book to themselves; while most are merely registered in annals, a mere signature, the lives of women are registered not at all. Of all my friends in this life, among the dearest have been a brother and sister, both childless; he the famous Poliziano, she the unknown Poliziana. Both are dead, but while he is honoured (albeit insufficiently) by an epitaph in stone, no one can show me even the grave of Maria.

I brought with me to England a chest of papers, books and other things, some of which lie below a false base since my soul has not the strength to confront them. When I replaced Poliziano's Account of the Pazzi Conspiracy, which served me in my book about that event, I looked for my journal, begun in 1482 and titled presumptuously with the words 'A Record of my Times', to aid me with my continued story, since Erasmus has written from Paris demanding it, eager to know what I can tell him about Savonarola. But beneath it I discovered Maria's notebook, rambling, fragmentary, written only for herself and not for posterity. Reading it evoked vivid memories, such vivid memories, of a time of war. This is not history as such – how can it be, when it deals with women? – and yet it needs to be written, as a memoir only, perhaps, and not for publication.

The great Hermes said, 'As above, so below.' Similarly, as without, so within. Women live enclosed lives, and yet the battle that took place between Poliziano and Lorenzo's wife was the microcosm of the battle Lorenzo was fighting against the Pope. It was not a trivial, domestic tiff. It was potent, and the energies unleashed within the house were not confined therein, or so Maria believed.

The truth of Poliziano's life is now under attack by Slander and Rumour. His enemies recast the truth; like worms that bore through books, they change a word here, destroy a sentence there, until a completely new story is written. He, the Chiron of our age, a centaur-teacher of mankind, has been turned into a hybrid monster. Therefore I call upon Minerva to aid me in my retelling, my song of truth.

TOMMASO DE' MAFFEI
Oxford, 1502

The First Book

MONTEPULCIANO

1

From the notebook of Maria Ambrogini,
called 'Poliziana'

Sexagesima Sunday

I TRY SO HARD *to love you, Lord God, and I fail. The fault is your*
own, for being invisible. It would be easier to love smoke – at least I
can see it and smell it if not touch it. It would be easier to love an idea
or dream, because I can think it. But if you cannot be seen, heard, touched,
smelt or tasted, how am I to love you?

This evening the sky over the Val di Chiana was astonishing: milky grey
here, blue there, the clouds plum and apricot and strewn about like tattered
banners. Over in the east, where that mysterious line of water catches the
dying sun, it was orange and glowing. As the sun sank down behind our
high, dark city, every tower in the valley before me, every castle, farmstead
and hermitage capping one of the little hillocks shone like rich gold. Oh, how
I wanted to be out there, where so many bells were tolling compline in the
still air. Utter beauty!

I told Suor Agosta what I had seen, about the eagles flying in a heaven
as coloured as Joseph's coat, but she looked down on me with great disap-
proval from her high chair at her writing desk. 'These are worldly joys, child!
The world is full of misery, however beautiful it seems. The sky is only a
shadow of God's radiance. Our true heaven is beyond the sky and brighter
than anything you can imagine. Love God and abhor the world.'

Regretting saying anything – but oh, how can I keep such things to myself
forever? – I bent my head over my pharmacy labels.

'Child?'

'Yes, Suor Agosta?'

'How is it you saw the valley?'

3

'I was feeding the doves as is my duty, Suora.'

'The dovecote is not so high!'

It is true, but from the ladder to the elevated cote I can clamber up on to the granary roof which slopes over the convent wall in such a shallow line as to be near enough flat; flat enough to stand on. 'If I stand on tip-toe on the top rung, Suora,' I lied, 'I can just see over the granary roof.' And I hung my head guiltily.

'It is your duty to feed the doves, not to stand staring out to space, you idle girl! To love God properly you must do your duty.'

✢

It is not that I think you do not exist. Of course you exist and are everywhere. But I doubt that you love me. Just as the sun shines on everyone, saint and sinner alike, so your love, if you have it, is indifferent. Well then, so must mine be. That is only fair, is it not? And until you show yourself to me, even as a dove or in a burning bush, it will remain so.

At Easter my long probation shall come to an end and I shall take my vows as a novice; then, next year, when I am sixteen, I shall become a Bride of Christ. A vain and shallow wife of an invisible God, a God who, like a sultan, locks away so many wives for his own pleasure, whatever that might be! To my mind a life spent amongst women is no life at all. I may as well be dead. Who would want to end up like Madre Generale, bewhiskered, toothless and full of hatred of anything young?

Dear Lord God, you have enough wives. Wherever you are, free me from this place and this destiny, this prison for unwanted daughters.

✢

Carne-vale

A new postulant arrived while we were feasting in the refectory, eating pigeon, hare and cheese, as well as the usual bread and minestra. Some of the nuns were eating much more than was good for them, as if to store up for the whole of Lent, and it is sure to be a night of much noise and disturbance in the dormitory as they come and go to the latrines, knocking against beds in the dark, farting and groaning. The new girl, a very dark, skinny little thing, is called Lauretta. Like me she is an orphan though two years younger,

4

but she has spent those years on the Outside– and she has been married, wife to a mortal man! – and therefore seems older than me by far. I was sent to show her to our dormitory. Leaving my supper to the thieving fingers of my neighbours, I was glad to have the opportunity to talk to the frightened girl alone.

'Where do you come from?' I asked her as soon as we reached the silent cloisters.

'Cagnano.'

'So do I! What is it like? I was only five when I was sent here.'

'Five? Why?'

'I do not know. I presume my parents died. Someone must have paid for me. What is Cagnano like?'

'But it is only twenty paces away!'

'And beyond our walls. Tell me quick, before anyone comes, for here we must have God's words on our lips all the time.'

'Cagnano is horrible.'

This told me nothing that I might see, touch or imagine. 'In what way? What does it look like?'

She shrugged. 'Like anywhere else, only it is steep and in the shadow of the city much of the day. There are two cities, you know.'

'Where?'

'Here! One above the other. Cagnano is in the lower part and catches all the slops and waste of the upper city. It's just behind the lower wall and stinks like a drain.'

I was shocked. I came from a good home, I am certain of it.

'What is your family name?' Lauretta asked.

'Ambrogini.'

'Oh!' She stepped back as if I were poisonous.

As we neared the dormitory, I could hear someone following us – the Madre Generale herself to judge by the clipping tread she has, like a bird of prey hopping round a carcass.

'Your family name?' I whispered urgently.

Lauretta was staring at me with frightened eyes.

'Yours?' I insisted.

'Del Mazza,' she whispered. She flinched as she said it, as if expecting

me to strike her, but I was only raising my arm to the latch of the dormitory door. Before we could enter, old beaky was upon us.

'Lauretta del Mazza, daughter of that murderous family of villains, come here.'

Lauretta went to meet her in the shadows of the cloister, lit only by the wax torches held by myself and the Madre Generale.

'On your knees, girl. Renounce the past and all will be well. Your only father now is God.'

'Thanks be to God!' Lauretta sank to her knees as if with great relief.

Here, then, is another of them, someone to whom being in a convent is a liberation and a source of joy. Once again, as ever, my hope for a friend, someone I can talk to, who will understand and share my soul's longings, is dashed.

✟

Suor Agosta reads bad books. Not all the books in the library are Holy Scripture or the missals, psalters and antiphonaries which she copies in large letters, more often to be sold than used, since we already have our own. And sometimes she paints beautiful capital letters or pictures. But when she rests from her work, she turns surreptitiously to smaller books with more delicate script and these she reads as pricked up as a hare to the sound of anyone coming. Sometimes when I cannot sleep I go to the library and read them myself. Suor Agosta has taught me to read and write in Latin and thus it is easy enough to understand Ovid's Metamorphoses. These tales of gods and their lusts are fun! I especially like the one about Daphne who, to escape the pursuit of the god Apollo, turned herself into a laurel tree. We have laurel trees in the triangle of garden behind the dormitory cloister with their leaves dark and shiny all year round, and flavoursome in the pot. But if I were being chased by a god, I would not run away! It is hard enough to see gods, without running away when you do.

Zeus took the form of a swan to ravish Leda. Imagine!

And he came upon poor naked Danae as a shower of gold!

But no, Our Lord God is a gentle god and does not ravish his brides. They do say that some feel ravished, like the one called Maddelena who was an anchorite on this patch of earth before our convent was built.

6

They say it can happen, that you be taken by ecstasy. Perhaps I shall run away.

These stories of Ovid give me awful dreams and I wake up feeling full of shame. I would like to confess to Suor Agosta that I share her enthusiasm for the ancient pagan poets but I dare not. Not yet. One day I shall. For now I fear she will deny it and report me to Madre Generale.

The story I like most is that of Orpheus, the singer who loved his wife so much that, when she died, he went to hell to beg Pluto to have her back. Pluto, as charmed by the music of Orpheus as all the wild animals of the wood, agreed, but on condition that Orpheus must regain the upper world without looking back. I like the idea of a man so musical that all the wild beasts approach him without fear. It was the same with the blessed St Francis. I tried singing to one of the rats in the granary but it ran away. I lack holiness. Even the rats know that.

✠

Lauretta is also going to be made a novice at Easter. Though she is younger and will only have been here a matter of weeks, her progress is speeded because she is a 'voluntary'. This means more, I think, than that she chose to come here; it means that she wants to be here. Suor Agosta told me that Lauretta has been purified by suffering and that her heart is open to God's good grace. She left it unsaid that mine is not. I try, dear Lord, I try and try, but love is not something you achieve by effort. Is it?

I think Lauretta has been advised not to associate with me, to keep company only with the devout, and so she walks past me as if I do not exist. But I dog her steps, for I am determined to find out as much as she can tell me about the Outside and about my family since she obviously knows them.

This evening as I was treading on her heels in the cloister she turned on me. 'What do you want? Leave me alone!' She kept her eyes cast down to the stone-flagged floor. 'It wasn't my fault! I had nothing to do with it!'

'To do with what?'

'Nothing!'

'I just want to talk to you.' I took hold of her sleeve and placed it to my nose. It smelt of the musty camphor of the chest of robes, but there was another scent there, more subtle. 'You smell of the Outside.'

'Oh, just like your brother – all poetic and fanciful.'

'What brother?' I grasped her now as a beggar does a rich man. 'Tell me! I have a brother in Cagnano? Twenty paces away? Is he older than me or younger? Does he look like me?'

She was gazing at me now, searching me, trying to establish if I were truly so ignorant or only pretending to be. 'You have two brothers and two sisters. Yes, you look like them. But your poet brother – I've never seen him. He's famous and lives in Florence and has taken the name of our city as his own.'

I tried to speak but could not. Lest Lauretta see me cry, I ran away to the library. Suor Agosta found me making the ink on my labels for acqua vitae swim in a puddle of tears and she spoke sternly to me, saying, 'Our Lord did not cry on the cross!'

✝

Second week of Lent

I have the story now. I had to bend Lauretta's fingers back to get it, but she told me in the end. My eldest brother is called Angelo. He left Montepulciano for Florence not long after I was born and now he is a famous poet living in the household of Lorenzo de' Medici, who even I have heard of. My other brother, Derio, is a merchant and lives in the family house with his wife Cammilla and two baby sons. My sister Lucrezia is married, as is my younger sister Saracina, though she be but fourteen.

'Was my father a great man?'

'He was the chief magistrate and Gonfaloniere of the city.'

'But he lived in dirty, dank Cagnano?'

'Please! Leave go of me! That was his contrada. But he lived in one of the tall houses on the border.'

I knew it! I let her go and left her grimacing over her sore fingers while I ran off to feed the doves, skipping all the way, at least until Suor Cecilia saw me and, with a nod of remonstrance from her gentle head, reminded me of decorum.

'I am the daughter of Ser Benedetto Ambrogini,' I told the doves, 'and the sister of Angelo of Montepulciano. There! I told you I was someone and not just anyone. After Lent they shall make me a novice. In a year's

time I shall take my vows and become indistinguishable from anyone else within these walls, but I shall always know now, in my heart, that I am the daughter of a great man. But why did he send me here, why? Do you think perhaps I was his favourite, that he offered me up as a living sacrifice, as Abraham did with Isaac? I think that must be so. I was his little darling, as you are mine.' Thus I speak to the doves, somehow driven to idiocy in the presence of domestic animals and birds. It is something about their muteness and their loving trust. They say it is the same with babies but I would not know. I have only seen baby Jesus, and him a wall painting. But I coo to the doves and they to me as I stroke their soft feathers.

The roof of the granary is runnelled with terracotta pantiles. I tread between their rows carefully to find a good place to stand. There are great cities in the world such as Siena, Florence and Rome, but all I know is that Rome is south and the other two are north, but how far I know not except that, as I cannot see them, they are not close. Here I may watch the eagles wheeling and clouds pass by in stately procession. Sometimes the Val di Chiana is full of mist and then the little hills seem to float like islands. Sometimes the Chiana is flooded greatly, at which times I can see it; other times I cannot.

If I turn towards the city above us, I can see what I now know to be its upper part circled by a tall forbidding wall of stone. The lower part and Cagnano is obscured by the convent wall. Twenty paces away lives Derio and his wife Camilla and their two small sons. They could tell me every-thing I want to know, but how may I reach them?

✣

Third week of Lent
Spring is coming. From the granary roof I can see a trembling greeness coming upon the bare trees and smell a sweet fragrance of grass and new herbs in the air, but in the convent we celebrate this blessed season with a forty day fast and my stomach is grumbling all the time. Every waking minute I think of food. Oh, it is not total starvation. We have a bowl of plain pasta every day, but it does not stop me dreaming of cheese and ripe figs. Hurry, Easter! The sense of frustration is rising in me like sap and I am so greening with it that it must be obvious to the others. I am a cricket waiting to leap, a bulb

9

straining to flower, a cow ready to calve, a sun about to rise. I am all pent-up potential contained by walls.

Suor Agosta told me a story she said had been told to her, but I know she found it in one of her illicit books. It is of the hero Odysseus trapped in the cave of a terrible cyclops, a giant with but one eye. The cyclops keeps his sheep in the cave and Odysseus and his men escape by hanging below the sheep, holding on by gripping their fleeces. What a wonderful idea! Alas, we have no sheep, only a couple of donkeys with short, rough hides. She also told me the story of the Trojan horse, but that was a clever way of getting into a stronghold, not out of one.

✠

Lauretta continues to avoid me, slipping away adroitly whenever I approach. She has befriended Suor Cecilia and follows her everywhere, adopting all her gestures and stances. Lauretta desires to be holy, but she has a secret. It sits on her soul like a toad and I can see its shadow. There is to be a communal confession before the Reconciliation of Penitents and the Paschal Vigil and I hope to hear what it is she conceals.

✠

Madre Generale asked Lauretta what name she shall adopt when she takes her vows in a year's time. Avoiding my gaze, she said, 'Suor Benedicta.' Madre Generale was pleased and told me that 'Benedicta' means good speech, as if I could not work that out for myself. She then asked me what name I will choose. I told her 'Eurydice'.

'Stupid child! You have ten days left to grow up, or else suffer another year of probation.'

Ten days, then, to make a decision, whether to embrace the invisible God or escape this place.

✠

One person who will not be speaking the truth at the Confession is Suor Emilia, that rosy dumpling of a woman who creeps out at night to meet Martellino the stableman in the granary. Sometimes when I am on the roof watching the moon cross the sky, and gazing at the hills bathed in her light,

I can hear them in unholy congress, whoofing like a pair of bellows, groaning and smacking like the pedals of the organ. By the sound of it there is little pleasure in lying with a man, but Suor Emilia is as greedy for it as I am for ripe figs.

✝

I have a new longing. I long to be with my brother Angelo and the desire is gnawing in me to run across the hills with him, shouting and hollering, playing Crusader and Saracen. I would be the Saracen. I would not mind. But I would shoot him before he kills me and see him roll about groaning, clutching the arrow that has gone clean through his chain mail and out the other side. 'Die, you pale-faced infidel!' I would cry, but it would be my last words before Derio, Sir Angelo's dashing squire, creeps up behind me and takes off my head with one slash of his sword. My rolling head would cry out the name of the Prophet and then fall quiet. All would be quiet. And then we would jump up laughing to chase each other over the meadows and play it all over again.

Why, God, did you deny me my childhood? For what crime was I incarcerated at the age of five and denied the green grass to roll in, the horses to ride, the great views unimpeded by walls? Why did my parents have to die, and what killed them? Plague! It must have been a terrible fever that took my brave and noble father and his dear wife. Or a foul contagion of the kind that comes up from the marshes and makes its victims delirious and sweat so much that they end up dessicated like dried fish. That must have been why they sent Angelo and me away. They wanted to save us. We were their favourites.

✝

Sheer Thursday and Pedilavium
Madre Generale washed the feet of the nuns while I held the bowl for her. It is a great thing she does. All those feet! Some long and slender, some knobbly and old, broken yellow toenails and hard skin. Madonna! I could not do it. Suor Agosta read from the Gospel of St John the Evangelist and I tried to picture what it would be like to have Jesus wash your feet. I think I would want to wash mine first, before he came to me with his basin and

11

towel. But he pounced upon those poor disciples and they had to reveal their feet just as they were!

Afterwards Madre Generale sat in her chair in the Chapel and told us the meaning of the event. 'When Simon Peter asked Him, why only my feet, Lord? Why not wash the rest of me? Jesus explained that the rest of him was already clean. The feet are the place of the sins we cannot cleanse away by ourselves.'

My guilty toes wriggled in my sandals.

'Therefore he commanded the disciples to do as He had done, and wash each other's feet, which is why in the convent we love the Lord by serving each other. But for the purification of the soul, the Lord has given us Confession. Suor Emilia, come forward.'

'Holy Mother Mary, have mercy on me.'

'To what do you confess?'

'I have sometimes risen during the night to steal food, Madre, for I am very hungry.'

'How much and how often?'

'About two eggs a week, and then some bread.'

And… And… I prompted her silently, but she was content to add lying to her hoard of sins.

'Ten Hail Marys,' said the Madre Generale, 'and restrain your appetite in future. Our Lord spent forty days in the wilderness with nothing to eat. You can survive on what you are given.'

'I thank you Mother. Glory be to God.'

'Maria, come forward.'

'Holy Mother Mary, have mercy on me.'

'To what do you confess?'

'I… I… I do not love God. Not enough.'

The thorn-faced Madre Generale stared at me in contempt. 'Well, until you do, He cannot love you either. Your duties in needlework will be doubled and your pasta halved until your heart surrenders. Now, what about your sins?'

'I hurt Lauretta's fingers and I am sorry.' I should have confessed to having spied on Suor Emilia and Suor Agosta, but it did not seem right. Besides, I have another use for this knowledge. I was given only two Hail

Marys for the finger bending. The needlework punishment hurts far more.

'I thank you, Madre. Glory be to God.'

'Lauretta, come forward.'

Lauretta looked at me queerly as we passed in the nave.

'To what do you confess?'

Lauretta sank gracefully to her knees in a Cecilia fashion. Her head hung low. She was silent.

'Well, child?'

She mumbled something.

'Lauretta, speak up. Tell God what he already knows, in a clear voice.'

'The sins of my fathers, Madre, weigh heavy on me. I am stained by their guilt.'

'Speak out, child.'

'I am of the Del Mazza family, born in exile but brought back here when the period of banishment was ended.'

There was a whispering in the Chapel and several of the nuns shuddered at the sound of Lauretta's family name.

'She is the daughter of the blacksmith at the Cagnano gate,' Madre Generale told us. 'That villain who with his kin kept the contrada in terror for many years. And what did they do when they returned?'

Lauretta mumbled again.

'Speak up! Clear your conscience and your soul.'

'Maria's father, Ser Benedetto Ambrogini…'

So that was his name! Bene-detto-o. Good speech – the same as Benedicta. If it was his name, it should be my chosen name, not hers!

'Ser Benedetto was the chief magistrate, and it was he who had sent my father and his brother into exile for brawling. When they came back, they ambushed and murdered him.'

Her words suddenly disappeared echoing down a tunnel. Everything went dark – black, then red, then green. I was hot as in a sudden fever and about to vomit. I stood up and fell over. I never did hear her penance. All I remember was Madre Generale saying, 'Leave the past outside the gate, child, and it will trouble you no more.'

✣

13

Tenebrae

I went early to the Chapel to prepare it for the Mass. There I found Lauretta alone, saying the rosary. I sat beside her in silence. Her breath quickened.

'Confess it to me and your guilt will be removed,' I told her.

Her head went lower over her rosary.

'Lauretta?'

Her voice faltered in her repetitions.

'Let me wash your feet free of this sin you cannot cleanse yourself.'

She gazed up at me with eyes haunted by her ancestors.

'Lauretta,' I said softly. 'Please trust me.'

Abandoning her prayers and now fiddling nervously with the beads, she began to tell me the story of the Ambrogini and the Del Mazza.

'My family were blacksmiths, yours were drapers, at least, they had their origins in haberdashery. So we come from the same low stock. But your grandfather did well for himself, and he had his sons educated in the law. Your father excelled in his studies and eventually became chief magistrate and Gonfaloniere, leading city processions carrying the banner of Montepulciano. I think my father hated him just for that, that he was a lawyer and not a draper, even though your father remained loyal to Cagnano, his family contrada.'

'What is a contrada?'

'It is a district of the city – there are eight of them. It is where you are born, where you live and where you die. It has always been so. Ser Benedetto moved into a tall fine house at the highest part where four ways meet, one of them leading to the upper city. He was a great man, but it was my family that ruled the contrada. No one did anything without my father's say so. He organised all the games and sports and festivals of the contrada, the horse races, the barrel-pushing contests, and some would say he arranged who was going to win them, too. The men of my family are brutes, always drunk and beating each other up. My father hated yours, not only because of something that happened in the past, I don't know what, but because your father believed in goodness. Ser Benedetto was strict with his own family, allowing no one to carry arms because he wanted to set an example to the rest of the city. My father and uncles used to jeer at him for it and call him a coward. But it takes a brave man to go unarmed, not a coward. When he

14

sat in court, he always made wise decisions and just ones. Everyone deserved what they got from him, not least my father. After stabbing my uncle in a fight, my father was called before the magistrates and banished for a year. A year's exile is not so hard to bear, especially when you have relatives in the place of banishment. For us it was Livorno. That is where I was born.'

'What brought you to the convent?'

'I was married to a man as brutish as my father. When he died, just a few weeks later, God forgive me, I rejoiced. I had a dowry, a small one, but I could use it to buy a place here, and I would rather be here than anywhere in the world.'

I was astonished. 'Why?'

'Because there is goodness here. Your father was exceptional. You don't find goodness in the world very easily.'

'And have you found it here?'

'Yes, in Suor Cecilia. And in others. Many of them practise virtue.'

'You should not have to practise virtue. It should flow out of you naturally as from a fountain.'

'There. The daughter of Ser Benedetto speaks truly.'

'Well it does not flow out of me, not virtue! I am a wicked, wicked girl who should have been a boy. That is what they tell me.'

'Don't believe all you are told.'

I asked her to tell me the story of my father's murder, promising not to faint or be sick, but she did not know much.

'Girls in the world have no more freedom than girls in the convent. We are kept a casa all our lives, except for going to church and some special occasions. All I know is that my father broke the terms of his banishment and came back and, at some point, succeeded in his vendetta against the Gonfaloniere. That's all.'

'Was your father tried and hung?'

'No, he escaped. It was two years before he dared to come back and, when he did, the Ambrogini were waiting for him.'

'Angelo? My brother?'

'No, a cousin called Maso and his brother Bastiano. They did the deed. Angelo was still a boy and they did it for him, giving my father like for like. An eye for an eye, a tooth for a tooth.'

'What did they do?' I whispered.

'Sawed his head off while he was still conscious. Good riddance.'

Her words were fading again. A head was rolling down the hill, and the black and the red and the green were flashing.

'Maria, breathe deeply. Put your head between your knees and breathe deeply.'

In real life, in real death, the slain do not jump up to chase each other laughing.

✝

At the end of the Mass, Suor Cecilia played the portable organ while we sang the Miserere. With her sweet angel face she looked as pretty as a wall painting. Lauretta could not take her eyes off her, but as we sang the words of the psalm, she slipped her hand into mine, as if begging my forgiveness for the sins of the past.

Have mercy upon me, O God, according to thy loving kindness; according unto the multitude of thy tender mercies blot out my transgressions.

One by one the candles were snuffed out and the shadows deepened, the darkness drawing ever closer.

Wash me thoroughly from mine iniquity; and cleanse me from my sin.

Suor Agnese moved silently with the snuffer, and little puffs of smoke and the smell of tallow came forth from her actions.

We sang a line each. Mine was: Behold, thou desirest truth in the inward parts: and in the hidden part thou shalt make me to know wisdom.

Suor Emilia sang, Behold, I was shapen in iniquity; and in sin did my mother conceive me.

Since Madre Generale was directing this, it is clear she knows more than we tell her.

Lauretta: Deliver me from bloodguiltiness, O God, thou God of my salvation.

Together we sang, The sacrifices of God are a broken spirit: a broken and contrite heart; O God, thou wilt not despise.

When all the candles were out we stood in darkness and thus the Paschal Vigil began. Some nuns wept during the night, whether from exhaustion or contrition I could not tell. But I went into a world of trance, half dream, half waking, and saw my father nailed to a cross, and the head of John the Baptist rolling down a hill. San Giovanni Decollato, *I muttered to myself over and over,* San Giovanni Decollato aiuta mi.

☩

Easter Saturday
The trees are in leaf, the air soft and warm, the doves doing what doves do in the spring, fluttering, cooing, coupling. They make less fuss about it than Suor Emilia and Martellino.

Tomorrow I shall be admitted into the novitiate. From tomorrow onwards I am going to have to struggle to acquire virtue, or else be like those who have given up and indulge themselves in error with or without any torment of conscience. Worse, I am going to have to pretend to love God when I do not. Are You listening? Worst of all, I shall be condemned forever to this henhouse of clucking women.

Unless I have the courage to go.

My plan is simple, not clever. It involves no sheep or wooden horse. It has come naturally to a daughter of Cagnano.

2

The eve of Easter
'*SUOR AGOSTA? The books you read are the filth of the devil. How come you have not have the courage to confess your sins?*'

She looked at me in absolute shock.

'*You choose to read pagan poets rather than Holy Scripture because these stories of rape and seduction ignite your blood.*'

The twenty years of her seniority; the authority of being in charge of the library – it all vanished. She pleaded with me like a girl.

17

'It is not true, Maria!'

'Are you not always telling me to love God? But what is it that you love?'

'Literature! Poetry! Words and language! Beautiful language…' she put her face into her hands and wept.

'The most beautiful words are Holy Scripture.'

'Maria! What has come over you? You sound like Madre Generale. Are you about to take everything seriously? Will you jump from being a rebel to a bigot? You would not be the first. Maria, do not let faith become cruelty. That happens too often.'

I softened. 'Suora, I will keep your secret. You may trust me.'

Then I let her have the conditions of my loyalty.

✟

'Suor Emilia. I notice in your washing that you have shown no blood these past two months.'

'Maria!'

'Is it the stableman?'

'Maria!'

As with Suor Agosta, Suor Emilia's usual character dissolved like sugar in water. She began weeping and confessing all in one, sobbing and spluttering, begging God to forgive her and me to keep her secret.

'It will be plain to all soon enough.'

'No, there are ways. At the mineral baths. A douche. I will lose the child.'

'A bastard it might be, but better it lives than is murdered.'

'Please, Maria! What is it you want? I will do anything.'

✟

With the shears kept in the room where we cut cloth and bandages, Suor Agosta has cut off my hair, not to the crop of a nun, but to a man's length. I shall enter the world of men as a boy. My breasts are small and easily flattened with a bandage which she has tied round me. Suor Emilia brought me clothes of the eldest son of Martellino, and my accomplices have procured the ladders and ropes required to make a mundane escape by the light of the full Easter moon.

✟

18

Resurrection

City gateways have doors the same as convents! – only, bigger, deeper and guarded by soldiers. As I slipped through the shadows to the Cagnano gate, which is not twenty paces away but more like a hundred and all uphill, I saw them before they saw me and returned downhill, past Santa Maria delle Stelle – how sweet and peaceful it looks from the outside – to find shelter somewhere until morning. I could hear wolves howling, a sound that makes me feel secure in my dormitory bed, but now I felt real fear. The moonlight silvered the path in stripes and I stopped in terror as a badger walked across it, followed by another and another. Such strange creatures that I had only heard about before. Surely the sound of my thudding heart would alert all the wild animals – wild men, too – and they would come, not to listen to my song but to tear me apart and eat me. Snakes, scorpions, spiders, bandits – what dread things hide in the night, waiting only for me to sit down and rest? A new sound made me stop and listen, but I could hardly hear above the sound of my heart, but at last I knew it for water, water dripping into a pool, and I came to a natural fountain where spring water trickled from a hole in the rock below the city walls to fall into a stone trough made by man. The place was lovely in the moonlight and the beauty of it, with its new ferns and creeping ivy, displaced my fear. I may not love God, because I cannot see him, but I believe in him and, surrendering my fate to His Will, I settled down by the plashing water to spend the night.

I thought I should not sleep but I did, and in my sleep I had a dream, so vivid I took it to be real. In the moonlight appeared the figure of a man, tall and strong. I was not frightened of him and went gladly to meet him. He opened his arms to me.

'Father!' I felt such unfathomable love as could pour out of me like spring water.

'Noli me tangere!' *he replied urgently.* 'Do not touch me!'

Ser Benedetto – he of the good speech – to be seen but not touched. And soon he could not even be seen but had faded to nothing.

✠

I was awoken by a bee, early to work in the dawn. It poked into any flower it could find, humming and buzzing in the contentment of happy labour.

Above, the city bells began to ring for Prime and there came the sounds of the people rising: shutters thrown back with a bang, street criers announcing the first hour, someone barking out a greeting and a crude joke to a neighbour. I sat by the fountain looking out over the Valdichiana, watching a view of paradise emerge in the growing light. As far as my eye could see there were rolling hills, valleys, slopes given to newly planted vines, ploughed fields, terraces. I breathed in the dewy fragrances of herbs and flowers and I breathed out joy. I am free!

In the distance, on the road leading up to the city, travellers became visible; with streams joining them from the villages, it soon became a river of peasants and merchants, pilgrims and pedlars, all making their way up to the Cathedral high on the summit to celebrate Easter morning and the Resurrection of Our Lord. I hid deep within the curtain of ivy and more than once was nearly flushed out by a sniffing hound or a startled horse come to the trough, but I remained unseen until the crowd was so thick that I could slip out and join it without anyone noticing. I passed freely into the city through the Gozzano gate and left the stream at once to enter the main thoroughfare of Cagnano, the contrada marked by the sign of the black dog. Everywhere there were flags or emblems in wrought iron of the dog, stamping this place with its identity. The street was filled with shops mostly making and selling pottery, and I could see where the monastery pharmacy gets its pretty decorated jars from. Asking a man where I would find La Casa Ambrogini, I was directed to the top of the street.

I walked up the street almost hopping with excitement, drinking in all the noise and bustle of a world still in shadow while the sun was yet hidden by the great battlemented wall to the left. The world of men! Apart from the visiting priest, and the monks who come to collect our produce for the pharmacy – the curative water from the spring under the Chapel, the tinctures of dandelion and myrtle for the cure of the stone, the labels I have written out so laboriously – tarrasacum, mirtillo, cammomilo, calendula *– apart from those and the stableman and his sons, this rare and exotic creature called man is as fascinating to me as would be an elephant or a sphinx. I tried not to stare as I passed them, nor draw attention to myself, but my eye kept glancing up, entranced. Here he was, that mythical creature of my imagination, rarely as beautiful as Apollo,* *too often as hideous as a cyclops or a gorgon: an old man climbing a ricketty ladder to attach an awning to a hook; a bored and lazy youth sweeping the outside of a shop; a baker in a jaunty cap delivering loaves; a monk strolling jovially along, nodding to passers by and greeting them by saying, 'Christ is risen!'*

'Christ is risen!' he said to me, beaming. Distracted as I was, I forgot to respond, 'Alleluiah, He is risen indeed.' Instead I said, startled, 'Is he?' Then I hurried on lest I be accosted as an escaped slave or an infidel.

I walked through groups of men exchanging news, passed one peeing into the channel in the cobbled street (it is true – they do have a member that we do not!) and a few boys kicking a ball about, apparently lost in the delusion that they were the best players of the best contrada in the city; two soldiers dicing, a man without legs propelling himself about on a board on wheels. The more I saw the greater the mist of disappointment. These are not gods but humans, just like us. The smell that saturated the stableman's clothes, a smell of sweat beyond the stink of mule and donkey that had seemed so strange during the night, was now general. Even male urine smells different to ours, and its pungent odour makes Cagnano vivid and repugnant to the nose. And yet, they are still human and not the altogether different creatures I have supposed.

At last, at the top of the street and the meeting of the four ways, I came to my family home. It is not the palace of my fantasy but a large square house with an open loggia under the roof, a solid building that must last forever, unlike the family within it…

I knocked at the door and was admitted by a servant.

'I wish to see Ser Desiderio.'

The servant invited me in cordially and asked my name.

'I am kin.'

'I can see that,' the old man said with a smile. He led me not very far, into an office at the front of the house on the ground floor and there, at a desk and writing in a ledger, my brother Derio. Although I have only seen my reflection in a copper pot or basin of water, I know it is not a beautiful face but an interesting one; now I saw a truer reflection: large nose, thick eyebrows, and round black eyes. He gazed at me with a frown. 'Who are you? What do you want?'

'Ser Desiderio,' I said, glancing at the servant who was hovering curiously. 'I would speak to you in confidence.' While the servant shuffled off I glanced about and took in the office of a merchant of cheap and utilitarian fabrics and haberdashery. From rods between arches hung samples of ribbons, lace, girdles and purses.

Derio had climbed off his high stool and was coming towards me. 'Do I know you?'

'Ignore these clothes. I am your sister, Maria.'

'God Almighty!' He was shouting furiously before I could say anything more.

'Do you know what this means? They will extend your probation! Would you be a postulant forever? Cammilla!' he shouted out of a window looking on to the narrow well of the house. His wife's name bounced off the walls of three storeys. 'Cammilla!'

'Coming, husband!' came a cry in return.

Before long I could hear her running down steps and hurrying across to the office. 'What is it? What is it?'

'It is this!' he said, catching me by the scruff of my shirt as if I were a rabbit or kitten. 'It is my sister Maria. She has run away from the convent. Close the door. We don't want the servants to know.'

Cammilla, a buxom young woman with a face as cheerful as a pomegranate, did as she was told and then came to me in delight. 'How wonderful! How wonderful! Oh, Maria, you look just like your brother. Not your sisters. They take after your mother. But oh, look at you, dressed as a boy. Mother Mary! And half-starved. Well, it is a feast day and we shall fatten you up.'

'What am I to do?' said Derio, his anger dissipated by his wife's simple joy. 'Should we send to the monastery and report finding her?'

'Not on your life!' said Cammilla. 'Not until we have fed her and dressed her and heard her story. What is the matter with you? Just because you are the son of a magistrate doesn't mean you have to live by the letter, not in your own house. Live by the spirit, that's what I say. The poor girl has been beaten up and abused and we must give her haven. Maria, Maria, come with me upstairs. Oh, what joy! I never in my life expected to meet you. Come with me.' And she bustled me out and up the stairs to her own small and cosy

22

chamber where an infant boy played with wooden bricks and a baby was being rocked in a cradle by his nurse.

'Assunta, take the children to the loggia. They need air.'

The little boy left his bricks and came over to me with his arms wide open. I picked him up and he sat in my embrace staring at me sombrely. The nurse took him from me and he struggled. 'No! No!'

'I will see you again soon,' I promised my new friend, this nephew.

Cammilla was burrowing in one of her three clothes chests, pulling out gowns and chemises which were all voluminous. 'Sister,' I said. 'I shall stay as a boy for the time being. It would be best.'

'You are trying to hide your bruises. I understand. There is no need to feel shame, Maria. A cruel bunch of harridans, the nuns of Santa Maria delle Stelle. Well, let us see what Derio has.' And she began to burrow again in another chest.

'They did not beat me,' I told her.

She held up a shirt to me. 'Yes, I think this will be fine.'

'I said they did not beat me.'

'And you will be hungry. We are not supposed to eat until after Mass, but I'm sure some milk and bread would not be a sin in the eyes of the Lord.' She went to the window open on to the well. 'Beata!' she shouted. 'Bring milk and bread at once.'

As I changed, she saw my bandage and gasped. 'Child! What did they do to you?'

'Nothing!' I laughed. 'This is just to flatten me.' I put on my brother's clothes which, though large, did fit well enough, once laced up tight.

It was Derio himself who brought the food in, saying that the fewer people who saw me the better. He looked discomfited to see me dressed in his fine shirt and hose. 'This is not right, not right.'

'Brother, I shall leave you in an hour and not trouble your conscience any more, but first I want to know everything about our family and its past.' I was frustrated in this room, looking out as it did only to the interior of the house. It seemed Cammilla spent much of her time here, as penned up as in any convent.

'Everything in one hour? It is not possible. Besides, we must get ready for church, and I do not intend to dress with you in the room. Go to the

23

loggia and wait to be called.' It seemed as if my presence had placed a great burden on him and I went as directed, glad to find the air again.

The loggia goes round all four sides of the house. Here the family dine on a summer's evening but now it was a place for the hanging of washing. The little boy ran to me as I emerged and I picked him up again. 'What is your name?'

'Lat–tan-zio,' he said, pronouncing his name as if in love with it. While he stared at me as if at a great mystery, I gazed at the view. I could see the water on the eastern horizon clearly now and knew it to be a lake. Walking round until I had a view of the city, I looked down on an unrelieved pile of stone, huddles of houses and squalor. The forbidding walls, two circles of them, seemed to shore the city up. Convents, castles, cities: all prisons. But below in the street it was more colourful with families coming out in their best clothes and organising the people of Cagnano into a procession.

When Derio came up to join us, I asked him, 'What is that lake in the east?'

He looked amazed that I should not know. 'Why, that is Trasimene.'

Trasimene! 'Where Hannibal routed the Romans? Here? In our land?' Having read Livy on my own at night, I had had no teacher on hand to tell me, in an aside, 'By the way, all this happened just over there.' History, which has always been fused in my mind with mythology, suddenly leapt into focus and I was filled with wonder. My expression touched my brother and he softened.

'You did not know?'

I laughed. 'I have more holes in my knowledge than a colander!'

'At least your ignorance is surrounded by knowledge. For Cammilla it is all one big hole. She would not know Hannibal from one of his elephants.' He smiled for the first time. 'Father used to take us out on the hill and read the story to us from- from- '

'Livy.'

'Yes! I was not very good at my studies. Not like Angelo. He was the apple of Father's eye. I was always more interested in catching birds than learning my lessons, but Angelo drank up, absorbed everything Father could tell him. Those two used to walk along, Angelo running to keep up with his father's strides, both of them talking incessantly and oblivious to me, trailing along behind very bored indeed. It was better when our cousin Maso came to live with us. Orphaned he was, when he was fifteen, Angelo nine and me seven. But he was my best friend and taught me how to ride and shoot. He could not bear history either.'

'And I? How old was I?'

'One, I think.' He smiled. 'You and Saracina came later. Lucrezia was the eldest of us. You and Saracina – I only remember you as swaddling babes. Angelo used to hang you both up on meat-hooks in the kitchen where it was so warm that you would stop bawling and sleep. You used to hang there like a wasp's nest. Ha! That's all I remember of you.' He snapped out of his reverie as bells began to sound. Led by the great Cathedral bell, soon all the bells of all the churches and chapels were tolling, calling everyone together.

'The procession! We're late!'

He caught up his son, who wriggled squealing under his father's arm like a suckling pig, and led us downstairs, the nurse following on with the baby still at her breast.

Outside the house the street was now filled with the people of the contrada, more or less orderly and in line behind the statue of Our Lady which, borne aloft on a litter, was to lead us to the upper city and the Cathedral. Lattanzio was lifted up on to his father's shoulders, as were so many boys of his age, who, like the wobbling giants on stilts in the procession, had the best view of everything. I walked along with Derio, already eager to avoid Cammilla and her enthusiastic concern for others. Besides, I wanted more of our story from him. My attention, however, was divided, pulled this way by everything going on around me, and that way by what Derio had to say. The people, as we moved slowly along, chanted the Ave Verum.

The processional way was a serpentine route leading ever upwards, the longest and least direct way possible (many tunnels run up through the upper city wall, but we took none of them). We picked up or were picked up by other processions from other quarters, and the contrada flags of so many vivid colours and emblems – the griffon, the lion, the eagle – made streams of colour in a sea of people slowly advancing on the Cathedral while the bells continued to toll and reverberate.

'Our father was the Gonfaloniere so we always walked at the very head of the people in processions. You would have thought we were sons of a prince.

25

Look at me now! A merchant of woman's stuff, but one step up from a
pedlar.'

'But you have a fine house.'

'It is Angelo's.'

'Does he ever visit Montepulciano?'

'I have not seen him since he left. But he often writes and enquires after
our affairs and never charges me rent. If it were not for Cammilla's dowry,
I would be a poor man indeed, living in a house without furniture. If only
I had learnt my lessons…'

'Saracina is a strange name.'

'Angelo named her. She used to scream so much. "You infidel!" he used
to say. "You Saracen!", and the name stuck. We shall see her in church, no
doubt. We always see them on Easter Sunday.'

I felt clammy with excitement. 'Never any other time?'

'Not unless there is a baptism or burial. We each have our own churches.'

What did this mean? 'How is it you never meet at other times?'

He looked at me strangely. 'They married well and remain a casa except
for Sundays. Is this one of your holes, Maria?'

'Do you mean all women are enclosed?'

'Of a certain class. Poor women go about like prostitutes, but they have
to earn a living. The Cagnano women are always out on the street, or
hanging out of their windows gossiping. But Cammilla is a Contucci and
is forbidden such conduct. Nevertheless, the way she knows everyone's
business, I often suspect her of disobedience, but she must get the gossip from
the servants. Even that is a mystery to me. Do you know – perhaps you
could explain to me, how my wife, who never listens to anybody, knows
everyone's business down to the most intimate detail? How does the
information gain entry into her noddle?'

'Perhaps you are mistaken to think the information is correct.'

'Ha! You mean she makes it up? Excellent! Yes – that explains everything. Ah, you are Angelo's little sister indeed.'

'What happened to Father?'

'Oh, I could not tell you that. No, too terrible. Not for the ears of a girl.'

'Please!'

But by now we were ascending the steepest of streets and I had no breath

26

left, unused as I am to such exercise. I puffed and panted all the way. The street led into the piazza, which itself continued the great ascent, rising in a steep slope of cobbles. It was filled with the faithful, bowed by the effort of the climb, converging on the steps up to the Cathedral, surely the largest building in the world.

'Oh! So big!'

'Well, it is the House of God.'

I am old enough now not to be easily caught by such turns of speech; I had no expectation of meeting the one I seek within those great wooden doors. We followed the crowd, pressed like olives in the crush, into a vast grey, smoky space. There were paintings and candles and all manner of rich things. At the altar was a fat bishop and many priests, deacons and canons but, as I suspected, no sign of the resurrected Lord. Once inside the Cathedral, the crowd parted to segregate itself into male and female. Ignorant of this custom and bewildered by it, I was about to go with Cammilla when Derio pulled me back.

'Oh! I nearly forgot!' I said and went with him to stand with the men.

'My cousin Marco from Siena,' Derio explained to a friend who greeted him. I nodded dumbly.

As the crowd fell quiet when the choir began to sing the Introit, Derio nudged me. 'Over there, by the pillar. That's Lucrezia.'

My eldest sister is a matronly woman of about twenty five years with several servants attending her. She was dressed very finely in green silk but I could not see her face for the light veil she wore.

'And there,' my brother whispered, 'standing three behind her, the girl in a blue gown. That is Saracina.'

She had her hair up in a coif.

'She is married?'

'Yes, by one year, and to the Tarugi, one of the best families in the city. Her guardian was generous with the dowry.'

Saracina's face was bare and I stared at a black-haired girl dressed beautifully in fine silk and brocade. I hoped I might look like her as soon as I could grow my hair again and wear a gown and chemise.

Derio pointed out Lucrezia's husband to me, a sickly man with a yellow complexion, standing near by. I could hardly attend to the Mass for staring

27

at these members of my lost family. They all stood apart from one another, as if the Ambrogini ship had been dashed on rocks and all its parts scattered, one piece even being hurled even as far as Florence. I am growing fond of Derio – and he of me, I think – but my sisters seem remote. I have no feelings for them. For too long I have dreamt of throwing myself into their arms and finding love, familiarity, security. But now I saw them as distant and was surprised at my own indifference.

The Mass was made splendid by choirs and much music. How powerful the sound of so many voices – this was a mighty ocean compared to Suor Cecilia's sweet trickling stream. But the words of the Mass, they were the same, the same Father, Son and Holy Spirit. 'Spiritus Sanctus,' I once asked the padre. 'What does it mean?'

'Holy Spirit.'

'Yes, I know that, but what does it mean?' He pretended not to know what I meant by 'mean' and dismissed me as 'a child troubled by the devil's questions.'

I looked around the Cathedral, so vast it surely contained everything, but saw neither Father, Son nor Holy Spirit. They were depicted here and there in the many wall paintings of the many side chapels, but Actual Visible Presence – no sign of it. Instead what I saw in the host of faces all around me was a portrait of the seven deadly sins. The faces of the poliziani, as the natives of Montepulciano are called, are hard, but I could see a subtle form to each one of them that was easily identified. I saw pride, vanity, covetousness – especially amongst the women, with their eyes flickering about, evaluating each other critically and unkindly. None of them was listening. Why should they? They had heard it all before, over and over again. Indeed, now that I had caught a glimpse of this world and could see it more clearly, the words and music of the Mass seemed to be a mere background to the noise of the thoughts and emotions of the so-called 'faithful'.

Amongst the men I saw cruelty, lust, gluttony and sloth. This is an ugly world indeed, for all its rustling silks and bright jewels, and the edge went off my happiness and sense of liberation. I have read Suor Agosta's copy of Dante's Divine Comedy and know precisely which circle of hell or purgatory each of these souls is headed for.

When it came to partaking of the bread, however, there was a change in the people, as if the Mass had finally overcome their bestial natures; as we shuffled into queues I saw care and consideration in these blighted souls. Mothers looked after their children, the young gave aid to the elderly and infirm, adults looked down fondly on toddlers who, lost in dreams, were having serious conversations with themselves.

Lattanzio insisted on walking with me to the priest at the station, taking my hand possessively and leading the way on his bowed legs. All around the Cathedral various queues were snaking their way towards more priests than I could imagine, each one with his basket of the Blessed Sacrament, which was warm and newly baked. When we came to our celebrant, I opened my mouth wide. Lattanzio copied me, but the priest tapped him kindly on the head and gave him a blessing. I began to fall in love with my nephew, his warmth, his trusting grip, his Ambrogini nose, his mud-puddle eyes, his simplicity. And my love reached out to include the priest. Not stopping there, it began to embrace everyone in view, and my loving gaze was returned in kind by anyone who met it. Where now those ugly faces?

Afterwards, outside the Cathedral, everyone was gathering into the clans of kinship and greeting each other enthusiastically. Cammilla was already on her way towards the Contucci when Derio pulled her back.

'But I want to speak to my mother!'

'We cannot risk Maria being seen. Come, we are for home.'

'But I want to speak to Lucrezia!'

'And keep Maria's secret? You could not do two such things at once!'

I could see Lucrezia. Her veil was now drawn back and she had the face of a righteous woman, one who lives by the law and would turn me over to the authorities at once, saying, 'What else can I do?' Though I was sorry not to meet her or Saracina, I consider my brother's decision to have been wise. Lucrezia, who was staring expectantly at Derio, thinking he would approach her, looked surprised when he did not, but led his family off on the shortest route back to Cagnano.

✣

I have been given a pallet in Monna Cammilla's chamber where I may sleep as if I were her servant, which, Derio says, is what I am while I remain in his house. A proclamation has been read in the city squares announcing the

29

latest runaway slaves and 'a defecting postulant from Santa Maria delle Stelle, fifteen years old, a daughter of the Ambrogini family.' So now all the servants know and have been sworn to keep my secret, for Derio has come to think that it is important that I should know the outside world for what it is and decide for myself which is best. 'Or else you will ever be a reluctant nun which is of no use to anybody.'

'How shall I know the outside world cooped up in this house?' I asked.

'It is as much as you would know if you were a wife. You cannot change your sex, Maria, and at some point you are going to have to reconcile yourself to that.'

He has had some of his cheaper fabric made into a gown that will fit me.

✠

This evening, after supper had been cleared, I sat alone with Derio and Camilla at the table and at last I have drawn out the story.

The Del Mazza family hated the Ambrogini because of something that happened in the past, Derio does not know what, some minor insult. When the Del Mazza brothers were caught fighting each other they were sent before the magistrates, of which Ser Benedetto was the chief, were fined four hundred lire and sent into exile. A few months later they came back and ambushed my father as he was leaving the house.

'He was able to reach a neighbour's house,' Derio told me, 'and to get the door barred behind him, but the frustrated bandits began shouting that if they could not have him then they would take his sons. Angelo and I were upstairs in our own room and watching all this from the window. I am sweating now just at the memory. The girls and Mother had been sent away as a precaution. You? You were not yet born. Suddenly Paolo del Mazza espied us and shouted, 'There they are! The whelps! Get them!' And the gang crossed the street to our house and began throwing themselves against the door. Angelo had been instructed by Father as to what to do in such an emergency and he sprang into action, but I, shame to say, I just stood there wetting myself. Angelo shook me out of my fright and dragged me upstairs to the loggia. There a plank had been placed into the loggia of our neighbour's house and we had to cross it! Our neighbour was calling encouragement to us from the other side – indeed everyone was setting up a clamour

and throwing buckets of stuff down on the attackers. They could not see the plank from where they were: it was at the side of the house.

'"Out!" said Angelo. "Come on Derio – get on to the plank on your hands and knees." I was so little, Maria, only five or six years old. I started to cry and expected Angelo to beat me, but he kissed me on the head and told me the angels would look after me. He told me to be as brave as Achilles or Hercules. He knew all the names of heroes from his studies with Father, but they meant nothing to me. "Have no fear," he said. "I shall be right behind you and, look, there is Ser Giovanni waiting for you." Well, my hands were sweating so much I thought I was sure to slip off and fall to my death in the alley below. "Fix your attention on the plank," Angelo said, still calm. "Think of nothing else but the plank." And so I began the journey across and can remember now, as clear as day, all the details of every knot and grain of that piece of wood, its roughness and its splinters. Angelo was behind me and Ser Giovanni ahead, his arms outstretched. In fact it was not as hard as I had supposed – we were across very quickly and into safety. Ser Giovanni pulled the plank into his own house but, to my horror, only to project it out again the other side to the next neighbour. And so we went on, escaping our persecutors by going from one house to the next, walking over roofs, bridging alleys with the plank, until we were far enough away to come down and run into the upper city, where the bandits dare not go.'

The Del Mazza were caught and the terms of their exile lengthened to two years, but the Ambrogini lived in perpetual fear. Ser Benedetto took his sons out of school and taught them himself, though Derio thinks this was not just a matter of safety.

'Angelo was dying at school like a plant without light and water. All the catechism and abacus left him parched and wilting. It was from Father that he learnt what he called 'proper' Latin.'

'Proper' Latin apparently is the tongue of the ancient poets and not that of the Christians, Church Latin. I realise now that Suor Agosta has taught me 'proper' Latin or else I could never have read Ovid and Livy by myself. As for Church Latin, I had presumed it was simple because it was so repetitive. Another hole in my knowledge patched!

'Angelo used to say that Church Latin hurt his ears because it is coarse and barbaric. You can see why he was not popular with other boys. So Father

31

took us out of school and taught us poetry, history and law – stuff like that. I could not follow it all. Father and Angelo conversed entirely in Latin and did not always remember to translate for me. Before long they had decided to learn ancient Greek together as fellow pupils. Ser Benedetto had learnt the alphabet, which is different to ours, from a refugee of Constantinople.'

'Why a refugee?'

'It was sacked by the Turks in '53. Did you not know?' He looked at me as if unable to comprehend how anyone could be so ignorant. 'Even Cammilla knows that, do you not, my love?'

Cammilla, when not engaged with children and servants, muses a lot, and she muses a great deal when Derio and I are talking, lost in her own little world, the contents of which I cannot imagine.

'What, my dear?'

'What happened in Constantinople in 1453?'

'It was sacked by the Turks, dear. And it will be us next.'

Derio told me that the Ottoman Empire is expanding and, having taken Greece, Italy was next in their sights. 'And they will do to Rome what they have done to Jerusalem and turn St Peter's into a mosque!'

'Holy Mother help us!' said Cammilla, going back to needlework and picking at it nervously. This was something she clearly did not want to think about and soon enough the look of blissful dream had come back on her face.

'Are Turks Saracens?' I asked Derio.

'No. No more than we are crusaders, but it is the same old fight. Anyway, when Maso came to live with us, I escaped this Babel of foreign languages and went out with him everywhere. Maso was training to be a soldier and I wanted to be one too – until it happened. And then I wanted to go down a hole and never come out again.'

'I have heard the story, but not in all its detail.'

Derio would not tell the story in his wife's hearing and sent her away to her room. Alone we sat at the table and the gleam of the polished wood became the stage of my imagination, where I saw it all play out before me. I saw the Del Mazza return from exile to set up their forge again inside the Cagnano gate, mending horse-shoes, making contrada emblems, grilles for windows, all manner of iron-working. Bang – bang – bang went their hammers all day long. I saw my father telling his sons to stand up for themselves and not

32

show any fear when walking abroad. He steadfastly refused to allow anyone in the family to carry weapons but said they were to live at all times by his principles of peace. Cousin Maso, who disobeyed him, went everywhere with a sword at his hip and a knife in his belt. I saw the loggia on that evening in May when, after supper with some friends, Ser Benedetto decided to go out and check the property of his dead brother – Maso's father – and Mother pleading with him not to, saying it was too dangerous.

'I am not going to live as a prisoner of fear,' Father insisted. And Maso told her that he would protect his uncle 'to the death.' They took Angelo's hound, Ercole, with them. This infuriated Angelo, who wanted to go with them himself, but Father said it was a walk for men only and Angelo was still only a boy. He and Derio hung out of the window. The colour of sky was fading fast, the swifts were circling with their piercing whistles, bats darting past too quick to see. Suddenly the boys heard Ercole barking. He was coming closer and closer, barking wildly, until, turning the corner of the lane from the gate, he could be seen below, throwing himself up in the air as if to reach Angelo. Without stopping to ask permission, Angelo flew down the stairs to the door, unbarred it and ran out. Ercole leapt, barked and ran off, clearly expecting him to follow.

I saw Angelo finding blood on the road just outside the Cagnano gate and, further along, Maso staggering, apparently mortally wounded, his shirt all ripped and bloodied, and him shouting, 'Murder! Murder!' Angelo stopped to help but Maso pushed him away. 'Not me, you idiot! Your father!' I saw Angelo running on blindly, careless of his own safety, to where men were shouting; suddenly halting at the scream of his dog. One scream and then silence. And by the Gozzano fountain – the name apparently of my resting place in the night and the home of my father's ghost – Paolo del Mazza pulled my half-dead father's head up by its hair in his fist and…

I fell forward on the table to smother the images. 'I know the rest, Derio.'

'Thanks be to God, for I do not like to tell it. Angelo saw it all, though luckily they did not see him. He disappeared after that and it was two days before he was found, wandering about on the hillside like a colourless wraith. By the time he came back to the house, everything had changed. All the furniture and books had been sold to repay Mother's dowry, and you and Saracina had been taken away by uncles. Maso recovered – it had just been *a slight wound – and went south with his brother to find a war. I was sent to another uncle's house, an Ambrogini uncle who was a draper. You went to a Salimbeni house, relatives of our mother. But Angelo, he came back to find his world utterly destroyed and all his hopes in ruins. He was sent to Florence to become an apprentice cobbler in the workshop of a cousin.'*

'And Mother? What did she die of?'

'Die? Monna Antonia is not dead. As is the custom, she returned to her family. As soon as Father died, Salimbeni aunts arrived to work on our mother. She had neither the strength nor the means to resist. Immediately after the funeral, the Salimbeni took her away along with her dowry, or the value of it, which meant the house was stripped and all our goods sold off. Within the week Monna Antonia was married again, this time to a tax collector.'

'I thought we were orphans!'

'Mother may as well be dead so far as we are concerned, but in fact she lives. I noticed her in the crowd on Sunday.'

I wanted to ask him more about her, but somewhere a cock crowed and Derio looked up startled. 'What hour is it?'

As he rose to go to his bed, he said, 'The last I saw of Angelo, he was on the back of donkey and being led away by a priest bound for Florence. He swivelled in the saddle and shouted one word. My clever, brilliant brother – in his extremity he had only one word.'

'What was it?'

'Mamma!' And Derio choked suddenly and covered his face with his hands, the hardened merchant suddenly a boy again himself. His tears evoked my own and we hugged each other, two members of a broken family, temporarily reunited. 'She would not come out of the house!' he said, his voice high. 'She did not say goodbye to any of us!'

When I reached my own bed, I cried alone, the tears welling up from some unknown source, fathomless, effortless gushes of warm tears that soaked the straw of my pallet. Two hours later I rose up with a face like a puffball.

✝

Derio lets me use a spare desk in the office since what was once Ser Benedetto's study is now a guest room, not that Derio ever has any guests. Though he keeps telling me I am to help Monna Cammilla in her various tasks, he uses me himself as a clerk and secretary. My writing skills are now put to the service of the drapery trade, but my knowledge of herbs and simples is of equal use and often I am called upon to treat a child with colic or a scullery boy who has burnt himself at the cauldron or spit. Derio says I have until Ascension Day to make my mind up, whether to return to the convent or have him find me a husband. The dowry would be more than he can afford. Ascension Day is two weeks hence.

As to how Angelo made the transition from cobbler's apprentice to famous poet, or what poetry he is famous for, Derio is ignorant. Angelo writes frequently – I have seen his letters, written in a beautiful hand – but they are full of practical family matters of property and such like, and not a line of poetry in them. He must think his family incapable of interest in anything other than mundane affairs. Several times I have written to him myself, but I cannot get it right and have wasted much parchment.

✤

It is a very tedium to live in this house. If I had been raised here, I would have been as ignorant as Cammilla, and as engrossed with the minutiae of motherhood. I no longer blame her for being so interested in everyone else's business. It is so much more interesting than her own.

✤

Day follows day, and I am not sure I can wait my allotted span, but often think I shall just go back now to Santa Maria delle Stelle. Only pride makes me remain.

✤

Ascension Day
I awoke this morning feeling utter relief and had packed my scrip before I had dressed. But then Monna Cammilla came to me in tears saying that the baby is very sick indeed. It is true: it has a fever. I sent a servant out to pick the necessary herbs, which are fresh and abundant on the hillside, and made a tincture and a compress. Cammilla will not hear of me returning to the convent until the baby is well.

✤

Terrible news has just come from Florence. On Sunday, at the Cathedral, a rival family made an attack upon the Medici! Both Lorenzo and his brother Giuliano are slain! Of Lorenzo's companions we learn only that 'many are dead.'

✠

More news. Lorenzo survived. The attackers were the Pazzi family, but there is evidence that the real heart of the plot is St Peter's, Rome. They are saying that the Pope wants the Tuscan territories for his own and that the Medici stand in the way of his desires. Dear God in Heaven, can this be true? The Vicar of Christ a mortal land-grabber and murderer? The baby recovers but I am no longer as eager to return to Santa Maria delle Stelle, for I must know my brother's fate. Cammilla keeps crying and saying Angelo has gone to his grave, but we do not know that for certain, and I must know it before I return to the place where not even the Sack of Constantinople is heard of.

✠

Glory be to Almighty God! We have had a letter from Angelo. He tells us in vivid detail of the attack – in his true, poetic voice at last – of how the murderers struck as everyone dipped their heads in prayer when the sanctuary bell was rung. The Medici brothers were standing apart out of sight of each other on either side of the octagonal choir in the great Cathedral of Florence. Angelo was standing with Lorenzo, who was attacked by two priests. Priests! At Mass! Dear God, what kind of world is this? Where do we find any sign of our faith in practice? All is show and pretension, corruption and deceit. I can hardly bear it.

We await more news. All we know is that Florence is in turmoil and there is rioting, but whether the people are for the Medici or against we do not know.

✠

There has been another letter from Angelo. With his particular knowledge he is aware of things long before the rest of the world. He says there is certain to be a war between Florence and Rome and that Montepulciano, standing as it does on the border of Tuscany, must be in danger. He advises Derio to move to the house of relatives in Siena.

36

'How do we know there is going to be a war?' Derio says, not at all willing to suffer any interruption to his business. But then, this morning, there were two proclamations in the city. One, coming from the Pope himself, informed us that Lorenzo de' Medici is an infamous dog who has committed the sacrilege of murdering an archbishop; that as a result, he is excommunicated, and all Florence with him if the people do not give him up. The other, coming from the Priors of Florence, told us that a papal plot to murder the Medici has failed, that many of the conspirators, including the Archbishop of Pisa, have been brought to justice and hanged. Clergy in the territories of Florence, including Montepulciano, are instructed to ignore any threats of excommunication, 'since the devil himself, this false Pope, has no power over us,' and to continue as normal.

Derio has ordered that all his possessions be packed into crates. I am to return to the convent tomorrow. He says it is the safest place for me.

3

IT ALL LOOKS so different, as if I am seeing it for the first time: the lowness of the buildings apart from the Chapel, with all the dormitories and cells but a single storey high, the place arranged like a little village with cobbled lanes running from Chapel to Library to Refectory to Cloister. Pots of basil are out on window ledges and canaries sing in little cages hung from eaves. Everywhere birds cheeping, in trees, bushes and on the roofs. The warmth of the sun has penetrated the creamy stone and turned it into honey.

✢

'Forgive me, Madre, for I have sinned.'

'Have you seen the world for what it is?'

'I have, Madre. It is an ugly, brutal place full of injustice and nowhere is there sincerity of faith.'

'You were at your brother's house, that we knew, but we left you there.

37

It is better that a soul comes to God of its own volition, and not through the volition of others.'

'Why did my uncle send me here in the first place?'

'Because you were such a clever, bright little girl, and he wanted you to be educated.'

There are many holes in my knowledge, but that it is not one gaping void like Cammilla's I have my Uncle Luca to thank. I repented my sins and begged forgiveness of my uncle's spirit. My probation has been extended to Advent. It is not so long to wait, and the Madre Generale has said that my novitiate can be a short one if my repentence and change of heart are as genuine as they seem.

I have apologised to everyone publicly, and even more profusely in private to Suor Agosta and Suor Emilia. Suor Emilia is growing very fat indeed, for the douche at the mineral baths has not done its work. I have promised to help her in whatever way I can, even if it is only by being a friend. As for Suor Agosta, I threw myself on her and confessed that I had read her books in secret and loved them as much as she did. 'Teach me everything you know, for I want to learn about heroes such as Achilles and Hercules.'

Delighted, Suor Agosta sat down with me and told me about the poetic tradition from Homer to Virgil and up to Dante.

'You often complain about how you cannot love that which is invisible, and I find it just as hard. If I love poetry it is because it is the voice of the human heart, and in that I can detect the presence of God himself. It is the same with Suor Cecilia: she hears God in musical harmony and so she serves that. The vacancy that frightens you, Maria, is inside yourself. Find your talent, serve it and you will be loving God.'

'I love to write, Suor Agosta.'

'Then write. Here in the convent you are free to do so. Out in the world it would be impossible.'

'Not impossible but certainly prone to interruption and subject to dis-approval.'

'I think perhaps you have served your term with labels. I shall think of something else for you.'

The Second Book

MARS ASCENDANT

4

A FTER THE ATTACK on the Medici in April, Florence threw off any semblance of civilisation and plunged into the hell of revenge. The stench of human mortality reeked in our noses as we made our way through streets wet with the blood and littered with the butchered, decomposing parts of the slain. Eighty complicit men were killed on the day, some by justice, most by the mob. Dogs and pigs grew fat on the remains. The corpses of the main conspirators twisted on ropes hung from the windows of the Palazzo della Signoria; others were propped up, naked and rigid, as trophies in shop windows. Two of the Pazzi family had contrived the plot, but all the Pazzi suffered for it. Eleven of the men-folk, apart from the infamous Jacopo and Francesco, were executed, many more were imprisoned. Since all of us close to Lorenzo felt his own ruthless, passionate need for revenge, we did not question the legality of the perfunctory trials. None of us doubted that the Great Judge would condone. Surely the whole world would understand that what had been done against us was a crime against God.

Even as he was recovering from the shock of the attack, Lorenzo was snarling the name of the man he suspected to be at the heart of this: Girolamo Riario, nephew of Pope Sixtus and Count of Imola. It was days before the confessions were made that proved him right; worse, those same confessions implicated the Pope himself. Erstwhile monk and theologian, Sixtus had encouraged the Pazzi to rid Florence of the Medici. Now surely we were in Dante's Inferno. Both rumours and authentic reports rushed into the city, all saying the same thing: far from displaying any guilt or contrition, the Pope was massing his armies against us, and calling on the help of his ally, the King of Naples.

✣

I awoke to the sounds of the day, carts trundling to market, someone nailing something to the church door, and the crier's bell: *ker-ling, ker-ling, ker-ling.* Elena and I lay rumpled in a tangle of sheets, late arising as usual. I sat up and stroked the hair of my Pazzi wife, thanking God for her. 'May the seed of the Pazzi perish,' was the cry of the people in the streets, and the government were complying. While all her sisters, cousins and aunts were being rendered homeless by the edicts passed swiftly, stripped of their dowries and proclaimed unmarriageable, she alone was safe, given to me by Lorenzo himself as a favour for the loyalty I had displayed during the attack. In two cases he had overruled the edicts. His brother-in-law, Guglielmo de' Pazzi, was allowed to live, though confined to his villa, and Elena, an illegitimate daughter of Jacopo de' Pazzi, he gave to me as wife, along with a small house. This was my prize for saving Lorenzo's life at the cost of that of my own brother, who had been one of the conspirators. I thank God that I had not had time to think when I made that choice.

For a month after our swift, nocturnal marriage, Elena and I had enjoyed shuttered solitude in this house. Despite all that was going on in the streets, despite the destruction of both our families, such was our love that we lived in a bubble of contentment. Each morning I found it difficult to greet the dawn with anything more active than a loud, contented sigh.

The sound of the bell came closer and closer until the crier arrived in the small piazza which our house fronted.

'What is it?' Elena asked, turning over sleepily.

I went to the window to find out, opening our protective shutters cautiously.

'*… and he is pronounced to be culpable, sacrilegious, excommunicate, anathematised, infamous, unworthy of trust and incapable of making a will. All his property is to be surrendered to the Church, his houses are to be*

42

levelled to the ground and made desolate, that none might ever after dwell therein.'

I turned back inside. 'The Pope has excommunicated Lorenzo!'

Elena sat up in outrage. With her brown hair tumbling about her shoulders and her legs submerged in linen, she looked like a dishevelled sea-maiden. 'That's not possible! What is his crime?'

I smiled gently on her outrage. When it came to right and wrong, she could transcend family loyalty. Whatever worthy reasons her father may have had to justify his actions, he had murdered and thereby damned himself in his daughter's eyes.

I leant out dangerously far to catch the rest, but everyone in the street was too distracted to notice a Maffei at a window, or to suspect a Pazzi inside. They converged on the crier to hear the message the Pope was sending us, and all of them wore that same look of offended intelligence as my wife.

'All ye citizens of Florence, be it known that unless you offer up your leaders to justice, this interdict will be extended to include the entire city and all its people, from the date of the first of July. From that date, Florence will be stripped of its archiepiscopal rank and pontifical dignities; mass will be prohibited; no one will be eligible for the sacraments of baptism or burial; all holy festivities will be banned.'

'What has Lorenzo done?' a man opposite shouted down from a balcony.

'He is accused of murdering an archbishop,' the crier called back.

'Would that be the same archbishop tried and found guilty of murdering our Giuliano? The one that dangles from the Palazzo della Signoria?'

'The same.'

'The archbishop who was executed for crimes he committed with the blessing of the Pope?'

'The same!'

Utterly provoked, the people moved even closer to the crier shouting angrily.

'I am only the messenger!' the man claimed helplessly, now

ringing his bell like a leper. 'I, too, am a Florentine. To the devil with this Pope and his threats!'

The crowd at once began to cheer and became as boisterous in their support as they had been in their hostility. I left the hapless man and his jangling bell and hastened into my clothes.

'What else did he say?' Elena asked.

'Apparently if Florence refuses to give Lorenzo up, we shall all be excommunicated on the first of July.'

'What does that mean?'

'We cannot celebrate mass or perform baptism or burial. And no holy festivals.'

Elena stared as if at ghosts. 'No baptism?'

'That's the least of it!'

'Where are you going?'

'To Lorenzo, of course.' I leaned over the bed and kissed her. 'I shall not be long.'

'Will you be safe?'

I tied on the ribbons of blue and silver that marked a member of the youthful *brigata* of the Medici party. 'I shall be safe. Be sure to bar the door behind me.'

I demonstrated the locking device, as I had done so often before, as if she had the understanding of a cretin. I was so young, a mere eighteen – too young to be married. The sense of responsibility weighed on me. Elena, even younger, considered herself too young and too in love to be widowed and, not listening to my instructions, which she already knew by heart, clung to my back until I had to struggle free. Telling her to trust in God, I left.

✝

Out on the piazza the crowd was gathering about a large printed sheet tacked to the church door. This news was too potent for me to stand back and look on the thick ugly letters with critical disgust, telling anyone who would listen that the press was the devil's invention. I read the papal bull quickly with my temperature rising as anger ran like fire in my blood. While I stood there, mentally raging in the face of the Pope, countering his every accusation against us with one of my own, the local baker stepped forward, pulled the sheet from its nails and ripped it up. '*Il papa è un bastardo!*' The gathered crowd shouted their agreement.

And thus it was on every piazza and at every church I passed on my way to the Palazzo de' Medici on the Via Larga: all business abandoned while people read the papal bull or had it read to them. Market women were calling on the aid of the Virgin Mary, the way women do, while the men argued with each other about how we should respond to the Pope. I cursed the invention of printing, that it should allow such calumny to be so widely broadcast. The closer I came to the Via Larga, the denser the crowds, and at the end I had to push my way through to Lorenzo's house.

✢

Once inside, I found the courtyard resounding to the activities of the Medici bank as usual, but a queue of men, including even the Chancellor of Florence, had formed at the desk of the secretary, Niccolò Michelozzi, anxious to see il Magnifico and offer support. I joined the queue behind the chancellor, Bartolommeo Scala, a short, neat man who wore his hair close-cropped in the manner of a Roman senator. He was bearing the gift of some of his poetry written in praise of Lorenzo. 'It does not take me long,' he said to the Gonfaloniere beside him, beaming over his work. 'It just pours out.'

'You have a gift, Bartolommeo,' said the Gonfaloniere.

'Truly a gift from God, and all such gifts must be returned. I only ever write for others. They seem to like them, Lorenzo especially. He has inherited his grandfather's exquisite taste.'

Despite being one of the richest and most powerful men in the city, when he reached Niccolò Michelozzi, he was told he had to wait an hour like everyone else. Scala was still blinking with amazement when Angelo Poliziano ran into the courtyard and straight up the stairs.

'Why does he not have to wait an hour?'

'Angelo has special privileges,' Michelozzi replied as he wrote Scala's name in the day book.

Bartolommeo Scala was not a man used to waiting. With an hour to waste, he wanted to know why Angelo Poliziano had special privileges.

'I discovered him myself ten years ago,' said Michelozzi, 'in a shoemaker's shop in the Via Saturnia.'

'Yes, yes, I've heard the story, Niccolò, ad nauseam. But why does he have special privileges? He is only the prior of an insignificant parish.'

'He is young Piero's tutor, and he is translating Homer.'

'Following on from Carlo Marsuppini, who did not have special privileges. And besides, does this golden youth not despise translation and think we should all be multi-lingual? Why is he translating Homer and not teaching us all Greek?'

'Ideals soften with age, as you well know.' Niccolò shifted impatiently. He had too much to do to waste time with Scala. 'If you want the truth, Angelo has special privileges because Lorenzo loves him, and who can explain love?'

'Love?' The Chancellor of the Republic looked at first puzzled and then shocked. 'Greek love? Platonic love? Lorenzo? But he is a married man, a father!'

'Ah, Tommaso...' said Niccolò, noticing me and writing my name in the book.

Scala's eyes fastened on me, and since I was young and a companion of Angelo Poliziano, he obviously thought he was looking on a catamite and scowled.

'Platonic love,' I reminded him, 'is chaste, or it is not Platonic.'

'Hhhm.' Scala did not believe it. 'Hhhm. So those who have to make appointments must consider themselves unloved? Hhhm.'

'Lorenzo considers Angelo his master in poetry,' said Niccolò.

'While in Lorenzo our beggar boy has found an endless source of provender. Yes, I see, I understand.'

Michelozzi was annoyed by Scala's cynicism. 'Be assured, Ser Bartolommeo,' he said, 'Angelo is the *compare* in this household, the

46

tent companion, Patroclus to Lorenzo's Achilles. If you want to wait less than an hour to see il Magnifico, you would do well to befriend him.'

Niccolò told me that Lorenzo had asked to see me as soon as I arrived.

'Why *him?*' said Scala. 'He's only a scribe, a philosopher's lackey. Mere Chancellors must wait. Well, mark my words, Niccolò, within the day it will be me Lorenzo wants at his side.'

✝

Entering Lorenzo's chamber, I heard voices coming from the studiolo. The chamber was dominated by a huge painting by Paolo Uccello of the Battle of San Romano, a work full of horses and spears in the new art of perspective which had thrilled Lorenzo when he was a child. I suspected that he now spent more time in contemplation of the wooden crucifix sculpted by the master Donatello which hung on the wall facing his bed. I joined Lorenzo and his companions in the adjoining study, the place most private to him, a small room with painted walls which was dark, secluded, protective: the womb of his studies. With him, besides Angelo, was Marsilio Ficino. Lorenzo tall, well-shaped and commanding; Angelo short, his dark eyes ever on Lorenzo, anxious to please; Ficino both the shortest and the eldest of the three, golden haired and perpetually smiling. The crowsfeet at the corner of his eyes had been etched in by his good nature.

'The people are with you to a man,' Angelo was saying as I entered. Lorenzo, finely dressed even at this early hour, looked relieved.

'I have been at the Piazza della Signoria where the bull was read out by the papal herald,' Angelo continued. 'He was lucky to escape with his life.'

'Surely the Pope knows that Florentines are intelligent men quite able to distinguish for themselves right from wrong? My fear is not that the people will believe these lies, but that they will choose to obey the Pope out of simple self-interest.'

'Then you do not know your Florentines. They will never give you up.'

'Tommaso, thank you for joining us,' said Lorenzo, touching me affectionately on the arm. 'We are discussing events.'

It seemed a symptom of the times that these three should be considering such mundane matters as excommunication and the threat of war. Whenever they had met together alone like this, it had been to explore the subtle workings of the human soul and to examine causes rather than effects. Angelo the poet, Ficino the philosopher, Lorenzo the philosopher-poet, each of them dedicated to the ennobling of the human heart through poetry; to the ascent of the soul through philosophy. Lorenzo had been born to a work begun by his grandfather, Cosimo, which was to bring unity to Italy and restore the country's former glory. 'And,' old Cosimo had told him when Lorenzo was a boy, 'that is not done by military might: it is the work of love and wisdom.'

That great aim, which was behind all the efforts and activities of the Medici, was now under attack. While the courtyard boiled with priors, lawyers and merchants concerned about the loss of liberty and livelihood, here in this inner sanctum Lorenzo was quietly discussing with his closest friends and advisers how to protect his secret work.

'It is not stupidity on the part of the Pope,' said Ficino. 'It is greed which has made him prey to evil. It is the devil himself who wants you dead.'

'Must it come to war?'

'There is no alternative if justice is to prevail.'

'How close are you to finishing your translation of Plato?'

Only here, only in this house and in this man would the fate of a book override all other concerns and considerations. Ficino, naturally, saw nothing surprising in this, but was relieved that Lorenzo shared his own preoccupations. He had been twenty years on the translation of Plato from Greek to Latin and now, just as he was finalising his revisions and making the work ready for publication, Florence was threatened with war.

'I need about a year. With help, six months.'

'I want you to leave the city and reside in your villa near mine. With right so overwhelmingly on our side, if war does begin, it cannot last long, and you will be safe at Careggi, peaceful and secluded. Tommaso, you are already commissioned to help Ficino in his work; I am asking you now to be wholehearted in your service and to be available to him at all times.'

How easy that would have been a year ago! Now it was impossible to be wholehearted, not if it meant living apart from Elena. I felt like a man strung between two horses being whipped off in different directions. 'But my wife, Magnifico...'

'When I say "all times" I mean daylight hours! You may return to her each evening after your work is done.'

Ficino nodded in agreement, his startling blue eyes regarding me kindly. His own celibacy did not prevent him from appreciating my dilemma. 'Of course you may,' he said.

'And I?' Angelo asked.

'I need you with me,' Lorenzo said. 'If I do not have you beside me when I face what is coming I shall go mad.'

Gentile Becchi, the Bishop of Arezzo, entered quietly.

'Ah, Gentile,' said Lorenzo, turning to him at once. 'Have you read this bull? I want you to frame our response...'

As Lorenzo and the bishop began at once to discuss what to say, Angelo and I left the room with Ficino and went to the library where Lorenzo's companions, the *brigata*, had gathered, along with other men waiting to see Lorenzo. The Medici possessed so many books that they were kept in several locations, but in the city house were Lorenzo's favourites, and the library glowed with the colours of bindings, each leather dyed according to the subject it covered. It was a Byzantine, jewelled place presided over by a marble bust of Plato. On this day the luminous and usually tranquil sanctum of learning resounded to an anxious discussion on war, for the brigata knew well enough what the response to the Pope must be.

'Ah,' said Baccio Ugolini as Angelo entered. 'Here comes the chief priest of the Muse. He will tell us what war means.'

'Not I!' Angelo retorted. 'What do I know of war?'

'But you are translating the Iliad.'

'War in ancient Greece is far removed from what we call by that name. Then it meant a generation of young men slain on the battlefield. It meant heroic deeds, skill in arms and immense courage. It meant striving for glory, at the risk of pale, endless death. But what does it mean now, in 1478? – infantry making their way through swampy valleys, lines of cavalry on the high ridges, all held together at the centre by a trundling cart bearing their city's standard and its holiest relics; captains on hire from other states, mercenaries, sieges, little or no engagement; ruin for farmers and landowners, hunger for the city dwellers...'

'True enough,' said Niccolò Michelozzi. 'The only survivors in modern warfare are the soldiers. They alone reap any benefit.'

'War these days,' said Bartolommeo Scala, 'is a matter of careful planning and administration.'

Baccio disagreed. 'It is a matter of artful diplomacy.'

Francesco Sassetti, the manager of the Medici bank, was convinced it was a matter of economics. 'The richest man will win, and Lorenzo is as rich as Croesus.'

'Well,' said Angelo, 'whatever it means, were Achilles and Patroclus to be transported here, now, they would wander Tuscany in vain if they sought glory.'

He left the group and went away in a corner to be by himself.

'What is it?' I asked, following him.

'All this talk of war.'

'It frightens you?'

'It annoys me. Life is short, time so precious, everything so transient and ephemeral. Lorenzo is a poet, not a war-lord. All his time will be taken up by these events. What time will he have left for poetry? And yet without poetry he will find it difficult to live. At least I know my function in this conflict: to stand at his side as a living reminder of the true life, the life of literature. Perhaps I shall write an epic of his heroic and illustrious deeds; be his Plutarch. Yes.' He brightened a little with this thought.

My eye was caught by a book standing closed on a lectern, displayed to attract attention. Bound in red Moroccan leather, edged with a silver frame and clasps, decorated with cloisonné enamels depicting the Muses, it announced itself as a treasure. What might lie herein? The Word of God? I opened the book delicately, feeling I could only defile it by my touch. It was Lorenzo's collection of Tuscan poets, including some of his own sonnets. Its sublime script had been decorated by Francesco d'Antonio del Chierico. I had heard of this book, the making of which was handled by my old master, the bookseller, Vespasiano da Bisticci. The commission had come in a time of want, when there were so few commissions about that I had gone to Rome to seek work. In the time of Cosimo de' Medici, Vespasiano had built an industry to serve the sudden passion for copies of antique books. But Lorenzo, inheriting the vast collection, had small need to commission new works, and these days Vespasiano laid off more scribes than he hired. Lorenzo had arranged for a Book of Hours for his new wife and, after that, almost nothing. While I was in Rome I heard from Florentine friends about Lorenzo's commission of a new book called *La Raccolta Aragonese* – a collection of Tuscan poets – intended as a gift for Federico, Prince of Aragon, son of the King of Naples. Here it was completed. I stood breathless before it. Here were the sonnets of Dante and Petrarch, a Life of Dante, and a commentary that Lorenzo had written himself, the whole work gathered together by him as an anthology – a posy of flowers – to represent the literary heritage of Tuscany.

Angelo joined me and looked on the book sadly. 'This represents all of it,' he said, 'all Lorenzo's hopes and aspirations bound into one volume.' He told me about the poets of the thirteenth and fourteenth centuries of the *dolce stil nuovo*, or 'sweet new style', whose careful poetry aspired to a mystic ascendancy to God by way of Love. It had begun with Cavalcanti's *Donna mi prega* and culminated in Dante's *Vita Nuova*. 'They may be understood on the literal level as the yearning of a poet for his unobtainable love, but on the symbolic level...' He thumbed through the pages –

Poliziano's reverence for the word did not extend to pictures – until he came to Lorenzo's commentary on four of his own sonnets. 'It is all in here, Lorenzo's profound understanding of the *stilnovisti*. No one else has understood them the way he has. The School of Poetry founded in Tuscany by these men and annihilated by the Black Death is being revived by Lorenzo.'

I understood this on the literal level. Angelo astonished me with what he said next.

'He is being aided by Dante himself.'

'How so?'

'The same way that Plato guides Ficino.'

I turned towards my friend with my mouth open. This was a secret of the bed chamber. Who else could know this but Poliziano? Angelo laid his finger across his lips, signifying that I was to keep the secret. 'It is true. We have nothing by which to understand these works, and yet Lorenzo does understand. Where does that knowledge come from, if not from the author?'

'What is it that he understands?'

'The meanings of the words in their essence. He has discovered that the key to the stilnovisti is buried in their language. For instance, if they use the word *gentilezza*, we may take it to mean kindness or amiability, but the root *gens* signifies all that is born – generation, genius, genus, genuine, gentle. By it the poets refer to humanity in respect to its true state, born of God, humanity in its most noble aspect. You may read these poems on all four levels: literal, allegorical, symbolic and anagogic.'

'What is "anagogic"?'

'It is where mind and meaning are one: the understanding is full, total and no longer to be conveyed in words. The anagogic meaning of *gentilezza* for you would be when you realise the divine source your own humanity. There would be nothing to say about it, you would simply radiate glory.' He raised his eyebrows and smiled.

So now I knew what he and Lorenzo discussed when they spent nights together; now I knew what kept Lorenzo at his desk in the little studiolo adjoining his chamber, whether here at the Palazzo in the city or in any one of his villas. At each location he had a private study to which few were admitted, and no one at all in the absence of Lorenzo except one man: Angelo Poliziano.

'Is this why you have taken to writing in Tuscan?'

'It is Lorenzo's wish. He wants to revive Italy, to create a nation, through the Italian language. Since Tuscan is Italian in its finest form, he wishes me to continue the work of Dante and Petrach in making our own vulgar tongue as lofty and capable of expression as Latin. It is a high aspiration. I share it, but not in my heart. I believe a man finds God in what makes him happy: for me that is the Latin and Greek of the ancient poets. That is my *theologia poetica*. I would rather be reviving good Latin than good Tuscan, but who am I to choose what I do? A slave, like the very best of the Roman grammarians. I do share his aspirations, however. I do believe as he does that language makes the man, and that the best work for civilisation is literary.'

I had turned the pages and was now gazing at one of the pictures. A young man swimming from a sinking ship was grasping at the branches of a laurel tree.

'Laurentius – Lorenzo – the protector of all that is good and beautiful. He is our refuge.'

On another page I found a painting of *The Triumph of Fame,* a golden chariot drawn by four white horses and carrying Eros. Throughout the picture and in roundels in the margins formed by the tendrils of belladonna were famous lovers: Aristotle, being ridden like a mule by Phyllis, Hercules domesticated by Omphale, Danae and Jupiter. In a roundel at the bottom of the page a fair young woman picking leaves from a laurel tree.

Angelo pointed to her. 'Gentilezza,' he said, and the picture jumped out at me at a different, higher level of meaning, as if thrown into deep perspective. Angelo turned, biting his lip thoughtfully, to gaze on his companions still heatedly discussing war.

'Love, not war,' he muttered, 'we must remember that in the days to come.'

'Is this book not intended for Prince Federico of Naples?'

He turned back to me. 'It was, it is, but Naples is the ally of Rome.'

A cold shiver ran through me. I was still reacting to the Bull of Excommunication and had thought no further. But it was true: if we were heading for war with Rome, then we were heading for war with Naples also. And Naples was governed by a brute of a king who had a brute of a son – not the poetical Federico but his elder brother Alfonso, the Duke of Calabria. Stories abounded about the cruelty of King Ferrante and Prince Alfonso, stories to terrify children with. And grown men. Florence was a mighty state that won wars. Why, it had vanquished my native Volterra with a short siege. But as Volterra was to Florence, so Florence was to Naples. King Ferrante had a standing army; the Duke of Calabria had been born wearing spurs.

'Angelo,' I said. 'We can never win against Naples!'

'We shall win. It cannot be otherwise.' He laid his hand on the *Raccolta Aragonese*. 'This is God's work that Lorenzo is about, work on behalf of all humanity. God will not let us lose.'

'So what do we do? Find a good round stone and a sling?'

He smiled. 'We shall meet like with like, set Goliath upon Goliath. The King of France has a claim on Naples; he has a standing army; and he is most fond of Lorenzo. My only fear is that in the coming months Tuscany shall become a battleground, and Lorenzo will be so caught up in negotiations that he will have no time for his beloved, his *gentilezza*. It is that which makes me sigh.'

As Virgil was to Dante, so Dante to Lorenzo. When Lorenzo called for us later and we joined him in the sala, I looked at him afresh, half-expecting to see the shade of Dante close by. Ficino had told me of the line of philosophers that stretches across the ages from ancient Egypt to the present day; now I began to glimpse the similar tradition of poets. Lorenzo was about thirty at this time and an imposing figure. Though he stood amidst a crowd of men, even a stranger could have identified him at once. Radiating glory. He stood so well, his back straight, his chest proud, and the grace of his movements were those of a dancer. Though his expression was sombre it softened as soon as he saw Angelo. He clasped his friend briefly, introduced him to others and then stood together with him, no longer a solitary figure, now one of the brigata.

We went with him to the Palazzo della Signoria where he was to address the priors.

The great hall, painted from floor to ceiling with the emblems of the city and scenes of famous moments of Florentine history, was filled with its leading citizens uniformly dressed in the crimson *lucco*: merchants, leaders of guilds, bankers and lawyers, each one of them, I have to say, elected by the will of Lorenzo. Left to the people, democracy is a squabble: to function at all it needs a guiding hand. It had been the opinion of the Pazzi family, since they were not among the elect, that Lorenzo was a tyrant, and thus they had sought to change the leadership of Florence by murder. Now the Pope was provoking us to war for the same end: to get rid of the Medici.

As Lorenzo entered the hall, a hush fell upon the priors. He considered them gravely and began. 'I have no wish to discuss the past, to excuse myself or to accuse others. Upon these matters the State has pronounced its verdict. I only wish that cruel memories might be forgotten. It grieves me to the bottom of my heart that the Vicar of Christ, at a time when all Christ's servants are in mortal peril from the Turks, should descend to persecuting a private individual, and to wage war against a state to which the Church owes so much. Within me two sentiments struggle for mastery: my gratitude for the steadfastness with which my country protects me, and my grief that by another's guilt I am the cause of trouble for my city, which I love more than my life. For me it is enough that my conscience is free of any sting of remorse. For my city I hope that the aid of God and the providence of our citizens will easily and shortly deliver Florence from present toils.'

The men ranged along the benches listened in silence and reflected on the truth of his words. Should Florence refuse to offer

Lorenzo up to the Pope, war was the certain outcome. This would be a mighty interruption to trade and many private fortunes would be lost. Not one of them, however, was so self-interested that civic pride was not inflamed by the threats from Rome.

Lorenzo cleared his throat and continued. 'I have come to you here today because there is something I want to say to you, as if to all Florence, directly. It is this: If the city believes that my own death or exile would serve the public safety, I offer you my life.'

A spontaneous, unanimous protest came from his audience: 'No!'

'My life,' Lorenzo repeated, above the rising clamour. 'My life, my property, the blood of my children…'

'No, Lorenzo, no!'

'Freely and frankly I will offer these things.'

Feet began to stamp the floor to underline the response. The answer was no, a thousand times no.

Ser Bartolommeo Scala, justly famous for his oratory, took it upon himself to frame the reply. 'Lorenzo de' Medici, son of Piero, grandson of that great Cosimo whom we chose to call *Pater Patriae* – Father of his Country – it is perhaps correct to refer to yourself as a private citizen, but you are more than that to your city. You are her first born, the son above all others. It is your duty to live and die with your republic.'

Scala looked to his fellow priors and received their approval.

'A special council must be elected, a Ten of War, to administer the coming events. I do not think I am being a prophet to say that you will be asked to lead it, for you, though but a private citizen, have the ear of all the kings and princes of the world. We shall look to you to guide us, and to fight our war with those skills in diplomacy for which, Lorenzo, you are so justly famed.'

Scala's words met the continuing approval of the chamber.

'As a prior of this city, and its Chancellor,' he continued, 'I shall make it my business to see that you are protected in such a way that you may live in peace and security. The death of your dear brother affected us all most deeply. None of us wish to suffer any further loss of such magnitude. I propose to the Signoria that a guard of twelve men be appointed to accompany you at all times.'

Though the chamber approved his words, Lorenzo was quick to refuse the suggestion. 'No. To treat me thus is to treat me as royal. No! I wish to walk these streets of our republic free and unencumbered.'

But the government of the city had made up its mind: Lorenzo must be protected. Henceforth, wherever Lorenzo went, he must be surrounded by armed outriders.

Genuinely displeased, Lorenzo left the Palazzo and returned to his house, enjoying perhaps for the last time his freedom to walk alone with his companions. But what Scala had said was true: he could not walk abroad now without expectation of ambush. Though he might regret its necessity, he did appreciate the security a bodyguard would bring.

✣

As Bartolommeo Scala predicted, Lorenzo was elected into the Ten of War, as was Scala himself. At once the ten chosen men met to plan their measures to defend the city. They had little experience and the city was quite unprepared for war. Through the efforts of Lorenzo, Florence enjoyed a strong alliance with Milan and Venice, and to those two cities they decided to ply for aid; having no army, Florence must rely entirely on hired soldiers.

As was the tradition, chancellors of Florence were literary men, well-versed in the ancients and masters of Latin. Scala – who was, after all, the son of a miller – prided himself in having a way with words and presumed that his literary skills were beyond question. It was with relish, therefore, that he set himself to compose letters that would win this war, and one of the first letters he wrote was to the Duchess of Milan. A man always prepared to do things himself, and fired by enthusiasm for his task, he did not bother a secretary but wrote the letter in his own hand; and having written it he dispatched it, but not before having a copy made to present to Lorenzo. As I happened to be in the office on the ground floor,

I was given the task. Scala's style was his own, and it was not always easy to grasp his meaning, but in one phrase he seemed to be saying the opposite of what he surely meant to say. I felt all the hairs of my body stand up, prickling with fear. But Scala was a man who you would correct at your peril. If I were to draw his attention to the mistake, he would be winching out my bowels on a windlass within the hour. So I wrote the copy and prayed like a man in a sweating fever. The prayer was answered, but not before the original letter had been dispatched to Milan on the fastest horse.

Angelo walked in and, as Scala was present, I summoned my friend with my eyes, laying down my quill pen so that it pointed to the line. Angelo affected to pass by my desk, ask me what I was doing and pick up the copy of Scala's letter. Scala was delighted.

'What do you think?' he asked cheerfully.

Angelo did not reply. He was reading and re-reading the one line, the colour draining out of his face. He went to speak and hesitated.

'Well? It is only a slight thing so there is no need to be envious. I, after all, am a generation older and have had more practice. That is all that makes the difference.'

I watched my friend's face moving, could see the inner contention. Angelo was a disciple of Truth and a knight in the Order of Language, but like me he feared to say anything that might upset Scala. Then courage began to flow in him and to straighten his spine with resolve. He pointed to the clumsy phrase and, speaking with the utmost bravery, said, 'If I understand your meaning correctly, here you have muddled subject and object, easily done in the passive construction.'

Scala blinked rapidly. 'Well, a mere slip. It was done in haste – it just came to me all in one. Your sensibilities are so rare you are the only man in the world to have them. No one else will read that line the way you do.'

'I did,' I said. Scala's glance demoted me to wormhood.

'The mistake is serious,' Angelo continued firmly. It was so serious that, if Scala was going to be defensive, Angelo could no longer

58

worry about hurting his pride 'This letter will achieve the opposite of what we desire. The duchess will consider herself insulted and send her armies against us. I can rectify it soon enough – it will only take a moment's work. Hand me your pen, Tommaso.'

Scala blanched and took the letter from him. 'This is a copy. The original is already on the road to Milan.'

Angelo paused. He was only half the age of the chancellor, and knew that his rights did not extend so far as to give orders to have the letter intercepted. But seeing Scala entrenching for a battle, he put out his hand.

'Give it to me.'

'You upstart! How dare you!'

Angelo snatched the letter from him and dashed off to find Lorenzo. A moment later everyone in the house could hear Scala being summoned to go at once to Lorenzo's chamber. He went through the house with the air of a man wishing to get his execution over with quickly. Since I had been a witness, I followed. In Lorenzo's chamber, Angelo was sitting at the desk writing a new letter to the Duchess of Milan in a beautiful style with perfect syntax. Scala looked on him wrathfully but swallowed as he turned to face il Magnifico.

'My good friend,' said Lorenzo gently, 'I realise that it was your haste to do us service that resulted in this blunder. It is small, but significant, and I am going to have your letter intercepted on the road. I hope you do not mind?'

Scala remembered why he loved Lorenzo and was grateful. 'I trust young Homer is making all the points I wished to make.'

'Naturally. You are the politician – he is only a poet.'

Scala was mollified. 'I hope you consider me a poet, too, but you are right. My real skill is in administration.'

'With that there is no argument, and I need you with me as my private counsellor. I am looking on you, Bartolommeo, to win this war for me.' Lorenzo took him by the arm to escort him back to the door. 'You will not take it amiss if I ask Poliziano to check any future correspondence at this level before dispatch?'

'Magnifico,' said Scala, the blood rushing to his face as he bowed. 'Your wish is my will.'

After Scala had left, Angelo had Lorenzo sign the new letter and seal it. 'I hope I did right,' he said.

'Of course.'

'Scala was so angry he could barely see his way out through the door,' I said.

This made Angelo laugh in a high, ringing tone, not because the joke was funny but because of the tension in him that was now released. We did not know that Scala was still outside the door but, when we left the room a moment later, we found him there, looking like a child of Night.

'Still here?' Angelo asked smiling.

At the time it was such a small thing, one man's tiny grammatical mistake, and a shout of laughter, but that is the nature of a seed.

✠

'Lorenzo is my god,' Angelo Poliziano once told me. 'He adopted me, looked after me, educated me, raised me, cultivated me. I am his creature.'

'Have you no other god before him?'

'Of course I do! But in this world, Lorenzo stands in His place. He is my Lord.'

For his lord this courtier did many things. He was Lorenzo's companion during all hours of leisure; he was one of his secretaries during hours of state craft; he organised the games and entertainments of the house; when Lorenzo was journeying, it was Angelo who wrote Lorenzo's letters to his wife; he was the tutor of Lorenzo's eldest son and the authority on literary matters for the entire house. With his days thus occupied, he stayed up after hours to study and to write.

Though short, Angelo was of good figure. He had one slightly squinting eye, and a large nose, both of which he presumed barred him from the affection of girls. His hair, long and straight, had a raven sheen, and his dark brown eyes reflected a variety of moods and emotions, but when he was with Lorenzo, they were puddles of love and admiration. He was beloved by the women of the house, the favourite of Lorenzo's mother and the confidant of Lorenzo's wife, but this was no weight in the scales against the rejections he had suffered from various objects of his adoration. He seemed destined to pine under closed windows or sing plaintive songs under empty balconies. If a man is what he thinks he is, Angelo Poliziano was beyond hope in matters of love. And as the years passed, and his love poems drew forth no response, his natural love of women began to grow spiteful. He began to pretend that he did not like women at all, but considered them at best vain, at worst stupid, and an unnecessary distraction from the literary life, rather like war. His heart became dedicated to study, books and reading, for books are inanimate and do not have the power to reject the reader.

But with the coming of the bodyguard, he felt separated from his lord, and the days of the brigata singing love songs under balconies were ended.

I told Elena about it, how there were guards not only at the gate of the Palazzo de' Medici, but also outside Lorenzo's chamber. 'Even Angelo has to ask permission to enter, now.' It was just a piece of information, something to say, and I was not making much of it, but Elena did.

'Nothing must come between those two,' she said.

'What do you mean?'

'You told me what Ficino said, that this war on earth is being fought in heaven, that it is a battle between the light and the dark. Surely evil thrives on separation. Do not let anything come between Angelo and his lord, not even bodyguards.'

I was often surprised at how much my wife knew, given that she was even more cloistered than most wives. Despite being in the house all day with only two maids for company, she often told me things about the Medici family I did not know myself. There seemed to be a network of information passing from maid to maid, beginning in the Medici scullery and filtering out through the city to its furthest reaches. One night as we sat upstairs she told me that Lorenzo's wife was not speaking to her husband but had locked herself away in her chamber.

'She is always locked away in her chamber,' I said. 'It is what she prefers, to be alone with her maids and the children. Besides, at the moment she is still in confinement following the birth of her little girl and, until she is churched, she is bound to keep to her room.'

'But it is true, is it not, that when Lorenzo addressed the Signoria he offered the city his life, his property and the blood of his children?'

It was the great talent of Elena to make me feel stupid despite my education. It had not occurred to me that anyone would think Lorenzo had meant what he said. 'It was a rhetorical flourish, nothing more.'

Elena gazed at me intently. 'I do not think that Monna Clarice understands rhetoric or its flourishes.'

5

Florence, July 1478

WE ENTERED WAR with great confidence. Fragments of the various printed copies of the papal bull wiped many a Florentine arse. Archbishops and bishops told Lorenzo that, since the devil has no authority in heaven, any interdict the Pope might make could be safely ignored. When Naples declared war on us – which it soon did – we sent ambassadors to France. Had it been a war with Rome alone we could have won easily with the aid of our great ally, Milan. Naples, however, had a standing army under the command of Alfonso, Duke of Calabria, who, as a baby, had been drawn from his mother as a knife from its sheath. We needed help. King Louis of France was very affectionate towards the Medici; besides which, he had a claim on the throne of Naples stronger than that of its current occupant, Ferrante of Aragon. It was time for the French to move and, as they swept south, to vanquish the papal armies on the way. The outcome seemed certain: victory. Did we have God on our side? There was not a man in Florence who was not convinced of it.

The city took on great colour. Everywhere flags and banners were put out with the emblems of the *contrade*, of the city, of the guilds, of the saints. Hastily formed militias paraded through the streets, stepping boldly to the drum, while in the fields by the city walls they practised archery and swordsmanship. This was all mere display since, in fighting any war, we had to rely on mercenary forces bought with hard cash, but it did what it was meant to do and gave the city of merchants a swaggering, martial air. Wagonloads of grain were brought into the city to shore us up against any siege; the walls were manned; the gates closed at night. Oh, noble Florence, how fine you looked in that hour.

Those forces we had so far hired, under the command of *condottieri*, were sent to various strongholds in the south of Tuscany. When the enemy crossed into our territory near Montepulciano, we had a castle or fortress at the head of every valley well-defended to meet them. What we did not expect was to be attacked on the inside. When that happened, our confidence suffered a tremor.

Siena, in the south of Tuscany, was a proud if small republic with a history as long as that of Florence, and a talent in art that some said surpassed ours. It had a bell tower that was higher, a central piazza that was more beautiful, a grape that was superior; but it did not have our wealth since we had more or less blocked its trade routes north. Attempts had been made between our two cities to live in harmony, and only recently Siena had, in order to please Lorenzo, refrained from executing the murderous and vengeful cousins of Angelo Poliziano. But it was no surprise when Siena announced its support for Rome and Naples, though we were taken aback to discover that the first incursion into Florentine territory was Sienese.

'Perfidious Siena!' Lorenzo thundered when he heard the news. He dispatched Baccio Ugolini to tell the Sienese that all trade with Florence was stopped and that all loans from the Medici bank were being recalled.

The forces of Rome entered Tuscany at Cortona under the leadership of Federico, Duke of Urbino. Now the duke was familiar to me as the figure of nightmares since he had led the attack on my native city of Volterra six years previously. Then he had been in the pay of Florence and seemed to us, the besieged, to have been the warrior face of Lorenzo de' Medici. But now, in the hire of the Pope, he was the enemy of Florence.

The mighty duke was nearly defeated by us at a battle at Lake Trasimene near Cortona. It was an unlucky place for Romans – many of his soldiers had visions of their ancient forebears being attacked by Africans with elephants. This place, which had been the site of Rome's defeat by Hannibal, was surely cursed. If it had not been for the discipline of Urbino, our modern Romans would have fled. They rallied when they were joined by the Neapolitans under the Duke of Calabria, and caused the Florentines to retreat on Arezzo. After that, the Neapolitan contingents struck out across the hills to raid the rich wine towns of the Chianti valley.

The officers leading the armies of Florence were second-rankers but intelligent, and were commanded by two counts who had the ability to fight and win wars, but the Council of Ten in Florence was adamant that someone of higher rank was needed to lead its forces. Since the enemy had two dukes, Florence would not be content with two counts. And so Lorenzo secured the help of Ercole d'Este, Duke of Ferrara.

✝

The great Florentine festival of its patron saint, San Giovanni, was postponed until July. In the melting heat of high summer, the city came out to pretend everything was normal. A party of us went out from the Palazzo Medici to watch the horse race in the streets and see the strange buildings that had appeared overnight in the squares like monstrous fungi. Giants and demons strode about on stilts to terrify children.

'What is that?' asked Lorenzo's son, Piero, holding his tutor's hand.

An enormous structure was passing on a cart, a monument to whoredom, a figure of a raddled woman with her breasts exposed, wearing the papal tiara. The little boy who, even at the age of six, had a fascination for female anatomy, was enchanted. With a lascivious grin, he shook back his thick, pale hair which was forever falling in his eyes.

'Why, it is a portrait of the holy father,' said Angelo Poliziano wryly.

Piero, precociously aware of his status, ordered us to follow the cart; and then, as much a child as an heir to greatness, pulled us along. The cart went to the Piazza della Signoria where men took the effigy and placed it on a pile of faggots.

A fool dressed as a cardinal hailed the exultant crowd. 'Why are you laughing, Florentines? Are you not now excommunicated? How can you laugh, you who are refused the sacraments and are destined for hell?'

People began to pelt him with hard bread and bad eggs.

The authentic Archbishop of Florence then appeared in person, coming on a processional cart from his palace and led by an escort of angels blowing trumpets. Standing on the chariot, he addressed the people and told us that he had instructed the clergy to perform the sacraments as usual.

'We shall ignore this interdict of the Pope, since the words of a false man have no power over us!'

Wild cheering erupted and the bonfire was lit. Little Piero stared with his mouth open to see the strange, exciting figure of a breasted pope engulfed by flames, crackling and disintegrating in a fierce heat.

Since hearing that the enemy was grouping in the valley below

Montepulciano, Angelo had grown morose, distracted by concern for his relations in his native city. He jumped violently when a fire-cracker went off behind us. 'Have you seen enough? Do you want to go home?' he asked Piero.

'No!'

'Yes. Come along.'

'No!' Piero pulled backwards with all his weight. 'I will stay! I will stay!'

'Your mother is waiting for you.'

'I do not wish to go back to her!'

'Why not?'

'She is always crying,' he complained, his face rumpling with distaste.

'It is grief, Piero, at your uncle Giuliano's death. Women always weep.'

'I wish to see…' Piero looked about him for inspiration. 'The tumblers!'

'Your father commands you to return,' said his tutor sternly. The mere mention of Lorenzo was always enough and Piero acquiesced moodily.

We began to make our way back through the crowds to the palazzo and, while Piero was distracted by a passing woman dressed as Salome, I told Angelo what my wife had told me, that Monna Clarice had heard about Lorenzo's speech to the Signoria when he had offered to his country 'my life, my property and the blood of my children.'

'He meant it rhetorically, of course,' I said. 'Any man would understand that. But women take things literally, and that is why Monna Clarice has become distressed.'

'Ah, is that the reason?'

'I thought you would have known. Does she not share her troubles with you?'

'Only by letter when Lorenzo is away. At home, I rarely see her, apart from meal times. If I share Lorenzo's company with any woman…' and here he lifted his chin to indicate that I would have to guess the rest since he could not speak in earshot of the boy.

Lucrezia Donati. That was the name of Lorenzo's mistress, a beautiful woman he would have married had the choice been his to make.

✢

As July progressed, and the sun became so fierce that we all longed to be in the hills, it became obvious that our danger was worse than we had supposed. Lorenzo, who had friends in every state, every country of the world, found that his letters asking for help were showing him the worthlessness of friendship with kings and princes. Our ally Milan had her own troubles; Venice could only muster 3000 men. As for foreign princes, with the Turk pressing on the borders of Christendom, no one wished to become involved in a small Italian squabble, whatever the merits of Lorenzo's case. Besides, his opponent was the Pope and that caused, well, *difficulties*. Soon enough we realised that our defiance of Rome was indeed to be that of David against Goliath. But still, we would win; with the help of God – and the King of France.

✢

We, the household, the family and the companions of the Medici, were called to attend a meeting with Lorenzo in the sala. As I arrived I met Angelo on his way through the house to 'gather up the ladies' and went with him. Passing through one of the upper galleries opening on to the courtyard, Angelo cocked his head to one side, as if listening to something. A *lira da braccio* was being played, though it was difficult to hear above the uproar of barking dogs. Leaning out we saw Baccio Ugolini, just returned from Siena, singing below; while in the garden beyond, dogs greeted a servant who had come out to feed them. To sing here and play on his lira da braccio was something Baccio Ugolini often liked to do, for the proportions of the beautiful courtyard were harmonious and amplified any sound so that it carried throughout the house. Baccio, who had no time for commerce and banking, and did not

67

much care for wars, was seeking to replace the harsh sounds of the day with music. He was singing a hymn that Angelo had composed himself, pulling the bow across the taut strings in a drone while his tenor voice rose up to the open sky on its updraft. Suddenly, like one bird joining another in flight, Angelo's own voice was joining the song, and now there were three lines of melody to listen to and multiple harmonies that began to play on the soul. Even the dogs stopped barking as the two voices and the lira each followed its own line and together formed a spiral of sound that wrought a charm in the place, offering a sense of the sublime to those in trouble and misery. The hymn was Orphic, addressed to Apollo, and could change the state of hearts. Mine was melting in a sweet grief, an ineffable sadness that beauty could be enjoyed at such a desperate hour. At the end, Baccio looked up, his face radiant.

'Meet us in the loggia,' Angelo told him from the gallery.

We found the rest of the *brigata* there, speculating on the future, each man concerned to know Lorenzo's plans for him. Angelo and I arrived enjoying the rare confidence of already knowing, but as we entered the cool, vaulted arcade in the garden, Bartolommeo Scala was assuring the rest that he alone knew Lorenzo's plans.

'I have been deputed to command the armies,' he told us pleasantly.

'What has happened to Duke Ercole d'Este?' Angelo asked.

'Well, when I say *command…*' Scala began.

'You mean some other word.'

At this the men laughed with no regard to the feelings of the chancellor.

'At least I shall be in the city, attending my lord Lorenzo,' said Scala, bringing his face very close to Angelo's.

'As shall I.'

'Have you not heard? Lorenzo is sending the family away,' said Scala. 'Everyone knows it. And to be sure, you will be going with them.'

'What makes you think that?' Angelo demanded.

'Because all the women are being sent away.'

The brigata grew hushed and tense. Angelo gazed at his enemy. 'I think I misheard.'

'No you did not. Lorenzo wishes to protect his most beloved. It is natural, and most commendable. I am a modern man and not disturbed by these things. You do not have to pretend with me. So away you go, my pretty boy, to safety with the women.'

The absurdity of being called pretty made Angelo laugh. 'Now I know you are joking, Bartolommeo,' he said.

Baccio Ugolini also began to laugh, to help clear the air. 'Enough of your dear wit,' he told Scala. 'I have business with this man.' He drew Angelo out into the garden.

'Is it true?' Angelo gasped. 'Am I being sent away? And Lorenzo has not told me?'

'No one knows Lorenzo's plans,' Baccio said. 'Scala is making it up, taunting you.'

'That self-appreciative jug of pig fat! What is he accusing me of? Does he think I am Lorenzo's catamite?'

'Just as he thinks I am yours,' I said. 'In his view we are like amorous whelks, one stacked upon another.'

'Scala is the least of your worries,' said Baccio. 'I have news: the enemy has destroyed the bridge at Chiusi and is camped but two miles from Montepulciano.'

Angelo leapt like a touched cricket. 'Is my city safe?'

His alarm only mounted as Baccio described the sixty squadrons of knights, and as many infantry, camped at the base of his native hill.

'Do you have kin there?' Baccio asked him gently.

'Of course! Three sisters and a brother, plus innumerable others. The whole city is my relation.'

'You never speak of them.'

'I left so long ago that they seem like strangers to me now.'

'So you will not be leaving us to rush to their aid, then?'

'The Medici are my kin,' Angelo said. 'Their needs come first.' He left abruptly to find Lorenzo's wife.

✠

Monna Clarice was a daughter of the patrician Orsini family and spoke in the Roman dialect. If she was not having a baby every nine months it was due only to the custom of churching. A year separated each child, and they ranged from eight year old Lucrezina to the baby Contessina. The two gaps in this linear progression showed where children had been that were no more. This constant state of pregnancy had exhausted Clarice at an early age and thus she remained aloof, preferring the company of her women and her religion to that of her husband and his friends. Lorenzo and his wife were so curiously detached that it was a wonder to the rest of us that she had so many children. Coarse jokes abounded. Whenever Lorenzo left the sala to relieve himself, some wit would say he had gone to father a child and would be back anon. Others said that he was so fertile and she so fecund that they only had to look at each other. My favourite was Angelo's: 'If Lorenzo were a bee, with that much pollen he could not fly.'

Chosen to be Lorenzo's bride in order to inject a strain of nobility into the Medici, Clarice had nothing in common with her husband other than their children. Sometimes she made an effort and joined us for dinner, but soon enough she tired of our wit and erudition, made an excuse and left. If she was very caring about Lorenzo's friends, it was only to compete with her mother-in-law for our affection. Nevertheless, Angelo enjoyed her ministrations. Plagued by frequent headaches and stomach upsets, he found in her a ready supply of sympathy and herbal remedies. But there were only two men in the household for whom she seemed to have genuine affection. One was her spiritual guide and confessor, Bishop Gentile Becchi; the other was the house chaplain, Matteo Franco. When we entered her chamber, Matteo was singing with her the canticle of St Francis for the Birds.

'He has chosen for you a dwelling
In the pure region of the air.
And without your needing to sow nor reap,
You are delivered from all care.
He sustains and governs you.'

Her room had painted walls of deep blue and gold, a coffered ceiling of painted wood and a floor of coloured marble. Images of the Madonna were everywhere: in paint on the wall and on the bed head, in wood in a niche, in blue and white glazed terracotta above the door. On the several huge marriage chests ranged round the walls were propped birth trays, each one a gift following the birth of a child, each depicting some holy scene: Ruth and Boaz, Esther, Judith and Holofernes. It had long been the fashion to have scenes of mythology on cassoni and trays, but not for Monna Clarice. She abhorred the pagans and filled her room with scenes from the Bible.

On a low table a candle burned next to her greatest treasure, a Book of Hours opened at the day's page, richly illuminated, a gift from her husband at their marriage. I edged closer to it, for it was a book as beautiful as the *Raccolta Aragonese*. Its pages had been painted by the same artist, and yet how different it was. Its script was of the old kind – confusingly called *lettera moderna* – the script of the Church, with square, graceless letters. Ah, this was a beautiful example of it, to be sure, but nevertheless the script itself spoke not of harmony and proportion but of earnest piety. The borders to the page were as striking as in the *Raccolta,* but the symbolism here was of a more mundane kind. All the images spoke of union between the Medici and the Orsini: a pruned branch (Medici) and roses (Orsini); a bear (Clarice Orsini) hugging a laurel tree (Lorenzo de' Medici). But within those luscious borders of red and green, a text and illuminated capitals that could have been written in a scriptorium a hundred years ago.

It had been a month since the birth of Contessina and Monna Clarice had not yet been purified at church. I felt like an intruder in this warm and feminine chamber. My anxiety at having married too young was exacerbated by this papable reality of a woman recovering from childbirth. Angelo took off his cap respectfully and turned it round and round in his hands, impatient for the opportunity to speak, trying not to look at the wet-nurse who, with Contessina feeding at her ample and exposed breast, was being watched unblinkingly by Piero. The duet of Clarice and Matteo moved seamlessly into another canticle of the saint, the one on Love.

'Love, Love, who has so wounded me.
I can only utter one cry, Love.
Love, Love, it is the cry of the whole world:
Love, Love, it is the cry of everything.
Love, Love, you make me suffer so.
Love, Love, I cannot bear it.
Love, Love, you give me so much,
Love, Love, I think I will die.'

Monna Clarice was serene and beautiful in her way, her pale complexion set off by autumnal hair. She always looked mild and calm, but today, though her expression remained placid, she was rocking back and forth in evident agitation.

Her daughter Luigia toddled towards us, gurgling with delight. Angelo caught the child before she fell, raised her aloft and dandled her in the air. Then, as the hymn ended, he gave the child back to its nurse. 'Monna Clarice,' he said. 'Your husband awaits us in the sala.'

'Thank you, Messer Angelo, but as you can see I am a-bed.'

'Do you think you could rise? It is your husband's express will.'

'Very well. I shall be along presently.' She looked at us with her usual passivity, as if she had no will of her own but had been born to suffer life and wait patiently for death. It was a look that appealed to most men and made them feel very protective. Angelo himself was always very solicitous, though in a slightly patronising fashion that a brighter woman might have noticed. I seemed to be alone in finding this quiescence more irritating than nettle rash.

✝

I always kept my views to myself until I was home and then I would let fly.

'Why is she so exhausted?'

72

'She has just given birth!'

'It was a month ago. The chamber is stuffed with servants and nurses who feed the babies, wipe their bottoms, put them to bed, rock the cradle, get them up again and play with them. She is married to the finest man in the world and yet she strives to be an object of pity!'

It would never have occurred to me that events were striking Monna Clarice differently to the rest of us. Never occurred. Not because it was impossible to imagine, but just because it never occurred. We were all united against Rome the aggressor, and together we railed at the injustice of the Pope. To view the matter any differently was inconceivable. But since I had married and taken Elena de' Pazzi to my bed, I was privy to a woman's wisdom and alternative point of view.

When I told her later about Monna Clarice singing the canticles of St Francis, she exclaimed, 'That poor woman! What must she be suffering?'

'Idleness?'

Elena jabbed me in the ribs. 'I mean the suffering of the soul, not the body. The Pope has accused her husband of – how does he put it? – "dog-like savagery" towards holy men of the church.'

'How do you know that? Have you read the bull yourself?'

'It is on the church door.'

'Elena, I told you not to leave this house!'

'I have obeyed! My maid went out and had someone read it to her. Lorenzo is accused of sacrilegious murder and is excommunicated. Poor Clarice! What must she think? She is the most pious of women, and her husband is excommunicated. You say she was rocking like an idiot while Franco sang the Canticle of Love? And you are surprised?'

'Elena, Elena – I still do not follow. The Pope is the devil incarnate and cannot speak one single word of truth. Every Florentine knows it.'

'But Monna Clarice is from Rome. Stand for a moment in her

shoes. To her the Pope, the Vicar of Christ, is her spiritual father. And he is accusing her husband of sacrilege.'

'As the wife of Lorenzo she cannot entertain such thoughts, but be loyal to her husband. Is that not what St Paul enjoins us? Men, serve the Lord; women, serve your husband.'

'And that is why Clarice is torn in two, since God and Husband are in opposition.'

Understanding suddenly, I sat upright in my bed with sweat on my brow. No wonder Monna Clarice could not rest. Elena began to sing softly the words of the saint.

'Love, Love, my heart is broken
Love, Love, my heart is wounded,
Love, you are my life:
Do not forsake me,
For you have made me faint
All-embracing Love.'

She stroked my back gently, inviting me to lie down. Few men are blessed with a wife whom they love. In that respect, I, Tommaso de' Maffei, was the wealthy man, and Lorenzo de' Medici the pauper.

But I am wealthy no longer and have lost my fortune. *You have made me faint, all-embracing Love.*

✠

Everyone assembled in the sala was edgy, all voices slightly sharp and high, all smiles too wide, all eyes troubled and flickering from this face to the next. Only Angelo looked calm, confident in the presumption that he knew his fate, and everybody else's. The family, he knew, was to be sent away to safety, all the women and children, most likely in the care of Lorenzo's uncle, Ser Giovanni Tornabuoni. Lorenzo's companions, the brigata, would be sent hither and thither in various ambassadorial roles; Angelo alone would stay with Lorenzo, as was obvious, right and natural. Lorenzo himself had said as much.

Angelo stood beside Lorenzo's mother, Monna Lucrezia, always a favourite of hers and, since the death of Giuliano, almost an adopted son. He held her hand to give her courage, not that she needed any. Lorenzo took out a list. 'It has more corrections and alterations than one of my sonnets,' he said. 'This has not been easy, especially since my beloved mother steadfastly refuses to do what I would have her do.'

'I am staying, Lorenzo. Let there be no further argument.'

'Very well, but I want you to stay at our villa on Careggi, not here in the city. Mother!' he said, as she opened her mouth to object. 'It is close enough. I shall see you every day.'

'Make certain you do, or you shall not win this war.' Monna Lucrezia, who had learnt more from her father-in-law, Cosimo, than her husband had, was the member of the family most expert in statecraft. Lorenzo acknowledged this with a nod.

'If I did not believe that, my Amazon queen, I would not be acquiescing to your demands but would be sending you to safety. Ser Giovanni, dear uncle, may I ask you to reside with your sister and be a companion to her?'

Angelo, realising that there was nothing he could give Monna Lucrezia that she did not already have, relinquished her hand. He was staring at Lorenzo with a slight frown. If Ser Giovanni Tornabuoni was to go to Careggi, who, then, was to be the one to attend Lorenzo's wife and children? Matteo Franco? Monna Clarice herself, looking as wan as moonlight, was staring at her husband with a dim sense of foreboding.

'My wife and children,' Lorenzo said, 'I shall be sending to our loyal friends the Panciaticchi in Pistoia. And for their protection I shall be sending my dear and faithful companion, Angelo Poliziano.'

At this, Monna Clarice swooned, falling back into the arms of her servants like Mary at the foot of the Cross. Emotions flickered over Angelo's face as if he were a candle in a wild draught. While all attention was on Monna Clarice, he muttered an excuse and left the room. I found him in the marbled antechamber, pacing up and down, trying to walk off his fury.

75

'Stop!' he said, before I had even begun to speak. 'None of your wise platitudes! The philosophers might abjure shows of emotion, but I am not a philosopher. I am a poet. Leave me.'

I told him that I understood, but he interrupted, exploding: 'The shame of it! In front of everyone! To be sent away with women and children as if I were a eunuch! How can I hold my head up now? And why did he not warn me beforehand? Why? And why does she faint away at the prospect of my company? I shall be the butt of the brigata's jokes forever more. I thought she was fond of me!'

'Lorenzo wants you safe.'

'Did Achilles send Patroclus to safety with women? Where would the Iliad be had he done so? No story at all.'

'Well, there would still be the sack of Troy.'

'I must fight!'

'Fight what?'

'The enemy! I must be with Lorenzo to the death.'

'You? Fight? What with?'

'I speak metaphorically, numskull.' He buried his face in his hands and groaned. 'I do not understand.'

'If you would only let your passions subside, you could see his reasoning clearly enough for yourself. He needs a surrogate father for his children…'

'Ser Giovanni…'

'And a tutor for his sons…'

'Ah…'

'Little Piero needs you. Lorenzo is adamant that all our work suffer no interruption. That is why, despite the war, Ficino is to continue with the Plato translation. And your contribution to the great enterprise? Why, it is to raise the philosopher king, the wise leader for the next generation. That is why you are being sent away.'

Though Angelo still could not understand why Lorenzo had not told him in advance, he was nevertheless comforted and, taking me by the shoulders, he kissed me on both cheeks. 'Man of reason,' he said. 'I thank you. But did she have to faint like that?'

'She has hardly been out of bed since she gave birth. Her legs are probably weak.'

Satisfied by my explanation, he returned with me to the sala, his composure regained.

✝

Montepulciano, July, 1478

My most invisible God, I must confess to you what I cannot confess to others. I have been on the roof again. How could I not? You know how long I have resisted, how I have spent the summer within these walls and never complained either inwardly or outwardly, but have sought my joys in the new companionship I have formed with Suor Agosta, and the instruction she is giving me in the properties of herbs and the laws of poetic metre. She told me that to love one's duty is enough; it is not for me to worry where that love goes or by whom or what it is received. And therefore she has given me duties that I may love, and Lauretta will be writing the labels from now on. But this morning, as I was feeding the doves – a duty I do love and refuse to relinquish – I saw smoke curling into the sky in so many columns they were like pillars in a cathedral of smoke. How could I help it? How could I not make that little leap from the ladder of duty to the roof of disobedience?

There are camp fires all along the river, from south to north, and I know what my Sisters do not know, that Rome is advancing on Florence.

Oh, I would know so much more! What is happening outside? Is Angelo safe? Did Derio and Cammilla reach Siena in safety? Will the soldiers attack us? It is a seething, writhing, worms' nest, this frustration.

✝

There is so much smoke now, from burning fields and villages, that everyone knows what is going on. The padre came to speak to Madre Generale. He assured her that we shall be safe, but for the sake of others we must pray all day and all night, taking turns, each of us to be in prayer for at least three hours at a time.

The granary has been filled and the Madre says we can withstand the famine that will follow the passage of the hostile army. And no, she says, they will not come up the hill. Their goal is Florence.

I cannot sleep. It is impossible. This is like waiting in a cave for the cyclops to come home. My most ineffable and ghostly God, forgive me. I must spend the night on the roof, with my book and my pen in my scrip, since these are my treasures and all I have, and I love them as my family and my God.

6

Florence, July 1478

IT IS OFTEN remarked that the best courtier has only one family, that of his patron. If this were true, then Angelo was the best of courtiers since his own family was a distant, shadowy thing that inhabited the past, a list of names with no faces. There was nothing in his life to divide his loyalties. But in the week before he was due to depart with Monna Clarice, there came a visitor to the palazzo.

Maso Ambrogini, a wandering mercenary, stood hollering at the gate for his cousin. I came out of the office to see what was going on.

'He can't come in,' the porter said. 'Lorenzo's orders. He's a murderer.'

'I acted where justice failed!'

Angelo ran down the stairs to the courtyard. '*Gesumaria*,' he said, recognising his cousin. 'You.'

'Angelo, I have news.'

'You know Lorenzo will not have you in this house.'

'That was before his own brother was murdered. Does he still have the same views about vendetta now?'

Angelo glanced at me. I shrugged. Maso had a point, given how many rotting corpses of the Pazzi were still swinging by their necks from high places.

'Nevertheless,' said Angelo, 'we shall walk together in the street.' He beckoned to me to go with him and I fell into my habitual step, that of his companion. Although I had been assigned to Ficino, within a week Angelo and I were to be parted, and I intended to spend every minute with him that I could. We went up the Via Larga as far as the Monastery of San Marco while Maso told his news. His brother Bastiano was back in prison, this time at Volterra, and Angelo presumed that Maso's visit was, as usual, to get money from him to pay fines. But Maso had come for a different reason.

'Something has happened at Montepulciano.'

'What?'

'You must know that the armies of Rome and Naples have crossed the border near Montepulciano? They have been fighting at Lake Trasimene.'

'Yes, but the city is safe, surely?'

'There is nothing to be gained by attacking it, but while the commanders are studying their maps, trying to decide whether to advance up the Chiana valley or whether to come west, the soldiers are getting bored. They are roaming the countryside doing what soldiers do,' – here Maso raised his eyebrows knowingly – 'but even a wretch like me can't condone what they did at the Convent of Santa Maria delle Stelle. They raped the nuns. Fair enough game for any hunter, but it was particularly vicious and many of them died. Santa Maria delle Stelle – does the name mean anything to you?'

'No, nothing. Should it?'

'It was the home of your sister, Maria.'

'Oh God!' Angelo put out his hand to steady himself against a wall. 'Maria is dead?'

'I don't know.'

'We must write to Derio!'

'*Write*? The fate of your sister is unknown and you want to write *letters*? Is there no marrow in your bones? This is a matter of your family, cousin, your own sister. Why, even now you should be running for your sword, but here you stand planning letters. Admit it, you're too afraid to make the journey.'

'I am reluctant to travel through battlefields? Who would not be?' Angelo threw up his hands. 'Sister she may be, but I have no face for her, no memory. She is just a name.'

'So you will not go?'

'I cannot go. My duty lies here with Lorenzo.'

I was impressed that Angelo did not mention that he was about to be sent away to Pistoia. Loyal and discreet, as ever.

'She is kith and kin, fifteen years old and utterly alone.'

'If she's alive.'

'No marrow in your bones, no heart in your breast.'

'If I paid you, would you go for me?'

'I would go without pay – but since you've offered...' he held out his hand for his cousin's money.

'I shall have to pay you later. What is in my purse would not buy a sparrow.'

'And what shall I do if I find her?'

'Get her placed in another convent of course, or married. Though I am not sure I can raise a dowry. How much would you need? How much for a dowry?' Angelo had little money of his own: I could see him wondering if once again he could call upon Lorenzo's generosity. Lorenzo had already paid the fines to Siena for the release of Maso and Bastiano, and had not been happy to do so, given the nature of their crimes.

'How much will you want?'

'Nothing. I realise how poor you are.' Maso glanced at Angelo's fine tunic and hose. 'Your house will do.'

'*My house?*'

'That one amongst the properties of your benefice that you kept for yourself. You don't live in it. It lies empty. I need a base, Angelo, for my business.'

'And what business may that be?'

'A simple trade Bastiano and I have been building up over the years. Very lucrative, especially now, but I need a base.'

'What trade?'

'Military equipment.'

'Arms trading!' This was synonymous in Angelo's mind with

grave robbing, since the market place for the trade was the battle-field after the battle.

'We have to live. While Bastiano is in prison he cannot look after his wife and children. And then I have a wife and children in the garrison at Volterra to think about. We've done great deeds for you in the past. In fact, we have done your duty.'

'And you have been paid for it.'

'No, no. All you paid was the fines put upon us. But we have not been paid any recompense for our time and effort. Come. You don't need that house. You sleep on feather mattresses embroidered with the Medici emblems. One little house, Angelino, that's all I need, and Maria, if she lives, will be safe.'

'What will you do with her?'

'I don't know. That's for you to decide. Find another convent, or a husband.'

'But the dowry!'

'Florence has a fund for dowerless girls.'

The fund was for those in real need. Was Angelo one of them? He thought not. He enjoyed every material comfort, but he lacked substance, a fortune he could call his own. Nevertheless, it was true that Lorenzo had the power to dispose of the dowry fund.

'Take what you need,' he said at last and wearily. 'Take what I have. But I will have no burden put upon me, Maso. No ties. I must remain free. To serve Lorenzo, I must remain free.'

'So the duty falls to me once again,' said Maso, satisfied that the deal had been struck. 'Me and not you, O privileged one. It falls to me, the bandit, the outlaw who Lorenzo will not deign to have in his house. I will be the one to risk his life and liberty – it seems to be my job in life to do your duty. First I avenge your father's murder and now I rescue your sister. By the way, I shall need expenses…'

As Angelo emptied his purse into his cousin's hardened, grimy hands, Maso gazed on him as the common man ever gazes on the scholar – with utmost contempt.

✟

I do not know why, except that his grandfather had set a precedent with his own wife, but Lorenzo forbade Monna Clarice to enter either the library or his study. She never complained, nor made any comment, but dutifully avoided both places. I once asked Angelo about it, but his only explanation was that she was a pious woman who would be disturbed by the breadth of her husband's interests. 'But if she cannot read Latin and Greek, how would she know what all the books are?'

Angelo had no answer to that but said it was the rule, and that was that, and were he ever to marry, he would impose the same rule, 'Or else have one's concentration repeatedly broken with so much chirruping of *what are you doing? – when are you stopping? – what do you want for your supper?*'

I told him that such questions are the very sound of love. He said if that were so, then love is inimical to man's peace. Which it is, of course – there is no arguing with that. But who wants peace when you can have a woman in your arms?

On the day before the family's departure, I was surprised to find Monna Clarice standing outside the library door, as immobile as a statue of the Virgin.

'Madonna?' I enquired.

'Oh, I am waiting for Messer Angelo,' she said demurely. 'I think he is within.'

I went inside and found him packing a chest with books from Lorenzo's collection. 'For Piero's education,' he explained, 'Cicero, Demosthenes, Plato, and I thought I might read Suetonius, *The Lives of Notable Poets*. And then I suppose I ought to take some holy books for the edification of the soul. Jerome, perhaps.'

I told him he had a visitor waiting for him outside. When he went out, he left the door ajar and I could hear Monna Clarice gently enquiring about his needs and requirements. After much questioning about clothes and linen, and some very clipped and efficient answering, Angelo returned.

'Dear God! Imagine having to be interested in such things. Is the lot of women not pitiful? Where was I?'

'Naked and unhoused,' I retorted.

'Eh?'

'That is where we would be without them.'

'Elena told you that. I am going to put a muzzle on that glorious *bellezza* of yours. Is it not a great shame that women have the power of speech? It ruins everything.'

Deep in books, we forgot all about women until we were joined about an hour later by Gentile de' Becchi, the Bishop of Arezzo. He apologised for being late and said he had been delayed by Monna Clarice.

'Did she want to know about your clothes?' Angelo asked.

The bishop looked bemused. 'My clothes? No. She wanted to know about the Bull of Excommunication, about what it said.'

'Did you tell her?'

'Have I done right?'

'I doubt it,' said Angelo gravely. 'What did she want to know?'

Gentile looked abashed. 'What the Pope means by "diabolical suggestion".'

'You have undoubtedly done wrong,' Angelo decided. 'To discuss such calumny with the superstitious is to throw dry brushwood on to a fire.'

'Oh dear.' Gentile, a large man given to shuffling like a bear, looked forlorn. Angelo took pity on him and said that no lasting damage was done, he was sure.

'There was something else she wanted to know,' Gentile continued. 'When the Pope says we must give up everything we possess, she wanted to know if this means our houses, villas and furniture.'

'Of course. What else could it mean? But it will not come to that.'

'Indeed, as I told her, and I also said that, since we have God's love, we are free to ignore the Papal instruction to abandon the sacraments, but I fear this example of republican democracy was lost on our lady from Rome. She looked quite confused. She said, "What if Florence does not have God's love?" You know, sometimes she quite floors me with her questions, but she is right, when you think of it. It is a presumption on our part to think we do have God's love.'

'Gentile!'

'And then she said that here in the library there is a statue of a false god. I suppose she means our Plato. How does she know that?'

'She was here a while ago, and I spoke to her with the door ajar.'

'Well, even if she could see the bust, how would she know it was Plato?'

'Who else would Lorenzo deify with candles?'

I glanced up at the ancient Greek portrait bust, inscribed *Platon* on its chest in Greek letters. The first time I had seen it, the light and shadows of the votive candles seeming to animate the bearded face with its sightless eyes, my heart had thudded with excitement that our philosopher was here, yes, accorded sanctity. But to Monna Clarice this was visible heresy.

'She is convinced that Plato is the cause of all our troubles,' the bishop continued. 'In her opinion, Lorenzo is worshipping false gods, and that is why he is at war with the Vicar of Christ. "My husband," she said, "with whom I am one flesh." And then she began to cry so hard that I had to sit with her in my arms until she was calm.'

'Women are very prey to their emotions,' said Angelo, his eye straying to a book on the poets of the silver age. 'Ah, yes. I shall take that one.'

✝

The existence of Angelo's benefice, the church of San Paolino, hidden in the maze of streets between Santa Maria Novella and Ognissanti, was unsuspected by many Florentines. It was frequented only by the dyers, leatherworkers and prostitutes of the area. If Angelo went there on the night before his departure, it was not to perform any service in the church but to collect rents. He sat in his chamber for an hour or more waiting for his tenants to arrive at the appointed time but, as usual, no one turned up. We soon left for the customary tour of the properties attached to the benefice, beginning with the house he had kept for himself. Maso had already taken possession of it before departing for Montepulciano and Angelo wished to give me instructions with regard to the house in the absence of both its owner and its tenant.

It was a tall, narrow building pressed between grander houses on the Via dei Fossi. Although Maso had only slept there one night, the place was affected by his presence, contaminated one might say, for he had left much behind. The room which Angelo had intended to make available to poets and philosophers of the Platonic Academy for their discussions was now filling up with the arsenal of an arms dealer: crossbows, halberds, even an arquebus – all the spoils of war, stripped from the dead to be sold to the living. We stood looking at these terrible things in silence.

The kitchen was empty, we were hungry, it was time to exact tribute from the tenants. Many properties in the backstreets of Ognissanti had come with the benefice of San Paolino, but there was not a tenant who had paid his rent in months. We went to a street parallel to the Via dei Fossi where stood the *bottega* of Angelo's friend from university days, Sandro Botticelli.

'Help us, starving exiles and pilgrims in this fine city of yours,' said Angelo at the painter's door, hoping he might gain by the laws of hospitality that which he could not gain by the laws of rent.

It always surprised me how well-built the painter was, given that he rarely remembered to eat. My good friend Filippino Lippi called out a greeting, a sound that always restored my spirits. He had his back to us since he was holding up a panel for Botticelli to view; when he turned, it was to confront us with a portrait bearing a likeness neither of us was strong enough to look upon. A sweet, reflective profile of Giuliano de' Medici, it smothered our jokes as a bucket of ash on a fire.

'Well?' Sandro asked. 'Is your silence a compliment?'

I hoped Angelo would speak, for I could not. If it was not true to life, it was true to Giuliano: the essence of his beauty had been caught in paint. Grief in Angelo transmuted into anger and he complained irritably that painters are alchemists who do not know the power of their own operations. Sandro accepted this as the compliment he had been waiting for, but Angelo was truly upset and his soul disturbed. The dead, he declared, should be left alone, and not be brought back to haunt us.

The two painters took us to the tavern opposite the shop to restore us with bread soup and strong wine. While Angelo and Sandro discussed posthumous portraits, and a terracotta panel of the Resurrection that Lorenzo had commissioned from Verrocchio, Filippino and I exchanged opinions on the war and its progress. He drew a map in the sawdust on the floor, showing how armies advanced and what he would do if he commanded the Florentines.

'Lorenzo is useless,' he said quietly to me. 'He should stick to banking.'

'He is not very good at banking,' I said. 'I am convinced that, if he could be what he wanted to be, he would be Angelo Poliziano and a poet.'

'He would only be Angelo Poliziano if Angelo Poliziano had great wealth, numerous properties and Lucrezia Donati for a mistress,' said Filippino. With our backs to our companions, we grinned at each other.

Oblivious to us, Angelo was describing for Botticelli the relief commissioned of Verrocchio and how it was to be modelled on the lunette of Della Robbia above the sacristy in the cathedral, the place where Lorenzo had taken refuge as his brother died on that sulphurous day. He told his friend about the two Roman soldiers, the figures always shown on the left of the sarcophagus in Resurrection scenes. In Verrocchio's version, one was to appear to be sleeping, the other yawning, 'But in truth they are to be portraits of Giuliano and Lorenzo, and those who know will read the picture differently, seeing not sleeping soldiers but one brother dead and the other screaming, while above them, Christ rises from the tomb.'

Sandro Botticelli shivered. 'I have heard that Lorenzo prays for resurrection.'

Angelo dipped his voice so that no one beyond our table could hear. 'He has had made a little image of Osiris, the Egyptian god who was dismembered, and carries it with him everywhere as a talisman. I tell you, if he could find a magus who could effect the Lazarus deed, he would sell his soul.'

'So I have heard.'

'It is a madness, a temporary madness. It will pass...' Angelo said, and we all understood that he spoke from experience. 'Something has changed in him, he is not the same man. You can see the agony etching deep into his skin, every day deeper, like acid. The madness will pass, but...' Angelo struggled to express what he sensed in Lorenzo. 'His joy has gone. He so loved life, but now he seems hard, even brutal sometimes. Why, he shouted at me yesterday as if I were Pope Sixtus himself, and all I had done was mention my cousin Maso.'

It was the opinion of Botticelli that Giuliano's death had been a form of sacrifice. 'The more I think about it, the more I am convinced. Giuliano, the best of us, slain at the altar of the cathedral – Isaac offered up to God, at last. We are all changed. I cannot put brush to panel now without thinking... We have wasted far too much time being frivolous. It is time to serve God in all we do. God and the spirit of Giuliano.'

Grimacing at the taste of the rough wine, Angelo told him how he had been given the duty of taking Lorenzo's family to Pistoia and looking after them. 'I am to continue as Piero's tutor, and to take Lorenzo's place as father in the family. So with this pernicious liquid you are poisoning the man whom Lorenzo trusts most in the world.'

'Trusts most not to bed his wife, you mean.'

'Ha!' Filippino was surprised to hear such wit from his master.

'I had hoped that you – unlike everyone else – would be above that kind of comment.'

'And I thought you of all men would never abandon the Muse.'

Angelo barked at Sandro. 'Abandon her?'

'You are giving up poetry to become a nursemaid.'

'Sixty years ago, a certain book was found in the Monastery of St Gall by Poggio Bracciolini. When he brought it into Florence, it was paraded in triumph. That book was Quintilian's *On the Education of an Orator*. It formed Lorenzo's education, it formed mine, and it is now to form that of his sons. Nowhere in that sacred text does Quintilian refer to the role of the educator as that of nursemaid.'

'Most noble words. But your Muse is a jealous goddess who does not approve of such stoic virtue. She wants you for herself. To follow the path of art is to be a little bit selfish and utterly single-minded.'

'The days when a man could live solely by the art of his pen are long passed,' Angelo complained. 'If ever there was such a time.'

Sandro refilled our cups. 'I sometimes think God hates poets even more than he hates painters. At least painters can set up shop and sell their wares. You benighted souls – mere puppets of patronage. Our patrons commission us to paint. Yours pay you to teach boys, act as secretary, bursar, chaplain, to compose noxious odes in praise of visiting donkeys, in short anything but write the verse you have it in you to write.'

'How can it be otherwise when the patron, himself a noble poet, is so hobbled by worldly concerns? While Lorenzo yearns for time to concentrate on his sonnets, how can I hope to have such time myself? And yet, now I think about it, that is what he has given me. For what else shall I do all day once my lessons with Piero are over? In his magnanimity, Lorenzo has removed me from all peril and danger and given me time to write.'

'Phoo! When did you last keep company with six children under the age of eight? Write? Ha! I wish I were a betting man. God definitely hates poets. Whatever spare time you have, I wager it will be less than when you were a cobbler's apprentice.'

Forgetting his resolution not to drink too much of the wretched wine, Angelo reached for his cup, staring at his friend wildly. 'What are you saying? That I would be better off away from Lorenzo?

I cannot believe it. You cannot be serious. He is the best of all patrons, best of all friends.' He drank and his face stretched as if it were an agony.

'What about your Homer?' Sandro Botticelli asked. It was a question as sharp as a dagger.

Angelo muttered something in reply.

'What was that?' Sandro asked cruelly.

'I said, I am working on Book Five.'

'Liar. You haven't done anything in Latin or Greek for years. While you are serving Lorenzo in his life's work, you have abandoned your own. Now you only write in Tuscan.'

'It is well for you that I do!' Angelo retorted.

If it was unkind of Sandro to bring the matter up at this hour, he was unrepentant. He stretched wearily and said, 'I do not know if anyone has told you this before, but what you should be aiming for is a professorship.'

'God preserve me, I was not born to put men to sleep.' Angelo stared across the room in grim frustration. He called to the mistress of the tavern to see if she had anything better in her cellar. 'The best you have,' he said, 'and be quick.'

Not only vanquished in argument, but by a painter – an artisan in a grimy apron – Angelo stared at the new wine being poured into his hollow cup. He tasted it, and grimaced again, but not so violently. He nodded to the mistress of the tavern and she left the flagon on the table. He had drunk too much, despite the need to keep his head clear for when he met Lorenzo later to receive his instructions. He should be at the palazzo even now, yet here he was, suffering Botticelli's knife to plunge into the most tender parts of his soul.

'Patronage,' said the painter, 'a curse upon it. It is just another form of slavery.'

'Constraint is the mother of art. Leave a man to himself and he will waste his time in pursuit of his desires. Remove his freedom, restrict his time, forbid him a family, and then his talents will prosper and grow.'

'If that is true, then your being sent to Pistoia is a blessing from which we may hope great things.'

The wine was beginning to swamp our brains in pleasant clouds. Filippino's head was propped on his hand, his eyes only half open. I too was nearly asleep. We both jumped violently as Angelo shouted, 'Of course it is not true! What is Lorenzo thinking of, sending me away? I, his Patroclus, his Jonathan! Why is he sending me away with his wife? You can imagine what the others are saying. Tell them, Tommaso; tell them the gossip behind my back!'

'Our friends of Lorenzo's brigata are calling him a eunuch.'

'Lorenzo may as well castrate me and have done with it. Dear God in heaven! Sandro – when he announced it I could not believe my ears. *Pistoia?* I nearly followed Monna Clarice in her faint.'

'Hush,' Sandro said, stroking his friend. 'Have some more wine.'

I slapped my hand over Angelo's cup. 'He has had enough. He needs to keep a clear head.'

It still took another hour to part company, for Sandro grew morose and was certain we should never meet again. The coming war, he said, was Armageddon. 'Everything we have worked for shall be destroyed.' He looked at Angelo unsteadily. 'You,' he said, 'are my priest, the priest of the Muse and of Beauty. Through your words, I have visions. We see the same world, live in the same world, you and I. I paint the roses of your imagination. You cannot go away and leave me, I will not have it. I want to walk in that realm of Aphrodite you have painted for us in your Tuscan words, Angelo. What shall I do without you but miserable Annunciations?'

Angelo smiled. 'Do not let the agents of the Church hear you say that.'

'We live in a world of dogma and suspicion. But Truth, she is beauty itself. You must not go. Do not leave me. Who will tell me about the great painters and sculptors of Greece? Who will describe for me satyrs and centaurs? Do not go, please do not go!'

'Ficino remains, and our Tommaso, and other friends of our Academy. It is I who will be alone, not you.' So saying, Angelo

Poliziano embraced Sandro Botticelli in a farewell so prolonged and mournful they had to be pulled apart by us, their servant and apprentice.

✢

Lorenzo was awaiting us on our return, his arms full of his younger son, Giovanni. The two year old, who had woken while Lorenzo was visiting the nursery, was now draped over his father's chest, his head heavy on Lorenzo's shoulder. As we entered, Lorenzo's annoyance blazed silently from his eyes. 'I have been waiting for you for hours,' he told Angelo, his voice low so as not to awaken the child.

Angelo apologised and explained about the wine of Ognissanti and its papaverous qualities.

'Fatherhood is not something one delegates,' Lorenzo said, bouncing from foot to foot to keep his son somnolent. 'I cannot say to you, here, take him and feel in your heart what I feel. It would not be possible. You do not know what it is like to discover your wife is pregnant, what feelings rush in your blood, how the natural duty to protect turns a man into a drawn crossbow, ready to fire at the least danger. All I can do is to ask you, my friend above all friends, to take my wife and children to safety on my behalf. You could at least have been sober while we had this conversation.'

Angelo went to the wash basin and tipped a jug of cold water over his head. He returned to Lorenzo, towelling himself dry, with enough wine still in his veins for him to speak the truth.

'I expected us to face this war together. How could you make such a decision without telling me? Oh, I know I am not a warrior except in my dreams, but then neither am I a eunuch to be trusted with your wife. All week I have been at the mercy of the wits in this house. Have you not heard the Maenads baying for me? They are delirious with the scent of my blood. That oaf Scala actually told me this proves I am dispensable, as he has always supposed. "Personally," he said, "I would have you in exile, but this will do, this will do." So do not blame me if I escaped for a few hours.

Besides,' he concluded, 'I needed to put my affairs in order. I do have them, you know, affairs of my own, family matters. But I am now ready to leave in the morning.'

Lorenzo paced the room, gently bouncing his sleeping son. He paused at the lectern where rested the copy of Quintilian that he kept in his room at all times, and he quoted from it: *Reasoning comes as naturally to a man as flying to birds, speed to horses and ferocity to birds of prey. Those who are dull and unteachable are as abnormal as monstrous births, and few in number. See that the child's nurse speaks correctly and do not allow the boy to become accustomed even in infancy to a style of speech which he will subsequently have to unlearn. There should be attached to the boy one person who has some knowledge of speaking who can correct any errors.* Have you forgotten your duty so soon, and the role I have given you? Why do you listen to what others say? You know the truth. Whatever you and I want – and do not forget that I too have to suffer my own decisions – your duty is to be with my son.'

Angelo sighed and apologised. 'Do you remember when we were in Mantua, when we visited the schoolroom of Vittorino da Feltre? It was as if the place still bore his radiance, the glow of a great teacher, and we bathed in it.'

'Of course I remember. His spirit filled us like the Holy Ghost.'

'That was the day you asked me to be Piero's tutor. The promises I made that day I strive to keep. Forgive me for what I have said. I am sorry, Lorenzo. I will go happily to Pistoia, for the care of your son – both your sons – is my life's work. You will want me to take on the education of Giovanni when he is of age?'

'Be assured of it. With all that is happening, I am even more convinced that we have chosen the right course.' Lorenzo switched to speaking in Latin, so as not to be understood by Giovanni's nurse. However discreet the woman sitting in the corner might look, Lorenzo knew better. *'Men raised on ancient literature are much less likely to behave like beasts than those raised on the creeds of our superstitious faith. Ignorance is the enemy – but do not tell my wife I said so.'* Lorenzo turned his attention to the details of Angelo's duty. He spelt out how the children should be raised on ancient literature but brought up in the faith, what prayers to use and when; the finances of the family, which childish desire might be indulged and which curtailed; he gave advice on the temperament of his wife, especially when with child.

'Is she with child?'

Lorenzo shrugged, but a smile played at his lips. 'Not yet. But whatever her condition, I advise you to leave Monna Clarice to the care of her companions. I notice you always flinch when I read that part where Quintilian says that a child's parents should be educated and speak well. I know what you think about my wife's dialect, and I have done what I can to improve her. But do not try to correct her yourself. I ask you only to correct the mistakes the children pick up from her. Never confuse my wife's lack of education with a lack of wit. When it comes to knowing what is best for the children's material welfare, listen to her as to an oracle.'

'When shall I begin to tutor Giovanni?'

'He will be three in December. You can begin then.'

'I would be happy to start now.'

'Your happiness would not last a day. The pleasure of teaching a child still learning to speak soon palls. No, leave it to his mother to teach him to recognise and name the alphabet, and just keep a discreet ear on his speech, cure it of any taint of the Roman dialect. Indeed, let him hear your Tuscan as much as possible, as well as your Latin. You will be as a beacon to my sons. I could not find a better model for them. So for now let Giovanni grow accustomed to hearing you speak, then, in December, you can begin to teach him to read. As to the girls, I would have them instructed in Latin, so allow them to attend those lessons which are relevant, as Vittorino da Feltre himself recommended. Of course, my wife would benefit greatly herself from our educational programme, but she has chosen to reject it. She would rather be piously illiterate than profanely literate. That is her choice. But she is a clever woman, Angelo. Do not judge her on her preference in literature. She is the mother of my children; I love her as I love myself. I am asking you to protect her, with your life if needs be.' Lorenzo laughed gruffly. 'It may not be as emasculating as you think, to be in the country protecting my family. But I hope for your sake that this war *does* make a eunuch of you, that you see no battles, but instead spend the coming months in peace, enjoying the leisure to study. It is the least I could give you, in reward for your loyal friendship.'

Lorenzo handed him his son. Giovanni stirred but soon fell back into his contented, trusting sleep, his head resting now on a different shoulder. The weight of the boy was not as strange a sensation to Angelo as Lorenzo perhaps supposed, for he remembered it from his own boyhood, when he had carried round his sisters. Fatherhood is innate in all men, not just in fathers. What Lorenzo could not pass across, however, was that which Angelo would most require to fulfil his duty: the father's authority.

After a while, Lorenzo took the boy back and gave him to his waiting nurse, who had sat on a bench throughout, struggling to stay awake. Once she had left with the boy, there was a moment's awkwardness. Angelo clearly wanted and expected to spend the night with Lorenzo, taking this last opportunity to stay awake until dawn, composing songs to the lute, translating verse, discussing obscure etymologies, for in the night they were not patron and servant but the closest of companions and the best of friends. I could see the transformation taking place, the dropping of roles and the nonsense of the day. They were as impatient as lovers to be left alone, so I excused myself, saying I was away to my wife.

'And I,' said Lorenzo.

Angelo jumped as if stung.

'Monna Clarice is expecting me. This is our last night together for who knows how long.' Lorenzo wore the face of a man who chooses duty over pleasure.

Angelo and I exchanged a glance. We both knew that Clarice had been to San Lorenzo on this day in a small family procession for her rite of purification. It was incumbent upon her husband to take the opportunity to sow more seed in her fertile ground.

'How long will you be?' Angelo asked, still hopeful.

'I shall spend the night in her bed,' Lorenzo replied. 'We must rise early tomorrow for you are to depart at dawn.'

Angelo went to his own bed in the chamber he shared with other members of the brigata, walking in silently and without the light of a candle, hoping the others were asleep. But they were still awake, waiting for him, for they had not yet exhausted their jokes at his expense. When at last he went to sleep that night he had a dream in which he was castrated.

7

Florence and Pistoia, July 1478

THE PINK AND CREAM façade of Santa Maria Novella stood out in the dawn light like a temple to antiquity as a long line of horses, mules and donkeys made its way across the piazza towards the Porta del Prato. This new frontage to an ancient church, formed from sacred principles of geometry, represented a dream shared by Lorenzo and all his friends, that that which was most fine, the ancient knowledge of the Romans and the Greeks, should be brought back to life. Until our own age, the arts of grammar, poetry, oratory, painting, sculpture, architecture and music had become almost extinct. When Leon Battista Alberti had set up the new façade to this old church, with its glowing marble and singing numbers, he set up the programme we now so avidly follow. Santa Maria Novella had been the start of the New Rome that the Medici envisioned for their city, a city now under threat from the Old Rome of a corrupt papacy.

The procession was a subdued one for the Medici, and made at dawn to attract small attention: six covered wagons surrounded by an armed guard carried the family and their servants, while a long train of more wagons carried their furniture and possessions. At the head rode a poet who had just that week turned twenty four. I felt proud on my friend's behalf but my wife, who stood beside me to see them off, said that Lorenzo had chosen the wrong man.

'Why do you say that?'

'This is a task for an uncle of the family, some elder to whom authority is natural. Angelo will not survive this, Tommaso. Look at him. He is too young.'

I told her she was merely trying to guess the future and had no reasonable grounds for her views. 'It is we who may not survive, trapped as we are in this city. If I had had my way, you would also be in that train and attending Monna Clarice, but my request was denied.'

'I thank heaven for it. They would not want a Pazzi with them, and I would not want to be separated from you at such a time.'

She was hooded by her cloak, her face hidden from the Florentines. Putting my arm around her and feeling the warmth of her, remembering our intimacy of the night, I longed for immortality, for Arcadia, for somewhere to roam with her in meadows, free and out of danger, alive and together for eternity. On this day Marsilio Ficino was retiring to his villa on Careggi and I would have to leave Elena alone in the house until dark. I was frightened and could hardly bear not to have her always in my sight. The sinews of my anxiety felt taut beyond endurance. Absorbed thus by my own concerns, I forgot about Angelo and the disappearing family, consigning them to a fate I presumed must be a happy one compared to our own. The gates were closed behind them. Florence awaited the future.

I took Elena home and instructed her as usual on the locking and barring of doors; then, meeting Father Marsilio as arranged, I too went out of the city, to Careggi.

On the surrounding hills there was no sign of being at war. Peasants laboured in the fields, scything the hay and loading it on to ox-carts. Wasps crawled over the fruit of plum trees while bees meandered, intoxicated in an air laden with the scent of roses and honeysuckle. A gentle breeze soughed in long grass and olive groves, while buzzards hung still in the sky. If Angelo sometimes dreamt of being a warrior hero, I had no such fantasies, and was very content to be given such tremendous desk work at this time, in this place. Careggi – a Tuscan corruption of *caritum ager* – the field of the Graces. As soon as we arrived in his secluded villa built right into the rock of the hill, Father Marsilio wanted to begin work, but I had a question for him. I followed him about like an altar boy as he performed an oblation to the gods and refreshed the house by burning frankincense and attar of roses.

'What use is this work, if we are to be destroyed?' I asked, inhaling deeply of the sacred scents.

'This is why we are hurrying, Tommaso, to complete it before we die.' He smiled and handed me a quire of paper to tap into order.

I tried my question again, in a different form. 'What use is it to the world, when the world is a murderous bed of greed and iniquity?'

'Is that what the world is? I see it as a sweet and harmonious song of love.'

A third time, coming in from the east, as it were. 'Should we not be down in the city, defending its walls?'

'There are soldiers to do that, and we are not soldiers.'

And so for the last time, and from the fourth quarter, I approached with an objection. 'Should we not be at prayer for peace rather than translating philosophy?'

'This is not a work of escape or forgetting. We are not wrapping ourselves in blankets and pretending the war is not happening. This is the greatest work of all, coming to completion at a time of darkness; it is the very song of Orpheus, and needs to be sung.'

He spoke about the *prisci theologi*, the chain of ancient theologians who had prepared the Gentiles for the coming of Christ, a chain that includes Hermes, an Egyptian sage contemporary with Moses, Zoroaster, the prophet of Chaldea, Orpheus, Pythagoras and Plato. And now, since the words of Christ were being neglected and forgotten, the work of those theologians had become vital once more, and for this reason Cosimo de' Medici had charged Marsilio

– when he was still a boy – to bring Plato out of Greek and into Latin. This work was his life's work, and it was on the eve of completion.

'The Christian faith is true,' he said energetically, 'but its priesthood is corrupt.'

'How will Plato help that?'

'Think of a church such as Santissima Annunciata, where you can see nothing for the accretion of votive offerings, wax effigies, and the like – everything dark and obscured, full of cobwebs and shadowy. Or one of the icons of the Greeks, so ornately framed that one can barely see the picture. That is our Church, with the truth of the Gospels obscured by the abstractions of the theologians, the ignorance of priests and the superstition of the laity. How may we see Truth in such a setting? Were we to tear away the coverings, the pain would be too great, too terrible. It is better to shine the light of Reason, by which men may begin to see for themselves and distinguish the truth from the untruth. For that we need Plato and his beloved Socrates. As soon as this work is published, Latin Christendom will benefit from the knowledge contained herein and come alive to the teaching that once paved the way to Christ, and will do so again. For to be sure, with Byzantium lost to the Turks, and the Latin Church now home to demonic forces, a return to Christ is imperative for our people, the Christian flock.'

I was satisfied and asked no more questions.

✛

As Angelo's task in raising Piero de' Medici was a part of this great work, he too was singing the Orphic song. That was the intention of Lorenzo; but Lorenzo's wife thought otherwise. As soon as the Medici family was but a short distance from Florence, Monna Clarice changed her nature as completely as Proteus, the ancient shape-shifter.

'It was about a mile,' Angelo wrote to me. 'If you want to know the range of a man's influence over his wife, it is about a mile.'

A mile along the road to Pistoia, the meek, unassuming wife of il Magnifico demanded that the travellers stop and rest. Angelo returned from the head of the line to tell her that he had planned a rest further on, half way to their destination.

'She looked at me like Medusa. I turned to stone. We rested.'

And that was that. Authority was established, and it lay with Monna Clarice.

✛

Caro amico, Angelo wrote from Pistoia. 'Our host, Ser Andrea Panciaticchi, spares no effort in making us all at home. The palazzo is newly built in the antique style and is very beautiful, with ivory-coloured walls and stone doorways carved with garlands of fruit. Marble floors carry the sound of distant footfalls while the cheeping of birds in the garden echo in the house and amplify its peace. Stillness seems to exude from the palms growing in urns on the landings of stairways. Ancient statues on pedestals celebrate the Rome that first created such standards of cool elegance fifteen hundred years ago. This is a house of peace and repose and I am sure we shall all be quite happy here, as much as we can be, separated from Lorenzo.'

He told me that he had much leisure and was looking forward to reading and writing a great deal. The only thing he seemed to write, however, was letters, both his own and those of Monna Clarice.

✛

It takes marriage to make a man realise that a woman is more than an object for man's use. I had spent years in the Medici palace and had never spoken to Clarice d' Orsini. More often than not she only appeared in the distance, passing across an open door in a receding infinity of doorways. I sometimes wondered how she might respond to love-making, and discovered my imagination could not stretch so far. I thought it must be like having St Ursula stiff in your arms. I knew Lorenzo's mistress, Lucrezia Donati, much better, for being a friend and lover of Lorenzo, she was equal

99

to his companions; she knew my name and would greet me affectionately, as she greeted all of us, and we responded in kind. It was all too easy to imagine having Lucrezia Donati in your arms, and we envied Lorenzo his great fortune. As for the other one, the pale shade, she was simply the mother of his children.

I said as much to Elena one night, having read to her one of Angelo's plaintive letters, and found myself pinned down by her in a very wrath of objection.

'Why do men change the law to suit themselves, when they apply it to us so strictly?' she cried, her hair flying about like a Maenad's. 'How dare you condone Lorenzo's adultery so lightly – and that poor woman! Who knows what she suffers?'

As none of us knew, Elena made it up. Night after night she wove a picture of Clarice Orsini for me, out of the threads of information she gleaned from gossip and stitched on to the fabric of her innate understanding of female nature. It was an effective image she created. Imagine Clarice then, on the night before her departure to Pistoia. Lorenzo came to her, as she had begged him to. After the birth of the baby, after the purification, he took possession of her once more. Usually he would then leave for his own chamber but on this night he sat with her and talked, talked as he had never done before. She wondered where Poliziano might be, that Lorenzo was talking to her like this, and chastised herself for the thought, having decided long ago that it was bad enough being jealous of other women without being jealous of a man also. So she put aside her fear and anger to caress her husband and bring him solace in this midnight time, hoping for something that had been denied to her throughout their thirteen years of marriage: that Lorenzo might fall asleep by her side and that she might wake to see him beside her in the following dawn. But as ever she fell asleep first and when she awoke he had gone, his place cold.

Now she is in the Palazzo Panciaticchi in Pistoia and looking out of the window towards the great square. The view is strange. The place is strange. Even though she has with her the children and most of her possessions, along with her old nurse and her closest companions, Clarice feels alone in this alien place. It is not as bad, however, as that last time she moved house, from Rome to Florence, from girlhood to being the wife of a man she had never met. That terror, though she might sometimes smile at it now, still haunts her dreams. All those people, all those unknown people, cheering her progress along strange streets, helping her dismount, meeting her, touching her – oh, how the Florentines *touch* – calling her variously, 'daughter', 'sister', 'wife'. And she, in the extremes of isolation, thinking repeatedly, 'I am Clarice d' Orsini; I am Clarice d' Orsini.' But she was not. She had become a Medici. That family with flat noses and intense eyes, with the heraldic arms of five balls on a shield, who paradoxically were princes of a republic, untitled yet supremely powerful. 'I am Clarice d' Orsini.' She should have been the wife of a duke or marquis, not a banker. That Lorenzo was the richest man in the world was beside the point. He had no rank. 'I am Clarice d' Orsini, daughter of Jacopo Orsini of Monterotondo, sister of a Cardinal, and of the Count of Pitigliano.' But the words became meaningless as her identity was subsumed by the Medici.

Lorenzo's face, with its very square jaw, and the perpetual frown occasioned by breaking the bridge of his nose in childhood, could be rather frightening in repose, but she rarely saw him in repose. Instead she saw Lorenzo active, Lorenzo engaged, Lorenzo exercised. He was never still, always in demand, and always responding wholeheartedly. When the children had begun to arrive, he had thrown himself passionately into fatherhood. Clarice forgot who she had been and became grateful for who she had become, which was the mother of the children of Lorenzo the Magnificent.

That her husband had a mistress she knew well enough, despite all Poliziano's careful smokescreens. At first she had kept her pain to herself, but then she had confessed it in a rush to her mother-in-law. Monna Lucrezia had spoken to her at length of this, the worst pain a woman must suffer next to childbirth.

'*Must* suffer?' Clarice asked sharply.

Monna Lucrezia took her hands in her own. 'He is a man, and

when a man's needs become pressing, there is nothing a woman can do. Think of it: you are confined, or, having delivered, you are waiting to be churched. Months pass. Men cannot wait that long. His mistress, Clarice, is Lucrezia Donati.'

'I know,' said Clarice, choking on her tears. 'It was obvious, even from the start, even at the wedding. Before the wedding. When he would not write to me, his betrothed. Too busy to come myself, he said. Too busy! I know it is Lucrezia. I have always known.' Her tears became convulsive. Monna Lucrezia embraced her tenderly.

'Clarice, Clarice, I had no idea.'

Clarice turned her face, sanctified by tears, to her mother-in-law. 'Why did he not marry her if he loves her so much?'

Monna Lucrezia cleared her throat. 'You must blame me for that, for I would not allow it. His father and I, we were adamant. Florentine girls – they are vain; they are weak; they die young. This passion for Lucrezia – it was an infatuation, we said. We were determined that our Lorenzo would marry a Roman girl.'

'So your choice of me was politic!'

'Of course.' Monna Lucrezia straightened her back. 'Should I be ashamed of that?'

For the next two days, Clarice had kept apart and was fervent in her prayers. When she had emerged into the family again – and Lorenzo not having yet missed her – she went to her husband to offer her blessings to Lucrezia Donati, who had just given birth to her first child, by a husband Lorenzo had found for her himself. 'If it please you,' Clarice whispered to Lorenzo, her words coming despite herself, 'I would be godmother to the child.' Lucrezia Donati's husband was absent, away on business, as he so often was, commissioned by Lorenzo to perform various acts on behalf of bank and state in faraway places. So Lorenzo stood in place of the father at the baptism, and his wife stood as godmother. When Clarice held the baby and stared into its eyes, she did not see, as she had feared, Lorenzo's own image there. Even so, and despite all her prayers calling for the power to forgive, she could not look at Lucrezia Donati, but had her eyes fastened either on the baby or on the floor.

Lorenzo praised her for her magnanimity. She accepted the praise but secretly berated herself for failure, for she had not forgiven, nor risen above jealousy, or else she would have been able to meet the other woman's eyes. And it had been the same with that other contender for her husband's love – Angelo Poliziano. She had tried so hard to like him, to be magnanimous, but she could not forgive him for being her husband's preferred companion. She might know her husband's body, but Poliziano enjoyed an intimacy of the soul she could only dream of. And it was an intimacy that was corrupting.

It was not good, this poetry. She said so often enough to Lorenzo, and he would gaze at her fondly as if at an idiot. She had said to Monna Lucrezia, 'This ancient poetry is a pollution of the mind,' and her mother-in-law had laughed like a girl.

'I am serious,' Clarice insisted. 'To read Ovid is to corrupt the Christian soul.'

Monna Lucrezia persuaded her that the children were not being fed on Ovid nor on anything similar. 'It is all Virgil, Homer, Plato, Cicero – the very best, my dear, the very best.'

Clarice was not convinced, but she knew it was useless to continue arguing. She schooled herself to be outwardly content while remaining inwardly true to her own holy faith. Let these pagan Medici do what they will. She would not be subverted, not in her heart, and neither would her children so long as she had any power over them. But in the way stood their tutor.

'And now,' she thinks, as she gazes out over rooftops towards the spire of an ancient Pistoian church, 'we are alone together, you and I.' She tries to stop her thoughts, to go no further. She needs distraction and rings the little hand bell on the table, bringing her companions to her side. For she does not want to think any more about how bad things are becoming, about her God and her husband, and how they are at war.

✠

Caro amico, – What news of Montepulciano? Has my cousin Maso returned? Send me what news you have, since Lorenzo is unable to write but rarely. I hesitate to write of my own troubles, since they are so small but, like the motes in the eye, they seem huge. Yesterday I attempted to explain to Madonna Clarice why I am educating her son with the texts of Virgil and Plato. She said she was not happy for Piero to learn Latin from Plato. 'Have no fear of that, Madonna,' I replied, 'since Plato wrote in Greek.' How I miss you at such moments! – here there is no one to appreciate my wit. I crave to hear Matteo Franco's laugh, even if he does squawk like a peacock in season. Madonna was completely unmoved and said that, if my purpose is to teach her son Greek, then I should use the Gospels. I told her I cannot, for they are written in demotic Greek and not the pure language of the ancients. And then she said, 'Why does my son need to learn a language he will never use? Whatever kind of Greek the Gospels are in, that is the kind of Greek he needs to know, surely?' and went on her way before I could respond.

I do not want to go against the wishes of my patron's wife, but I must, if I am to obey my patron. We continue with Livy and Virgil, Statius and Aesop, Plato and Demosthenes.

Piero is enjoying his studies, as much as any small boy who would prefer to be outside playing with bows and arrows or learning to ride. We alternate the hours of the day between exercises for the mind and exercises for the body, and he is a better athlete than scholar, but we persist. He declines and conjugates well in both Latin and Greek, and I test him on the paradigms every day. As well as the precepts of grammar, I am teaching him correct pronunciation and elegant diction, and we commit to heart the moral sentences of antique authors so that the substance of his being may be refined. It is like sculpture, cutting away that which is shapeless and has no use, to reveal the hidden, living form of the true man within. And so gradually the anger and petulance of childhood will disappear, and a cultivated youth emerge.

It is the received wisdom of the schools that the seed is from the father, but often to look at this sapling is to see the mother. This is a question I intend to pursue, if I can find any of the books of Galen here. I have been to several houses in Pistoia, and met the learned men of the city, and may avail myself of what books they have, but the books of the whole city collected together do not amount to one shelf in Lorenzo's library.

If this is leisure, then it is being spent in a desert. *Vale*. Angelo at Pistoia.

8

Montepulciano, July, 1478

I MOVED AMONG those ruined nuns with my senses quite dried up. It was beyond tears, beyond grief, to see what men can do in lust, if it was lust, and not some destructive evil which flows through men rather than from them. Suor Cecilia was dead, as were three others. The rest were desecrated in mind, body and soul. I brought my sisters what relief I could, but gave them no words, for my throat was parched of speech. I was found by the magistrates and, a day later, taken to the house of my sister Lucrezia.

'Oh, Maria!' she said at our reunion, 'Maria, Maria, Maria!' And then began to cry and lament, for her husband is close to death. 'I cannot help you. I cannot help myself. As our mother suffered, so must I. Now it is my family that will be broken up and cast to the wind.'

It was as well that I was with her during that night. Even as her husband was struggling with the dark angel, Lucrezia was weeping for her future. Custom demands that she return to her family, but Angelo is in Florence and Derio in Siena. Twenty thousand soldiers lie between us. Honour prevents her from living alone with her children for, as she puts it, 'widows are prone to debauchery.'

I blinked. My sister does not look prone to debauchery. She read my expression and shrugged briefly. 'It is something that comes upon you as soon as you are alone. How am I to know? I have never been alone. But it comes upon you as sure as menstrual blood. A woman alone heaps dishonour on her family.'

She has her dowry and can marry again, if she can find anyone to broker it, but she will lose her sons. 'Maria, I could not bear to be parted from them. Can you understand? No. How could you understand? You have a virgin womb.'

In the third hour of the night, her husband died. Lucrezia set up a wail of lamentation that had very little to do with him. I sat in vigil at the bedside, resting deep in my soul where I was vesting myself in an armour of courage. At dawn I told her my plan.

'We shall walk to Florence, all of us together, to join Angelo.'

'You are insane!' she gasped. Her world is so tightly stitched at the seams that she has no conception of a life outside of law and custom. She is quite walled about with her ideas of what one can and cannot do. 'Insane!' she repeated.

'We shall go in the dark. The Madonna and her stars will guide us.' I wanted to tear the veils from my sister's eyes and show her the value of recklessness in an hour of need but she was as frozen as Lot's wife. She refused to listen to me and busied herself with the funeral arrangements.

Saracina came to the funeral with her husband, Bernardo Tarugi. Afterwards she spoke to Lucrezia, offering to take her in until such time that Angelo or, more preferably Derio, since he was married, could look after her.

'And the boys?'

'We cannot bear the expense,' said Saracina's husband firmly. The boys must either be split up and sent to uncles, or sent together to the orphanage. I thought Lucrezia was going to faint.

'And me?' I asked.

'You must come to us for the time being,' said Bernardo Tarugi, 'until we find you a place in another convent.'

'Leave us now,' I told them. 'Come for us tomorrow.'

'Two women alone in the house for the night?' said Saracina, shocked.

'Our virtue will not be compromised nor our honour lost in one night. Come for us tomorrow.'

✝

106

I could not sleep in the night for the sound of my sister sobbing. I lay awake watching the room gradually fill with moonlight until all things were visible. The moon pulled on my soul, drawing me up from the bed, drawing me up from my fate. Fate and Destiny – what is the difference? – you can choose the latter, or smother it with fear.

'Lucrezia,' I said. 'Come, let us go.'

'Go where?' she said, her words stumbling.

'Out, away. Let us sail away on the river of moonlight.'

'You are insane.'

I grasped her by the shoulders. 'What is left for you if you stay? Remarriage at best, at worst a living death as servant of your younger sister. Either way, without your sons. A recipient of charity and mercy, ever grateful, never complaining. A life of sewing! Lucrezia, take the chance! How much money do you have? We shall have to bribe the guards at the gate to let us out.'

'I cannot go.'

'This is your choice, Lucrezia: whether to live a day as a lion or a year as a sheep. Which shall it be? Either way we shall die, but I would rather meet death out in the open than already entombed. Will you come?'

'How can you even think of it? There are wolves and bears in the forest, wild mercenaries on the road, and you've seen what they can do.'

'And then there is God, who governs all things.'

'It is God's will that we be obedient. Break the law and take the consequences.'

'Lucrezia, you have lost everything. What do you have left to lose?'

Suddenly she looked at me directly in the eyes, and a light shone there not seen before. It was bright only for a moment, but in that moment I got Lucrezia from her bed and dressed. We tried no disguises. She put on a travelling cloak and I the habit of a postulant. We roused the boys and within the hour we were out of the city.

The road down the hill was clear. The valley and its sea of hillocks was transfigured by the moon, and all the sleeping people were unaware of it. That pentecostal light was frightening: it was the light of the imagination, and thought-figures began to move in it.

'Santa Maria delle Stelle, be with us, look after us, let your dark cloak be our shield and protection.' So I prayed. The first steps from the city were *taken in terror. We had to learn to trust the darkness and its silver queen, allowing the night to embrace us and the light to guide us. The fear of the dark endured, but with each step we whittled away at it, learning how to become creatures of the night and travel in the darkness like the badgers, the way lit by the moon casting her strange pewter light over the landscape. Having once caught my foot in a rabbit hole, I realised why pilgrims use staves and made one from the branch of a tree so that I might become at least three-legged in this world of sensible quadrupeds.*

My senses quickened as if coming alive for the first time. The touch of the ground was full of information and, apart from those occasions when I trod inadvertently into mire or ordure, I led the way surely towards a stream that leads down to the Chiana with a strange confidence that would not have been present in daylight. It was as if each step, taken in full alertness, passed us on to the next step, one step after another leading the way; as if my feet knew better than I did where to go.

At dawn we found an isolated beekeeper's hut fenced about in a small parcel of land on the hillside. The beekeeper was absent and, feeling guilty and intrusive, we ate from the harvest of his garden and drank his wine. Despite being fearful of his return, we were too tired to stay awake and slept on his pallet. The day passed without incident. As we left in the evening, we thanked providence for our shelter and tidied it up for its owner, putting flowers in a jug on the table and wondering what he would make of it.

On the second night the way was easier and we were growing used to our pilgrimage in the dark. The armies had not yet passed this way and so there were fruit on the trees, crops in the fields, and we could eat like any thief in the night. As we followed the stream, the moon travelled the sky and kept vigil over the world, for no one else was abroad except the night creatures.

Above, dimmed by the brightness of the moon but still visible, were stars like pearls on dark velvet. We walked in the ghostly light, gaining a rhythm which caused a deep peace to settle on us. I was beginning to prefer the badger world to my own, for here in the dark and in solitude I was not strange, awkward or a postulant. Here I could walk freely with my head bare; I could live the life of a nymph or goddess, be a prophetess in a cave, part of the living, breathing creation, feeling the pulse of the world. As for Lucrezia, rather than pass through this rent in the veils of life, she carried her world and her sons with her like a cocoon, and fretted all the way about what was ahead and what was behind.

'Smell this,' I said.

'Smell what?'

'Everything. The earth itself. Is it not wonderful?'

Scent is manifold, a texture of odours filling all space, and most of them sweet, even that of decay. In time I even became able to detect the pats of dung and avoid them. I had left the convent, the city and the artificial life, my fate and its artificial religion. Perhaps once men found it necessary to withdraw from the world in order to find God, but the ideal was a mortal one, subject to corruption, so that convent life now was nothing but a waste at best, an hypocrisy at worst. This life of the forest and the dark road, of fear and courage, of solitude and spirit, was a living faith that exalted my soul in a perfume of leaf mould and wood.

Lucrezia sniffed the air. 'Sulphur,' she said.

And she was right. Our land is a healing place where hot springs throw up a curative mud. We had come to an ancient spa circled around by brick arches shaded by pines and holm oaks. Filled during the day by the arthritic and the gouty, it was deserted at night. Water trickled gently from a fountain. Spirits seemed to play there, whispering, darting past so quickly they could neither be seen nor even glimpsed. It was as if the air hinted at them. Drawn in to the magic circle, and going towards the fountain to drink, I tripped over what I took to be a tree root. But the tree sprang to life at once, jumping up as a man. I screamed and Lucrezia ran off, running hither and thither I swear just like a sheep. The boys set up in a wail.

'Come back, woman!' the man commanded, holding me fast. He was only my height but had the grip of a giant. Lucrezia obeyed. Moaning, crying, trembling all at once, she came as a lamb to what must be her slaughter.

He peered at us. 'Gesumaria – a nun? A mother and sons? What are you doing out alone at night?'

'We are pilgrims,' I told him.

'And I am John the Baptist. Tell me the truth!'

'Don't kill us, don't kill us, don't kill us,' moaned Lucrezia, falling to her knees and embracing her terrified sons.

It seems I have the gift of seeing hearts: the inner person is always clearer to me than the outer, if vague smoke can be said to be 'clear'. For vague smoke is what I see when a heart is not to be trusted. I cannot see why but must rely on this subtle sense and bide my time until I know. But good hearts can be seen clearly. There is something in the person's eyes, in his voice, that tells you. A scent, a sound, I know not, but I trust the knowledge. This man was both clear and cloudy all at once. Loyal, I thought, to those who dare trust him.

'We are on our way to Florence,' I said, 'to find our brother Angelo.'

'What is your family name, Suora?' he asked.

'Ambrogini.'

'Ha! It is my own.'

'Angelo?' I cried.

'Maso!' Lucrezia jumped up. 'Maso! Is it you?'

Maso took my face in his callused hands. There were tears in his eyes. 'Oh, you are safe, Maria? God be praised! Maria. Maria, Maria. Last time I saw you, you were being carried off in a basket like Moses.'

And so I met my cousin, come to look for us, at an ancient spa in the Val di Chiana by moonlight.

✠

Maso renewed his smothered fire. While the exhausted boys slept curled up together under a blanket, we spent the hour until dawn talking. He wanted to know what had happened at the convent. Lucrezia had been too distracted by the death of her husband to ask, and so she heard my story for the first time. Something about the hour, so silent and enclosing; something about my audience being both family and yet strangers – I was able to tell the tale in a matter-of-fact way that surprised me. Perhaps we only need dramatic effect in speech when there is no drama. In this instance the drama spoke for itself, and the plainer the language and more level the tone, the more it shouted out. Maso swore repeatedly under his breath, and most colourfully. He declared that he will not rest until he has tracked down those Romans and eviscerated every one of them.

'Maria, I promise you, I'll give them rape with my sword.'

'No, no, no,' I cried. 'That is not the way of Our Lord.'

110

'Turn the other cheek?' Maso threw back his head and laughed. 'Oh, Maria, you have been locked up too long. The world is no convent.'

As Lucrezia had begun to doze, I asked him to tell me about what happened with father.

'That is not for a girl's ears.'

'The other night in the convent, these ears lost their virginity. I have already heard the tale from Derio. I would like to hear it from you, about the attack itself.'

'I was the only one armed, so I stayed back to take on the attackers. I yelled at uncle to run for his life, but he would not leave me. I took on four men with a sword in one hand and a dagger in the other, but they were so wild and fierce I could only be defensive. I took a wound, a slight one, but I roared out that I was hit, that I was dying, because I knew that while Ser Benedetto thought there was any hope for me he would not save himself. That was the kind of man he was. "Run! Run!" I shouted to him. "I am already dead!" He hesitated a moment and then ran off, but it was too late. His friends had already disappeared, and he ran alone down the road towards the Gozzano fountain.'

'What happened next?' I expected him to be coy about gruesome details, as Derio had been, but Maso was not coy.

'They were waiting for him there. They plunged their knives into him: arms, legs – all the non-vital parts, sticking him like a pig to drain the blood from him, weaken him, yet keep him conscious. And then Paolo del Mazza, standing behind him took hold of his hair in his fist and pulled back his head to bare his throat and…'

Maso paused. It was a story easy for him to recount in a tavern, but not here, in the midst of birdsong as the day began to rise in all its innocence.

'Oh my poor Father!' I buried my head in my hands and sighed for the man who is known to me in the heart but not through the senses.

'Several years later,' Maso continued, 'my brother and I caught Paolo del Mazza and killed him in the very same fashion, keeping him conscious while he died, sawing slowly through his neck.'

I was silent.

'Does that please you?'

'Our Lord permits no acts of vengeance.'

'But does it please you, Maria?' Maso was very concerned that it should.

'It does not bring him back.'

'But is something satisfied?'

'Yes,' I whispered, 'some mewling thing is quietened by it.'

'Good,' he said, and sat back on his heels.

With the creeping dawn and the rising of the sun, his face gradually emerged from the chiaroscuro of firelight into the clarity of day. He has long curling hair and round, open eyes, but the firmness of his mouth, the scar by his eyebrow and the rough stubble on his chin tells of a man you would cross at your peril. I did not believe he will really hunt down those who attacked the convent but it is true, something in me wishes he would. His promise may be empty, but the passion of it means much to me.

'Come,' he said, rising. 'The spa attendants will be arriving soon.'

While I roused Lucrezia and the boys, Maso unloosed the tether of his hired horse, threw the saddle on its back and buckled the girth strap. These were earnest sounds, the whoomph and click of commitment.

'Lucrezia, you can ride with the boys. Maria and I will walk.'

'No!' Lucrezia was walking backwards, shaking her head. 'No,' she said again, this time miserably. 'I cannot go. How could I go? It is not right. Maso, please take me back home, please.'

'Home where?' he said cruelly.

'To Saracina.'

'And the boys?'

Lucrezia's face crumpled in grief. I embraced her and promised her that I would find Angelo and compel him to send for her. 'Beg Saracina to keep the boys for six months. Just six months. If we do not send for them by then, well…'

She grew pink and radiant with hope, then hugged me in return. 'You are a good little sister, Maria. God go with you.'

I waited near the spa while Maso rode back to the city with Lucrezia. A few hours later he returned. A few hours! Was the distance we had covered from the city so short? I thank Providence for my cousin, knowing now that Lucrezia and I could never have reached Florence in a lifetime walking by night.

We set off at once for a lake, not the famous Trasimene, now out of sight due to the flatness of the land, but a smaller one into which the Chiana flows. My first time on horseback! High above the land, nervous and unstable, I had a fine view of the meadows and marsh cows, usually lovely beasts, white and sturdy, but now looking bony in the haunches. The ride was too short and taken at a mere walk. I wanted to throw my leg over the saddle and trot, canter and gallop, but at the inn where he had hired the horse, Maso lifted me down. I said goodbye to my Bellerophon and the poor old nag snuffled my palm.

We went to a jetty on the lake and took a marsh boat to travel through the reed beds. The oarsman seemed to make the long, flat boat skim over the water, past fishermen casting out their nets, through white water-lilies with their faces open to the sky. Oh, this was freedom, this was joy! There were birds everywhere. 'Herons, I think,' said Maso when I asked him. The oarsmen knew their proper names: grey heron, egret, crested grebe. Large birds with wingspans greater than my own length, with legs that bend the wrong way at the knees; little birds bobbing on the water; single birds; birds in pairs; flocks.

Maso only had eyes for humans. He scanned the horizon and quizzed the man about the movement of armies.

'They passed on yesterday. Goin' up the Chianti I hear.'

'Siena's no obstacle,' said Maso. 'They'll take Florence from the west. Perhaps Pisa first, cutting Florence off from the sea. These are grim times for Lorenzo.'

'Look, there, lassie!' the oarsman said to me. 'Did you see it?'

It had been as darting as the spirits of the spa. All I saw was a flash of coloured feather.

'Kingfisher,' said the oarsman. 'That's good luck that is, to see him. Your journey will go well.'

We crossed the lake to a jetty at the north bank where we took a river boat going to Arezzo. From the boat I looked back at the hill high above the Val di Chiana, its dark crown of a city. Free at last, I drank in through all my senses, but as we made our way slowly northwards, following the line of the border between Umbria and Tuscany, my joy soon faded. Scent turned to stink, music to noise, vision to reality, for Tuscany suffers war. On the boat there were soldiers from Naples dicing with soldiers of Cortona on their way to join Florence. There was no enmity between them, only camaraderie, for soldiers have no argument with each other. Their aim is to earn money and stay alive and thus, so Maso told me, they avoid engaging in battle as often as they can. Soldiers, being hired, may escape battles, but the land cannot escape war. We saw fields burning, the corn eaten by sheets of flame; we saw villages deserted and piles of dead animals. Famine and disease were evident everywhere, and the air was filled with smoke. The harvest this year will be one of ash.

9

Pistoia, August 1478

ONE BY ONE our fortresses began to fall in the south. One day Niccolò Michelozzi told Lorenzo that the towns of Calciano and Rincine had fallen.

'How many of the enemy are there?'

'About twenty thousand.'

'How many do we have?'

'Five thousand.' Niccolò moistened his dry lips with his tongue. 'Without Siena to help us, the enemy can now reach us directly by the Chianti valley. There is nothing to oppose them.'

Lorenzo looked at his secretary with hollow eyes. War. It meant tireless negotiation, the payment of sums both secret and overt, the hiring of good captains. Lorenzo had done all this. He had done more. He had consulted astrologers and timed all his actions according to the planets. He had spent his own money – too much of it – to hire Este of Ferrara. But the man had not yet arrived, the Florentines forces, divorced from the command of Count Orsini, were out of control and plundering the territory between Siena and Volterra, and the Chianti valley seemed to be a funnel down which the enemy was about to pour.

'Have we heard yet from France, Niccolò?'

'We are expecting the ambassador tomorrow.'

'All shall be well when we have France.'

✢

On all roads north, across the mountains, over the Lombard plain to the Alps; on all roads east to the seaports of Pisa, Livorno and Genoa, went couriers, some at great speeds, delivering letters to both neighbouring and foreign states. Letters on parchment and vellum, sealed with red wax and lodged in leather bags stamped with the emblems of the Medici and Florence. Lorenzo was calling in all his debts of generosity and kindness, every loan he had ever advanced, every favour he had done. Couriers resting in inns boasted of the distances they covered and the efficiency of their relay systems; one man claimed he could reach France in three days, another that he could get to England in the same time. But once a day a courier from Pistoia plodded into the courtyard of the Medici palace, full of complaint that he was having to do once a day what he used to do once a week, namely delivering correspondence from his town to ours. Each day he brought letters from Lorenzo's wife, written by Poliziano, and letters from Poliziano himself; each day he saw the heroes of his profession galloping past him with their horses in a sweat.

He began to grow ambitious and cut down on the three hours it took him from Pistoia, a town so close you could see it from the top of the Duomo, nestling in the foothills of the Appenines beyond Prato.

One day as he was galloping towards Florence he came up behind an embassy from France resplendent in the colours, its pennants, embroidered with the fleur-de-lys, fluttering cheerfully. Accompanied by a military escort and moving along at a sedate pace it filled the road and forced our Pistoian courier to go by fields to overtake them. Galloping over corn stubble, the courier's horse stumbled and threw its rider. The courier fell awkwardly and cried out in anguish as his leg snapped. Some soldiers from the escort

115

came to his aid and he eventually arrived in Florence carried by the entourage of the ambassador, Phillipe de Commynes.

✠

Angelus Politianus Tommaso Maffeo suo S.D.
I am as an exile here in Pistoia, longing for my friends and my patria. There is no one of interest in this house to talk to above the age of six. Here there is no Gentile Becchi on whom to spring a practical joke, and no Matteo Franco to spring a joke on me. No strain from Baccio's lira weaving through the house; no bellow from Lorenzo, *Where is Angelo?* No running up the stairs to find that – oh, glory! – he has an hour to spare, and is sweeping his desk with his arm, sending bank rolls cascading to the floor. No Marsilio Ficino to appear suddenly round a corner to remind you of God. No Monna Lucrezia, calling the best out of you with her admonitions. Just Monna Clarice, her silence and her criticism.

Here the city bell is not the *vacca,* and the campanile was not built by Giotto. There is no dome on the Cathedral, and no river Arno sliding heavily by. Fra Angelico did not decorate the cells of the local monastery, and Botticelli does not disturb my studies to ask about the attributes of Hermes. This is Pistoia, where the pigeons flutter as you walk across the empty square; where the dust eddies in whirlpools; where the Tuscan language is corrupted by the local dialect; where, in the hot part of the day, it is as if everyone has died of plague and will never be seen again.

Vale. Angelo in limbo.

✠

Ser Andrea Panciaticchi, the host of the Medici family in Pistoia, was always busy. He had letters to write, accounts to do, taxes to evade. His favourite books were the heavy ledgers ruled in columns in which he made entries with devotional regularity: the book of accounts, in which each item of expenditure was listed, down to the last denari; the book of *ricordi,* in which he outlined family affairs in bald, unemotional prose; the book of memoranda, in which he noted matters of business to which he must attend.

The purpose of his life was to lay the foundation for (the Panciaticchi) lives to come. His memorial would be a marble tomb and the wealth of his descendants. What he desired above all things was security, and in his worship of Caution he locked himself up in a small world where few risks need be taken. His safe home had become his prison.

Angelo's idea of accounting was to feel the weight of his purse as it hung from his belt. It was either full or empty. If he ever counted coins it was usually in astonishment, wondering how he had been so deviously robbed.

Thus, despite not having much time, Ser Andrea dedicated himself to the task of instructing a poet in the keeping of books, for it was with horror that he had discovered that this young man, who was to act as bursar to the Medici, that famous family of bankers, had not heard of the newly-devised and revolutionary double-entry system. Night after night Angelo was drawn from his studies to be shown how to balance the family finances that had been put in his care. At such times he would look up at the moon and wish to howl.

'It seems to me,' said the older man, 'that you have no financial experience.'

'When it comes to money I am a virgin,' Angelo agreed.

'Why is that?' Ser Andrea asked.

'Because I have never had any.'

Ser Andrea stared at him uncomprehendingly. Angelo resisted giving him a graphic account of poverty, of how it feels to live a life of self-denial not for any spiritual purpose but out of necessity, of the absolute shame of prostituting one's talents – writing dull letters for stupid men – to buy bread and notebooks. The two men stared at each across a gulf of incomprehension.

'But you are a prior with a handsome living,' said the merchant.

'I had a few debts,' Angelo said simply, 'which have not yet quite cleared.'

117

'Is it your family?'

'I would be a father to them if I could, but it is impossible. The living is not that handsome. But yes, some of the debt was incurred by my cousins.'

'Well,' said Ser Andrea brightly, 'with this system of double-entry book-keeping, you will find yourself so in command of your finances that you will pay all your debts and still be in profit. And then you will not have to depend on Lorenzo so heavily.'

Angelo made a noise – a stifled cry – which he covered by pretending to sneeze. 'Pollen,' he explained.

✟

On the instructions of Monna Clarice, Angelo took the children through the rosary each evening, going through the prayers mechanically. It had been years since he had recited the rosary prayers himself, and he soon discovered why: repetition sucked the soul out of them. The children were like mouthing fish, and had discovered the trick of sleeping and chanting simultaneously. He fell quiet. Lucrezina, the eldest child, prompted him with the next line.

'No, I think it is enough,' he said, laying the rosary beads aside.

The girl was shocked. 'We have not reached the end!'

He shrugged. 'The ceiling will not drop on us. There is nothing to be concerned about. Man has free will, and it is my will that we all fall into the lap of Morpheus, the god of Sleep.'

'I am not tired,' Maddelena lied. She was five years old and very conscious that her brother Piero was receiving instruction denied to her. 'Tell us the story you told Piero this morning. The one about the strange beast.'

He had found it in *The Ethiopian Romance* of Heliodorus the day before and shared it with his pupil. 'It was a camelopard,' he now told all of them, 'and seemed to be made of the bits and pieces left over when God created the world. They called it a camelopard because it had a spotted coat like a leopard, and a funny head like a camel. When it arrived, the people were about to make a sacrifice in the temple precincts. At the Altar of the Moon stood a pair of bulls, and at that of the Sun a team of four white horses.'

'Ahhh…' sighed the girls, feeling sorry for the sacrificial victims.

'When they saw that alien, unfamiliar, unheard-of monster, the camelopard, the sacrificial beasts were terrified. The horses reared up and burst their halters. The bulls ripped themselves free of the ropes that were tied to the rings in their noses, and sped away in headlong fright.'

'Ow!' cried Maddelena, rubbing her nose, horrified at the thought of having a brass ring ripped out of it.

'Ow!' Giovanni echoed, rubbing his own without being quite sure why, except that his sister had done it. At once the centre of attention, he laughed and beat the air with his pudgy arms.

The children wanted to know what a camelopard looked like. Angelo tried to draw a picture, but the children hooted derisively at his efforts. 'Maestro?' Maddalena plucked at his sleeve. 'What do you think a camelopard is? Does it have parents? Are its mother and father also camelopards, or is one a camel and the other a leopard?'

Angelo stared at the girl, amazed at her brightness. Piero never asked questions like that. He wondered what the answer was. His first thought was that it was not possible to make a third beast by mixing two others, but then he remembered mules. At last he decided that, a coupling between a leopard and a camel being inconceivable, a camelopard must have camelopard parents.

They made him tell the story again. Maddalena, who had adopted the camelopard as her own, made the picture which the master had drawn 'walk'. Giovanni squealed as she rocked the picture towards him and pushed it in his face. He was the affable kind of child who squealed when it was expected of him, especially by sisters. Left to himself, he would have said and done nothing. There was some excitement running among them now, and sleep seemed an increasingly dim prospect.

'It is time for our last prayer,' said the master, whose favourite hour this was for a reflective walk in air now cool after the blazing day.

The children groaned and returned to their knees.

'Why do you groan?' he asked.

'Prayers are boring,' said Piero.

'Not if you make them up yourself. I shall start, then each of you follow in turn.'

'What do we say?' Lucrezina asked in alarm.

'Ask God for that thing you want most. Almighty Father in heaven,' he began, and then pointed to Piero.

'Please send me a pony.'

'Stupid!' hissed Lucrezina. 'Please protect our father,' she offered.

Maddelena bit her lip and thought hard.

'Hurry up!' said Piero. 'My knees are hurting.'

The master told the boy to be quiet and the girl to take her time.

'Giovanni?' the master prompted.

'Please God, I want kisses,' lisped the child.

The children crowded round their little brother to answer his prayer. Giovanni was triumphant in his success.

'He is only two!' Lucrezina told the master with great pride.

Angelo dipped his head in his hands and asked God that everyone else's prayers be answered just as promptly as Giovanni's. He felt a jab in his ribs and opened his eyes to Maddelena.

'Ask him for what *you* want,' she said. All the children were staring at him now with interest. He cleared his throat.

'Dear God,' he said, 'keep Lorenzo safe and help him win the war so that we may return home very soon.'

'Tell him what you really want,' Lucrezina said.

'That is what I really want,' he protested.

'No it isn't,' said Piero. 'What you really want is a wife.' Having said this, the boy then pulled a face as if he chewed on gristle.

'Ah...' sighed the girls.

Though Angelo denied the accusation, the children were

insistent and would not let him rise until he had asked God for a wife. 'It is wrong to petition the Lord for yourself,' he told them. 'If it is God's will that I should marry, then I shall find a wife. For now, let him hear my true prayer, which is for your father.' So saying, he began to sing quietly in Latin one of those hymns excavated from ancient texts by Ficino. It was addressed to Selene, the moon. It could do no harm, only do good, and no one in the room was wise enough to know the difference between a Christian and a pagan hymn. It calmed him, calmed the children. Once it was finished, they went unprotesting to their beds. Sleep still seemed a long way off, however, and Angelo was beginning to despair of his walk. He tucked them in and told them how Morpheus and his invisible servants pour a kind of glue in your eyes which sticks your eyelids down, and how dreams come to disconnect your mind from reason, and to fill it with wonderful pictures. His words were effective. One by one the children fell asleep. And so did he, his head resting on his folded arms.

In their sleep, they all rode on camelopards in the land of unfettered imagination.

✠

A Tommaso de' Maffei, caro amico, – You know my views well enough for them not to sound harsh in your ears, but I cannot be tolerant of a Church that condemns its children to ignorance. We have such fine scriptural literature, both in the Gospels, and in holy fathers such as Augustine and Jerome. But who is this man Jacopo de Varraze, the author of a book more popular than the Bible? Why, you will tell me, he was the Archbishop of Genoa a hundred years ago. But the title of archbishop may be as easily bought as a round of cheese, and has never in living memory been conveyed by merit. That title alone does not give him the authority to fill the minds of our children with rank superstition. You know how I feel about those stories of his, how I want to throw buckets of whitewash over paintings of legends such as the finding of the True Cross, because it is worse than apocryphal: it is fantasy.

Ah! I hear you say. And stories of centaurs and cyclopses are not fantasy?

This is the pass we have come to here in Pistoia. Monna Clarice accuses me of corrupting the children with ancient fables, and instructs me instead to fill their heads with stories of miracles. Which of us is right, Tommaso? Please decide. Or better still, ask Ficino.

Do you remember how the Madonna liked Matteo Franco to read to her at night? She makes me do the same, only we do not read St Francis, but from that contemptible book *On the Misery of the Human Condition* by Pope Innocent III. She seems to think my soul will benefit from it, but without doubt my soul prefers the sweet music of the lyre to reflection upon the vileness of childbirth and the putrefaction of the human embodiment. Indeed, my poor soul shrinks in repugnance.

She thinks our life on earth is a suffering to be endured; I think life is a blessing to be celebrated; she thinks, Our Lord Jesus Christ having died for us, the least we can do is weep. I think we should cast off our sorrows and know Christ for that nimbus of light that is the radiance of the world soul. Such ideas are, however, the stuff of heresy and I must keep quiet. And suffer. And weep. Such is my vile lot here in Pistoia.

I am aware as I groan that others are suffering real hardship. Send me news of Lorenzo, and of Montepulciano. *Vale*. Angelo in purgatory.

✞

He tried to study, but found concentration difficult. It seemed as if, somewhere between Florence and Pistoia, the Madonna Clarice he knew had been spirited away and replaced by this creature who sucks the confidence out of poets. A physician would say that her predominant humour of phlegm had transformed into yellow bile, but can humours change so dramatically and in a moment? Lorenzo's quiet, compliant wife was become a termagant, and it was a metamorphosis more improbable than anything dreamt of by Ovid. But how could Angelo find fault with someone who spent three hours each day reading the Offices of Our Lady? Though fault there was, no matter how thick the drapes of piety. He wrote and told Lorenzo that his position was impossible if he had no authority.

A few days passed. He tried to write a poem but found himself lacking both time and inspiration. It was too hot. His Muse had fled. Spurning the delights of small town life, its apathy, its wind-whipped dust, its blistering streets – and double-entry book-keeping – Calliope had fled back to the great city. And who could blame her? Without her, however, Angelo's lively, urban mind became a slough of inertia.

He heard nothing from Lorenzo but was summoned to see Lorenzo's wife.

He was struck at once by the difference in her aspect. She who used to keep her eyes lowered and stumble nervously in her speech, conscious always of being considered a dim Roman by these superior Florentines, now stood before him like a queen. A servant fanned her to ward off the heat.

'I believe you have been making complaints about me to my husband.'

'Has he written to you? What did he say?'

'That is none of your business. Nor is it right that I should be the subject of your bitter criticism. In future you are to write nothing to my husband without showing me the letter first, is that clear?'

Not knowing Lorenzo's views on the matter, Angelo could do nothing but agree.

Clarice thanked him. 'You seem very dull and dispirited, Maestro. Is there anything I can do to help?'

'Only if you have a tincture to cure melancholy. Who could not be dispirited in times such as these?'

'Herbs do not cure a malaise of the soul. The only cure is spiritual reflection and prayer. Will you join me in reading to the children from *The Golden Legends* of Archbishop Jacopo de' Varraze? You will feel much better for it.'

'Madonna, nothing would persuade me to read such superstitious drivel short of an energetic bout of torture by the Sultan of Turkey.'

Under the expressionless gaze of Clarice's pure eyes, his joke seemed to fall echoing down a well. He raised his hands in despair. 'No, Madonna. No, I will not,' he said, and walked away.

✝

Magnifice mi patrone. Forgive these words, which I would have preferred to come from my mouth rather than my pen, but I have found no excuse to visit Florence that you will sanction. Therefore I must write. The position I hold here is becoming untenable. Everything I do or say is objected to by Madonna Clarice, my teaching is interfered with, my very soul is under her investigation and declared to be wanting. Piero is becoming the victim of opposing forces and does not know whom or what to believe. I cannot do what you have asked me to do, unless you vest me with the authority with which to do it.

My lord, you know my love for you and will forgive my anger. It is the situation, and our fears, which prey on all of us and make us fight. Please let me have your answer by return.

Your servant, ANG. POL.

✝

Such was Lorenzo's friendship with the King of France that he received the ambassador, Phillipe de Commynes, in his own house. They greeted each other amiably without use of formal titles.

'Well, Phillipe, you bring us good news I hope.'

The Frenchman looked him straight in the eye and told him he did not. 'My King has considered the matter very carefully. He says that your cause is just and that you deserve the support of every honest man, but that he cannot lend you his forces.'

For Lorenzo it was as if there were an earthquake happening. The floor was surely tipping?

'As you know, His Majesty has a rightful claim on Naples, but if he were to send his army to claim what is rightfully his, well, that is a big affair. He says it would devastate your country. Forty thousand men marching through, wanting food and shelter: Italy would be destroyed. Lorenzo, Lorenzo, he will do all he can, I promise you, but there will be no invasion as you had hoped. I am instructed to travel on to Rome and tell the Pope that if he does not stop this war then we shall demand a Grand Council. King Louis has the agreement of the Holy Roman Emperor and the King of England in this. Lorenzo, all the monarchs of Europe desire your success. Be assured, we will bring down this Pope, but by negotiation, not by war.'

'It is too late for that!'

'Believe me, it is not too late. We shall do all we can, and you will be victorious.'

Lorenzo had planned a banquet for the ambassador. Now he had lost his appetite and had to sit through twenty courses when all he wanted to do was run out into the streets and find help. He felt like Atlas, with the weight of the world on his shoulders suddenly too much. He needed to speak to his mother, to the Signoria, to Scala, Este, anyone! He could not sit exchanging pleasantries at an hour such as this. Suddenly Commynes leant towards him and said softly in his ear, 'If you need to leave, I shall understand.'

Lorenzo jumped to his feet. 'Forgive me, ambassador, I have so much work to do.'

'I understand,' said Commynes.

✢

Angelo went to see a learned man in the city, renewing his search for a copy of the works of Galen. Though he failed in his search, he succeeded in finding good company, and returned to the Palazzo Panciaticchi at dusk in a better humour. He saw a man he recognised leaving the house with a brace of partridge and looking most cast down. It was the father of the Pistoian courier, who had brought the family this gift only to be turned away, accused of wanting to poison everyone.

'I just wanted to thank Lorenzo for keeping my lad employed even though he broke his leg in that fall from his horse.'

Angelo ran up the fine stairs two at a time. No matter that she was a woman and the wife of his lord, it was time to confront Clarice. He could hold back no longer. Fired by the power of the ancient poets – rhetoricians – to whom speech was the fiercest weapon, he went up the stairs like a shot from a bow and into her room without knocking.

'Madonna! I am in charge of this family. You do not dismiss gift-bearers, accusing them of wishing to do us harm. Such ignorance! Such rudeness! It may be the way of the Orsini – it is not the way of the Medici. You should have spoken to me first.'

'As I would have done, had you been present. You do not leave this house without my permission!'

'Do not speak to me like that. I stand here in Lorenzo's place. And Lorenzo, as you well know, seeks your permission for nothing.'

She responded to his words with a shriek so piercing that it, as he put it, 'loosened the bowels'.

'You, stand in my husband's place? *You?* I need someone I can trust! Someone with authority! Not you, a servant! I want Giovanni Tornabuoni here with me. Do you hear? I *demand* it!'

✝

Elena, weary of the four walls at home, rode out with her maid to Careggi at the end of the day, bringing a letter from Angelo in Pistoia. I was simultaneously delighted and annoyed, for though I loved to see my wife, I preferred her safe at home.

'I have told you never to leave, that you must stay in with the doors bolted. Elena, Elena, when will you do as I say?'

'No one recognised us. Why should they? I do not have *Pazzi* branded on my forehead. Here, a letter from Angelo.'

Already in a bad mood, as I read it I began twitching with indignation as if flea-bitten. 'That woman!' I declared. 'That stupid, stupid woman!'

Elena wanted to know if Monna Clarice were safe and well.

'More so than she would be if I were looking after her. The wonder is not that Angelo has lost his temper but that he has kept it this long.'

Ficino wanted to know what was happening and I gave him the letter to read for himself.

'The last thing Lorenzo needs is a fight among his own kin,' I said. 'We should be united in our support of him. What can we do, Father, to resolve this trifling dispute?'

'Trifling?' said Elena. 'I would not find it trifling to be away from home during a war and in the care of someone who shouts at me in front of servants.'

'Is it any wonder he is shouting? She countermands his every order, intercepts every step he takes.'

'Stop!' said Ficino, 'before you two get any more trifling your-selves.'

We stood looking sheepish under his command. 'What can we do?' I repeated.

'Watch and wait,' Ficino counselled. 'We do not know the whole of it.' He looked out across the vista of Florence to the scene of distant hills, but what his eyes were seeing, I could not tell. We left him there, as still as Socrates, watching and waiting.

10

Arezzo, August 1478

ON THE BOAT *there was a pilgrim who wore the pilgrim's broad-brimmed hat and carried a staff and scrip. The journey passed quickly with his stories. He is on his way back to his home in Verona from Rome; he told me of the Holy City and all its sacred sites, of where the early Christians had their first churches and where they were eaten by lions. He has been to*

Jerusalem twice and told me of his journeys in the land of the Arabs, of the sites and relics he has seen and his adventures. Today he was aiming to see a marvel somewhat closer to home. He said that at Arezzo, in the church of San Francesco, is a most marvellous sequence of paintings by a master called Piero, a man who still lives but paints no more. He told me about the legend of the True Cross that the sequence depicts, how Adam's staff grew into a tree which became both the Cross of the Crucifixion and the tree on which Judas hung himself.

'St Helena, the mother of the Emperor Constantine who converted to Christianity,' he told me, 'discovered the Cross in Jerusalem and brought a piece back to Italy. There are several fragments and I have seen them all.' He spent his life going from shrine to shrine, communing with the saints and praying for the people.

Maso disapproved of my listening so avidly to all the pilgrim's tales, saying it would fill my head with superstition and give me a lust for wandering. When we arrived at Arezzo, where the Chiana meets the Arno, he made me stay on the boat while he went into the town to find lodging for the night, saying that atrocities had occurred in the wake of passing armies and the city was not yet safe. As soon as he was out of sight, I joined the pilgrim, who had said that San Francesco is close to the river and that I could be there and back before Maso returned.

There were several people gathered in the chapel reading the walls, pointing to the various scenes and explaining the story to each other. The pilgrim could not stop talking, pointing to this and that, reading the story to me, telling me how much of it he has seen himself and what this and that reminded him of. To be free of him I said that I wished to pray and I knelt down at the altar until he had fastened upon some other hapless individual. When at last the pilgrim had bored even himself and gone off in search of new wonders, I rose up to stare at the magnificent walls in peace. Of a strange, ethereal reality, not of this world but from behind it, the scenes of Adam, of Solomon and Sheba, of the Emperor Constantine in battle, reared up above my head to a dizzying height. I had my head so far back I stumbled over a blind man sitting there alone. I apologised in an abstracted fashion, hardly sparing him a glance. One by one, each scene transported my soul until I forgot about my hunger and weariness. But the scene that drew my eye again and again was that of the Queen of Sheba bowing her head before King Solomon.

There was a fineness to the queen's features, though it was not that which made her beautiful. It was the very quietness of her as she, monarch of her own realm, surrendered herself into the hand of this bearded king, and he accepted her solemnly. It was the surrender of the noble horse to the will of the rider, the kind of surrender that amplifies and does not diminish. She was not becoming a slave of Solomon: she was making him a master. By giving him her gifts, her wealth increased, for he gave her wisdom.

A priest came from the sacristy with a bowl of bread and fruit. As he passed into the chapel, he touched the shoulder of the blind man sitting in the shadows and put the food into his hands.

'There is a young nun here who seems transfixed by Solomon,' he told him.

The blind man nodded and smiled. 'I know. She has trodden on me more than once.'

The priest crossed to me and told me that Solomon was a portrait of Cardinal Bessarion, who had died about six years before. 'He came to Italy in the train of the Emperor Palaeologus for the Great Council that sought to unite the Greek and Latin churches; but Bessarion made his own pact with the Latin church and converted.' The priest kept nodding and looking at me sagely, as if to say 'there is much more I could tell you.'

But I was more interested in the story of Solomon and Sheba than in the models for its figures, and it annoyed me to have my reflections interrupted by this well-meaning but intrusive man. Could no one let me alone to enjoy the paintings in peace? The priest offered to read the story to me.

'Thank you, I am already familiar with it.'

The priest steered me towards the blind man. 'There is enough in that bowl for two, is there not, Piero?'

The blind man nodded and held the bowl up towards me. My hunger had returned and I took some fruit while the priest went to the lectern and opened the great book. He began to translate the text into Tuscan, but I told him I knew Latin well enough.

'Ho! A woman who knows Latin? Well, listen. Hear the story of a woman who laid down her pride.'

And when the Queen of Sheba heard of the fame of Solomon concerning the name of the Lord, she came to prove him with hard questions.

And she came to Jerusalem with a very great train, with camels that bare spices, and very much gold, and precious stones: and when she was come to Solomon, she communed with him of all that was in her heart.

And Solomon told her all her questions: there was not any thing hid from the King, which he told her not.

And when the Queen of Sheba had seen all Solomon's wisdom, and the house that he had built,

And the meat of his table, and the sitting of his servants, and the attendance of his ministers, and their apparel, and his cupbearers, and his ascent by which he went up unto the house of the Lord; there was no more spirit in her.

And she said to the King, It was a true report that I heard in mine own land of thy acts and of thy wisdom.

Howbeit I believed not the words, until I came, and mine eyes had seen it; and, behold, the half was not told me; thy wisdom and prosperity exceedeth the fame which I heard.

Happy are thy men, happy are these thy servants, which stand continually before thee, and that hear thy wisdom.

Blessed be the Lord thy God, which delighted in thee, to set thee on the throne of Israel: because the Lord loved Israel for ever, therefore he made thee king, to do judgement and justice.

And she gave the King an hundred and twenty talents of gold, and of spices very great store, and precious stones: there came no more such abundance of spices as these which the Queen of Sheba gave to King Solomon.

As he read, I sat beside the blind man and shared the bread and fruit with him. I now interpreted the picture as being the moment when Sheba communed with Solomon of all that was in her heart.

'Sheba,' the blind man said, 'was modelled on the mother of the artist, a woman called Francesca, the wisest woman known to him. Francesca devoted her life to the fruition of her son as an artist.'

'Did Solomon and Sheba marry?' I asked.

'I think not,' said the blind man. 'Not as we understand it. But they found unity of the soul, and that is a very sacred marriage indeed.'

I gazed on the blind man, who seemed to be enjoying such peace and repose. 'You know these paintings very well,' I said, 'for a blind man.'

He smiled. 'One does not need eyes to see.'

'If I were to commune with you, and you were to tell me all you know,' I said to him, 'what wisdom would you tell me?'

'I have not always been blind, but now that I am, I like to sit here and listen to the paintings.'

I gazed at him, wondering if he really could hear paintings. I realised suddenly that he could, if he had painted them himself. 'Master Piero?' I asked, and he turned his sightless eyes on me. His eyelashes were strangely webbed together, as if a spider had been at work there, and there were splashes and stains of food on his clothes of which he was oblivious. Who cared for him now, I wondered, other than the priest? I took his ancient hand in my own, a hand which had once held the brushes that painted these walls. It was gnarled, its veins like ropes, and it looked like a beloved and devoted servant; one of Solomon's men, happy in the service of art. 'Who painted these pictures truly?' I asked. 'Was it this hand? Was it these eyes that are now filmed over? Was it your mind? From whence the vision, Master Piero?'

'Ah,' he said, and tears moistened his dry face. 'I have the vision still. I just cannot share it any more.' He turned his face to the priest and grasped my hand as he did so. 'This woman,' he said. 'She is beautiful, no?'

'She has the inner radiance of one of your angels, Piero.'

'So why?' he demanded, turning his face to me, 'are you alone?'

I told my story briefly, saying that my cousin would be looking for me and that I must go. The priest counselled me to take great care; he thought it was perhaps better that we wait in Arezzo until the danger was passed.

'It is not going to pass,' said Master Piero. 'You do not understand, Father Clemente. You think she is making a simple journey from Montepulciano to Florence, albeit threatened by mortal danger. You do not understand. What is attacking Florence and Lorenzo de' Medici is Lucifer himself.'

I felt so cold suddenly, as if a draught had blown at us from the crypt.

131

The priest thought Piero was referring to the Pope and objected, but Piero shook his head. 'I am speaking about the devil; the Pope is merely the devil's agent.' Piero then began to speak urgently, as if to convince me of something. 'There is in Italy, and there has been these past forty years, a brilliance of wisdom, Solomonic wisdom. Such things are rare and a very honey pot to evil. The devil wants Lorenzo, your brother Angelo, and all Florentines who are lighting the lamps of wisdom. I'm an old blind man. I can say these things when younger men must be more circumspect. But a devil is a devil, and I am telling you that, as you enter the land of the Arno, you are leaving all safety behind you. You do not flee to shelter, my dear, you flee from it.'

He held my hand gently in his. 'There is a brotherhood of men, not formally bound but united in Platonic wisdom. Cardinal Bessarion was a founding father but now, like Cosimo de' Medici, he is dead. It is the younger generation, younger and weaker, that is being attacked. There is no certainty that good will prevail. Think twice, my daughter, before you set forth. Take Father Clemente's advice and stay in Arezzo.'

I said that, on the contrary, it was now imperative that I reach my brother, especially if the danger was so great. Then the priest told me that Angelo was not in Florence, that it was common knowledge that he had gone to Pistoia with Lorenzo's family.

My spirits plummeted. I don't know how long passed – it seemed only a little while later, when I was gazing again on the image of the Queen of Sheba, that Maso found me, my uplifted face catching the light coming through the chapel window 'as if you had seen God.' He rebuked me for running off but I hardly heard him. Still in communion with Solomon and Sheba, I came back to myself slowly. 'Where is Father Clemente, and Master Piero?' I asked, looking about me, but the chapel was empty, with not so much as an apple pip to prove that I had had company. I told my cousin that I had been in conversation with Piero the son of Francesca; he glanced at me in disbelief and then rolled his eyes like a man left in charge of a lame cow. He brought me back to these flea-bitten lodgings. Tomorrow we must return to the river and a boat ready to take us up the Arno to Florence.

✣

In our journey, we glide past death as in a dream. Villages reduced to silence by malaria, to ash by soldiers. Cattle dead in the fields, bloated and stinking with flies. Thieves and robbers hanging by the neck from gibbets. And everywhere crows.

'Why do soldiers kill and burn everything in their path?' I asked.

'To destroy the food supplies of the enemy,' Maso replied.

'But what about the people?'

'If they are in the way, we cannot be concerned about them.'

I let it all drift past me, trying not to think or feel. I understand the world of men even less than I understand that of women. I watched the birds in the sky to keep my attention from what was on the ground, although my nose reminded me often enough. The only true escape is by the route of prayer and contemplation, by which I can spring wing-footed from this realm of shadows, if only I could concentrate.

I do not know what lies ahead for us. This brother we seek, to whom I have prayed so often to come and rescue me – I do not know him, how he looks or what he is like. I hear he is rich, and also that there is a fund in Florence for dowerless girls, so it is likely that he will find a husband for me; but it is Solomon I want, and not a husband as we understand it.

✜

Florence moved towards us along the river: great battlemented walls, many towers and spires, and an enormous dome dwarfing everything. Catching the sun like a jewel, Florence seemed as bright and otherworldly as an illumination in a manuscript; but its credibility as a heaven on earth, a New Jerusalem, was destroyed by the bloated face of a drowned man floating past. The mills along the bank were idle, the bridges quiet.

We disembarked at Santa Trinità. 'I will take you to Angelo's house,' Maso said. 'He will probably be there, or in the Palazzo Medici.'

'No, no, he has gone far away,' I said.

He looked on me contemptuously. 'And how would you know that?'

I did not reply.

Once inside the city, the bright vision was destroyed. The beauty of Florence is like cosmetic paint on a raddled whore. And Angelo's house, once *we arrived there, was empty, as I had predicted, nor was he to be found at the Palazzo de' Medici.*

'He has left the city,' Maso told me after he had made enquiries.

'I know. Pistoia.'

11

Florence and Pistoia, end of August 1478

THE ARMIES of the Dukes of Calabria and Urbino were active around Siena. Having taken Castellina and besieged Radda and Panzano, a small squadron advanced up the Chianti valley; finding themselves unchecked by any opposition, they arrived at Grassina, close to Florence. They looked down on the village, wondering whether to loot it or not, and the commander thought they might as well. There were not many of them in the squadron, but the effect of their action was dramatic. The peasants rose up like sparrows from a wheat field and flocked to our great city, there to frighten us with wild and exaggerated tales. For several days, before his spies told him the truth, Lorenzo de' Medici himself believed that the entire enemy force was within a short walk of Florence.

He was exhausted. He had had his fill of official councils, where everyone aired their opinion, all opinions were compromised, and hours later everyone staggered from the stifling chamber with nothing of any consequence having been achieved. Outside the council men pleaded with him to act but Lorenzo refused for, according to his astrologers, the hour was not propitious. Instead he invited certain men to dine with him at his villa on Careggi. He needed to relax in congenial company and gain a broader view on events. Ficino was one of the guests, and I attended him.

The Medici villa was hidden in a wood on the lower slope of the hill. To come upon it amongst the trees was to meet a wall, a high stuccoed wall with crenellations and no windows. Only above

134

the wall could one see the projecting eaves of the house. Its air was not so much forbidding, however, as secretive. The villa on Careggi was Lorenzo's seclusion and retreat. Entering through the gate in the wall one came upon a small inner courtyard with a well, some ground floor stores and offices, and a flight of stairs up into the house. Inside the walls one felt as secluded and protected as Lorenzo himself, and as welcome. Though it was cooler in the hills than in the city, it was still a hot night and we were to dine in the upper loggia.

We were taken by servants through Lorenzo's chambers, two small, comfortable rooms with several doors – and, I knew, at least one secret passage, for even when he was within his villa, Lorenzo did not feel completely safe – to the square loggia with a view over the garden. As I passed through the chambers, I noticed the door was open to the tiny studiolo. It was empty within; I could see Lorenzo's desk and standing on a pedastal a beautiful and very life-like portrait in marble of his mistress, Lucrezia Donati. (Small wonder these rooms were out of bounds to his wife.) I felt the absence of Angelo acutely, for I had never been at Careggi without seeing him either out walking in the garden or here, in Lorenzo's inner sanctum. Whenever Lorenzo had a meeting in his chamber, Angelo would be secreted in the studiolo. He had shown me the door once, how it had been so designed to sit in its jambs that sounds from the chamber were amplified rather than cut off. He had demonstrated this by standing on the far side of the chamber and speaking very softly while I listened behind the closed door of the studiolo. I had heard every word.

'We have signals,' he had told me. 'Certain words repeated. On hearing them, I come out on a pretext.'

'To save his life in an attack?'

'Potentially. But usually it is to save him from boredom. People fasten on fame, Tommaso. They feed on it, overstay their welcome, oblivious to the comfort or well-being of the one they profess to so admire. They are parasites and will feed on their host until he has no more to give.'

The open door… It spoke in silent eloquence of Angelo. The open door, the desk, the marble portrait bust. I wondered how much Lorenzo was missing his friend. Walking into the chamber himself, Lorenzo greeted Ficino and asked me how Angelo was faring, had I heard from him? Thus conversing, we went through to the loggia.

The sun was sinking behind the trees and the fragrance of the garden below began to waft upwards on the evening air. The rest of the guests were already at table; some of the men, such as Andrea del Verrocchio, Antonio Pollaiuolo and Leonardo da Vinci, were master painters and sculptors; others had professions such as cartography or engineering; and two men in the party were foreign ambassadors, but not here in their official capacity, rather as friends. Everyone looked relaxed and cheerful, for here was not an elegant banquet but the plain fare that Lorenzo himself preferred: bread, cheese, cold meat, fruit and olives, along with the best wine and oil from his own estates. If it was a great honour to be formally received by Lorenzo, it was a greater one by far to be informally received by him. We said grace and then transformed into peasants –the preferred condition of the true Tuscan – with our elbows on the table and not a fork in sight.

'It is only a small squad at Grassina,' Lorenzo said, breaking his bread, spearing cuts of meat and eating off his knife. Happily his disapproving wife was not present. His mother was, but Monna Lucrezia was eating with her fingers as any good Tuscan wife. 'There is no possibility of their attacking Florence,' Lorenzo continued. 'Nevertheless, we need to take our danger seriously, and I am calling on you to find some way for our David to beat the papal Goliath, using intellect rather than brute force. We have secured some help from Venice, but still our forces are much inferior, and we need the slingshot of native wit to fell this brutal enemy.'

I looked out over the hills, watching birds darting for insects. It seemed to be a time of utmost tranquillity. Swifts and martins dived in a limitless sky which grew paler before it grew dark, and it was difficult indeed to imagine that Tuscany had been invaded.

Though earlier in the week he had been telling me that all war was bestial madness, Leonardo da Vinci was now trying to convince Lorenzo of the feasibility of building a covered cart of wood which ran on its wheels by means of an engine. This, he said, the engineer in him overcoming the philosopher, was his Trojan horse, which would run into the enemy camp and destroy them all. Lorenzo found the idea very appealing, but thought it better suited to tales of romance and epic poetry.

Bernardo Bembo, ambassador of Venice, advocated tactics he had culled from the *De Militia* of Leonardo Bruni, one of the great chancellors of Florence in the previous generation. Lorenzo dismissed these as literary and impractical, but Bembo disagreed, showing him a passage in the book that described how Brunelleschi had diverted a river to flood Lucca. Lorenzo was more interested in diverting the influences of the heavens. Having engaged Duke Ercole d' Este of Ferrara to lead the armies of the alliance, he could not hand over the baton of command until the first propitious astrological moment could be found. It was one thing to challenge heaven with a war against the Pope, quite another to do so at an unfavourable time. Propitious moments, however, seemed few and far between, and any right astrological moment occurring before September 27th was occurring at night. Ficino counselled patience and told him to wait, and against all the advice of practical men, Lorenzo did intend to wait. While the armies gathered idly in their camps, Ficino studied the heavens looking for an earlier moment, but in vain.

After the meal had been cleared, one of the cartographers showed us how the enemy advanced. 'We thought that, having made their incursion at Montepulciano, the Dukes of Calabria and Urbino would advance up the Val d'Arno,' he said. 'Arezzo would stand in their way. Well, as we know, half the force has taken that route, with terrible consequences for Arezzo. But what we did not expect was for Siena to offer Calabria the Chianti valley unchallenged.'

'Then you have not lived as long as I have,' muttered Monna

Lucrezia, studying the map keenly. The cartographer pointed out each valley route and showed how the enemy approached. Despite recent shows of friendliness, Siena had gone over to the cause of Rome with such alacrity as to make evident the depth of the city's hostility. Indeed, it seemed that Siena preferred to be occupied by the enemy than go to the aid of the friend; preferred to do Florence harm than maintain her own liberty.

'We have lost Siena without any struggle,' the cartographer complained.

'Siena has lost itself,' Lorenzo's mother said. 'Think no more of it. They will regret this action. The best we can do is to pray for their souls, that they may be forgiven.'

Now, while the enemy marched purposefully through Tuscany, the allies, lacking central command, were making raids on Sienese territory and doing little else.

Surrounded by creative, inventive men, Lorenzo began to look at the familiar map with an entirely different eye, wondering if they could not block this mountain pass or sabotage that road, or dig an enormous pit into which an army could fall. Taken by Bembo's suggestion to divert a river, Leonardo sketched a plan rapidly in his note book, showing how to divert the Arno. By myself I was incapable of finding any fault with Leonardo's astonishing ideas but could only stare at his hand flashing over the page, only hang on each grave word of his technical explanations, as if in the presence of truth revealed. Lorenzo, however, dismissed it, saying it was hopelessly impractical since it could not work without causing an innundation of friendly cities.

'It looks as if we must fight as usual,' he said at last.

'But not before the twenty-seventh day of September,' Ficino said. 'Without doubt that is the heaven-marked day for our victory.'

Leonardo, put out by the rejection of his devices, closed his notebook. He leant over the map of Tuscany and asked what was happening in the Casentino valley.

'The armies are avoiding it, and for good reason,' said Lorenzo. 'There is a lot of sickness and contagion in the area.'

'What manner of contagion?'

Lorenzo winced and did not answer. He had enough fears without adding plague to them.

Monna Lucrezia, who looked upon the Casentini as her children, was offering a prayer to the Virgin to help them when the courier from Pistoia came in on crutches, his damaged leg stiff in wooden splints. He looked so hot and weary it seemed he bore very bad news. Lorenzo snatched the letter from him and tore it open.

'She sends you a hundred warblers,' said the courier.

'What?'

'Your wife – a hundred singing birds. Dead of course. They'll sing no more. I left them in the kitchen.'

Lorenzo screwed up the letter and threw it back at the courier. He failed to catch it. I jumped up to return it to the poor fellow, who thanked me miserably as he limped away. Lorenzo turned to one of the ambassadors. Philippe de Commynes sat back from studying the map and rubbed his eyes wearily. Had he been the king of France, and not just the king's ambassador, then he would have readily lent to Lorenzo the massive standing army of the French. As it was, Philippe was merely the mouthpiece of King Louis. On the eve of his departure for Rome, where he would deliver to the Pope a strongly worded condemnation and a threat of a Grand Council, he wore an air of hopelessness. He looked up at Lorenzo and said that, on his return, he would offer his retinue to help in defence of the city. It was then, I believe, that Lorenzo knew for certain that any hope he had left in France was vain, that King Louis had done all he was going to do for his 'beloved Florentines'.

✟

As the armies moved, fields and vineyards burned, our ancient olive trees roaring incandescently in apocalyptic flames. All roads winding through Tuscan valleys were busy with displaced people looking for food and shelter. Many tried to enter Florence only to be turned away. There were rumours of plague in the Casentino as well as in certain army camps, and the city guards were instructed not to allow in anyone who was sick. Since most people were sick from hunger or exhaustion, it was safest to turn away everyone. But Florence was Florence and such sanctions did not extend to merchants and their goods.

✠

Though in his arrangements for the family, Lorenzo had compromised in regard to his mother and allowed her to remain in Florence on the understanding that she reside at Careggi, within weeks this agreement had been forgotten and Monna Lucrezia was to be seen at his side at all times, even in the councils of the Ten of War, which took place more often in the Palazzo Medici than in Palazzo della Signoria. Visiting messengers and ambassadors to the Palazzo would find Lucrezia de' Medici sitting quietly, her thin lips compressed, her falcon eyes watchful. Her intelligent presence disturbed them and they expected her to speak at any moment as the Oracle at Delphi, but Lorenzo, without introducing her or even referring to her, would continue with business as if accustomed to having a lady sitting close by as keen as a judge. Messengers delivered news of the advance of armies, the destruction of fortresses, atrocities committed in occupied cities, the distress of peasants; ambassadors spoke of the intentions of kings and the bias of princes; anyone glancing at the lady met her steady, penetrating gaze.

From the centre of her silence, Lucrezia took in all that was happening, in the house, the city, the nation, all Christendom. Listening to a messenger from Milan tell of the struggles of the boy-duke to withstand the ambitions of his Sforza uncle, she grieved for the boy's mother and prayed for them both. A servant approached nervously to ask in a whisper if he could have the key to the spice box.

'It is on the hook on my bedpost. Be sure to put it back there,' she said, as if his request bore as much weight as the rest of the proceedings.

In a lull between visitors, Lorenzo turned to her. 'Mother, what should I do with regard to Milan? It is as much in need of help as we are.'

'Clearly we need to come to an understanding with Ludovico Sforza,' she said.

'But it is the duchess and her son who have the right. Sforza is a usurper.'

'Of course, but if Sforza succeeds in his ambition, we shall need him as a friend. Principles have a price we cannot afford at this time, Lorenzo. Let Sforza know he will have our support if we can have his.'

Her voice was deep and grave. She seemed immune to life and its tribulations as if, after the death of Giuliano, nothing worse could happen to her. She had learnt much from her father-in-law, Cosimo, more than his sons and grandsons had, for she had applied herself diligently to studying his wisdom, whereas his heirs had presumed to inherit it through the blood. Now it was she who was sitting like Solomon, relishing the challenge that haphazard events present to the faculty of reason, giving her views only when asked, and invariably surprising her son with their unpredictability. If Lorenzo gained a reputation for quick decisions that confounded the expectations of ordinary minds, it was because he listened to his mother as to a Sibyl.

✠

A Tommaso de' Maffei, amico carissimo, – What is the news from the city? Here there is no news but only a passing of days. I try and keep fit by taking daily walks with the children, but the Madonna objects and says it is dangerous. She seems convinced that our enemies lie behind every bush and, whereas Ser Andrea and I think there is no need to put a guard on our gates, she insists on it.

To keep the mind fit is the greater task. Each day I kneel at the altar of Memory, the mother of Calliope and all the Muses, and commit to her the declensions of foreign grammars, quotations of great men, tenets from holy scripture, pearls of wisdom from the wise, and as many lines from the poets as I can find time for. In olden days, it is said, before writing was invented, bards had whole libraries in their heads, and one man could recite all the Odyssey and Iliad. If true, then that indeed was a Golden Age, peopled by giants and heroes. For now, in our own debased time, I do what I can, spending hours in silent practice in the hope of an invigoration of mind and invention next time I put pen to paper.

I am pouring the wine of Virgil into Piero. He is a grumpy, reluctant student in everything except gymnastics and poetry. He drinks Virgil greedily and has the first hundred lines committed to Memory. The story of Aeneas founding Latium echoes our own story and I am able to explain much of current events by this means. 'Your father,' I tell him, 'is our own Aeneas, seeking to refound his civilisation.'

Whatever chance may bring, however many hardships we suffer, we are making for Latium, where the Fates show us our place of rest.

Latium, the ideal nation, the homeland. Latium, that country Lorenzo wants to build afresh as a new Italy. I wish I could say that when I look on Piero I see another Ascanius Iulus, the son of Aeneas, inheritor of all his father's qualities, but, despite Lorenzo's seed, despite the education I am giving him, Piero remains stubbornly himself, wilful, feckless – oddly endearing, as his mother – and with appalling handwriting that displays all his impatience with study.

Whenever she can, Madonna undoes my teaching, tells her son that Virgil is a pagan heretic and his stories untrue. I feel her presence throughout our lessons, just out of sight, behind a door, always within earshot of her son. If ever I were to chastise Piero, and he shout in pain or protest, Clarice would arrive like Alecto. Therefore I do not chastise him but try and mould him with reason, which of course does not work on a child so young, and as a consequence I fear that he will not grow into the philosopher prince we desire. He needs his father! I cannot take that role while Madonna trips me at every step, reminding me of my position as a servant and a dispensable one at that.

Yesterday evening I went out into the city to visit learned men. What I need is a copy of the works of Galen, for I wish to know if the ancients ever questioned the popular belief that the seed is entirely from the father. To be sure, when I look on Piero, I see an Orsini. But I would be more likely to find an honest man in Rome than such a book in this place. When I returned, I was accused of visiting a bordello. Madonna finds it inconceivable that a man would forsake his duty (she thinks I should be with the guard at the gate) and go out into a hostile city, where all food is poisoned and every shadow hides an enemy, to look for a book. She believes that men are driven only by lust. Well, perhaps that is so, but for some of us the lust is for knowledge, truth and reason.

But it is about the events of tonight that I write to you, desperate for the ear of a friend. At supper I asked Piero to recite Virgil, to show the company how well he is doing. He romped into the opening speech of Aeneas with a greater power of delivery than I had anticipated from him. The little six-year old so *declaimed* the Latin verses that the hairs stood up on my arms. Everyone was impressed, including his mother. Then, oh, how stupid of me, I asked him to translate the lines into Tuscan. He came to the part:

'O muse! The causes and the crimes relate;
What goddess was provoked, and whence her hate;
For what offence the Queen of Heaven began
To persecute so brave, so just a man–'

Monna Clarice stood up so quickly that dishes crashed to the floor. 'Heresy!' she cried. 'Blasphemy!' Now it had not occurred to me before that calling Juno the Queen of Heaven might upset anyone. We men have compartments of the mind, one for each faith or system of knowledge, and the wise amongst us do not seek to reconcile them but to accept each in its own context. But for Madonna there is no context. She has no sense of history or geography. Such is her grasp of natural philosophy that she believes in the sphinx, the basilisk and the blessed pelican, who feeds her young by plucking the flesh from her own breast. And therefore to such a shapeless mind clouded by ignorance, to speak of the Queen of Heaven as bearing hatred for a man must seem sensational.

Ser Andrea spoke to her soothingly, as if to a rearing mare, and told her that there had been a misunderstanding, that Virgil was speaking poetically.

'Then poets are liars!' she said.

How ironic, that this cloth-brained woman should come to the same conclusion as Plato. She left the hall at once and retired to her room. As soon as we decently could, the rest of us returned to our meal, but then came one of Clarice's attendants, running in to say that Madonna was very ill and that we must send for a physician. I went to her at once while a physician was summoned, but could tell at a glance that all was well with her. When the physician came, he agreed with me and gave her a mild sedative.

I spoke alone to her favourite slave, the nacreous Iride, and she told me something chilling. She said the Madonna believes that what we are suffering is heavenly retribution for the sins of her husband. She told me something else: it seems that Monna Clarice is once more with child.

Tommaso, these things must seem of small concern compared to the large matters in Florence. Certainly they will seem so to Lorenzo, and I will not have him bothered by them, but if you have the opportunity, plead with him to visit us. *Vale.* Angelo in Hades.

✠

Elena told me that all little girls are made to learn St Paul's words by heart: *'Wives, submit yourselves unto your own husbands, as unto the Lord. For the husband is the head of the wife, even as Christ is the head of the church: and he is the saviour of the body. Therefore as the church is subject unto Christ, so let wives be to their own husbands in every thing.'*

'If Angelo stands in Lorenzo's place, as he does, he is right to expect this obedience, but it is not forthcoming,' I said. 'Monna Clarice rejects him as her husband's deputy.'

'Perhaps for reasons other than the obvious ones,' Elena said. 'Think. These words of St Paul are all very well in an ideal marriage, but what if your husband is not a man of virtue? What if he lacks religion? What if, indeed, he is a pagan heretic? What then? Surely God does not want us to fall into perdition knowingly, in simple obedience to our men? Imagine how Clarice feels, if she suspects Lorenzo of such things. It is not Angelo she is rejecting, but Lorenzo.'

I laughed. 'Lorenzo? Irreligious? He *flays* himself for love of God.'

'He whips himself for his arrogance, so repeatedly that it is evidently no cure. Imagine, Tommaso, you are a mother and a wife who fears God above all things, and you have to look on as your husband is challenged by the Pope. How would you be able to tell which of them is right? – why, by looking around you. Clarice has looked around, and she has seen that Lorenzo's fortunes are collapsing, his allies are not offering the help he needs, and now we have plague in the city. You do not need to be an augur to read such omens.'

'Wait,' I said. 'As little boys, we were made to learn other lines from St Paul: *Husbands, love your wives, even as Christ also loved the church, and gave himself for it. Men ought to love their wives as their own bodies. He that loveth his wife loveth himself. Let everyone of you so love his wife even as himself; and the wife see that she reverence her husband.'*

Elena regarded me in wonder. 'Is that true? Where does it say that? I want to see it written.'

We went to the local church and its bible. In it I soon found St Paul's Letter to the Ephesians and read it to her, translating it into Tuscan, and Elena had enough Latin to see that my translation was true. She stood back, looking amazed, then suddenly she threw her arms round my neck.

'I am so lucky to have you,' she said, though I could not follow her logic. 'You make it so easy to be a good wife.' While she hung round my neck, burying her face in my shoulder and murmuring, I was turning the great pages of the bible, for I had remembered something in the first letter to the Corinthians. I found it in Chapter Seven.

The wife of an unbelieving husband should remain constant and he will be sanctified by her, and the children also. The loving wife makes the family holy.

Elena begged me to ensure that Monna Clarice had these words of St Paul brought to her attention. 'And how may I effect that?' I asked, bemused.

'I don't know. By Ficino or the angels. Somehow you must do it. Lorenzo's safety depends on it, as does Angelo's.'

'You and Ficino and the angels: between you...' I let the sentence hang, quite defeated by her unworldly powers of reasoning.

'Just do as I tell you, husband,' Elena said, wagging her finger at me. We fell on each other laughing, delighted with each other, and hurried from the church, fearing that our turn of thought would sully the holy place. That night she told me she had had no show of blood in the past month.

✝

Angelo, out one evening in Pistoia, found a copy of Galen with a scholar called Master Zenobio, and discovered that, in the opinion of the ancient physician, a child is as likely to take after its mother as its father: the seed does not determine the matter. He returned to the Palazzo Panciaticchi in a state of wonder and triumph. With both knowledge and fine wine running in his veins, his spirit was exalted, and the stars above were so bright that he could walk by their light at this, the time of the moon in its first quarter. Then, realising that he had no one with whom to share his joy of discovery, he fell into an abyss of loneliness deeper than anything he had experienced before. He stood in Pistoia under the stars wondering why fate had brought him to this. He went to his room and wrote to me about Galen. The letter revealed only the excitement of scholarly discovery; it was Elena who told me about the stars and the loneliness.

12

Pistoia, September, 1479
Angelus Politianus Tommaso Maffeo suo S.D.

I CAN BEAR it no longer. She can bear me no longer, but has persuaded Lorenzo to part with his uncle Giovanni Tornabuoni and send him here. The reason? She is with child again. She says she needs someone to look after her who is strong, capable, wise and sympathetic. The inference is, of course, that I am none of these things, can be none of these things while I am an unmarried man. It is of no relevance that I have read the ancient authors, Hippocrates, Galen – even Aristotle – on the matter of human reproduction. Ser Giovanni's first wife died in childbed and that gives him the authority of experience. The fact that she died and was doubtless the victim of medical practices of dubious value does not make it, so far as the Madonna is concerned, any the less useful for that. It is Ser Giovanni she must have.

It is too hot to argue. Summer in the valley – it has been unendurable. How I have longed to be in the hills with Lorenzo in a time of peace. I spoke to the Madonna yesterday and, to make conversation, mentioned that I long for winter, for, apart from its welcome coolness, it will be the time to begin the education of Giovanni. Tommaso, he is such a bright child and has mastered his letters already. But she grew red with anger and said that I will never be the tutor to her youngest son, that he is destined for the Church and will be brought up on the Psalter. To which I grew even redder with anger and said that what the Church needs is intelligent men raised on the ancient authors. 'Educated,' I said, 'to be able to distinguish good from bad, for the men we have now, raised on scripture, are undeniably corrupt.' To which she screamed, and her maids set up like chickens in a coop where a fox has entered. So she won the argument in her usual way, not by logic but by emotion. Everyone rushed to her aid because of her 'condition.' No one rushed to mine because I do not have a 'condition'. I have an opinion.

Tommaso, I need you. Please, if Ficino can spare you for a day or more, please come. I am dying like a plant without water. Come, as soon as you can. Angelo, Pistoia.

✝

On the far side of the mountains in which Pistoia nestled, lay Bologna. North of Bologna, and linked by the river Po, were the neighbouring courts of Mantua and Ferrara, both governed by knights who, at vast sums, hired themselves as captains to any of the great powers, and competed with each other in fame and grandeur.

Ercole d' Este, the Duke of Ferrara, was by his own account descended from Trojan princes and Charlemagne of France. He had an array of villas and palaces full of tapestries, paintings and gems all dedicated to sensory delight. He had the greatest chapel choir in Europe; and the illuminated Bible of his father, famous throughout all Christendom for its splendour, travelled with him everywhere despite being the weight of a small horse.

When I arrived in Pistoia I brought the news that the duke and his army were making their way through the Bologna pass and would be at Pistoia two days hence.

The announcement had a powerful effect on Monna Clarice. She rose from her bed at once and sent for tailors. Angelo begged her to rest and not to get excited, but she ignored him as if he had not spoken. Everything she had to say she addressed to Lorenzo's uncle, Giovanni Tornabuoni, who clearly provided her with the fatherly presence she so desired and needed.

Files of tailors began to crawl through the house. The more brocade and cloth-of-gold to be seen, the more Angelo dressed in priestly black. Everything about Este offended him. He had heard that, though the duke spared no expense in artistic materials, he paid his artists considerably less than the cost of their pigments and by the square *braccia*. 'And all this famed opulence is, of course, financed by war.'

Giovanni Tornabuoni strode up and down wearing a thunderous frown. 'I have told Lorenzo repeatedly to engage someone who fights to win. Why does he not listen? Prestige. He says we need prestige. No other reason. So now we have as our commander this duke whose wife is the daughter of the King of Naples. This cannot be allowed to continue. I have to stop it; I have to make Lorenzo change his mind.' So saying, Giovanni Tornabuoni sent a servant to prepare his mount. 'I will return to the city at once. Florence is a republic, a proud republic. If she can dispense with the nobility in her government, she should be able to do without them in battle also. Do you not agree?'

Angelo, who harboured more republican ideals in his breast than was usual in members of the Medici party, did agree, wholeheartedly. In his opinon 'duke' was simply the title of the great-great-grandson of a barbarian. There were better men with no title. 'Go with speed,' he said encouragingly. 'Tell Lorenzo that the boy David was not king when he killed Goliath. He was a shepherd.'

✣

The days still being hot, we escaped the heat and the bustle of the house and took the children to the cellar for a lethargic game of ball. I held little Giovanni in my arms to give him a better chance of catching it, not that he ever did. Despite its subterranean location it was a cheerful place, its vaulted ceiling whitewashed and decorated with a pattern of vine leaves, clusters of grapes and tendrils of ivy. We were making so much noise it was some time before we heard the sound, but when we did the game ceased and the ball bounced twice then rolled across the floor abandoned.

'Listen!' It was a far-off sound like rain on a roof.

'What is it?'

We all strained to hear, staring at each other.

'Drums!' Piero cried excitedly, already leaping for the door. 'Soldiers! *Milites!*'

Angelo caught and held him. 'Whose drums? We do not go outside until we know whose drums!'

'Ferrara?' I offered.

'Expected tomorrow according to you.'

Cautiously we emerged from the cellar and in the courtyard met Ser Andrea Panciaticchi running into the house from the piazza.

'All is well. Nothing to worry about. It is the army of Ercole d'Este,' he explained. 'A squadron has arrived a day early to set up camp here in time for the arrival of their lord and commander.' He despatched a servant to tell Monna Clarice not to be frightened.

'*Milites veniunt!*' cried Piero, showing off.

'Do you want to see them?' the tutor asked.

'Yes!' Piero cried.

'Yeth!' Giovanni cried.

'Yes!' chorused the girls.

The girls we left behind, but we took the boys out to the piazza to see the spectacle of an arriving army, neglecting to tell Monna Clarice where we were going, since she had already been told that there was nothing to fear.

We gained a fine viewing place on the steps of the Palazzo del Comune from where we watched the infantry of Ferrara run into the main square, crying 'Este! Este! Este!' The soldiers wore iron breastplates and helmets and carried body-length shields; their legs were flashing streaks of red and green. The dust they stirred up had not settled before a train of wagons came into view, bearing the tents and equipment of the camp. The Gonfaloniere of Pistoia came out to meet the sergeant in charge and direct him to the best ground outside the walls in which to erect his tents. The drums stopped and the formation crumbled. Now the square was a confusion of foreign infantry seeking wine and Angelo thought it best to take the boys back to the house.

With Giovanni riding excitedly on the master's shoulders, Piero and I trotted back to the palazzo in military fashion, laughing and shouting Este! Este! Este! We were met at the gate by a solemn porter. Knowing at once something was wrong, Angelo made the boys go to the cellar and wait for him while he raced up the stairs, drawn by the muted sounds of distress coming from the direction of Clarice's room.

Lucrezina was outside the door crying. 'Mamma,' she explained tearfully.

'What is it, Lucrezina? What has happened?' Angelo asked.

'When she heard the drums, she grew frightened and called for all of us to go to her. But when she heard that that you had taken the boys out to the main square, she fainted and fell hard to the floor.'

Lucrezina renewed her weeping.

'Child,' said Angelo, 'there is nothing wrong with your mother. She is well.'

I thought this callous, but Angelo rolled his eyes and said, 'This happens every other day. It is always my fault.'

A physician arrived in a flurry of attendants.

'The Madonna...?' he asked Angelo.

'In there. You will not find anything wrong.'

The physician ignored him and passed into the chamber.

'Do you know how much he charges us to tell us she is well?' Angelo complained, throwing himself down on a chair to wait for the physicians's verdict. A short while later the physician came out looking grave.

'She has had a terrible fright,' he told Angelo.

'But she will live and the baby is well?'

'I have given instructions for a drink of herbs that will soothe her.'

'Not common herbs we can find in the lanes for ourselves, I trust, but rare and expensive ones worthy of the Medici.'

The physician missed the sarcasm. 'Of course. Also a mixture of attar of roses from Turkey and spikenard from India could be used as a fomentation.'

'I shall send a caravan of camels at once.'

The physician laughed pleasantly. 'Master Angelo, the local apothecary has such things.'

'At a price.'

'Of course. But the wife of Lorenzo the Magnificent is worthy of the best.'

✝

We went to Angelo's room to converse alone, since that which he most needed was a companion with at least a modicum of intelligence, but all he could talk about was Monna Clarice. It was a torrent of self-justification unworthy of my friend, and when he put his head in his hands and groaned, 'It is torture. She is torturing me!' I thought he was making too much of it. I began to tell him of the evils befalling Lorenzo and Florence so that he could see his own concerns in context and know them to be trivial, but it only made him angry. A knock came at the door. It was one of Clarice's maids. 'My mistress wants to know if you have written to Lorenzo, and, if so, what you have told him.'

'I have not written to Lorenzo,' Angelo said. 'Tell her I do not intend to write to Lorenzo, or to burden him with insignificant events inflated out of all proportion. Tell her there is a war on. Tell her that her husband needs our support more than we need his. Tell her that she is dying more often than a cat and cannot have many more lives left. Tell her that if she does this to me again...'

'... and does not die, you will kill her,' I said.

Angelo barked with laughter, a sound which echoed strangely in the Panciaticchi house. It was the first joke he had heard since leaving Florence.

The maid, looking horrified, left quickly.

'She will report everything,' Angelo said.

I prepared parchment, quill and ink. 'You had best write to Lorenzo.'

✝

Monna Clarice, believing that Poliziano had not written to Lorenzo, had one of her more literate maids write for her, telling her husband what she had just been through, assuring him that she was well but asking for one of his own physicians. 'The Master,' she said, 'does not take my troubles seriously and doubtless omits to mention what goes on here.'

Angelo wrote to Lorenzo that there was nothing to worry about: Clarice had fainted but there was nothing seriously wrong with her. Lorenzo replied by sending his physician Stefano della Torre.

'Why have you come?' Angelo asked, directing him to Clarice's chamber. 'I told Lorenzo there was nothing to fear.'

Della Torre said that Lorenzo had had a letter from Clarice, and that his anger was towering. 'He cannot believe that you have taken it upon yourself to judge his wife's health. He is too angry to write today. Beware the next letter from Lorenzo de' Medici!'

Angelo waited outside Clarice's chamber, listening to the murmur of voices from within, the firm questions of the doctor and the weak replies of the patient. He could hear no words but the sounds told all. Piero came and reminded him that it was time for lessons but Angelo told him to go and practise the speech he was to deliver to the duke.

At last Stefano della Torre appeared from Madonna's room, looking grim. 'It is a matrix, a pain in the uterus, that is all. She is in good health but needs plenty of rest and hot fomentations on her back. She is not to be troubled with any reception of the duke.'

'So what I said was true.'

Della Torre glared at him. 'What do poets know of medical matters?'

'The realm of poetry is human nature. If you knew about that, you would be a better physician.'

Della Torre snorted angrily.

'Will you take some refreshment before you return to the city?'

'I would have you know that there is plague,' Stefano della Torre told him. 'However much I would enjoy a glass of wine in this parochial retreat of yours, I have much more pressing matters to which to attend.'

The doctor's news smashed the shell of Angelo's complacency.

'In Florence? Where? How many?'

'It began with two in the gaol but is spreading. About seven or eight died yesterday in the poor quarters. They are trying to contain it at the Ospedale La Scala. It is bad, but nothing like Mantua. Eighteen thousand dead there, including Ludovico Gonzaga himself.'

Angelo stood with his mouth open, unable to comprehend such figures. 'Were we not expecting help from Mantua?'

'Small chance of that.'

Doubt assailed Angelo then, huge and black, a crow blotting out the sunlight. For the first time he confronted the possibility of Florence losing the war. What if the fears of Clarice were well founded? What if the house of Medici was indeed close to annihilation? What then? The idea was unbearable and he sought his room. He had had angry letters from Lorenzo before, and usually justified, but this time the mere threat of one disturbed him almost more than anything else that was happening, exciting his fears and gripping his heart. He knelt to pray.

Lorenzo's reply, when it arrived early the next day, was a long and seamless argument on the duty of a friend to speak what is true rather than what he thinks to be true. It was firm and uncompromising: Lorenzo needed to know all that was going on, not just Angelo's version of events. Angelo replied at once, admitting the fault and begging his lord's forgiveness. The little crisis was over.

'Why is it,' he asked me, 'that when men are angry they shout and fight openly, whereas with women, all the feeling is hidden and rumbles on forever, like a thunderstorm that does not break? Why is it that, when a man fights with a woman, he risks losing not his pride, but his whole being?'

'You are exaggerating. Angelo, you are suffering from heat and boredom, that is all.'

He grasped hold of me. 'You do not understand. Even you. I had hoped… Listen, women are poisoners. They do not need phials of venom to do their work. It is already in their nature. A word here, a glance there, a timely swoon. I tell you, Tommaso, whether you believe me or not, Clarice works for my destruction. She blames me for everything. I do everything I can to please her and nothing works. Why do women hate me so?'

I wanted to fly home to Elena, to be with the woman I loved and restore my faith in feminity, but I agreed to stay a few more days to support Angelo in the ordeal of entertaining the Duke of Ferrara.

13

Pistoia, September 1478

DUKE ERCOLE D' ESTE rode into Pistoia under the banner of San Giorgio to be received by the city dignitaries and ushered into the Palazzo del Comune. The town hall was a newly built and proud edifice with a pretty courtyard so vaulted that its ceiling seemed to be the awnings of a tent. The Pistoians were proud of the architecture and decoration of this, their house of government, but Duke Ercole d' Este, who had built for himself the most beautiful house in the whole world, thought otherwise.

Along with his colourful entourage he entered the palazzo, hardly sparing the place a glance. A short while later an invitation arrived at the Palazzo dei Panciaticchi requesting the presence of Madonna Clarice at the banquet to be held in the evening, along with that of Angelo Poliziano the poet.

✢

While he was still dressing, Angelo had Piero practising how to bow with his hand crossing his chest in one graceful, flowing movement.

'Like this. There, good. Do it again. Good.'

Piero wanted to know why such efforts were necessary, and the master, who had been taught this skill by the boy's own father, told him about *gentilezza* and greatness of soul, but he wondered himself about the necessity to abase oneself before men of power. As much as Florence celebrated the ancient world, so much did it also retain a love of the more recent, chivalrous past, a period led by France. Not every Florentine bore the two loves in equal measure; in some degree or other each individual displayed a preference. Angelo so admired the ancients that he almost disdained the heritage of the troubadours. Chivalry, he said, has as its source a dream, an imaginary past to which its proponents look back. One might trace through generations of knights and find that each referred to a previous generation as being of a golden age, but that there was nothing at the source except an empty dream.

'Trace back any lineage and all that you come to is some power-hungry, land-stealing baronial ancestor in that misty period after the fall of the Roman Empire; in short, a barbarian.' Chivalry, he said, was nothing but the attempt of the barbarians to cover their actions with a semblance of morality. They invented codes of conduct impossible to keep and, rather than question the justness of war, they had become obsessed with the pedigree of knights, the colours of heraldry and establishing rules for battle. 'So long as a man was properly dressed and performed various inconsequential rites according to the prescribed manner, he could do what he would.'

The world of ancient Greeks and Romans, however, had a glowing, truthful heart. Their finest literature dealt with questions relevant to men of all epochs, and the answers to those questions defined morality. The goodness of man, his natural inclination to protect rather than to murder, his daily sacrifices of his own desires in the cause of the common good, this was the miracle of humanity, the natural law and the true religion.

The court of Ferrara, Angelo said, was an eclectic mix of ancient and modern: Christian and pagan images shared the same walls. Borso d'Este, the duke's elder brother, claimed he had created the heavenly kingdom on earth. 'And in Ferrara of all places,' Angelo muttered as he laced his hose to his tight jacket, pulling himself into the fine shape of a courtier. He had heard tell of paintings from

Flanders keeping company with frescoes by Piero della Francesca, of rooms hung with tapestries housing manuscripts with painted pages of Arthurian legend and Greek myth. The Este, thirsty for novelty and all things marvellous, collected everything. 'And now it is all being paid for by the taxation of Florentines.'

He wished he could approach Este in the toga of republicanism, bearing the scroll of the law, and greet him man to man rather than have to sweep the floor with his cap. It was, after all, what Lorenzo would do in the circumstance, and was he, Angelo, not here *in loco parentis*, Lorenzo's deputy? He could not imagine il Magnifico bowing before anyone less than a king or the Pope, and therefore, rightfully, neither should he; but of course, custom dictated that he bow so low as to kiss his own knees.

'Like this,' he said, doffing his cap once more with a flourish of his arm.

Piero looked superb. He stood with his neck held well back and his narrow chest pushed forward. From infancy he had idolised his uncle Giuliano; now with every new month he added to his age, he brought into play gestures and stances he had once observed in his uncle. But that apart, there was a beauty to the boy which was not from the Medici, but from the Orsini, as confirmed by Galen. Piero was his mother's son.

Together we went from the nursery to meet Monna Clarice as she emerged from her room. She was dressed in a new gown of cloth of gold, with sleeves of crimson brocade and emerald embroidery, and on her head she wore the hat once given to her by the King of France, presented by his ambassador, Phillipe de Commynes. Of all her lamentable old fashioned head-gear this was surely the worst, huge and ungainly. It is a feature of Oltramontane fashion that it looks eccentric when worn in Italy. A more graceful lady might have carried it off, but Clarice, walking with her head modestly lowered, looked like a horned cow moving slowly across pasture. Glancing up, she recoiled from our gaze.

'What is it?' she demanded.

'Your hat,' said Angelo blithely. 'Magnificent. Such a hat has not been seen in Italy since the days of Pepin the Bald. But surely my lady is not well enough to attend this function?'

'I make the effort solely for the sake of my husband,' she replied. 'Are you saying my hat is out of fashion?'

The tutor was wearing his most expensive doublet, one of blue made with tiny pleats running from shoulder to waist, which had cost him a month's salary.

'How is it that you always look as if you have slept in your clothes, Maestro?' she asked with a frown.

✝

Giovanni Tornabuoni returned from Florence in time to escort the family to the Palazzo del Comune. He told Angelo that his journey to the city had been in vain, that Lorenzo suffered from the sin of pride, that having engaged Este, nothing would now persuade Lorenzo to dispense with him. 'And so we are stuck with this fool,' he said.

We made the short journey with Clarice riding side-saddle on a mule. If she looked like a painter's image of the Holy Mother in flight to Egypt, then it was Ser Giovanni Tornabuoni walking beside her who resembled St Joseph. Angelo was left to follow in the rear with the rest of the servants. We were received in the court-yard of the Palazzo del Comune, under the billowing ceiling and hanging shields of the major families of Pistoia.

It was to be a small banquet: a mere sixty guests mingled with the duke's attendants in the sala. Clarice and Giovanni Tornabuoni were presented to him; Angelo Poliziano was not. The duke looked over the bowed head of the wife of il Magnifico and beckoned to the tutor. 'Here,' he said, 'sit by me.'

Servants altered settings adroitly to accommodate the duke's wish, though the Gonfaloniere of Pistoia could not see why a mere tutor was being so honoured. But the duke wished to discuss poetry, not war, and he kept Angelo from his food all evening. Roasted lapwings and linnets sitting in a nest of spinach went cold on the poet's plate as he was engaged in conversation on medals

158

and symbolism, on antique cameos and coins, and most of all on drama, for Este wished to revive ancient theatre. Lorenzo had the same wish. Angelo tried to draw the duke, to find out what he intended, just as the duke tried to draw him. They praised, they flattered, they stroked and they milked. Suddenly the duke sat back and regarded Angelo from a greater distance. 'You are utterly wasted in Florence,' he said. 'Come to my court. Leave this very day. I have met other men of your talent, your breadth of knowledge and ability, but I have never met one with such loyalty to his master.'

'That very loyalty naturally prevents my accepting.'

'Of course, it must, or else be shown to be false. But if ever that loyalty should – God forbid – lose its object, come to Ferrara. Promise?'

Angelo went and stood with his pupil as Piero delivered the speech they had been rehearsing to welcome the duke on behalf of Lorenzo. The duke steepled his fingers and listened with his eyes half-closed, the smile on his lips telling everyone how accustomed to flattery he was. As soon as Piero was done, Este leant towards Monna Clarice and apologised for neglecting her. 'You have a fine son there, Madonna, with a most excellent tutor. Goodness, you have a Chiron for your Achilles. Nothing is more important for our children than good education. I have a son too, a son and two daughters. We are very blessed in our children. I am having my girls educated. Are you? It is most important in my view. My Isabella is very musical, and is now promised to Francesco Gonzaga. It was a very marathon of a negotiation, but it was settled, and just before poor Ludovico died of the plague. Now, of course, his son Federico is the new Marquess of Mantua, *years* before we expected it, and my Isabella's husband will be the next one.'

Emotions passed like clouds over the face of Clarice. She had been trying to persuade Lorenzo for the past year to secure the Gonzaga prince for their own Lucrezina, but Lorenzo had said that at eight his daughter was far too young to be betrothed.

'How old is Isabella?' she asked.

'Just five, Madonna.'

'Mercy!'

'Tactics, that is my way, tactics and strategies, in the home as in the field. Look ahead and make plans. And that is exactly what I intend in my campaigns on behalf of your fair city. Tactics and strategies – that is the way to win a battle. Confound the enemy.'

'Better to confound him than kill him,' observed Angelo brightly, returning to his seat.

'Exactly so.'

'Especially when he is your kinsman. I believe your wife is the most beautiful daughter of our enemy, the King of Naples.'

'Ho!' said the duke, enjoying the challenge of this brave and cheeky Florentine. 'As with everyone, young man, I am related to several hundred people. But I am a professional soldier, and if I have relations in the opposite camp there is nothing unusual in that. These days war is humane – just a game of chess. We do not seek to kill anyone, and the worst that can happen to one's opponent is loss of face and financial ruin. Il Magnifico is paying me handsomely to fight this war for him, and I shall play it to win.'

Angelo thought that, with this oaf as captain, Florence must abandon all hope.

'Murdering the enemy is the method of barbarians,' the duke continued. 'Modern warfare is merciful, so lenient that you, a boy of what, twenty?'

'Twenty four.'

'Twenty four! And what do you know of war? In that heroic past which you so admire, you would have been dead on the battlefield by now, but these days you can sit in repose writing poetry and leave the fighting to us professionals.'

It was true. The days of real battle were far in the past. *Of arms and the man I sing.* With Lorenzo holding the baton of command, the baton was in the hands of a banker, and battle plans were laid in the Medici accountancy office. If Angelo were to sing of war, he would have to find rhymes for *perfidy* and *cowardice* as he strained to describe the actions of those men in besieged cities who, for a sum, opened up the gates to the enemy. *Of gold and the purse I sing.* But to say that no one died in modern warfare was an arrow so far wide of the mark as to be shot by a fool. The tales coming out of Arezzo made the stomach revolt.

While the duke continued to boast of the humanity of modern warfare, Angelo envisioned Montepulciano with its blessed vineyards in flames, its herds driven off, its proud people begging for bread, its women reduced to prostitution. Although these days no one died heroically, thousands died in want and all loss of dignity. The plague had come, and where was it flourishing? Why, in the Florentine camp. War and disease were companions who rode together. No one died? Thousands died. Eighteen thousand in Mantua alone, but to the duke only one of them had had a name. *Of alms and the man I sing.*

'So!' said the duke, slapping him across the back. 'When will you come to Ferrara?'

'As soon as my patron is persuaded to part with me,' Angelo said, meaning, 'Never.'

14

Florence, September 1478

I HAVE MADE my room a little sanctuary but my prayers are as dry as dust. Maso has joined the city militia and is on duty at the walls. When he returns at night it is always with friends, and they drink into the early hours and make such noise. I keep warning him to be careful with plague in the city, but he laughs in his carefree way and looks as immortal as he feels. 'It is confined to the Ospedale della Scala at the monastery of San Martino,' he says, 'and I am stationed at San Marco. There is nothing to fear.'

But there is: I fear him and his friends. All alone here with men. It does not take custom or the law to tell me this is not right. It is a surprise and a plunging disappointment to discover that I miss the convent and long for female company. Here there is nothing but loneliness. When I look out of the windows on to the street I see only soldiers. The few despondent traders and artisans left in the city – for most have fled to the hills – hurry past with their noses buried in pomanders. There is a smell of sulphur in the air, the odour, Maso tells me, coming from places where clothes and fabrics are being fumigated, but it is still the smell of Dis.

Maso went to market to get food and came back with lengths of cheap fabric so that I can 'dress like a woman and not like a nun'. I made him have them fumigated, not only for the sake of safety, but also to delay the task of cutting and sewing, for of all the tasks that are my womanly lot, this one of dressmaking is one I detest. But the stuff is here now, and the wretched business of cutting is over, so I must sew. I am being as slow as I can be, for I think it not wise to dress as a woman in this house of men; it would be best to continue looking like a postulant, even a ragged one. In the convent sewing was a great interruption to study, but now, with nothing to study, I confess I am beginning to enjoy making stitches as small as I can, the push and pull of the needle, the feel of the fabric; but to do it overlong pains the neck, and I would much rather be reading and advancing my Latin.

✦

Maso came home this evening in a terrible mood. 'It is all for him,' he told me. 'Everything. These people are suffering, they are dying – it was ten today – and it is all for Lorenzo. The only thing His Holiness wants is him, and the only thing Florence has to do to be spared is to give him up, but they will not do it. They would rather die. Explain it to me, explain it if you can. Is it pride?'

'They must love him, Maso,' I said.

'Faith, loyalty, that kind of thing? What people ever loved their ruler?'

'Angelo loves him.'

'As a dog loves its master at meal times. Loves him? He fawns on him. He has given up his right to his own life to be a servant of the Medici. I mean, here we are, family, desperate, and where is our brother? Looking after Lorenzo's family.'

'Does he know we are here?'

'Well, no.'

Maso cannot write and has not bothered to hire a letter-writer. When I suggested I might write the letter, he grew furious and said it was no use. It would have to be delivered to the Palazzo de' Medici and he is banned from the place. He is throwing up obstacles unnecessarily. Any of them would be easily overcome if he had a will to it. Meanwhile I am penned up here, stifled, bored. I have to make meals for him at night and have not yet found the stomach to gut a fish; have not yet succeeded in cooking anything without burning it. I tried to skin a rabbit but was overcome by grief. All that beautiful fur, brown and cream, each strand a silky perfection, the ears that yesterday could hear, the blind eyes that yesterday could see, the legs formed for hopping, all the effort of creation to produce this wonderful creature, only for me to pull it apart and boil it. I was not confronted by a dead rabbit but by the unfathomable mystery of life and death. All that growth, that perfection of form. What waste! It made me think of education, all the effort and toil to learn, that can be struck down and destroyed in a moment by the bony hand of death. Suor Agosta – where now her learning? Here was a dead rabbit, the dead body of a rabbit. But… Where was that which saw through those eyes and listened through those ears, the rabbit itself. Where was it now? Vanished? Oh, who is there I can ask such questions of?

Maso found me in a huddle on the floor, smacked me over the head, told me I am useless, a half-woman, and I could only agree with him. He made me stand up and watch as he took his knife and slit the belly of the rabbit open; made me take the skin in both hands and pull. It came away too easily. I gagged to see what was inside, but Maso made me look and pointed out all the organs to me, the heart, the liver, the kidneys. Such colours! Iridescent, like the inside of sea shells. In anticipation I had expected to faint away but as I stared into the dissected animal my wonder only increased. Who *made this?*

Maso chopped it up and threw it in the pot over the kitchen fire. All the colours disappeared into brown. We had rabbit stew for supper.

✠

Although it is not particularly cold at night yet, I have lit a fire, for in this task at least I have a talent and the fire keeps me company. Its shadows people the room; by the murmur of the logs, the shadows speak. This is a strange place in a strange city and it belongs to a strange man I do not know. I have looked everywhere for a sign by which I might know him but have found none. He owns this house without possessing it, an empty, forlorn place. I have tried to cheer it by dusting and cleaning but it accepts my attentions ungraciously and, as soon as I've turned my back, covers itself in dust again.

Brother… Brother. I have started addressing Maso as 'brother' since this word alone can remind a man that a woman needs his protection, but he just smiles oddly.

I regret everything. I regret running away from the convent; I regret all my years of petulance. I did not know freedom when I had it. I would give anything to be with Suor Agosta now, or even Madre Generale. Oh, I weep for them! Was it all my fault? I feel it is so. A dim and distant voice tells me this cannot be, but my heart throbs with guilt and regret. And after all my efforts, what have I attained? An empty house in a deserted city.

What do I want? Dear God, more than I can hope for.

✣

Dear Invisible God, your lost daughter calls on you with all her might. Forgive me my sins. Allow me into your fold. Show yourself now before my heart dies of misery. Show yourself. Fill this emptiness with your presence. Let me know your will. Speak to me, O God, speak to me. I am father-less, motherless, brotherless, friendless, godless. What can I do, what can I say to make you hear me? What is your will? That I sew? Then I shall sew. That I dust and clean? Then I shall dust and clean. That I skin rabbits for Maso? Then I shall skin rabbits and boil them in the pot. Since there is nothing else for me to do and no purpose to this, my life, let me do my duties without complaint, content that it is your will. Whoever you are. Wherever you are. My Lord.

✣

I can barely write this for shaking. Nor can I tell all. Just the boiled carcass of fact. There came into my room in the middle of the night one of Maso's soldier friends. I woke up to his hot, drunken breath on my face, the wet, fierce pressure of his lips on my mouth. He was grunting, scrabbling at me like a dog after a bone, his hands ripping away at my coverings. I struggled and tried to push him off but he was too strong and heavy for me. I tried to get my mouth free of his so that I could scream but he bit my lip. He held me down with one hand while with the other he pulled off his hose. I prayed then to my invisible God with every fibre of my body and soul. I did not hear the door open or Maso come in. All I knew was that the man suddenly rose up rigid, his head thrown back, his mouth open in a silent scream, his throat yawning wide and gushing with blood.

Maso pulled the corpse off me, leaving me lying there naked and vulnerable, covered in hot blood swiftly growing cold and sticky. I leapt up, grabbed a sheet and tried simultaneously to cover myself and clean my body, whimpering incoherently, not sure what was the more shocking: rape or murder.

'Did he enter you? Is your honour preserved?' Maso demanded, wiping his knife on the corpse.

I assured him that my virginity was intact.

'No man touches my kin and lives.' With that he dragged the body out by its feet, leaving a trail of blood behind it.

Now it is the morning of the night before. I have cleaned the house and washed the floor and the linen, but nothing will wipe this sin away. I do not know what Maso has done with the body, though I have qualms about drawing water from the well. I try and persuade myself that the corpse is in the river, which seems to be the graveyard for Florentines, but Maso had returned too quickly to have made the journey to the bridge. I don't know who the man was or if he will ever be missed. But at least I know now to trust Maso, no matter how crude his sense of justice.

15

AT THE FIFTH hour of the morning of September 27th, in the Florentine camp at Poggio Imperiale, Lorenzo de' Medici handed the baton of command to Ercole d'Este, Duke of Ferrara. But despite all pomp and ceremony, despite all the propitiousness of the moment, when Este led his men out of the camp, he took them on a route leading away from the enemy.

The duke advanced south like a cat walking a wall, gracefully avoiding all obstacles in the search for food and somewhere to sleep. The rules of warfare demand that, in under three months, the armies must retire for the winter; with that, as well as other delaying measures, these fair-weather combatants could, perhaps, hope for the continuation of this profitable affair until at least the following autumn.

Persuaded at last by his Florentine masters to change direction, the Duke of Ferrara spent the next three weeks marching fifty miles, but keeping at least a day behind his quarry, the Duke of Calabria. If there were no fire, however, there was much smoke, and the rest of Tuscany suffered its stench. Various hill top towns and outlying fortresses came under siege and no military relief was forthcoming. The solid Tuscans held out doggedly but the ruination of the harvest brought famine, the poisoning of wells brought sickness, and plague stalked the land like a rabid wolf. One resourceful condottiere of Rome encouraged the plague's advance by catapulting rotting corpses over the walls of the town he was besieging.

The poignant shadows of autumn began to fall across our valleys. It seemed as if the gilding sun was setting on our civilization and hell was beginning to gape beneath our feet. When the Florentine camp moved to Monte Sansovino, where the town was surrounded and besieged by the enemy, one by one the soldiers began to sicken and die. Two by two. Three by three. A sergeant entered the tent of the captain to deliver the news in a whisper. The captain blanched. 'Deal with it,' he said. 'Tell no one. The enemy must not know.'

And thus during the dark hours of each night, the Florentines took the dead from their beds and buried them in a lime pit. The captain, Galleotto Pico della Mirandola, walked the camp, trying to encourage his troops and himself. 'The enemy must not know,' he repeated endlessly, but no one listened. Fear got the better of them. The conscripts began to defect at night; the mercenaries simply rode off at the hour of their choosing. The only ones who remained were those who were loyal beyond all fear of death, those who had nothing better to do than die, nowhere else to go but the grave.

Lorenzo wrote each day from Florence, trying to instil faith. He sent the recipes against plague that Ficino recommended: steam baths, an airing of the tents, unguents, crystals of arsenic applied to the wrists, armpits, nostrils and throat. He prayed. We all prayed. But no amount of prayer could instil faith in Lorenzo himself. He looked on catastrophe, saw God's wrath and began to doubt himself.

The enemy, knowing of the Florentine disaster, offered a truce. Even though he knew that the eight days of peace were entirely to the enemy's advantage, Lorenzo could only accept. He sent a terse note to Angelo Poliziano at Pistoia. 'You are to remove the family to our villa at Cafaggiolo forthwith; but go via Fiesole and await me there.'

✝

Hearing that the family had arrived at Fiesole I rode across from Careggi. Angelo did not wish to be inside the villa so we sat together on the terrace wall below. The view over Florence was misty but you could make out the shape of the dome of the Cathedral, standing protectively over the huddle of houses. Wood smoke and the smoke of other things pervaded the air. Only the snaking river Arno reflected the light of the sun; everything else paled into cloudy lines that may have been sky or may have been hills, it was impossible to say.

Immediately below on the terraces some colour remained. Dark cypresses by chapels, pines huddling round the deep red roofs of villas – the kind of villa, Angelo said, that he desired for himself, somewhere secluded, but not isolated, a small house with a study as big as a hall. 'And no woman.'

'Oh, you do not mean that.'

'Believe me, Tommaso, I most certainly do. I have seen through all her guises now, and know her heart. I want no woman in my life.'

'One day everything will resume its right proportion and you will think differently.'

'If I were not so desperate for friends, I would push you and your complacent backside off this wall.'

He preferred Fiesole to Florence, which was natural for one born to hill life. It had been an Etruscan city, lost to the Romans in battle. Once, and not so long ago, he had only to walk on this hillside imagining Virgil and Ovid walking the same paths for every thought in his mind to arrange itself into verse. Now, he said, Calliope had deserted him.

'Or rather, my ear has deserted her. I cannot hear! How long can this aridity continue, I wonder, before I can no longer call myself a poet?'

In the library of the villa, tucked inside the book of the *Iliad* which he had presented to the Medici eight years previously, he had rediscovered his first letter to Lorenzo, in which he offered to translate all of Homer. 'My letter,' he said, 'which I have only ever remembered with embarrassment, has been kept in the book like a pressed flower. I read my youthful words with surprise and fore-boding, for they declared that I desire no other god, no other muse but only Lorenzo.'

He had no recollection of writing such words. 'And yet there they are, ink on parchment in my handwriting. What did I mean?

Did I so callously deny the Muse in favour of this human lord of Florence? Or was it the literary conceit of a nervous boy? If I really did change allegiance on that day, then it has been no creative divinity sustaining and inspiring me these past years, but Lorenzo himself. Is it any wonder then that I cannot write now, while my lord is in mortal danger? When will he come?'

He looked down on the road to Florence wistfully.

'Why do you not go into the city?' I asked.

'He forbids it. There are at least a hundred sick with plague and yesterday a man was found dead on the benches of Santa Maria Novella. The containment is not working. Lorenzo told me to wait for him here, saying that it is my duty to be with the family at all times.' If his voice betrayed no emotion, his face wore the fixed stare of Odysseus's dog. 'He will come soon. I just have to be patient. We are so close, here on Fiesole. Beloved Fiesole.' He turned to me. 'Do you know, just walking in the garden in sight of the Duomo was enough to make me sing again? Then one of her minions came out and stuck her finger in my windpipe. Said my noise was disturbing Madonna's rest.'

Below and to the west, the abbey bell began to sound the hour.

'Shall we go down to the library?' I suggested. 'For the evening approaches and I must leave before dark.'

While I went for the horses, Angelo called for his pupil. In the conflict with Clarice, he had taken the utmost care not to turn the boy against his mother, and converted every temptation to criticise her into a lesson in consideration for others. He did not disparage Clarice's beliefs and promote his own: he laid them side by side and trained Piero to make his own judgements. Piero made them, and discerning the difference between justice and injustice, was becoming inseperable from his tutor. When it came to grammar, he still writhed with reluctance, but in the realm of poetry he was ardent, had quite fallen in love with Virgil and was devoting himself wholeheartedly to the memorisation of the Aeneid. At his tutor's call, he shot from the house, tying up the laces of his jacket as he ran.

'Where are we going?'

'To the Badia.'

'What if Papa comes?'

'We shall not be long, and may even meet him as we go!'

Angelo mounted into the saddle and pulled Piero up to his place on the horse's croup. They rode together in great harmony, Piero keeping his seat with the ease of a natural rider whether the horse walked or trotted. For all Angelo's complaints about having to spend time with small boys when he would rather be writing, here was the man made whole by his relationship with others. Angelo Poliziano was born for fatherhood, even if it was not to be the usual kind.

✞

The cloisters were quiet, the monks spending the hour in solitary contemplation in their cells. The shifting light in the vaulting cast pleasing shadows over the stone slabs and clay tiles of the cloister floor. The graceful columns of the arches had Corinthian capitals, a design echoed in the shorter columns on the upper storey. I stood for awhile gazing out of an archway which gave a view over the monastery gardens and olive groves to Florence beyond. The archway led into a loggia where the Platonic Academy often met, and the view was one I had often looked on while Ficino stripped the veils of ignorance from our eyes, so that what began as a contemplation of Nature's beauty ended, through the Socratic technique of seeing beauty as separate from its object, as a vision of God. To see it now, the vivid green of grass, the black-green of cypresses, the colour of flowers, the movement of clouds, was to be at once reminded of the limitless depth of peace.

The monks of the abbey were custodians of one of the greatest collections of books in the world, amassed by Cosimo de' Medici. Though some effort had been made to catalogue it and put it in order, there was much work yet to be done. During summer months spent on Fiesole with Lorenzo (*that* was the golden age, if ever there had been one), Angelo had been adopted by Father

Abbot as the chief adviser in the task, for he knew all the authors, both ancient and modern, had read them, knew their chronological order, had an uncanny talent for dating a script and was unequalled in his ability to detect errors and counterfeits. He had free access to the place and a key, and we let ourselves in to a room off the cloisters to view this wonder of the world.

The room was pungent with knowledge. Knowledge of the many things, knowledge of the One, put down in writing over hundreds, perhaps thousands of years. Knowledge on parchment, knowledge on paper, vellum and papyrus; knowledge rolled or bound in books. Worm drilled, beetle-ridden, mouse-chewed: the wisdom of the ages, smelling of plant, animal and mineral. I inhaled deeply and felt immediate intoxication.

There were books there that dissolved your soul in beauty. Gold ink on blue vellum to catch the light; figures and scenes of astonishing reality; wreathed margins full of symbols; and everywhere rhythms of colour as mysterious as music. There were title pages that played tricks – making you think the paper was torn, or that a fly had settled on the cherries – designed to pull forth from our throats the ultimate praise a painter craves: 'I took that for real!' But for all their dazzling beauty, Angelo was not interested in these, considering them a dish overwhelmed by its sauce. His rare taste was for the unbound, the untitled, the indecipherable: books whose beauty was intellectual, not sensual.

'What is your desire?' he asked. 'An apocryphal gospel from the second century? Or a scrap of Aristotle written perhaps by the philosopher himself? The Laws of the Emperor Justinian? Or the Hymn to the Sun by Julian the Apostate? We have the mysteries of the Platonists, and all those original Greek texts Ficino has translated: the Poimandres of Hermes Trismegistus and the Dialogues of Plato, Proclus, the book on angels by Dionysius, the disciple of St Paul – as they say, but I have my doubts and think he was of the sixth century, and would prove it if you have an hour to spare – or would you like a text written in the very hand of the Venerable Bede? Then of course, over here, we have the Romans. I could find an early Pliny for you, and all the plays of Terence, and then there is Piero's favourite…'

'The Virgil!' The boy pointed to a book that was chained to the wall.

'The only earlier copy I know of is the one in the Papal Library,' Angelo said.

Having seen the one in Rome, I was keen to examine this, so Angelo asked Piero to climb up and unlock it from its ring. This Piero did with eager and enviable agility. He handed the book down to us with great care. Clearly the tutor's love of literature was now running in the boy's veins. Angelo turned its heavy pages so that we could study its script and illuminations. Piero watched me as I pored over his favourite book, anxious to see if I approved his choice. I did, saying that the script was very fine indeed, but Angelo said that one does not judge a book by its script. 'It has at least a hundred lines missing from the text.'

'How do you know that?'

'Because I have read it and missed them,' he replied simply.

Did he read every book he came across, no matter if he had read it before in another manuscript? The answer was yes, he did. Piero and I exchanged glances, half appreciative of Angelo's voracious intelligence, half disturbed by it. Angelo closed the book with the haughtiness of a sculptor dismissing the work of a rival. 'A hundred lines…' he complained.

'When we win the war,' Piero said, consoling his tutor, 'we can sack Rome.'

'What, and get that Virgil from the Papal Library and bring it here? Now that is the first valid justification for war I have heard. Remind me Piero, in the hour of victory. We shall go together to fetch it.'

'Just the Virgil?' I asked. 'If you are sacking Rome, there may be other treasures you could bring home.'

'Oh, I think we have everything else already. No, the Virgil will be sufficient. Although a few ancient statues would be good, of course. Lorenzo has been thinking of establishing a school for sculptors. Yes, we shall bring back some statues for him.'

Our happy voices rang in the vaulted cloister and, for a short while, we forgot how reduced our fortunes were becoming. As we left the abbey, we paused to look down on the city once more. The clouds had passed and now it dazzled like a jewel in the evening sun; even the red clay tiles shimmered. There the dome of the Cathedral, there the spires of Santa Maria Novella and Santa Croce, the bell-towers, the girdle of the walls. A map-maker could sit here and draw the whole city and its monuments, set against the blue hills in the distance. Florence. The heart of Tuscany, of Italy, of the Christian world. Here Truth was not scorned nor forced to beg in the streets, but was honoured and adorned; she was beauty, she was love. I saw her with Botticelli's eyes, that divine spark in the soul of Man, without which he is a brute. By its light we have education, culture, civilisation – those fine, fragile gifts of the Divine to his Creation. By the light of Truth, we create rules of combat which are fair, just, and do not include the use of plague victims as weapons.

We stood looking down on our city in silence, unable to comprehend the force that wanted to crush us and yet feeling its suffocating weight. They said that the Pope wanted Florence for himself, but Florence without Lorenzo was a ring without its gem. What the Pope really wanted was the light, and he mistook its source if he thought it was the city and its wealth.

'We are to go to Cafaggiolo tomorrow,' Angelo told me, gazing at the city as if for the last time. 'But he will surely come before we depart. Tonight probably.'

Having bid my friend farewell, I took the road down to the city. Angelo took Piero and did not return to the road but set off on a different path, one that would take him to the summit of Fiesole above Lorenzo's villa on a track used by few other than peasants. I knew that track: he had taken me on it once. It led past a natural fountain and over sites of tremendous antiquity, places where he could commune with the gods of his ancestors. And perhaps pray to them.

On my way to the city, my heart stopped to see a party of riders coming towards me on the road. The men were Roman, were armed, were led by a captain, and – oh, I could breathe again – passed me by as if I were not there. My heart pounded. The Lady Clarice! The children! Aghast at the lurid pictures of massacre being painted by fancy, I turned and followed behind them at a discreet distance. By the time I reached the villa, the men were dismounted but were not burning furze to smoke out the Medici family. Instead a sergeant was telling a servant that Count Niccolò Orsini had arrived to visit his sister.

I slid off my horse, my limbs dissolving with relief. Angelo found me there in due course as he returned from his ride. I told him what had happened, expecting him to find it as funny as I now did, but he looked towards the house with trepidation. 'Do you have to go back to Florence?' he asked.

'Yes. Why? What do you fear?'

'Being beaten up by a condottiere in full armour.'

'Oh, poets and their imaginations! Niccolò Orsini is a nobleman.'

'So what? Please, stay the night!'

Grumbling but acquiescing I paid a boy to go to the city and tell my wife where I was, and then I went to the kitchen to find some supper. Angelo preferred to join me rather than dine with the family.

'I could not bear to be with two members of the Orsini clan at once. I have asked for a bed to be made for you in my room.'

'Angelo! Your fears are unreasonable.'

'Anybody's fears are unreasonable. A man of reason has no fear.'

'Well, then.'

'You know me well enough not to expect perfection.'

I continued to mock his fears, but when we left the kitchen to retire, we met two of Orsini's men sent to find us. 'Come with us, Maestro,' one of them said to Angelo, taking hold of him. 'Count Orsini wishes to discuss certain matters concerning his sister.' Angelo struggled, trying to free himself. I jumped in to break the soldier's grip on him but was thrown aside by the other. I regained my feet and ran after them, absolutely refusing to be parted from my friend, whatever lay ahead for him. We were both shown into a small private chamber and the door was locked behind us.

Orsini was physically unremarkable. If it were not for his shiny armour and his title, one would have passed him by in the street. He stood by a table holding a small bundle wrapped in oiled linen. 'I wanted to see you alone,' he told Angelo, 'but if you must have a servant witness your humiliation, so be it.'

'Servant?' I cried, and was hit so hard across the mouth by one of the guards that I sank to the floor to nurse a cut lip.

'I have heard everything from my lady sister,' Orsini continued addressing Angelo, giving the bundle a single turn. 'That one of your low estate should have the effrontery to shout at an Orsini – admonish her and challenge her authority. Her superiority aside, she is with child. What possesses you? I know Florentines are arrogant, but such pride as yours defies belief. You shouted at her!'

He said this as if it were the most incredible thing he had ever heard.

'I could do little else since she will not listen to me.'

'Why should she listen to you?'

'In Lorenzo's absence, I am the voice of her lord.'

Orsini laughed, sincerely amused. '*You?* This very simple matter is only complicated by your friendship with my brother-in-law.' The contents in the bundle underwent another turn. 'You have offended the honour of my sister, my kin, my house; Lorenzo de' Medici not withstanding, I will have restitution.'

The cloth came away from two bald daggers that now lay on the table.

I tried to rise, but one of Orsini's men trod on my hand so effectively that I was pinned to the ground.

'I will not fight,' said Angelo hoarsely.

'Nor I,' said Orsini. 'My intention is to stab you in the heart. However, my sense of honour demands that I offer you the means

175

to defend yourself. I will do as I intend. If you truly do not wish to fight, then you will die.'

'Please my lord, I am a poet and not a warrior. Do not force this.'

'The choice is yours, Ambrogini.' Orsini picked up one dagger while pushing the other towards his enemy.

Angelo's hand closed round the hilt. To die or to kill – the choice seemed a double evil. But in the end, and with regard to the soul, it was no choice at all. He released the dagger and pushed it back towards the Count. 'Consider, my lord, if you wish to have murder stain your conscience.'

Orsini was astonished and wavered in his resolve. 'It is vengeance, not murder.'

'Weasel words. When the Lord said *Thou shalt not kill*, he had no nicety of distinction in mind but meant what He said.'

'Would you, apostate, remind me of the Ten Commandments?' Orsini was becoming so enraged that he *needed* to fight, but his chivalric honour prevented him from making the first move. He had to force Angelo to spring at him, and to make this frog jump he must provoke him as he himself had been provoked.

'You have a sister, I believe.'

'Which sister?'

'Maria. A whore, by all accounts, who offers her body to any soldier, monk or shepherd who comes her way.'

'That is not true!'

'Yes it is. A letter has come for you from the Signoria of Monte-pulciano, reporting her missing. It is said she ran off with a soldier.'

'What? When? What letter?'

'It is with Lorenzo. At this time! At this hour! Your damnable kin – bandit cousins and depraved women – to swarm him like flies at such a time as this.'

The knife was still in reach on the table. 'Say no more!' Angelo warned.

'She is a slut and a harlot. Through you, her shame besmirches the Medici.'

I could see Angelo fighting the urge to throw his full weight at the Count and to bang him against the wall. Forget the knife. It would be enough to break the man's nose. Some blood would be sufficient. A broken tooth. A bitten tongue. Anything to shut Orsini's mouth.

In all the years I had been his friend, not once had I seen violence in him. I tensed, thinking that, when he exploded, the force would be terrible, but he did not explode. Who knows what struggle was going on inside, but the man of reason won and he grew calm. 'These false accusations will not rouse me,' he told Orsini, quietly and with conviction. 'God knows my sister is pure and I will not fight. Kill us if you will, with your slander and viciousness, but the sin is all yours, and not ours. Hypocrisy – clearly an Orsini trait.' He turned, pushed the guard off me and helped me rise. 'I am leaving,' he said to the Count. 'If you wish to stab me in the back as I go, that is your prerogative, but I think that even you would not be so base.'

The Count was enraged: 'Ambrogini! You will have no further contact with my nephews!'

Angelo turned. 'On whose authority?'

'On my authority!'

'On what grounds?'

'Your heathenism is a corrupting filth that endangers their souls. We will have none of it.'

'Will you tell Lorenzo this?'

'All of it, and tomorrow!'

'I will be most interested to hear his response. Good night to you, your Lordship.'

'You upstart shoemaker! If you show any further disrespect to my sister, I promise you, I will have your hide made into boots!'

Angelo's lip curled in distaste. 'What imagery, from one whose only care is for the purity of souls. God go with you.'

✝

As he strode away, I had to walk fast to keep up with him. I asked him, as well as I could through swollen lips, where his courage had come from, and he said that his eye had fallen on a little roundel by della Robbia set in the cornice of the room. 'The one of a little baby in swaddling clothes,' he said. 'My sister Maria – she used to sleep better hanging up on a meat hook than in her cradle. It is my enduring memory of her. Every time I go past the foundling hospital, I see her image by della Robbia everywhere. And there it was, the same image on the wall, and I knew without doubt his words were calumny and slander. Maria is innocent.'

'Buth ow d'you know?'

'Sometimes I have access to such wisdom as our master Ficino enjoys: intuitive, based on nothing but an inner conviction. I do not know how I knew, I just did.' In his room he made me rinse my face in the basin and then checked the injury.

'Intuition is a wonderful gift. How else could I have known that I was going to be beaten up by Orsini?'

'Buth you weren' beaten. I wath.'

'The wise man does not meet violence with violence.'

'Thumtimes,' I told him, 'you are inthufferable.'

✟

The following morning, with a face as blue as if I had swallowed ink, I rode to Careggi to explain as best I could to Ficino why I had been fighting. He gave me another lecture on the habits of the wise man that put me in a mood of high dudgeon, and I was still glowering over my work when I heard visitors arriving. Ficino went out but I was of a mind to ignore them and carry on with my copying. Then I heard a voice so familiar that my head jerked up.

Lorenzo walked in, complaining about the stench of the city.

'And since I have no sense of smell,' he said, touching his flattened nose. 'God only knows what it is like for others. What have you done to your face, Tommaso?'

Considering it inadvisable to tell him that I had been slapped by a henchman of his brother-in-law, I pretended it was too painful to speak.

'Stung by a bee,' Ficino said. I was astonished to hear the priest

178

of Truth tell a lie, but understanding that Ficino did not want Lorenzo to be distracted, I nodded, looking most doleful.

'What were you doing? Kissing the hive?' Lorenzo laughed. When Lorenzo laughed, we were all expected to laugh. This I found particularly difficult and tears came to my eyes. Ficino sent me away to get some camomile balm for my mouth.

Despite Lorenzo's manner, which was brisk and full of good humour, we could see the reality behind the mask: here was a man needing solace and advice. I left them alone, and listened from the far side of the door.

'How long do we have together?' Ficino asked him.

'An hour, no more. I must go to Fiesole to see Angelo before he departs.'

They spoke of the difficulties of the war, of how the Dukes of Calabria and Urbino were overwhelming the Florentine forces. They spoke of Lorenzo's financial difficulties; they discussed the plague and its advances.

'Father Marsilio,' Lorenzo said quietly, 'I have a question: are these terrible acts of God retribution for my sin?'

Ficino demurred quietly, but Lorenzo did not want to be dissuaded from this idea. 'Why should it not be so? I have enough sin to merit such reward. Tommaso!' he called suddenly. 'Come in from the other side of that door.'

I entered sheepishly.

'You think I do not know when I am being spied on? Did you not learn the art in my own house? Stay here, I want to talk to you. How is your wife?'

I told him that she was pregnant but very well. I told him how happy we were in our house, which he had given us, and thanked him for everything he had done.

He looked wistful, as one who can give happiness to others, but not to himself.

'I have a confession to make to Father Marsilio that I would have you hear, too,' he said. 'As Volterra was six years ago, so Florence is today. I crushed your proud city, Tommaso, and when the

Volterrani cried for help, no one listened. Who would have believed then that the same could happen to mighty Florence? And yet Florence, which is vast in comparison to Volterra, is herself dwarfed by Rome and Naples combined. So here we are, and what we meted out is now being meted out unto us – retribution for sin. At first I thought the devil was after me, but now I think it may be God. For my arrogance I, the victor, am now the victim, and when I beg God to forgive my sins, He is as deaf to me as I was to you.' Saying this, he turned to Ficino and fell to his knees, begging him, as a priest, to give him penance and absolution.

I stared at him in horror, knowing in my bones he was wrong.

Ficino spoke. 'If you would destroy Florence, you do well to fall on your knees weeping. Up! Stand up, Lorenzo!'

'I am in prayer.'

'This is superstition infecting your brain.'

Lorenzo winced slightly and shifted his weight, for his legs were Medici legs and pained him. 'What then must I do?'

Ficino told him that he should concentrate on his goodness rather than on his sin. 'Take refuge in that, for goodness is God Himself. Lorenzo, you are no mere tyrant protecting a city for your own interests. You are the grandson of Cosimo, Father of our Country, and what you protect belongs to all humanity. The Pope is the agent of the devil, not of God. That has been clear from the outset, and it grows clearer with each passing day. Rise up, Magnifico, and fight.'

Lorenzo confessed then that which he had confessed to no one, which was that he was ruined, that he, once the richest man in Italy, had little money left. Worse, he had become a thief. As a mark of its charity, Florence had a state fund for dowerless women: he had just robbed it of seventy five thousand florins.

'Wars must be paid for,' said Ficino. 'So be it. Be sure to return the money when you can.'

Lorenzo looked astonished and then smiled wryly. 'If I am convinced that you are the true spokesman of God, Marsilio, it is because, like my mother, you never say anything I expect to hear.'

As he still showed no sign of coming to his feet, Ficino bent down and helped his patron up.

'Would you care to sit and tell me what is going on, without the passion and the drama?'

Lorenzo had brought his maps. He showed Ficino the lie of the armies and what the Florentines faced. Ficino unrolled his own maps, which were of the heavens, and studied both charts. He consulted his ephemeris and did calculations, but it was as much by inspiration and wisdom as by the position of the planets that he decided on Lorenzo's best course of action. 'You must go to the army camp.'

'Must I lead my armies, Marsilio, like a knight of old?'

'You are not a captain, but you are their leader, and a leader should visit his men to encourage them.'

'When should I go? I am on my way to Fiesole to see my family...'

'Now. At once. Mars is currently under the power of Venus, but it will not be so for long. You must leave within the hour.'

I was torn by contending forces. Ficino must be right; at the same time, I longed for Lorenzo to go by way of Fiesole. But I watched him take the path of duty, and it led back to Florence.

16

Florence, September 1478

TODAY CAME a deputation of neighbours a-beating on the door. I dared not open it, but unlatched the small portal instead. They were angry and accusing. Who was I? Was I a harlot living with the soldier who was squatting here? Just because it is a time of war, they said, does not mean that all rules of decency be suspended. I explained that I am the sister of Angelo Poliziano and this gave them pause, but then one claimed to know for a fact that Poliziano had no family of his own. I told them he has a large family, all in Montepulciano, that Maso is Angelo's cousin and that I have been brought to Florence for my safety, 'For I have been assured that this great city will be my protection.' To that they had no reply and went away grumbling.

And that has been the only event of this week, the only cause to pick up pen and write herein. At night, when Maso is not here, or is in a drunken sleep, I creep out to the piazza under the blanket of curfew and fill our buckets from the public well. Nothing will induce me to use ours.

Without books, I resort to memory and entertain myself by trying to remember all I can from what I have learnt, and in so doing I have discovered something: all those prayers learned by rote and repeated endlessly have meaning. Now they have meaning, and they give me someone to talk to. After an hour or more of this, I find a golden place within where there is peace and no fear, all is silent in a potent way, the silence of life. What this inner place is, I know not, lest it be the kingdom of heaven. Is this what they were teaching us at the convent? If so, how is it that no one learnt the lesson? Perhaps it takes isolation. Perhaps that is the reason why some of the saints chose to be hermits or anchorites, for the world's noise – even in a convent – drowns out this blessed silence. When I am in my kingdom, it is like sitting on a rock or a mountain and being unmoveable yet not solid. The body is poised in inaction. All manner of monsters rear up in the imagination, and terrible thoughts and fears arise to shout in my face, but nothing in me moves. I am impervious, immoveable, invulnerable. Seeing this, the spectres vanish.

They return, of course, for the state does not last. I am there for minutes or hours – the kingdom being timeless, it cannot be measured in time. But too soon the body twitches and the breathing begins again, and then my ghosts crowd back into the mind and jostle for attention.

What is the relationship of this condition to God? I do not know, but I think of it as His footprint in my soul. It seems to me now that the invisibility of God is the single most important thing about Him, but I do not know why. Oh, for someone to discuss such matters with! How long must I endure this waiting? How long before Angelo comes?

17

I RETURNED to Fiesole on the following day to bid farewell to the departing family and to explain to Angelo the reason for Lorenzo's failure to visit. My arrival coincided with that of Bishop Gentile de' Becchi. He was a quiet man, impeccably dressed and blameless of character, so familiar a figure in the Palazzo de' Medici that he seemed as permanent as the walls. Once tutor of Lorenzo and Giuliano, he had remained in the household as adviser and mentor, and to provide a check upon the spiritual exuberance of his erstwhile pupils. He never engaged in any contest of poetry or battle of wit, but took it upon himself to balance the wilder theories of the Platonists with theological opinions of the most rigorous orthodoxy.

If his complexion was a little grey and sunless it was because his world was the musty one of books, a world of incense and candle-light. Unique among the men of the house, he was happy in the labyrinths of scholastic logic, at ease with the driest commentary on a Patristic text, and more conversant with the semi-Pelagian heresy than with the Enneads of Plotinus. As a consequence he had often seemed to his younger companions to be rather dull.

All that had changed with the publication of his riposte, on behalf of the Florentine clergy, to the Bull of Sixtus V. Commissioned by Lorenzo, Bishop Gentile had convened a conclave of bishops to establish the right of the Florentines to follow the faith despite the mass excommunication the Pope had imposed. In the report of the Synod, Bishop Gentile referred to the Pope as the vicar of the devil, a pimp prostituting his own mother, the Church. He spoke not as a bishop to his pope but as a forthright and enraged Florentine. 'Pimp! Simonist!' he had written. 'Heretic! A sinner who would wash his stains with his own ordure!'

The response of his countrymen to his outburst had been

joyous. Copies hurried through the printing press had been tacked up on church doors to be met with hoots and howls of agreement. His obscenities were on everybody's lips. Now he tended to enter any room looking pink and abashed, trying as he was to regain his air of dignity whilst knowing that it was hopeless. He was engaged in writing a more sober argument against the Pope and arrived with a sheaf of papers he wanted Angelo to read for him. Knowing full well that, despite his newly unleashed power of rhetoric, his ecclesiastical Latin was still prone to solecisms, he gave Angelo his work shyly, then escaped to see Monna Clarice.

Angelo picked up the thick sheaf of paper and began to read the draft. Like a school master reading the essay of a young boy, he found many mistakes for his pen to mark. Reading on this super-ficial level, however, it took a while for him to realise the substance of the report. When it dawned on him he sat back in admiration. Here was another work of the roused man, a man of great courage. Gentile Becchi was risking everything, life, office and reputation, to make a stand for truth. This courage, literary, wordy, but courage nonetheless, ran down Angelo's own spine. He had become lost in a fog of petty, personal concerns and had almost forgotten that the scholars, too, were at war. There was work to do – great work. He went over the text again, revising it, making its arguments jump out so that no one could miss the points they made.

✣

Clarice's hands nestled in those of the bishop like a pair of trust-ing birds. Not only was Gentile her spiritual confessor, he was also the man who had, with Monna Lucrezia, chosen her to be the wife of Lorenzo. Thus he seemed to her to be her father in more ways than one. The bishop stroked her hands, encouraging her to speak.

'I cannot confess my heart without drawing down the wrath of heaven, for it is a sin to find fault with another,' she said. 'I should look to my own faults. There are beams in my eyes, Monsignore.'

'Messer Angelo complains that you do not do as he asks,' he said.

Such was Clarice's indignation that she forgot about her beams.

'Do as he asks? That wretch! How dare he? He carries such airs for a cobbler! He sneers at me and says I am stupid – and this before the children! He is impious, scornful, heretical. Monsignore,' her voice dropped a register, 'I fear he prays to the old gods. For to be sure I never see him at Mass in a public church. And,' she added, before the bishop could interrupt, 'at Pistoia he used to leave us – frequently and in the evenings – to go in pursuit of carnal delights. If, by the grace of our Lord Jesus Christ, my sins are being chastised by this man, I do not understand what I have done so wrong as to deserve this punishment.'

Bemused by the strange portrait she was painting of his friend, the bishop rebuked her mildly, saying that of all the misfortunes pressing on her at this time, Angelo Poliziano was the least of them. Continuing to hold her hands between his, he assured her of Lorenzo's devotion.

'Then why has he not come to see us?'

'He has gone to the camp. My darling girl, I cannot describe to you how busy he is. I do not think he sleeps above two or three hours a night. Now it is his express wish that we depart immediately for Cafaggiolo and I have come to escort you.'

'And Poliziano with us?' Clarice's eyes filled with tears. 'Monsignore,' she said abjectly. 'Please do not send me into the country alone with that apostate. I could not bear it!'

In his wisdom, Bishop Gentile thought that the family should attend Mass together at the Badia – the whole family together, including the tutor – in the hope of some reconciliation. Although the church was one of the most ancient in the environs of Florence, its interior had been recently remodelled and awaited the embellishment of wall paintings. Without any frescoes to distract the eye and mind, and under the soaring architecture styled on that of ancient Rome, the beauty of the church was a fit setting for his plan.

The church of the Badia was as beautiful as its cloisters. The whitewashed walls, the tall, slender arcades of dark grey *pietra serena*: in the dusky light they were more a vibration than solid stone. The proportions, founded on Pythagorean mathematics, evoked harmony in the soul. Whenever he had the place to himself, Angelo practised his poetry there, for to make a sound in that church was to be in direct communion with the angels, and so he recited to them the store of his memory and delighted them with song. But on this day he had to listen to the liturgy of monks, the music of the faith, and to feel his soul being disturbed – gently shaken, as one who is woken from his sleep.

Monna Clarice had been provided with a little stool and she knelt on this for the duration of the rite. The children knelt beside her, descending in height like organ pipes. Angelo stood behind them, the rejected father of this family, listening to a lively sermon on Solomon and Sheba, about which he wished to engage the abbot in discussion later. But when it came to the prayers, he found himself surrendering the intellect and its interests, for he was taken suddenly with grief, and he prayed to the Lord for the safety of Lorenzo, invoking all the powers of heaven to aid his friend and patron. He prayed for a speedy end to the war, for a Pauline flash of revelation to blind the Pope, for the clouds to part and reveal a heavenly proclamation of peace. 'And thus cause our days at Cafaggiolo to be few.' The thought of going deep into the mountains with Monna Clarice was seeding misery throughout his being.

If he had been avoiding going to Mass, the reason was soon obvious. He listened to the music of the liturgy, let himself be swept along by its cadences until his soul flowed like a river questing for the ocean. With the ringing of the Sacristy bell, the moment of communion, and the rising swell of plainsong, his heart had always begun to beat with an almost unbearable love; but it had been the ringing of the Sacristy bell that had signalled the Pazzi's attack on Giuliano, and at this, the first public Mass Angelo had attended since, the agony he had feared and tried to avoid engulfed him. There was no sound from him, no sob, just a drenching of grief that Giuliano, that beautiful god of the woods, had been taken so young, and that in the wake of his death so much trouble had come upon the family. Turning away towards the shadows, his face hidden in his hands, Angelo wept in silent desolation. As soon as he could he slipped away to the garden beyond the cloister.

Monna Clarice watched him go.

Outside, Angelo threw back his head to howl out his agony but the grief could not find expression in sound. It wracked him body and soul, making him twist and contort, bending double, now hugging himself to contain the pain, now tearing at his hair, and the only sound that came out of him was deep and inarticulate. When the spasm at last subsided, leaving him spent and panting, he stumbled to the loggia where the Platonic Academy sometimes met. The connection of the Badia with Ficino and his students, the housing here of a Platonic library, the reworking of the interior according to Pythagorean laws of number, the election of an abbot well-versed in the liberal arts, might have all resulted in a centre of philosophy with nothing but a façade of religion. But somehow it had become instead a place as porous as terracotta to permeating influences that, reduced to their essence, were single and unified. It was a House of Knowledge; it was a Temple.

According to Ficino, the teachings of Christ had been prefigured by ancient philosophers such as Hermes of Egypt, Orpheus and Zoroaster. Christ, Ficino had once said, was always here: it was Jesus who had a historical time and place. The pre-existent Christ: Angelo had felt immeasurable relief at the concept, for the religion that claims Truth for itself and denies all other faiths and traditions is an ossified system of belief and the stuff of bigotry. He preferred the river of faith in which those men of all ages who sought truth moved towards the ocean of God in their own streams.

The thought that this was his last day on Fiesole shot fresh pain through his wounded heart. This land of olives and cypresses, stacked logs and wood smoke, which the Platonists would claim to be a mere shadow of reality, was impossible to leave. He loved Fiesole above all places and would have clung to it like a limpet if it had not been for duty.

Piero came out to find him and, seeing his tutor's distress, the boy leant against him, using his warmth and his weight as a means of comfort. Angelo embraced his pupil gratefully and walked to the horses with him.

The Third Book

JUNO'S WRATH

Tell me, Muse, the causes of her anger.
How did he violate the will of the Queen of the Gods?
What was his offence?   VIRGIL

18

THOUGH IT IS as close to Florence as Pistoia, Cafaggiolo, being buried in the Apennines, takes twice as long to reach. The mountain range running diagonally across central Italy forms a great protective shoulder into which Florence snuggles, and, though it lacks the soaring, snowy majesty of the Alps that cut Italy off from France and the Holy Roman Empire, it is still a very effective divide. Beyond the mountains, on the eastern seaboard, are the Papal States, while to the north lies Bologna, Ferrara, Mantua, Padua and Venice: the flat world of the river Po.

At first the road wound gently up and down the hills beyond Fiesole, but soon it grew more steep and began to climb the first mountain. At each vertiginous bend, Angelo looked back anxiously to the train of lumbering wagons behind. The densely wooded, deep valleys, the rolling vistas of pine tops relieved only by the stone roof of a secluded monastery, the eagles circling in the cobalt sky, the autumn motley of oak and beech – these things, scenes he had so often shared with Lorenzo on hunting trips, were now a beauty that filled him with a painful longing for the unobtainable. He wanted things to be as they had once been, and to last forever. He could hardly bear the progress of his horse that, step by step, was taking him away from Florence. The further they went on the rising and falling road, and with the first mountain now behind them, he was being cut off from that person and that place that he equated with the source of his happiness, the source of himself. When Bishop Gentile suddenly reached out and touched his arm, he jumped, startled from his thoughts.

The sky ahead was darkening with storm. It began to grow cold and Angelo brought the party to a halt so that everyone could put on extra clothes, but he bade them hurry so that they might reach Cafaggiolo before the weather worsened: clearly they were leaving the autumn behind and riding into winter. Bishop Gentile went to the wagon that carried Clarice to plump her pillows and encourage her. With the wind rising, Angelo called to him to be quick.

'Madonna is not well,' said Gentile, his head emerging from the wagon..

Angelo sighed. 'We cannot stop, Monsignore. There are outlaws in these woods. It is too dangerous to linger. We must go on. Tell her to send word to the front if she needs to stop.'

Inside, the women listened to this exchange, and when the bishop rejoined them, Clarice's old nurse Marta was telling her mistress, 'He has all the sensitivity of a dried cuttlefish. When you're going to be sick, you're sick, and there is no time to send word to the front.'

Clarice was gulping air. 'Please Monsignore,' she whispered, hardly daring to open her mouth to speak. 'I can take no more bends in the road. We must stop. At the shrine of the Martyrs,' she said. 'You know the place – near San Pietro, where we always stop.'

The bishop decided to remain in the wagon and beckoned to one of his servants following on, telling him to deliver a message to Messer Angelo to stop at the shrine of the Martyrs.

The storm rumbled in the north, and on distant peaks trails of vapour fell from leaden clouds against a lurid yellow sky. Piero shared Angelo's saddle, riding in front of the pommel with his master holding the reins either side of him. Angelo was telling him a story as they went, the one of Ceres losing her daughter Proserpina each year to Pluto, the king of the Underworld.

'Now,' said the storyteller gloomily, 'is Proserpina back with her husband, and all the earth is becoming cold and dead, but in the spring she will return to her mother.'

'How long will that be?'

'About four months.'

'Shall we be at Cafaggiolo all that time? What is it like there during the winter?'

Angelo did not know; like Piero, he had only been there in the leafy season.

'I do not want to go!' Piero wailed suddenly. Angelo wanted to throw his own head back and wail in unison, but he was a man, and was raising this youngster to be one too. He urged his pupil to the practice of courage, patience and forbearance.

'I want to go home to Papa!' cried the boy. 'I want Papa!'

Swathed in his cloak, Angelo rode past the shrine without noticing it, his mind fixed on reaching their destination as soon as possible. A shout to halt came from behind. As he wheeled his horse about, he was reminded that Monna Clarice wished to pray at the shrine of the Martyrs.

'What, in this weather? For the love of God, tell her no.'

The wagons halted and Clarice was helped down. She gathered her children to her and made her way to the shrine. It was an ancient stone, scabbed with lichen, over which a thatched shelter had been erected by local villagers. The dead blooms of recent votive offerings lay scattered before it. Clarice, her children and her servants knelt; the bishop also. Angelo remained standing impatiently by the horses until a censorious glance from Gentile persuaded him to come forward. So he did come forward, and knelt down to pray, but soon became absorbed in a critical study of this object of veneration.

Gaudy statues and waxen images, relics and reliquaries, are aspects of our religion which Poliziano deplored. To his sunlit mind they were as stuffed with superstition as they were with dust and vermin. He did not need the gruesome corpses of saints on display behind glass to remind him of death, nor could he believe that the rubbing of the toe of a bronze saint would bring any alteration to his fortune; the annual liquefaction of miraculous blood inspired in him only intellectual curiosity; and as for the doll-like images of the Virgin in peasant churches – rather than evoke his adoration, they mightily offended him.

Lorenzo had once taken him to Santissima Annunziata, the large church near San Marco dedicated to a miraculous image of the

Annunciation. It is said that the painting, begun by a monk, was finished by an angel. The church is popular with rich and poor alike, its nave filled with the pious and prayerful at all hours of the day; but it is the taste of the vulgar that prevails, paid for by the offerings of the rich.

The fresco itself is adorned with lamps and tatters of prayer written on rags, the air is dark and smoky, the space filled with the jostling press of sharply-elbowed faithful muttering their selfish incantations: Angelo denounced the place as heathen. When Lorenzo pointed out to him the hundreds of votive images hanging from the rafters, waxen likenesses of the famous sons of Florence, Angelo declared great pride in his patron that no image of Lorenzo dangled overhead like the fruit of a hangman. Neither knew who was the more embarrassed when, passing from the church through the atrium, Angelo recognized amongst the waxen images hanging from the ceiling a familiar figure with a flat nose and square jaw. Lorenzo had laughed, had said that this contribution had been expected of him by the people. Angelo exonerated him by voicing his suspicion – correct, as it happened – that the image had been commissioned by Lorenzo's wife.

While the bishop intoned prayers to St Christopher, Angelo reached forward and scrubbed at the moss and ivy, trying to read what was inscribed on the stone. From the style of the letters alone it was obvious that the inscription was Roman. What he deciphered from those letters would have made him laugh in happier times; now, so dismal was the day that he grew increasingly serious and rubbed hard at the lichen.

Clarice could bear no more. 'For what reason do you disturb our devotions, Maestro?'

'This memorial before which we pray celebrates the lives of certain Romans.'

'Indeed,' said the bishop, 'Christian martyrs of Rome.'

'Unhappily not, Gentile. Look here: it lists the names of consuls and proconsuls of the time of the Emperor Decius Trajanus.'

Gentile de' Becchi leant forward in amazement to read for himself, and then jumped to his feet in revulsion.

'These were the very Romans,' Angelo told Clarice, 'who persecuted the Christians. It is a shrine not to martyrs but to the makers of martyrs.' Standing up he considered the stone with renewed appreciation. 'A wonderful relic,' he said, 'speaking as a historian. Lorenzo would find this fascinating.'

Clarice stared at the monument that had been vested with the prayers of the faithful for hundreds of years. She gazed up at the bishop. For her sake, he returned to his knees.

'Obviously by association this has become a shrine to the martyrs of Rome,' he told her. 'Your prayers have not been wasted.' He threw a warning glance at Angelo to say no more.

Angelo stood apart and waited, and then walked with Gentile back to the horses.

'Her prayers were true, even if the altar was not,' the bishop told him sternly.

Angelo agreed but longed for a time when knowledge might rise like a sun in the darkness of ignorance and enlighten the world. Meanwhile cold rain from a cloud-burst was running down the back of his neck and he must protect a woman whose own ignorance was not to be disturbed.

Arriving at last at the brow of a hill behind the village of San Pietro, they looked down on the Mugello, a broad river valley farmed for arable crops, at the head of which was the Medici castello of Cafaggiolo. The valley was in the shadow of a dense black cloud that rolled over the sky from the far mountains, so billowing, so rapid in its progress, that it seemed to be the chariot of Zeus himself. On the ridge above the castello, the Medici tower of Il Trebbio caught the sun and was gold against the indigo sky; even as they watched, however, the cloud reached Trebbio and overwhelmed it. The rain began to fall savagely as the riders descended to the valley, on their way to their new home.

Cafaggiolo had four towers, the two central ones lofty, the two side ones squat, bulging out just above the level of the castellated wall, each topped by a square defence room. With small windows like eyes, the towers looked like four giant heads watching the travellers approach. The rain lashing down was only a prelude to the storm. The first brilliant streak of lightning was accompanied by immediate thunder, of such dreadful whip-lashing cracks that one spare horse reared whinnying.

'It is only weather!' Angelo yelled above the thunder's roar. His message went unheeded by the female members of the party who, in a body, began to implore heaven for mercy. 'It is not sent against us!' he cried. 'It is oblivious of us!'

The lightning, however, was not as arbitrary as he supposed, nor was it sympathetic to the ratiocinations of natural philosophy. Purposefully it aimed at the castello, played crackling round its towers, while the thunder struck the valley like a hammer on an anvil.

'Zeus!' cried Piero, a sudden believer in all his master's myths.

'Vulcan, more like,' Angelo shouted, bending his head into the biting rain and continuing doggedly forward. 'He is the blacksmith of the heavens, the lame husband of Venus, who was betrayed when his wife fell in love with Mars. He is the one who makes all the noise.'

Clarice sat in the wagon, cold and yet sweating, lurching to its rolling motion, wrapped in blankets and prayers. From within the canvas the lightning was visible as blue flashes, and the beads of her rosary were hot in her hands.

Though the distance they had to cover was short, by the time they reached the bridge over the castello's moat no one on horseback had anything dry about him. The ferocity of the deluge had turned the road into a stream. They waded to their destination and as they came on to the cobbles beneath the portcullis, Angelo's misery was profound and complete. 'O blessed bridge to safety,' he muttered gratefully to the inanimate structure of wood, 'my thanks.'

Behind him, however, came the frightful sound of Monna Clarice, who had climbed from the wagon to disgorge repeatedly the contents of her stomach. Her maids shielded her with a screen of blankets, but nothing could disguise the sound, not even the thunder.

✢

It was the oldest Medici property – the family had its origins in the Mugello – and it reflected the taste and style of great-grandfathers. There were many halls, many rooms, many loggias, many galleries, many stairs; and everywhere it was empty of anything except large pieces of graceless, old-fashioned furniture. Some recent attempts to soften the place had been made and now there was a plaster finish on the walls, glass in the windows, and some architraves in the Roman style, but little else had happened. The floors were either of stone or tile.

The thick walls, the grilles at the windows, the towers, all spoke of a time, long since gone, when the castello had been to the valley as a toll is to a road: no passage could be made but it be known, and allowed, and charged for, by the lord of the castle. Times had changed; government now was by burghers rather than landowners, and a man's enemy was no longer his neighbour. Internecine warfare had died with the last century, and the enemy was more likely to be a neighbouring state than a neighbouring family, but perhaps we had been premature in the re-creation of our castles into pleasant villas.

The enlargement of boundaries, the creation of states, is progress in a fashion but it follows an ancient pattern. How far the Roman Empire exceeded what is now Italy in its frontiers! What was once an empire was not now even a nation but a bundle of independent states. In Lorenzo we had a prince with a vision of nation, who built up alliances for the sake of peace and co-operation, who kept in mind at all times the need to present the Turks with strong, united opposition. Now thanks to the papacy his work lay in ruins, and his family were retreating – regressing – to a castle.

Angelo wandered through the empty halls. No one lived in the villa; it was cared for by a factor who dwelt in a house in the grounds, and staffed by local people. Houses, he decided, are as prone to melancholy as men, and if ever there was a Saturnine house, this was it. He walked through sad rooms and met no one. The rain, gentle now, pattered on the shuttered windows.

'Touring your estate?' came a voice, making him jump violently.

'Oh, Gentile!'

'Did you think I was a shade?'

'What else might one expect in Hades?'

Gentile told him that Monna Clarice was very sick after the journey and that she was to be looked after with the greatest care.

'I shall be a very model of patience and tolerance,' Angelo sighed. 'Indeed, if I should ever become a saint, I shall owe it all to Monna Clarice.' He took his friend by the arm as they walked along.

'Think, you are the master of this place,' Gentile said.

Master of a castle! Angelo had dreamt of such things as a child; he wished ruefully that it was still a dream and that he could wake up from it. As he turned to the bishop, his sense of helplessness was visible. 'Where do I begin? What must I do? Servants keep asking me for instructions and I do not know what to say.'

'Whatever you do, do not leave it to the women.'

'But they are so much better at organizing things.'

'Nevertheless, let them know who is the lord here. Even if you delegate everything, be the delegator. The first thing to establish is meal times, and you need to allot rooms. Time and space – that's the first step. You should know that, as a poet. Set your scene!'

Angelo explained that he had been walking the house in order to discover what rooms there were, but Gentile said that he should have sent someone else to make an inventory, that the place where he should be was at the centre of the house – the kitchen.

Angelo went there and discovered Italy in microcosm: a hundred separate states of independent, self-serving activity. In the absence of the cook, yet to arrive from Florence, the kitchen staff had formed a republic and elected a weak man as chief. The house-steward had become a tyrant and was whipping the servants to the laying of fires. Marta occupied the great wooden table like a regent, obstructing the flow of all other activities while she had special things prepared for her queen.

Angelo shouted for order and tried to impose himself as the Holy Roman Emperor but he was too late by months. What had failed to become established at Pistoia could not now be established here. He looked upon the rebellious mob and quailed. Trying to allocate rooms, he was told roundly that Monna Clarice had everything in hand in that respect. The unpacking that he ordered had already been done by the maidservants. The only thing anyone required of him was the key to the buttery, and he had no keys at all. At which point, Clarice herself entered the kitchen, bearing the keys as only the mistress of a household may do.

'You must ask me if you need anything, Maestro,' she said, bearing the look of one who suffered greatly but was bound to do her duty. Recognising defeat, Angelo relinquished his claim to power.

'All I need,' he said, 'is to know when we shall eat.'

Told that he had an hour to spare, he escaped the scene. He had been allocated a small room to himself on the top floor and there he set about establishing a republic of his own at his desk, expecting to find contentment in this. But a thought niggled, a knowledge that, in some subtle way, he had just suffered a defeat from which he was unlikely to recover. His republic seemed to him as stable as that of Milan. Instead of reading, he spent the hour with his head in his arms, reviewing the history of Italy, wondering what was going to happen next.

19

ANGELO'S ROOM at Cafaggiolo was small, cramped and north-facing. He had moved some of the furniture about but it had not helped. Gentile rubbed his hands and blew on them. 'Listen, I have a good fire in my room. Let us go there.'

While Angelo collected the papers they were to work on, Gentile peered behind a settle: it seemed to have been placed so as to obscure a fresco of the Virgin and Child. 'But this is a fine work by Fra Lippo,' he said. 'Why are you hiding it?'

Angelo ignored the question. He wanted to start work and led the way to Lorenzo's chamber where the bishop was accommodated. The hangings had not yet been fitted to the bed but even so it was a splendid room with a fire blazing in its hearth. He spread out the papers of Gentile's response to the Pope on the oaken table and told him that it was a work of passion he truly admired. The bishop, however, saw all the marks in the text Poliziano had made.

'I thought I had combed out all its nits,' he said, 'but you have obviously found many more.'

Nit-picking, however, was not how Angelo thought of his particular skill. He laid out his pens, knife and ink with the diligence of a surgeon making ready the instruments of cauterization. Gentile regarded the instruments as those of torture. Almost lost in his heavy fur robes, he looked particularly mild and vulnerable.

'Your reputation in surgery precedes you, young man,' he said, his voice fluting. 'Luigi Pulci told me your criticism was the worst pain he had ever endured. Worse, he said, than having a wart burned off your backside with hot irons.'

'I was a precocious youth. Pulci lashed me so often with his cruel tongue that I took little care in gouging out his own errors. Please, sit down Monsignore. You have nothing to fear. We are simply going to make a great work tremendous and, as ever, that will depend on cuts rather than additions.'

Angelo knew Gentile's integrity, and if his grammar and spelling were faulty, he put no blame on the man. About the first mistake, which occurred in the second line, he explained to his friend in the mildest tones what was wrong and how best to correct it. If there was an error in spelling, if the word had an *e* when there should be an *i*, he gave the root of the word and its attendant rules; if a phrase was awkward, he suggested a refinement, and sought Gentile's agreement before making it; if the syntax was awry, he put it straight, and cited an ancient authority on the matter. Finding indeed that nothing hurt, Gentile relaxed and even began to enjoy himself, for this was a superb lesson in style.

Angelo's contribution to the work was not limited to editing. Once he had caught any point the bishop was trying to make, he suggested quotations from ecclesiastical sources of great obscurity, astonishing the bishop not only with the range of his reading but also with his powers of recall. Not willing to trust his memory, however, Angelo insisted that all these quotations be checked by Gentile once he was back in Florence.

The pulse of Gentile's intellect quickened as they worked. He watched his laborious paragraphs refine under Angelo's deleting pen. His arguments, made slack by the weight of words, tightened up until they hit a resounding note. With Poliziano taking infinite care to be gentle and inoffensive, the bishop simply watched as his work hatched out of mediocrity into something splendid.

They worked late; when the candles were low and sputtering, Gentile suggested tentatively that they might retire. 'Or do you make a habit of working through the night?'

'Sometimes.' Angelo stacked the papers reluctantly.

'Father Ficino warns us against it, you know, says it makes us melancholy.'

'I prefer the melancholy of too much study to that of none at all. My days are become so full of children that I have no hope of peace until nightfall.'

'I have noticed that they come to you with all their little cuts and bruises. Why do they not go to their nurses? Do you have some special remedies?'

Angelo smiled. 'It is simpler than that. They do not want their mother to know what scrapes they have got into and they trust me not to tell her. And then they like a good story while the splinters are pulled out.'

✝

When the bishop finally went to bed, he could not sleep; and when he finally slept, he became so drugged by sleep he could not wake again.

'Monsignore!' said Clarice breezily, entering his room at noon on the following day. 'Are you not well?' She fussed at his pillows and sheets. Though the bishop had been disturbed repeatedly during the morning by the sound of her workforce in neighbouring rooms, he regarded her fondly and allowed himself to be clucked over.

'Would you like a meal brought to you?' Clarice asked. 'I wish I had known – I would have stopped all the work on this floor. Have they disturbed you?'

'The sound of good work is no disturbance to the righteous. I look forward to seeing the results.'

'The house was filthy! There has been no one here for months.'

'You have lived too long under the shadow of the Magnificent Lucrezia, my dear. Your light has been hidden from us. I shall make a point of telling Lorenzo how virtuous is his wife, how she cares so well for her guests, how the house all but sings to the tune of her efficiency. I shall also tell him how beautiful she happens to look at the moment.'

A deep blush suffused Clarice's cheeks. She demurred and gave all the credit to Monna Lucrezia.

'Indeed,' said Gentile, 'I do recognise the master in the pupil, but the credit is still yours.' Reminded then of that quality of

202

intelligence in Lucrezia which Clarice did not mirror, he asked her if she were studying and, if so, what? Clarice said that she read daily of the blessed life of St Francis, and that she was also reading the holy work of Pope Innocent.

'You are reading these books yourself?'

'There is one thing for which I am grateful to Maestro Angelo: he has goaded me into reading for myself. He seems to find holy books repugnant.'

Gentile laughed at her joke. 'He is kept very busy with the children and needs time to himself for his own studies. But tell me, does your reading include the Psalter?'

At the name of the sacred book, Clarice curtsied. 'For one hour in the morning every day.'

'And do you understand it?'

'The words are sacred and will have their effect whether I understand them or no.'

The bishop doubted this and suggested that she ask the Maestro for help.

'He would no more read the Psalter than walk to Jerusalem!'

'Nonsense, my dear. He probably has it by heart in three languages. You know, if you were to learn Latin yourself, then you would truly become another Lucrezia.'

Clarice lowered her eyes discreetly. Gentile continued unabashed, telling her that in the few hours he had spent with Poliziano the previous night he had learnt more than in all his years with his own tutors. 'I most strongly recommend you attend his classes with Piero. What an opportunity. It would be a crime to miss it.'

'Monsignore! What wife or mother attends school with her children?'

An intelligent one, thought the bishop, like your mother-in-law. For Monna Lucrezia had regularly attended the lessons he himself had given Lorenzo and Giuliano.

'A girl must be taught to sew and not to read, unless she is to become a nun,' said Clarice, quoting an old proverb.

'But that is the law for girls, to keep them marriageable. Once a wife, my dear... Monna Lucrezia did not start learning properly until after she had married Piero de' Medici. And where would Florence be now without her wisdom?'

Clarice did not reply.

'So, shall I tell the Maestro that—'

'Definitely not!' she said, surprising them both with her vehemence. She averted her face and busied herself neatening the folds of her dress.

'Speak out, my dearest. The difficulties you two are experiencing are obvious to all. Speak Clarice, hold nothing back from God, who alone can hear your most private thoughts.'

Clarice kept her head down as she replied. 'Lorenzo wants Giovanni to begin studying with the Maestro.'

'Excellent!'

'How can you say so? Maestro Angelo will not be using scripture in his lessons. He says that the language of the Bible is corrupt and ignorant, that the boys must be raised on the pure Latin of Cicero. If I were to learn Latin, then the Latin of the Lord would be the only Latin I would learn. The question is, Monsignore, if Poliziano's studies in grammar do not serve to elucidate scripture, then of what use are they to a Christian boy destined for the Church?'

The bishop was about to correct her on the matter of the language of the Lord, to tell her that Jesus never spoke Latin, when he was suddenly nipped by her question. He had never had previous cause to suspect Clarice of exercising the faculty of thought. Startled, he regarded her afresh. 'Do you know,' he said jovially, 'I have no answer to that. But on my way back to Florence I shall visit Careggi and speak to Father Ficino on the matter.'

Clarice shrugged carelessly. 'If you think it will help.'

'No, this is important, very important. Dear God, it calls into question everything we are engaged in. What *is* the use of all this study if it does not elucidate scripture?'

Clarice was surprised – and at the same time not surprised – that no man had thought to ask it before. 'No doubt Master Ficino will have an interesting answer.'

'Really,' the bisop muttered as, within himself, he rose up from the flooring he had just received, 'I am certain that it is of use. Certain. All our greatest men have had their education founded on Cicero and Quintilian.'

'But were they saints or merely great men?' Clarice asked, felling him again like a wrestler who does not wait for his opponent to recover.

'You will be leaving soon?' she asked.

'No, not for a few days,' he replied distractedly. 'Angelo and I have work to do which is pressing, work of maximum importance. If we can stop this futile war by the use of reason, we shall do it. Where is he at the moment? Where will I find him?'

'I believe he is with the children, playing ball.'

✝

If the Florentine camp at Monte Sansovino collapsed one day in November, it was not because of decimation by plague, nor because of damage from bombardes, nor because it had been overrun by siege towers and ladders, but because the enemy captain was a clever man who let it be known that all lives and personal property would be safe if the Florentines surrendered. Destroyed by the single blow of an idea, the garrison yielded in a body.

In a few weeks, the armies were due to retire for the winter. Lorenzo, who awoke each morning under an ever-growing weight of despondency, faced the dark months with little hope. The idea that they might be the last of his life was pulling him into the pit. His intelligence told him that he was the victim of the Pope's greed, that he had the moral right to defend himself, but all other evidence, of the starry heavens and the signs, was telling him a different story and inside, within himself, Lorenzo began to collapse.

20

Careggi, November 1478

THE WIND was gusting round the house, making owlish sounds while the rain pattered against the alabaster windows. It was one of those days when it was perpetual twilight, but such light as there was, was beginning to fade. I was trying to complete a passage from Plato's *Laws* before leaving Ficino's villa for home. It was that passage in which he speaks of the golden cord of reason, and I had paused to ask Ficino what reason is when we heard riders approaching. We went out to meet them and found Bishop Gentile, on his way to Florence, quite drenched and much out of countenance.

'I had to leave that place,' he told Ficino, giving his sodden cape to a servant. 'I could bear no more, and I am very, very sorry to have been so weak. I should have stayed for the sake of others, but Marsilio, I am growing old and cannot spend my days becoming so confused. I need light, air, reason.'

'There is a great demand for reason this afternoon,' Ficino said, leading him in to the fireside.

The bishop drew off his boots and put them in the hearth to fill the room with steam. Settling himself into a chair, he told us wild and mythic tales of a rain-lashed castle in the Mugello where the lord's wife and the lord's companion were fighting, 'like two ill-matched beasts pent up in the same cage.' Monna Clarice, he said, was making a great effort to bring life into the house, having it cleaned and polished relentlessly. He told us of his first days there, and the good start he had made on his work with the help of Angelo, but how, as the rain continued to fall day after day, and all the family were kept indoors, Angelo grew morose and uncommunicative.

'I was hoping to spend much time with Poliziano but he was sulking like Achilles. Either that or playing with the children. One day I went to consult him and found him playing horses with a two year old, and when I drew him to the study, the child came with him as if magically attached. Up the stairs he comes, this man brilliant in the languages, with a toddler on his shoulders using his hair for reins. With his head twisting this way and that, Angelo promised me that Giovanni would not disturb us. "Did you ever grow up yourself?" I grumbled. "I was never young, Gentile," he said. But his faith was proved, and the boy sat there as if listening to every word while the master and I discussed theology and grammar, and all was well, as Angelo had foretold. Indeed, little Giovanni was as quiet and attentive as the most model student, and seemed to drink everything in whether he could understand it or no, but then suddenly Monna Clarice's old nurse swept in like the North Wind and snatched the child away, making him scream. Lorenzo, as you know, wishes and expects Giovanni to be educated by Poliziano, but Monna Clarice is absolutely determined that her youngest boy shall never come near him, this man who by my judgement is the finest of tutors. Now why is she acting this way? Marsilio, can you explain it to me? Those poor little boys are being pulled apart by these two contending forces and after a few days of such battles, I could take no more. I relinquished my duty, put it down like a hot coal, thinking I could not care less what Lorenzo has to say about it, for I have had enough. But now that I am so close to Florence, it seems I am beginning to care very much. What will Lorenzo say?'

With his sense of guilt now pulling his chin down to his chest, Gentile sat before us like an old bear too tired to dance any more. 'Truly, Marsilio, I would rather be in the pestilential, famished city than out in the country with those two. For there is death of the body and death of the spirit, and of the two I find the former preferable.'

I was agitated by Bishop Gentile's account, throwing light as it did on the battle between Clarice and Poliziano, and giving credence to Angelo's own account of his misery by calling it a 'death of the spirit'.

But then Ficino said, 'There is no death of the spirit. The spirit is immortal.'

'I speak metaphorically and probably inaccurately,' said the bishop, looking abashed. 'But you know what I mean, when the source of a man's motivation and sense of purpose seems to dry up.'

'Yes,' said Ficino. 'I know what you mean.'

'As long as I have known Angelo,' I offered, 'he has craved time. Now he has time he cannot work for want of energy, enthusiasm, stimulation. Monna Clarice is killing him.'

'Will you trust in God only occasionally?' Ficino asked me.

I did not understand him.

'You want to go to Cafaggiolo and rescue your friend?'

'Of course I do, and at once.'

'Leave it to God, Tommaso. Have faith.'

'Monna Clarice,' the bishop continued, 'has changed beyond recognition. Gone is the shy and diffident young woman who once seemed to live in the children's nursery. Now she strides about the house in the very semblance of her mother-in-law and is most efficient in her work: clear-headed, forthright, authoritative. Aye, authoritative. Believing Poliziano incapable of running the house, as he has been deputed to do, she runs it herself, and most magnificently. Furthermore, Marsilio, she has begun to think. Well, perhaps she has always had the power of thought and only lacked the power of speech. However it may be, she is now asking questions to which I have no answer. For example, what use are our studies if they do not elucidate scripture? Why do small boys need to know about Caesar's wars, or the battle of Thermopylae, or Troy, and not the battles of the Hittites, the Canaanites, or those of Solomon and David? Why are we insisting on teaching them ancient Greek and Latin grammar, but not the Greek and Latin, or indeed the Hebrew, of the Bible? These are good questions, Marsilio, coming from a woman.'

Ficino agreed they were excellent questions and we discussed them at length. Finally we concluded that we learn the ancient languages in order to read the ancient philosophers, 'who,' said Ficino softly, 'explain the secrets of the universe much more clearly than the Bible.' We all gazed at each other like heretics, knowing that such an answer must be kept to ourselves and certainly not offered to Monna Clarice.

'The Bible,' he continued, 'requires interpretation, hence we have theology. But philosophy…' Ficino grew reflective. The humour changed in him. On the hill of Careggi, within the protection of Florence, it was sometimes easy to forget that there is such a thing as heresy, that we may be committing it, and that the Church is obliged to stamp it out.

'Of course,' he said, 'ostensibly it is what this war is all about: according to the official Church, Lorenzo is a sacrilegious dog who needs to be put down. The Church fears the truth. Fears it, because the truth does not need the Church. Heresy – yes, there is such a thing, and we can all find examples of it – but Platonic wisdom is not heresy. It paves the way for the Christian truth. Yet it is deemed to be heresy by the ignorant, and ignorant men of the Church will try and eradicate it, because it is true and good and does not need the Church. That is why.'

I felt a wintry draught and shivered.

'We must trust in God,' Ficino repeated.

'God and Lorenzo,' said the bishop, rising to go. We accompanied him to his waiting entourage, who had been sheltering from the rain under the loggia, and watched them depart. Turning back inside, Ficino told me that he had found the bishop's account worrying but that he had not wanted to alarm him unnecessarily by dwelling on it. 'It is difficult to tell when we only have report to go by, but it is becoming increasingly clear to me that this dispute between Angelo and Clarice is not the trivial matter I had first supposed, that of a clever man being made to look a fool by an even cleverer woman. There is more going on here than it seems, and I am not surprised Gentile took fright.'

I shivered again. 'What are you saying?'

'I am not saying anything until I am certain of my knowledge, and my daemon tells me that I need to know more. Go to Monna Lucrezia and find out as much as you can. I want to know everything about Clarice d' Orsini, from the first moment she entered the family.'

Ficino noted my expression of surprise at what he had said. 'Forgive me, I meant guardian angel. See how easy it is, to make a slip that leads to the fiery stake?'

Hunched into myself under my oiled cape, I splashed down the path to the Villa Medici, my thoughts full of daemons which, as the Platonists hold, are elemental – either of the watery air, or of the airy air, or of the fiery air. Each man has his own, and I was wondering what mine might be when I met a courier on the way to Ficino's house, bearing a letter for me from Angelo.

✝

Tommaso, il mio amico carissimo, – The bishop has left here very suddenly and already I am half-crazed for want of his company and conversation. Such is my desperation that I went into the enemy camp and offered to parley, to put hostilities aside, but the captain said she was not aware of any hostilities. She then repeated the charge that the Church requires men of true piety and saintliness, and does not need to be reformed by pagan heretics. I endeavoured to make her understand, and told her that those who preceded Christ were not only capable of distinguishing vice from virtue, but had defined such concepts in the first place. I tried to make her see that it is as important to awaken reason in a man, so that he can make his own choices, as to inculcate him with a list of rules he must follow. I tried to tell her about Cicero and Quintilian, Plato and Aristotle, but she clapped her hands over her ears and began to recite prayers so loudly I could not make myself heard. Thus she drowned me out as if I were naming fallen angels.

This morning I began my education of Giovanni. It did not last one hour before Madonna walked in and took the boy from me. In that hour I had enjoyed the brightest intelligence one might find in a three-year old. Giovanni thirsts for knowledge.

Tommaso, I cannot convey the depth of my desolation. I am without hope. I am being deafened by the baying of ugly, self-righteous Maenads. Arguments that are won by volume and not by reason are unholy victories, whatever words are used. Help me. Another day of this and I shall go insane. I only stay for the sake of Lorenzo and Piero.'

✝

Monna Lucrezia seemed to be expecting me. 'I have had a letter from Angelo,' she said, putting aside her sewing. Whenever at leisure she had a piece of embroidery on her lap but I never saw anything completed by her; indeed it always seemed to be the same piece that she was working on.

'Ficino is concerned and is beginning to think that this rift between Poliziano and your daughter-in-law is more serious than a domestic squabble.'

'Indeed it is. What we have is a man of reason locked up with a woman of faith. They could learn so much from each other, if only they would both practise what they preach.'

'Ficino says the same. He says that philosophy and religion should work together, and that our task is to know the faith.'

Monna Lucrezia sighed. 'Would that we had the necessary peace for such useful reflections. I love Angelo as my son, and I admire his golden intelligence, and I would follow his opinion in anything with the greatest confidence. But do not expect me to take his side. I cannot, for I also love my daughter-in-law.'

'It is not a question of sides,' I assured her. 'It is, in Ficino's words, a question of health. He wishes to know more details of the life of Monna Clarice, including the date of her birth.'

Monna Lucrezia acquiesced and told me all she knew.

✝

Clarice Orsini was born when the sun was in Virgo in the year 1452, which made her Angelo's senior by two years. As a child she had not been allowed to laugh, not like the Medici girls laugh, 'but

211

then Medici women are freer than most,' said Monna Lucrezia, who had let her own daughters dress as boys when young, so that they could learn how to ride and hunt. But when she chose Clarice to be the wife of her son, she chose a girl who knew only how to perch side-saddle on a quiet horse, and not to ride. Lucrezia had wanted pure blood stock in the family, to cure the Medici of a certain roughness inherited from their farmer-ancestors, and so she had searched in the ranks of the nobility for a wife for Lorenzo.

'She speaks very little of her girlhood so we shall have to fashion it for ourselves.'

I wanted to tell Monna Lucrezia that my wife was good at painting such portraits of Clarice, but I could not speak Elena's name in front of il Magnifico's mother; for all her fine intelligence and rationality, Monna Lucrezia could not abide to have the name of any member of the Pazzi family mentioned in her presence. Monna Lucrezia never asked after my wife; indeed she pretended Elena did not exist. The two women I loved most in the world had yet to meet.

She went to the window and stared at the rain as if the running water drops on the dark glass acted like crystal as a medium of visions. 'Now, what do we see? A little girl, obedient to her father and her God, at prayer in a most devout way. She is slim, wan, humourless. She gazes at an image of the Holy Mother with ardour. When she looks on the crucified Christ she has tears in her eyes. She has nothing to do but to stay in and be good. She learns how to read but not how to write, and knows no Latin. When she is at Mass she listens to the priests speak in a foreign language, a sacred language she presumes to be the language of God. Timidly and cautiously she grows, perfecting such skills as she has. She is excellent in needlework, did you know that? I have never seen stitches so small. In needlework as in life she aims for invisibility. Her brothers go out of the house and return with the scent of the wind in their clothes, the glow of the sun on their skin. She does not mind. She likes to be indoors. She particularly likes to be alone in the chapel, where, if she closes her eyes, she can feel the hands of the Virgin Mary cool upon her head. She tried once to speak to the Orsini chaplain of her love of Christ, of her tears for His wounds, but he was angry with her, saying that these were the fevered imaginings of a young girl, so she never spoke of such things again, but it seems to her that in the house and in the world there are few who truly live the faith. Encouraged by her instructress, however, who was the abbess of a local Benedictine convent, she comes to believe that marriage to Christ is the highest goal for any woman, and marriage to a man a poor second. "Indeed, it is a punishment, my girl," the abbess told her, "a very purgatory."

'Although the lessons of the abbess concentrated on the learning of the psalms, the hymns, the Creed, the Litany of the Saints and the Offices of the Dead, yet the dear sister also told her something of the world, "For you will meet it soon enough, my love, and you might as well know what it is when you do." So she told Clarice how the world of the three continents is as flat as a trencher and that in the centre of the dish is Jerusalem, and how close to the centre is Rome. She told her of the far off places such as China, Persia, India and Norway, and of the places at the edge, where the spices came from and the slaves. She told of human monsters such as the Sciapods, men with only one foot, the Griphones, who used the bodies of their enemies as horse trappings, the Essendones who ate their parents, and the Gangines, whose digestion was so delicate that they fed only on the scent of apples.

'She heard about wonders such as the pyramids and the Colossus of Rhodes, but she wanted to know about places much closer to home. Accordingly the sister told her of fearsome Milan and its patricidal dukes, of haughty Venice, where they would sell a Christian to a Turk for the price of a loaf of bread, of beguiling Naples and its cannibalistic kings, and of upstart, arrogant Florence. "Ruled by a family of nobodies," the sister probably said, "made rich by usury, and they have the gall to call their city the New Rome. The New Rome! What is wrong with the old one? Are not St Peter and St Paul buried here? Do we not walk upon the bones of martyrs? Rome is the capital of Christendom, and that is the trouble of course, the Florentines are jealous. So they have invented problems which only they can solve, by something which they call the New Learning. New Learning! What is wrong with the old learning, based on holy scripture? New Learning indeed. Fancy name for heresy. That's what it is, my girl, heresy. Right here in Italy. They call it Greek study; well, the holy book is written in Greek, but do they study to read the Bible? Of course not. Plato and Aristotle – that is what they want to read. They are pagans, my love, barbarians, apostates!"'

I was impressed by Monna Lucrezia's powers of imagination, wondering how much was based on fact, how much inferred and how much pure fabrication. She wove and stitched pictures in her mind better than she did with her hands on linen. She guessed my thoughts for she said, 'The part about the Benedictine abbess is true enough, for I met the woman. At the sight of me, a Medici, she shrank inside herself like a turtle, for it seemed to her that I was the wife of the devil.'

She continued. 'Clarice had been visited, inspected, by many prospective parents-in-law. They either came together, mother and father, or just father alone. She felt their eyes on her hips, her breasts, on her long throat, on her lips, judging both her stamina for child-bearing and her ability to please their son. "Beautiful but cold," they said and went away. Then came I, accompanied by Gentile Becchi, the Bishop of Arezzo. Clarice kept her head down and would not look up. At the time, I took this for shyness, but what I saw, what I saw…' Monna Lucrezia fell quite and reflective.

'What did you see?' I prompted her. She turned and gazed at me and her eyes were extraordinary, luminous and unblinking.

'The mother of a pope. I left the Orsini house, returned to where I was staying and wrote to my husband Piero, who had been too ill to make the journey to Rome himself. "I think I have found her," I said.

'Clarice's father called her to him, to tell her that she was to be betrothed to the twenty two-year-old son of the ruler of Florence. As her father pronounced the name *Medici* she dropped to her knees with her hands clasped in supplication and begged to be sent to a nunnery, but he refused. "You are my treasure," he said, "my bargaining chip. Put you in a nunnery? God forbid! With you I may ally the Orsini to one of the most powerful families in the world. You will be the bride of a great man, my love, and not a hooded crow in some convent."'

Monna Lucrezia glanced away, avoiding my gaze. 'The next part I know well enough: the betrothal. Lorenzo was too busy to attend himself, and so his cousin Filippo stood proxy for him in the ceremony. He told us that Clarice shivered throughout "like a trapped animal fearing death." The ring was slipped on her finger by a stranger and she had no picture of the man who was to reside now in her heart. Filippo remained distant, business-like, and never met her eyes. When it came to the marriage itself, that was held in Rome and again my nephew Filippo stood in for Lorenzo, for Lorenzo was still too busy to come south for his wife.'

My own marriage being a rare one based on love, I could not imagine what would keep a man from his own wedding.

'Of course,' Monna Lucrezia said, 'Lorenzo was not really too busy to get married. Who is ever that busy? The truth was he did not want to marry, at least, he did not want to marry anyone who was not Lucrezia Donati. I was so taken up by worry, and by trying to persuade him to accept his family responsibilities, that I did not spare much time for that pale girl in Rome who was waiting for him. But you know how my son is – as stubborn as a tree whose roots have found their way under a mountain. In the end we sent Giuliano to collect her. A mistake, I now believe.' Her voice had been dropping by degrees and now came a shuddering intake of breath. 'Who could not love him, eh? My son, my Giuliano? He was seventeen at the time, tall, muscular, with wild black hair and those lustrous, cervine eyes. I am sure Clarice had never seen any man quite so beautiful. How did she feel, what did she think upon seeing him? That he was like her husband? That first image of Giuliano riding straight-backed at the head of a splendid retinue of Florentines into the castello at Monte Rotondo must have impressed itself on her heart like an intaglio design on a gemstone, to remain there for life.'

'She was in love with Giuliano?'

'She has never said as much, but who grieved most at his death, she or me? A god in heaven would have judged it a close contest.'

The party receiving the Florentines had included Clarice's uncle the Cardinal and one of her brothers who was a sub-deacon of the Pope. With such a strong representation from the Church, it was as if the sacred were receiving the secular and giving their daughter away to it. Clarice made the transition with an ease that surprised everybody.

'It was a political alliance, of course. In marrying Clarice Orsini to Lorenzo, Piero and I were aiming to strengthen the bonds between Florence and Rome and thereby to secure a cardinal's hat for our Giuliano. As they set out together on the road, Giuliano apologised for Lorenzo's absence. Formal apologies had already been made, but now he wanted to convince Clarice that Lorenzo was truly sorry not to have been able to come himself. He had been very busy with the joust held to celebrate his wedding, a joust that he happened to have won.

'"I have heard much about the joust," said Clarice. "Almost everything, except the name of the Queen of Beauty. Who was she?"

'Giuliano chose that moment to entertain Clarice with a trick that always made the ladies gasp and laugh: he suddenly fell sideways from his horse, or appeared to. Regaining the saddle, he found Clarice, in a mixture of shock and delight, laughing like a little girl. He threw his cap in the air and declared that she was the finest, most beautiful sister-in-law a man could hope for. He spoke lovingly of his brother and made much of his accomplishments, particularly the episode in which, through courage and intelligence, Lorenzo had saved their father from an ambush. He spoke of his brother's qualities: steadfastness, strength, loyalty, love of poetry, sense of fun, magnanimity...

'"Lorenzo is a man of much virtue and grace," he said, "but these are attributes of the soul. He warns you not to expect a handsome man, and asks you, in your kindness, not to judge him on his appearance."

'Clarice asked for a description, and Giuliano told her that Lorenzo was as powerful as a bull, with a strong face and broad shoulders; that he was narrow at the hip and had well-shaped legs; that his hair was thick and black; his eye dark and piercing. Giuliano struggled to describe the face of which he was so fond, the face which Lorenzo himself so loathed. He told her that Lorenzo's eyebrows are close knit and, due to a slight disfigurement of the nose, he appears to be perpetually frowning, that his jaw is square and jutting, and the lower lip protrudes while the upper is thin. "But," he said, "this is the description of a dead man. When you see these features in animation…"'

Clarice wanted to know how his nose is disfigured and Giuliano said that it is very narrow at the bridge, where there is a little twist in the bone, then it spreads wide, and is long and flat. Then he laughed and said that in detailing the parts he was losing the whole. 'It is not his looks that should concern you, but his heart.' He assured Clarice that she would soon grow to love Lorenzo.

'When she arrived here in Florence, I tried to speak to her, to see if she knew what to expect on the nuptial night, but she said, her face flaming red, that she already knew. I expect her nurse had told her, as mine told me, demonstrating the terrible lesson with her finger and a ring. After her arrival, it was still some days before she met her new husband. She was lodged at the Alessandri palace while she rested and prepared for the celebrations to come. She clung to Marta as strangers fussed about her, dressing her in the elaborate gown of white and gold brocade that Lorenzo had had made for her. Her head sank in embarrassment and she could not straighten up. That all eyes in the palazzo were upon her was bad enough, but when the members of a magnificent procession arrived to escort her to the Palazzo de' Medici, she looked as if she were being led to the stake. Fifers, trumpeters, a host of young men gorgeously attired, knights and their retainers, arranged themselves around the young bride. At the Via Larga, she was met by more splendid youths and maidens, but there was no sight of either Giuliano or Lorenzo. The significance of the first ceremony, which was the hauling of an olive tree through a window, made her blush hotly. The rest of the day passed in banqueting. She sat in the garden loggia with a host of maidens. In the courtyard were massed the principal citizens of Florence. In the hall young men danced with their ladies, while I played host to the elder women on a balcony. I felt so sorry for her, Tommaso, but there was nothing I could do except watch from a distance and pray for her. The food appeared hot on the table, our servants striding to and fro as well-drilled as soldiers. Presents were given to her: gold rings, lengths of rich fabric, pieces of silverware. Alone amongst these trinkets was an object which appealed directly to her heart. It was a small book of the Offices of Our Lady, written in gold on blue vellum, each page of text embedded in sumptuously decorated margins. Its binding was studded with crystal and silver. It was a present from Lorenzo, and by its choice as a gift he seemed to say, "I know you, as well as you know yourself."

'After the banquet my brother, Giovanni Tornabuoni, approached to tell her that, though there were days yet to come before she would be formally presented to the groom, if she would like to meet him now, he would take her to him. "His father, Piero, is very ill and Lorenzo is in constant attendance," he said. In a room on the second floor she was introduced to Lorenzo and his invalid father Piero simultaneously. I was there. I saw her face. As veiled as Clarice can be, she could not hide her feelings. Her eyes glanced from Lorenzo to Giuliano and back again repeatedly, as if she could not take in how different two brothers could be. Despite Giuliano's warnings, she still felt cheated. As for Lorenzo himself... He retreated into formality, took her hand, kissed it and called on God to bless their union. He told me later that her hand had felt like a clammy piece of dough resting in his palm. It was all he could do to resist wiping his hand on his jacket after he had let her go.'

218

Monna Lucrezia left the window and returned to her chair. 'Of the rest, discretion binds my tongue. I know what happened on the nuptial night because the servants told me; they told me that "Lorenzo did his duty." His duty! Let us leave the rest to the imagination. Suffice to say that a stallion probably covers a mare with more romance. Two months later we knew Clarice was pregnant. Ah, Tommaso, Tommaso, I am leaving much out. I had to stand by and hold my tongue though fully aware that, having done "his duty", Lorenzo returned to the bed of Lucrezia Donati. And of course, when we were certain that Clarice was with child, he had the perfect excuse not to trouble her at night. This went on for a year, for after the birth came the churching, affording Lorenzo further excuse to avoid his wife.

'But following the birth of my granddaughter, Lucrezina, things began to change. Something was born in Lorenzo's soul, a certain tenderness and the seed of fatherhood; then, by association, he began to love the mother of his daughter. For a year I had been on edge, wondering what damage I had wreaked on my family through my own desires, but then, one day in the following spring, I saw them together with Lucrezina, Lorenzo throwing his daughter up in the air like a ball, the child squealing with delight, and the mother smiling. I saw love between them and at last my heart came to rest. Clarice needs no image of the Holy Virgin to encourage love for her children: it flows from her as a natural spring. In respect to her children her love is constant, not wavering according to mood, and never admixed with fear. For them she gives all because she cannot do otherwise; her love for her children is unclouded, undemanding, natural. And that is why I love my daughter-in-law,' said Monna Lucrezia. 'Opinionated she may be, and usually mistaken in her opinions, but her heart is made of love. At least, in respect to the children.' She sighed. 'The question is, how deep is her love for her husband? How faithful?'

I said nothing, but waited for her to continue. She gazed up at the chimney breast rising from the hearth to the ceiling. On it were painted the joint arms of the Medici and the Tornabuoni, which

Lorenzo had left from his father's time and had not replaced with his own and his wife's.

'There is the custom of *tornata*,' she said.

'I am aware of it, of course.'

'When my husband Piero died, I was expected to return to my family, the Tornabuoni, but I was strong enough, wilful enough, sufficiently capable to withstand the custom and become both mother and father to my sons. I am so much a part of the Medici, I could not contemplate returning to my father's house, nor of marrying into another family. Nor can I contemplate Lorenzo dying young, as a result of these troubles. But I think Clarice can and does muse on such things, and that if Lorenzo were to die, she would return to the Orsini, taking her dowry with her. The Orsini would insist on it; no matter how much she would want to remain with her children, custom and the Orsini would extract her from Florence. What then for the children? Ruin and abandonment, unless the Orsini are willing to take on the expense of them. It was very madness for Gentile Becchi to read the Papal Bull to her. She is living in the future, is preparing herself for widowhood. She has allowed into her soul the idea that the Pope might be right; the devil has done the rest. I believe she has divorced herself from Lorenzo in her heart.'

Her words chilled me. 'Can it be true?'

'Lorenzo's work is so vital, so important. If it succeeds, it will bring a certain grace – *gentilezza* – to the world. I cannot believe God has abandoned us, since it is His own work. This war at Cafaggiolo – it is over the education of Giovanni? Angelo must win, of that there is no doubt. Giovanni is the boy born to be pope, but to be a good pope he needs the wisdom of the ancients as much as the scripture of Holy Mother Church.'

✝

I told Father Marsilio everything I had found out about Monna Clarice. He was most interested in the concept of semi-literacy, a state of intelligence he had little experience of, since he knew so few women. That Monna Clarice could read but not write, that she could read only in Tuscan and not Latin, and then only slowly, was something he found difficult to comprehend.

'But she wants to teach the children to read herself?'

'As I could teach any child to read Greek, without my being able to read Homer.'

'Are many women in this condition?' His own mother – who lived reclusively upstairs – was fully illiterate and yet the wisest woman he knew. With her shining example before him, he could not see why women should want to read and write. 'I suppose it is useful for the education of infants.'

'Indeed, for that it is vital, and it has no other application. Monna Lucrezia, however, who has a man's soul in a female body, reads and writes in Latin as well as Tuscan for her own pleasure, as does my wife. But Monna Clarice, who comes from an ancient family, with ancient ideas, considers literacy to be an unfeminine trait.'

'And yet she loves scripture.'

'With enviable devotion.'

Ficino stared thoughtfully into the air. 'Is it not remarkable that there is no Tuscan translation of the Gospels?'

'I believe the Church forbids translation into any vulgar tongue.'

'A most strange law, considering the needs of vulgar people.' Ficino remained thoughtful, but his mind was transparent to me.

'Father Marsilio, we have quite enough work to do completing your translation of Plato.'

Prophecy, he often said, is one of the four states of divine frenzy.

When he turned to me, his eyes were effulgent with prophetic light. 'Our fate depends on Monna Clarice.'

I laughed. 'How can that be?'

'Believe me, it is so. She is not a reflection of what is going on, but a cause. This separation between husband and wife: it must be healed. We must help Monna Clarice as best we may.'

'She considers us heretics – she will take no help from us.'

'Divine Providence will find its own way. There is no one route to God, Tommaso. Providence determines the capacity of each of us and adopts the best means to draw us to the path of Truth. Clearly what draws Monna Clarice is scripture.'

'What route will Providence find for Poliziano? Should he write in Latin or Tuscan?'

'Both, and Greek too, since he needs all three for his true vocation, which is not poetry but teaching. Have you ever seen a man so happy as when he is with those boys? He was born to teach.'

'He sees teaching as a necessity that takes up his time.'

'He is wrong.'

I hardly dared ask my next question. 'What does Providence recommend for me?' I asked.

'That you stop taking up my time with questions and get on with the work in hand.'

✝

The leaves which had been plucked early from the trees by fierce winds were turned to mud by seemingly continual rain. Despite the season, the plague was on the increase. This was no mild epidemic of the kind we suffered so often: this was far closer to the one that had halved the population a hundred years ago. This was the kind we had nightmares about. Everyone in the Platonic Academy and the Medici household followed Ficino's prescriptions for averting danger, and we averted it, but still we lived with the fear, a fear which became so deep-seated that we spent most days oblivious to it except when any thought arose regarding the future. How many funerals can you weep over before the tears dry up? Not many. Soon the reports of new deaths became stale and monotonous. We lived for the day, all thoughts of the future being thrown down a well without a bottom. 'Face what comes when it comes,' men said to each other.

There was no possibility for the spirit to lift. Even Ficino was brought low and suffered from melancholy. It was colder than usual, and we kept warm as best we could, wrapping up for work in gowns and blankets. I heard from Angelo that he was rewriting his account of the Conspiracy of the Pazzi, detailing those events that had brought this war upon our heads. In some mental Dis, a realm of shadows I dare not approach, lived my memory of Giuliano. For much of the time there were sufficient distractions to maintain forgetfulness, but sometimes in the night I would awaken suddenly and the pain of emptiness would be there, waiting, ready to devour me. It came in a sentence: *Giuliano is dead.* It came in a flashing vision of beauty disfigured, made repulsive. Worst of all it came in the smell of blood. I had not previously known that the nose has the power of recall or that smells can be remembered, but my last memory of my beloved friend was the sweet, clammy stink of blood. At such times I would wrap my arms round Elena and bury my head in her warmth, feeling the pulses of her body, the softness of her, the small, returning pressure of her own arms which said, 'I am asleep, but I know you are there.' At such times I became a philosopher, wondering about life and death, and how something so palapably present can vanish. Sometimes the wonder grew so vast that I cried, and my tears woke my wife, who turned over to take my face in her hands, kiss my nose and tell me how silly I am. If she let me, I would lay my head gently on her womb to try and hear the baby within, and on the day when I heard his heartbeat for the first time, then the wonder engulfed me. But in the morning I awoke to a sense of foreboding as deep as the wonder had been huge. The knowledge that we were bringing a child into such an uncertain world as ours made a father of me beforetimes, and I spent the day buying grain and oil that we could store against the famine that was bound to be upon us before the spring.

21

THERE ARE THREE classes of musician: those who play the music composed by others; those who compose their own; and those *improvissatori* who sing and play as the Muse dictates, in the moment and inspired. In the spirit of Orpheus, without recourse to preparation or rehearsal, the *improvissatore* can draw the breath of Zephyr and sing to the sun and the moon. Of course there are many impostors, those who rehearse in secret for their 'impromptu' performances, but Angelo knew at least two genuine cantors. One was Baccio Ugolini who, given any verse or lyric, could set it at once to music. The other was Marsilio Ficino.

When, after due preparation, Ficino took up the lute he was himself taken by the god, to sing hymns in which both words and music were as new to him as to anyone else. He plucked notes we could not anticipate, notes that made the soul vibrate in sympathy and, in the vibration, lose its identity and merge with the universe. Divisions such as inner and outer dissolved. His sounds penetrated the dome of heaven, passed through the firmament as if it were not there, flew on the wings of cherubim to the seraphim at the seat of God. Divine frenzy is contagious. In one of his letters, Angelo recalled an occasion when, having spent an hour listing to Ficino sing, he had come away with his horizons infinitely expanded and all the planets spinning in their courses. The experience heightened the language of his poetry, and kept it high for days, but then it faded. Angelo had often since implored Bacchus to take *him*, directly, but had never had the time for the god to answer the prayer. Now that he did have the time, however, he did not have the mood, and sitting with the lute in the hope of frenzy he found only languor. 'But then,' he wrote, 'this house is under the dominion not of Apollo but of Saturn.'

He put aside the lute and went to his bookshelf, and here was another idea incinerating under the light of reason: he always thought he preferred the company of books to men. He did not. That was only true when he had the choice. Now he would have given all his books for Matteo or Baccio or me to walk through the door, but the only company he had was a farm cat with an ambition to become domesticated. It crept into the house when Monna Clarice was not looking to curl up on his bed while he studied. Such were his longings for convivial friendship that he had even begun a notebook recording all the jokes and witty jests of Lorenzo and his companions that he could remember while the ceaseless rain lashed the windows.

With a reluctant eye he gazed at the improving literature of the Christian fathers he had brought with him, but brightened when saw the book of poetry from the Roman silver age which he had forgotten that he had added to the chest in Lorenzo's library. Taking it down he opened its covers and continued reading where he had left off some months before. The cat was asleep on his bed, but the moment when Angelo's attention came to rest on the text, the cat awoke. Sensing that the poet's consciousness had become focused, it yawned, stretched, jumped down from the bed and leapt up on the desk. Simultaneously Angelo stroked it and pushed it away, for it was standing on a quotation in Greek which had caught his interest.

'Not there. Move your paws.'

The cat ambled on a circular route which took it past the poet's face. As it passed, it nudged him with its head and then dragged its body and raised tail underneath his stubbly chin, purring ecstatically.

'Please, move, I think this is Pindar…'

The cat returned, its purring amplified.

'Madonna. It *is* Pindar.' Angelo scratched the cat absently between the ears. If he could have purred himself, he would have done. 'You can tell – indisputably Pindar – the irregular number of feet per line – the arbitrary disposition of the rhymes. Why has no one noticed this before? *Santo cielo!* – I have found a new line by Pindar!'

The cat suddenly flopped over sideways on the book and stretched out all four limbs.

Angelo stared at the sensuous creature incredulously. 'How can you do that, on a line of poetry that has been lost for two thousand years? Move!'

The cat writhed in luxury. Angelo capitulated to its sensual demands, leant forward, rubbed his cheek against its soft stomach and blew into its fur. Its claws caught affectionately in his hair and, through his cheek, he could feel the vibrations of a purr which had its origins not in the throat but somewhere deep within. He rested his head on the pliant cat and sighed. It was not the discovery of a Pindaric line that was gripping his heart and squeezing, but the overwhelming realisation that no one from here to the distant horizon would care. He could tell Piero that when Pindar was a young boy and resting in a meadow, a swarm of bees had come and settled on his mouth and there left some honeycomb. That would interest him, but the details of Angelo's discovery would not. He thought of Lorenzo in Florence, how beset his friend was with tribulation and as far removed from poetry as it was possible to be. A deep sigh issued from him, making the cat twitch in annoyance. Repelled by this maudlin human emotion, it rolled back on to its feet and jumped from the desk.

A knock on the door heralded the arrival of the tutor's supper borne on a tray by the slave girl of Monna Clarice called Iride. Her gown, he noticed, was the colour of new moss. She watched him with her dark eyes as he lifted the lid on a fine dish of chicken and beans poached in wine.

'Where are you from?' he asked.

'Spain,' she said, without the curtsey he had expected.

'Gypsy?'

She nodded briefly and laid the table for him.

He went to the window to look out on the rain and saw, coming from the direction of the monastery in the woods, a very biblical scene of a woman on a donkey, with a man leading it by the bridle.

'Has Monna Clarice been to the monastery? For what reason?'

'She said she needed confession, and to speak to the abbot.'

That Clarice should take it upon herself to leave the house, on whatever pretext, in her condition frightened and angered him in equal measure. It was an act of independence he could not countenance. 'This is torture. Why is she torturing me? What have I done?' he said out loud.

It was a rhetorical question. He certainly was not asking it of a slave, yet Iride replied promptly: 'You have taken the place of her husband.' He wanted her to explain but the sound of a little handbell being rung urgently signalled the return of her mistress.

'I must go,' she said, standing before him, facing him, and, despite her words, not moving. He wanted to say, 'Come back as soon as you can,' but did not dare. After a moment's hesitation, she turned and left the room, drawn away by the tinkling, angry bell.

Angelo, caught between a woman and a woman, did not know which one to think about, but soon enough it was Clarice who was occupying his mind to the exclusion of the seductive slave. He tormented himself wondering what Clarice had been saying to the abbot. She had gone too far, to speak to someone outside the family. This was an act of war and there could be no further attempts at reconciliation.

✢

In the morning, Piero appeared alone for his lessons. When asked, he told the master what he had been told to say by his mother, that Giovanni was not well. Piero was not good at lying and Angelo had only to pinch his ear to have the truth pouring from him.

'The abbot says Giovanni is not to study with you. Mother is going to teach him to read.'

'How? What with? I have the boxwood letters here, and the syllable exercises.'

'She is going to use the Psalter.'

'What? He is only just three years old!' Angelo stood breathing hard, trying to smother his passion. In vain. The passion erupted

227

and all reason was lost. He stormed into Clarice's room without knocking, his face dark with anger, his black eyes piercing. Clarice cried out and embraced her youngest son protectively.

'I have come for the child, and I will have no further argument on the matter. You are the wife of Lorenzo. You have no right to consult abbots without your husband's knowledge; even less right to act on such advice. And no right at all to raise a boy on a corrupt text. Giovanni will study with me, and without cavil from you.'

Clarice met the tutor face to face and held his angry eye. 'How dare you come in here? How dare you speak thus to me.'

She had her arms around Giovanni, and when Angelo reached towards the boy, she pushed Giovanni towards his nurse, telling the woman to run, run to the nursery, as if she were saving them from being murdered. Giovanni was carried off howling. Angelo was too concerned for the child to run after him; it would only frighten him further.

The two of them, the man and the woman, stood staring at each other in mutual hatred. 'Giovanni,' she said, 'must be taught by the Psalter.'

'The Psalter? As an instruction for language?' Angelo was so offended he lost all restraint. 'That debased text? One might as well ride the palio on a donkey.'

'You speak of a holy book!' Clarice cried, certain now of all her suspicions about this man. 'A holy book of the Bible, and you call it a donkey!'

'It is its language I object to, Madonna, and the blessed St Jerome who translated it would be the first to agree with me.' He tried to calm down, tried to explain to this idiot woman the cause of his dismay, but it was like trying to shout in a nightmare. His voice would not work. She would not listen. Everything was booming in his ears as if he were drowning. 'The Psalter is a translation of a translation.' Such an explanation needed to be set out calmly, not thundered. The hotter and more speechless he became, the cooler Clarice.

'My son will learn by the Psalter,' she repeated.

'Not while he is in my care.'

'But he is not in you care; he is in mine.'

'And you are in mine.'

'Ha. Look at you. What do you care for? Nothing but words and poems. Trifles.'

'You speak to the man who stands in the place of your husband, and you speak with impudence.'

'When Lorenzo judged you, he judged you on your mind. I have no doubt you are a very clever man, Maestro, but you are not intelligent, else why lose your soul to perdition so easily?'

This caused Angelo to hesitate; Clarice took advantage of his confusion. Armed now with the authority of an abbot, and certain that, when she spoke to Poliziano, she had the attention of the devil himself, she addressed herself to Satan and challenged him. She was filled with a strange and magnificent strength, and her faith seemed to course through her, as if all the saints and martyrs were with her; she felt as if she were fighting the battle of St Catherine against the idolatrous philosophers all over again. With an un-wavering voice, directed at the evil in the heart of this man, she said, 'I know who you are. I know what you are doing. Corrupter of souls. Priest of Baal.'

Angelo took a step backwards. 'What do you mean? I am a Christian. I have been baptised. Dear God, I am even in minor orders and a prior of the Church. What is your meaning? Do you not see me at Mass? Have you not heard me recite the Creed? You are wrong, absolutely mistaken. I believe in the one true God, just as you do.'

'I am not listening.'

'You are never listening. When did you ever hear anything I said?'

'Leave my room before I call the guard.'

'Not before we have resolved the matter of Giovanni.'

'There is nothing more to be said.'

'There is one more thing to be said: you are acting contrary to

229

the will of your husband, which is that I should tutor Giovanni.'

'My husband is in error.'

'It is not for you to judge him.'

'Indeed it is not, it is for the Lord. And what the Lord's judgement is could not be more clear.'

Angelo gasped. 'What are you saying?'

She ticked off her fingers. Excommunication. War. Famine. Plague. 'What are these things if not retribution for his sin? Yes, I act contrary to the will of my husband, as I must if I am to act in accordance to the will of God for the sake of my children.'

✝

Alone in his room he faced an imaginary Court of the Inquisition and argued long and eloquently on the value of the New Learning. He justified himself repeatedly but in the repetition his arguments began to pall. Over and over the same ground he went, to drown out a faint, female voice which said, *Priest of Baal.*

'The Psalms,' he explained to his inquisitors, 'are temple hymns of the Jews written in Hebrew. Our Roman Psalter is a translation of a translation, done hurriedly into Latin out of Greek by St Jerome – so they say, though I have my doubts. If Jerome did do it, he surely despaired of it, and later he made another translation, this time into Latin direct from the Hebrew. That version of the Psalter is now in use everywhere in Christendom except Italy. Out of perversity, out of ignorance, out of the sheer torpid weight of papal obstinacy and clerical stupidity, the Roman Psalter is here preferred. Jerome's bones would rattle in his tomb if only he knew. This book, for all its holiness, is a translation of a translation. If one were to teach the Psalter, it should be taught in Hebrew, because any translation of a book, however holy, is not a fit text on which to raise the young. We must give them the fine, the pure original. To teach Latin from translation? It is unthinkable. Latin from Cicero, Greek from Plato, that is our plan. To raise up a boy to think for himself, to judge true from false and right from wrong. Then may he read scripture in whatever language he pleases.'

There was an edition of St Jerome amongst the improving books he had not yet opened. Ficino had once told him that, when seeking the inspiration of Truth, one should always open a book at random and the answer would immediately be found. Sure enough, on opening the Jerome randomly, his eye fell on a passage of extraordinary relevance and one which seemed to promise his vindication.

Very many years ago, for the sake of the kingdom of heaven, I had cut myself off from my home and my parents. Despite the fact that I was on my way to Jerusalem, intending to conduct myself as if I were on a military campaign, I just could not give up my library, which I had amassed for myself with such great care and labour in Rome. In my uncertainty, I used to fast so that I could later read Cicero; and, after frequent night vigils and floods of tears, induced by the memory of my past sins, my hands used to grasp Plautus; but when I had recovered my mental equilibrium and started reading the Prophets again, I discovered I was put off by their uncouth style…

Angelo found himself utterly in agreement with a saint and father of the Church. Uncouth! Precisely. He could not have put it better himself. *I was put off by their uncouth style…*

Jerome went on to describe a time when he was close to death and in a vision was brought before the Great Judge.

He interrogated me and I informed Him I was a Christian.

'You lie,' He shouted. 'You are not a Christian. You are a Ciceronian, for where your treasure is, there will be your heart also.'

Angelo felt the hairs on the back of his neck rise. He read on to discover that the prostrate Jerome was whipped by the Lord until he cried for mercy, until he vowed, 'If ever again I read or even take up a secular book, I have denied You.' From that time, Jerome said, he read Divine works with as much enthusiasm as he had previously read the books of men.

Angelo slammed the volume shut. Two selves contended within him. To give up all that he valued? He could not. 'It is my talent. It is God-given. I cannot give it up – I must not give it up.'

He paced his room in agitation. The rain droned outside. He was trapped by the place. His preference for literature over God, this fault in his soul that he had concealed throughout his life, was now being laid bare. This self-revelation, not difficult to deal with in itself, was made excruciating by having been revealed by a semi-literate woman who had called his poetry trifling. Had it been shown to him by mentor, friend or confessor, then it could have been cured by surgery of the soul – a cutting out of corruption which, though painful, would have healed easily in the company of friends who had their own amputations to endure. He did not mind being corrected, not when he respected the corrector, but to be put straight spiritually by Clarice? It filled him with bilious resentment.

He was dallying, as he had always dallied, with knowledge. Where men sought knowledge to bring themselves closer to God, he sought it for its own sake. He had left the path – if, indeed, he had ever been on it – and had become lost in the undergrowth of scholarship, a briary tangle of thorns which he enjoyed untangling. But Clarice, in the simplicity of her faith, appeared to be passing by on that straight path. To be overtaken by a woman, a mindless, stupid woman... He paced about, breathing hard, fearing that the path was lost to him forever, that to the man of knowledge the way of simple faith is ever closed.

As for the way of knowledge, he had been a raw youth when he had discovered Plato and the Greek writers. It seemed he had found a clear road to heaven in the company of like-minded men. Had he moved at all on it? It seemed now that, having been offered Plato, he had at once turned to study Homer, and from Homer to Virgil, from Virgil to Cicero, from Cicero to Ovid, then to anyone he could come by, requiring of his authors only humanity, not godliness – and, of course, the finest literary style. But what does literary style have to do with God?

To his teachers of philosophy, knowledge of Man is a necessary step in realising the Divine, so they had encouraged Angelo in his studies, but they had never invited him into their inner circle. He always presumed himself too young and thought that, when he grew up, then the doors to the inner sanctuary of the Platonic

232

Academy would be opened for him; but they never were. Ficino, who loved him like a father, had seen the blemish on Angelo's soul and left it to Angelo to see it for himself, but even far-sighted Ficino did not know it was going to take so long, or that the powers of God would have to use the wife of Lorenzo de' Medici to smack the young poet in the face and wake him up.

Now he sat at his desk fully awake and smarting from the blow. Everything was clear. On his desk lay open Suetonius *On the Lives of Notable Poets*. This book he now closed slowly and deliberately. A new life was about to begin. But where a wise doctor such as Ficino would have prescribed a ride in the country, a good meal in the company of jovial men and some light reading of Plato, this patient, who was treating himself, decided to fast and to read the Bible for the rest of his life. Angelo reached towards the holy book. His hand stayed in mid-air. Suddenly recoiling from the resolution, he came to his feet so quickly that his stool fell over backwards. He wanted to tear down the walls and scream into the hills, but a soft, familiar voice spoke to him, saying, *It will not work; it will not satisfy; if you tore yourself to pieces nothing would be achieved.*

He flung himself helplessly on his bed, the temperature of inner fires rising.

✟

The following morning he did not get up. He felt hot and nauseous; each time he raised his head, a strange power forced it back to the pillow. He tried to disappear inside himself, to find that interior cavern of the heart where all is peaceful and nothing moves. Intermittent hammerings on his door punctuated time. Suddenly he felt a cool hand on his forehead, opened his eyes but saw her not.

'What ails you?' came her kind voice.

'Lady, I desire oblivion. Where have you been?'

'I have never left you, but I could not be heard above the din. This despair is unseemly. Have I not given you my gifts? Why do you spurn me?'

'Calliope,' he said. 'Help me.'

'I am not Calliope. This sickness is from sloth, sloth comes from doubt. I am Pallas Athene, the one whom you doubt.'

'What of the one true God?'

'The name of my father also.'

His eyes opened then and were staring.

'I did not give you your talents for you to abuse them,' the inward voice continued. 'Teach the pure language, Poliziano, the pure language.'

'What of the one true God?' he repeated.

Laughter came from the goddess as water from a hillside spring. 'Do you think He speaks a debased tongue, He, the source of language? He, the father of the Greeks, the Romans, of every living thing? He is Life itself. Honour Him by loving Life. Honour Him by doing in His Name that which you are fittest to do. Worship Him with your talent.' Her voice was a harbour in a storm, a seat in a market, a kiss of encouragement. The agitations of his soul began to quieten. 'You were not born to be a saint,' she continued, confirming his own suspicion. 'Leave those things to others. You are my poet, you are my high priest. What, you ask, does literary style have to do with God? – I shall tell you. Beauty is God. And to bring forth true beauty, the poet must have a pure heart. It is not for you to choose between wisdom and eloquence, but to unite the two. That is your work.'

He began to breathe easily and deeply.

'Incidentally,' she said, withdrawing, 'the apple is mine.'

He sank into a slumber and dreamt of marbled halls. In several rooms guests were mingling, but he seemed not to have been invited to their banquet. Then suddenly an apple, a golden apple, rolled across the floor towards him. He picked it up, and read upon it the words, *For the fairest.* He looked for his lady everywhere, to give her the apple, but she had become three and he was not sure which of them was she. One had all the beauty of wisdom; one had all the beauty of majesty; and one had all the beauty of form. *For the fairest.* The answer seemed obvious and he approached the one

234

with the most beautiful form. But his hand stayed mid-air and, as if moved by an invisible force, he turned and offered the apple to the one with the beauty of wisdom. As he gazed on her, Pallas fell in love with the eyes of Poliziano, and his poetic heart. But the majestic one of the three filled with malignant fury. *Shirker!* she cried.

He tried to rouse himself but felt stupefied.

Shirker!

He opened his eyes and met the blazing ones of the Queen of Heaven who stood before him.

'What are you doing lying in bed? Are you completely lost to idleness?'

'Madonna… I am not well.'

'Not well?' With one hand in the small of her back, and one resting on the swelling dome of her belly, Clarice stretched backwards to relieve her spine. Six months pregnant and the baby kicking in her womb. Not well. What did men know of being not well?

'Get out of that bed you idle degenerate.'

✢

Hearing the chapel bell ringing, Angelo made his way there, his head dizzy, thinking it must be time for prayer, but the place was deserted. He came to the sala and found Monna Clarice dictating a letter to the monk from the monastery in the woods who had been summoned by the bell.

'What are you doing, Madonna?'

'Writing to my husband.'

'It is for me to write your letters.'

'But Maestro,' she said, 'an hour ago you were far too sick. Your recovery is truly miraculous.'

Angelo wondered if she might be poisoning him, slowly.

The monk looked from one to the other. 'In my opinion,' he said gently, 'there are too few of you for this castello. You should remove to the tower house of Trebbio.'

For Clarice and Angelo alike the fortified tower on the ridge was

235

the last resort; to go there would mean that all hope was lost. 'No,' they said in unison.

'Things are not so bad here,' said Angelo. Trebbio was far too small. The way he felt now, the Gonzaga palace at Mantua would not provide sufficient space for him to share with Clarice; indeed, the Lombard plain would be too narrow a confine.

'Trebbio is too small,' Clarice agreed. 'If the staff did not keep deserting us, we would not be so few in number here.'

Angelo had not heard about the desertions and offered to go to the village to hire new servants. As he went, the rain, which had ceased for the night, began again, a constancy of water from a dreary sky, but he rode through the flood hardly noticing, for a miracle of the mind was occurring, a spark of inspiration, that divine impulse which comes as if from nowhere, without warning, unfurling like a banner and revealing a poem. Pallas was with him, inspiring him, strengthening his heart. *You are my high priest.*

He went about his business as quickly as he could, hired four men and cantered back to the castello. Overcoming the desire to sit staring into the flames of the fire, he cleared his desk of all its clutter, found some clean sheets of parchment, placed them square to the edge of the desk, put ink pot and pen close to hand. Here, in the midst of misery, happiness had arrived. Offering his thanks both to his muse Calliope and her sister Pallas, he dipped the pen in the pot and began a new poem, one dedicated to Giuliano de' Medici.

22

Florence, December 1478

LORENZO READ the letter from his wife written in the hand of a monk. Though it was midwinter and the armies were in retirement, he was still too busy to respond to Clarice's appeals for him to visit her. Indeed, the more Clarice called for him, the less inclined he was to go. In this weather the journey to Cafaggiolo would be too perilous, too time-consuming, for causes too trivial: a thousand excuses ran in his mind to obscure the truth, which was that he did not want to go.

He sat staring into the fire, the muzzle of his hound laid across his lap. It was not that he did not love her, he did love her, the kind of love based on implicit trust. The love of a father for the mother of his children. To go to Cafaggiolo, over the muddy mountains in the freezing rain on collapsed roads, just because she wanted him to? – No. He was too tired. It was too dangerous.

He read the letter again, and listened to what she had to say with regard to the tutoring of the boys. He could do this much, he supposed, to appease her: he could compromise. There was no reason he could see, in his weary state, why the boys should not learn from the Psalter as well as from Cicero. He rubbed his face and sighed. He would not vex Angelo by asking him to take on the task. Better if he sent a man to act as chaplain who could guide the boys through the psalms. He fell to wondering who to ask, then remembered a man whom Clarice had been bringing to his attention in the hope of promotion, for reasons indefinable except that Clarice would emulate her mother-in-law and give her support, Virgin-like, to supplicants in need. He called Niccolò Michelozzi to him.

'Who was that priest for whom Clarice was requesting a benefice?'

'Ser Alberto Malerba, Magnifico.'

'Send for him.'

✝

A week later, and the verses of a song to the memory of Giuliano de' Medici still taking shape in his mind, Angelo was gazing blindly out of a window, his inner sight fixed on the images aroused by some divine creative force, when he became aware that the bridge over the moat was lowering for a party of riders. If visitors were expected, why had he not been told? If they were not expected, should he not be running down the stairs now, wielding a sword? Before he arrived at an answer to these questions, he recognised the head of the party as Bishop Gentile and jumped down the stairs two at a time to meet his friend in the courtyard. Gentile introduced him to Ser Alberto Malerba. Angelo apologised but could not recall whether they had met before or not.

'You *are* expecting us?' said Gentile, trying to read Angelo's blank expression. 'As requested by Madonna Clarice, Alberto has come to help you with the children.'

The bishop told him the news from the city, all of it bad, but Angelo was hardly listening. He was looking at this limp young priest with pimples, he whom Monna Clarice evidently considered to be his spiritual superior, trying to understand the world and its justice. As Ser Alberto spoke, saying how pleased he was to be given this unlooked-for responsibility, and how he prayed God for help in his lofty task, Angelo felt his temper coming very swiftly to the boil. Too swiftly. Feigning a return of his fever, he said he must leave them at once. 'I think I'm being poisoned,' he gasped. The young priest looked astonished. 'Beware the women in this house,' Angelo warned him. 'You reside here at your peril.'

He ran through the castello, taking out his wrath on doors and curtain hangings. Clarice had written to Lorenzo, telling him the children were in spiritual danger. Lorenzo had sent Malerba without saying anything. He pulled a curtain back across a door with such force that the curtain rings screeched in protest. He stormed through the east wing like a frustrated soldier looking for something – anything – to rape or kill. Suddenly he found himself in a room which, though empty, was familiar. Usually hung with burgundy and green velvets, Monna Lucrezia's room was now bare of everything except the bed and the pictures on the wall, but there was a scent in the air like lemon blossom, the odour of her spirit. He sighed. His anger dissipating at the mere memory of her, he fell face down on to her bed, missing her so much that tears welled out of his eyes. He imagined how horrified Lorenzo's mother would be if she could see him now, for Lucrezia loathed displays of emotion, and yet, dear Lucrezia, how she inspired them.

Clarice, entering by the far door, found him thus and exclaimed: 'Maestro, I have been searching for you everywhere. We have guests. What are you doing lying on that bed? And your face!'

'What of it?'

'It is full of beard. Have you not seen the barber today?'

'It is cold, Madonna. There is ice in my ewer.'

She bestowed a kindly smile upon him, and advised him to return to his room and his fire. 'I will have some hot soup sent to you. And some hot water, along with the barber.'

'Oh, how sweet you are, as soon as there is a bishop in the house,' he thought.

'When you are presentable, you must come and meet my Alberto Malerba. He is going to instruct the boys in catechism, and teach Giovanni to read by means of the Psalter. My dear husband has seen sense at last. I trust you will not be sour and bitter about it, Maestro.'

☦

Whatever he might think about Malerba, Angelo was glad to have Gentile's company and sought him out, but the bishop was in the very deeps of melancholy and wanted to be left alone. Florence, he said, was doomed; the city was on the very precipice of destruction. All conversation was vain in the face of such a prospect.

With the children now in prayer seemingly for hours on end, Angelo had even more time to himself than he could wish for. He tried to keep cheerful by finding passages in the epic poets that would revive the spirits of the boys as soon as they returned, but often they did not return. Day after long, weary day, he was being sucked down further into despondency. He wrote out his poem but it was a shadow of what had heard spoken in his mind. Sometimes he went to the sala in the hope of meeting someone, but Clarice kept to her room and so did the bishop. Occasionally Malerba swept past trailing the odour of righteousness, but he had nothing much to say for himself except how grateful he was to God and Monna Clarice. Angelo went into his own retreat. He tried to continue the spiritual disciplines that had formed his days in Florence, the times of prayer and contemplation, the times of study and composition, but he was overcome by such melancholy torpor that whenever he turned to such practises, sitting on the settle which obscured the wall and its painting of the Virgin and Child, he ended up leaning forward, resting in his chin in his hands, lost in thought. And dozing.

Suddenly he started awake, telling himself in a clear voice that he must do something practical, even if only to write a letter.

✝

To Madonna Lucrezia at Careggi.
The news we can send you from here is thus: that the rain is so heavy and continuous that we cannot leave the house and have exchanged hunting for playing at ball, so that the children should have exercise. Our stakes are generally the soup, the sweet, or the meat; and he who loses goes without. Often when one of my scholars loses he pays tribute to Sir Humidity. I have no other news to give you. I remain in the house by the fireside in slippers and greatcoat and, were you to see me, you would think I were melancholy personified. Perhaps I am but myself after all, for so much have I taken our calamities to heart that I neither do, nor see, nor hear anything that gives me pleasure. Sleeping and waking they haunt me. Two days ago we began to spread our wings for we heard the plague had ceased; now we are again depressed on learning that it still lingers. When at Florence we have some sort of satisfaction, if nought else than that of seeing Lorenzo come home in safety. Here we are in perpetual anxiety about everything. As for myself, I declare to you that I am drowned in weary sloth, such is my solitude. I say solitude because the bishop shuts himself up in his room with only his thoughts for company, and I always find him so full of sorrow and apprehension that my melancholy is only increased

in his company. Ser Alberto di Malerba mumbles prayers with the children all day long, so I remain alone, and when I am tired of study I ring the changes on plague and war, on grief for the past and fear for the future, and have no one with whom to air my fantasies. I do not find my Madonna Lucrezia in her room with whom I can unburden myself and I am bored to death. Our sole relief is in letters from Florence. However, I am trying to arm myself with hope and cling to everything in order not to sink to the bottom. I have nought else to say.

✠

As he signed his letter, there was a knock on the door and Iride entered diffidently with a tray bearing a bowl of meat stew. 'From Madonna,' she said. 'And she asked me to ask you if you would prefer to move to another room? She thinks this one is too dark for you, and that you do not like its decoration.'

Angelo could feel her eyes on him but dared not look up. Iride's unseemly gaze stirred him in sinful ways. Disguising his fear as religious scruple, he was trying to avoid her.

Iride peered behind the settle. 'Of course she means the painting. Why do you keep it hidden? It is a fine painting, the Virgin and Child…'

'Yes! I know that. Leave me now, and take the tray. I am not hungry.'

Affronted, Iride withdrew at once. Angelo ran to the door. 'Iride!' But she had passed from sight. Returning, he pulled the settle from the wall. It was indeed a fine work, by Fra Filippo Lippi, one of the great artists of the previous generation. He knew how angry Filippino, the painter's son, would be to discover that a masterpiece of his father was being deliberately obscured.

Turning the settle completely about, he sat as a man who has decided to brave his wound. It was like an ache in the pit of him that he had learned to live with but had now become inflamed. As he looked on the Mother of Christ he tried to picture his own mother, but could not. She had faded from his eyes like a shade in

Tartarus, pulled away from him by the Fates. He could never understand what he had done wrong that she should abandon him, and as much as he was sorrowful he was angry. He stared at the soft, downcast eyes of the Virgin, and thought how his own mother lacked all natural love. Monna Antonia had cut all ties to her offspring and married another man – a tax officer! – within a month of her husband's death. To look on this painting, on the subject of this painting, on the Christ child so loved by his Mother… It was as if he were a cripple, with both legs amputated at the knees, looking on a magnificent portrait of an athlete. He felt blighted, cursed in a way which other men were not. He had a mother who, quite against nature, did not love him, and he presumed the fault was his, that he was unlovable by women. Had it not been proved repeatedly by experience? Was he not now surrounded by women who magnified that view a thousand times? He bent double over himself, contending with a pain that was eating the very marrow of him. 'Holy Mother Mary,' he whispered, 'help me.'

✝

Squalls of rain drummed on the ground. It was impossible to leave the house. Clarice moved through its rooms like a ghost, listening to the shouts as her children exercised in the hall with their master. She wondered what use fit bodies were going to be to them, other than to send them to their graves with taut muscles. She looked out of windows in every direction. The cloud-covered mountains held the enemy. All around, in secret winter camps, they waited. They knew where she was, she and her sons. They would be here in the spring. And so would the new baby.

She walked the house, trying to focus on her prayers, but bead after bead of the rosary passed idly through her fingers while she walked with her thoughts. If God saw fit that she die, she and her babies, then so be it. She must resign herself to it. Besides, this was the realm of shadows and not the true home. This earth, this place of vileness, pain and cruelty. She paused outside the door of the bishop but decided not to trouble him. He could do nothing for her now, being quite lost to despair himself. As for Ser Alberto Malerba, he was a pleasant enough young man, but his eagerness to please was beginning to irritate her. Clarice walked alone, making her way back to her room, where it was warm and bright, where Marta, Iride, the nurses and all the children waited for her. But as she turned a corner, she met Poliziano crawling on all fours with Piero sitting astride his shoulders, and Giovanni running beside them, waving his arms excitedly.

'I'm the centaur!' Piero exclaimed, beating his chest.

'And I'm Hercules. I'm going to KILL him,' Giovanni cried, firing imaginary arrows into the air. The sight of Clarice's feet brought Angelo to a halt. Such small feet, such small, sanctimonious, angry little feet. He kept his head lowered, knowing he was in trouble.

'Get down,' Clarice said quietly. 'Piero, get down.'

'Ma-donna…' Angelo rose up slowly, dusting his knees and hands.

'On all fours! I cannot believe my eyes! A tutor, on all fours! Why, you are still a child yourself. How could Lorenzo have employed such a boy to look after us? *Centaurs*? What impious games!'

Humiliated in front of his pupils, Angelo asked Piero to take his brother to the nursery. The boy, faithful as a squire, nodded and pulled his little brother away.

Angelo straightened to face her. 'Madonna…' he warned, but he heard the threat in his own voice, and suddenly every stoic philosopher he had ever read was rushing to his aid, to help him check his anger. He was not going to shout. All the years of study had forged a part of him into steel, and now he knew its strength for the first time. This was a pregnant woman. A stupid, small-minded, poisonous woman, a bigot – but one with child. He held his ground, and neither quailed in her gaze, nor expressed challenge or contempt.

'You are wrong,' he said calmly, 'and I pray God that you see your error.'

'Do you take His name in vain before me, blasphemer? Get you from this house!'

'You do not have that authority. You are stuck with me, and I with you, but for the sake of your husband, we must endure. Now, let me pass.'

Clarice did not move.

'LET ME PASS!' he thundered.

Such was his tone, so forceful and uncompromising – so like Lorenzo – that Clarice moved out of the way as if picked up and set down by the wind. He glanced at her balefully as he passed. Tears were springing to her eyes.

'Madonna…' he said, conciliatory.

'DO NOT TOUCH ME, DEVIL!' she cried. Servants sprang out through doors as if they had been hiding behind them, waiting for this moment.

Knowing he could do or say nothing that would convince anyone of his innocence, Angelo turned on his heel and left the scene. Faith without reason, he decided, was a very force of destruction. He was under attack as Lorenzo was, and by the same forces. He shivered at the thought and went to find the bishop.

'I am Oedipus, being driven to blind myself and go into exile,' he complained. 'I am Orestes, pursued by the Furies, so insane that I bite off my own finger. I am Orpheus, being torn limb from limb by the Maenads.'

But the poor bishop, distressed by his own morbid thoughts, told him he was maddened by too much reading.

'You should take a walk,' he offered.

'A *walk?* You think gentle exercise will free me from my dire fate?'

'It is all in your imagination,' the bishop insisted. 'You read too much.'

✝

The gods in heaven disported themselves. Pallas Athene ran among them to protect her beloved, and begged the gods to stop their play, but their lightnings flashed and their thunder rolled and their waters poured. She flew on winged feet to the Mugello, to give her aid to the nymph of the River Sieve, the terrified object of the lust of Zeus, but she could do nothing but watch as the muddy, swollen, violated river rushed through her course, rolled over her banks and spilled out over the valley. At the place where the Sieve met the Arno, the little river became a torrent. The Arno, already glutted with the constant rain, could not contain the flood and churned towards Florence. In that city the river's channel was constricted by several mill-weirs; the surge smashed against the first of them, went over the banks and into the streets. At the last bridge, where the arches were blocked by debris, the Arno leapt over the bridge, and spilled out sideways, flooding San Frediano on one bank and Ognissanti on the other.

It was the eve of Christmas. Bells that had begun to sound the call for the *Missa in Nocte* broke off and began to toll the alarm. Putrid waters carrying human waste inched up stairways, sending people fleeing to the rooftops. From this vantage point, the Florentines watched bolt after bolt of lightning split the sky and crackle round the Duomo. The Florentines – that confident, faithful people who had disobeyed the Pope, ignored his bull of excommunication and continued with their devotions – looked on in horror as their city was attacked by heaven.

At the Ponte Vecchio was a statue of Mars that had been there since Roman times. It was said that if ever it were to fall, Florence would be in mortal danger. At midnight, it toppled into the water and, despite its weight, was swept away by the boiling torrent.

✝

When Lorenzo heard that the tributary that had flooded the Arno was the Sieve from the Mugello valley, he fell into the jaws of self-doubting, for the Sieve was the river of his ancestral home and such a sign from God could not be ignored. Was the Pope then right? Was he was the iniquitous son of perdition? Which one, out of a long list of sin, was bringing all this on his head? Was it Pride? Should he have humbled and abased himself before the Pope, whatever the Pope's own crimes? Perhaps his whole foundation was wrong, along with everything he believed, everything he stood for. He had entered into battle with Rome like David or St George, but now heaven itself was bent on his destruction and using his own beloved river as the instrument. The city, his dying city Florence, was being washed away.

Alone in his chapel on the first floor of the palazzo in the Via Larga, Lorenzo prostrated himself on the floor in front of a wooden crucifix that had been carved by Donatello. 'Lord, which of my faults has deserved this punishment? If I have erred, it was not wilful on my part, but the product of ignorance. If I have erred, it is because I was born to err, being Man. Punish me, O Lord, but spare my people. Have we grown too vain? What have we done, that it should come to this? Do we offend you with our love of beauty? Is Florence a Babel, built to challenge you? It was not our intention. But twice now in six months I have heard screaming in these streets. It is enough. I surrender. I surrender to You entirely. You have my brother, now take me. Let me bear your wrath alone. Spare my people.'

He seemed to be speaking into a void. He heard nothing but his own words, and they sounded rather contrived. He beat his fists on the floor. 'Are you deaf? Must I make you hear me?' Jumping to his feet, he stripped off his jacket and shirt, and from the cupboard took out the flail. He ran the knotted leather over his hand then, flexing his arm, he cracked the whip hard against his back, splitting the skin in five places. Convinced now of his guilt, and yet unrelieved of it, he swung the whip again, hard enough this time to make himself cry out. But still the guilt remained. A third time, and with such force that he brought himself to his knees. When he had lashed himself until he could endure no more, he added yet more lashes and then collapsed, faint with pain. Face down on the floor and seeing his blood on the marble, he thought of Giuliano. Then suddenly, at last, an inner voice was truly speaking to him. In loud clarity, it said: *Trust in the Lord. The time is not yet.*

✝

On the hill of Careggi we stood outside Ficino's villa watching the storm that played on Florence. I was in awe of the elements. The sky was rupturing with light from north to south. Trees were on fire. The whole land seemed under attack. Ficino reminded me of Plato's myth of the cave, said that what we were watching was a mere shadow of reality.

I had been working for Ficino for only a few months, but it had been long enough to dispel the unrealistic awe I had once held him in. I had grown used to working for a man who was fully human and whose wisdom was practical. I had also come to realise that Ficino had a sense of humour that could be engaged at any time. Being told that this storm, quite the most dramatic I had ever witnessed in this land of storms, was a shadow of the true reality, I crowed with laughter, and found that my derision amused Ficino. Surrounded by men who called him 'master' and who treated his every word with terrifying respect, I believe the philosopher enjoyed my irreverence and found it a relief. In my heart I was the most obsequious of Ficino's disciples, but it had become my role to play the part of Everyman – the objector to wisdom. Standing now in a land which seemed to be inside a drum being beaten passionately by the gods, and to be told that the realm of the senses is a shadow of the 'intelligible world of ideas' provoked such fierce rebuttal that I half-choked on it. In the face of this destruction, Plato's theory seemed preposterous.

'Be content, my young friend, it is so,' Ficino assured me, smiling broadly. 'Look beyond, look behind this reality – what do you see?'

'I see fury.'

'Whose?'

'Nature's.'

'Indeed. Is our lady not full of wrath?' Ficino asked. As if in

247

response to this, hail began to drive at us; flinching under the stinging rain, we hurried back inside the house. 'So what has made Nature so wild?' Ficino asked, throwing a log on the fire and blowing on his frozen hands.

I was shivering noisily but, in fear of chilblains, I kept away from the hearth and looked for warmth in the wine jug. 'It is my experience that a woman's anger usually stems from neglect. While I dally here in the gardens of philosophy, my Elena is at home sharpening knives.'

'Have we neglected Nature?' Ficino asked, ignoring the point I was trying to make, but another deafening crack of thunder had me turning to look out again at the brilliant roots of wrath searing the sky. I wondered how Angelo was faring in the Mugello, and with these thoughts came a despair which was not my own. Filled with sudden and inexplicable melancholy, I told Ficino that I would neglect Nature no longer, that I was going home to my wife.

'Elena will be terrified, alone in all this,' I lied. I left hurriedly, braving the storm to reach my house, the warmth of my bed and the comforting embrace of my beloved. But it was not Elena who needed shielding from fear, it was me. As I came down the hill of Careggi, however, I found that the meadows outside the city had become a sea, albeit a shallow one. In the dark I could not see where the road was: it was too dangerous a journey to make on horseback. A man, Florentine through and through, approached on a boat and offered me passage at a rate undreamt of by a professional ferryman. I gave my horse over to his boy to return to Careggi and climbed in, remarking on the transfiguration of the countryside.

'This is nothing,' said the man. 'Wait till you see the city.'

23

THE BOAT TOOK me to hell. Turbid water filled the ground floor
of every house near the river, including my own. Boats were everywhere – I had no idea the city possessed so many – rescuing goods
and merchandise. The people who had escaped to the top floors
were shouting down on the boatmen that they were looters and
robbers. Merchants and shop-keepers cried in anguish to heaven
that they were ruined. It was the feast of Cosmos and Damian, but
that was not why bells tolled everywhere. Their urgent *bong-dong
bong-dong* expressed appeals to heaven.

The ground floor of my house was rented to a leather-worker.
The water had brought in as much as it had taken out. Books were
floating about, a finely-carved chair, a picture frame, a jousting
lance, a child's doll and a bobbing flotilla of apples. The water had
redistributed everyone's possessions – all wealth was equalised in
ruin. But the finest piece of flotsam was a small rowing boat much
like the one I had arrived in. The leather-worker was salvaging
everything he could with the help of his family and of Elena. Her
belly huge with child, my wife stood on the stairs, her skirts tucked
up and her legs bare, taking armfuls of sodden skins from those
who brought them to her. I had left her in confinement and here
she was, wet, cold and lifting great weights. I told her sharply to
leave everything and to return to bed.

'You think I can rest while our neighbours drown?' she said.

'Elena! Put those skins down!'

'No! Not in the water! They are my living!' cried the leather-
worker.

'Forget your skins, my friend,' I told him. 'Take the boat and go
out and make your fortune.' When I told him how much I had
been charged, he dropped his own armful of skins into the water
and clambered into the boat.

'An oar, I need an oar! Or a pole! There, that lance will do.'

I gave him the jousting lance and pushed him and his craft out of the door.

'Bring it back in the morning,' I told him. 'I shall need it.'

At last I could devote my attention to Elena. For the past few months I had coddled her in the nest I had made, keeping her warm, bringing her food. The role usually played by mother and grandmother, sister and aunt, I played alone. I did not know I was supposed to find a midwife in advance, nor did Elena. I was rabbit-scared by the prospect ahead of us, full of mortal dread, and here stood my treasure soaked with filth and slime, shuddering with cold. 'Upstairs!' I ordered her. 'Let us get the bath tub filled.' And then the full horror struck me. 'The wells…' I muttered.

Elena turned and looked down on me. Tears were coursing down her cheeks. 'This is our Armageddon, Tommaso. This is the end.'

When we reached our sala I found that the fire had been doused by the sheer volume of rain that had come down the chimney. I made her remove her wet clothes. I dried her, used olive oil and a knife to clean off the dirt and wrapped her in blankets and furs before I did the same to myself. Then I took her to bed and cuddled her, giving her all the warmth I had, stroking and stroking her until her shivering ceased. In the large swell of her belly I could feel our child, its anxious movement gradually quietening, its little heartbeat steady. There was nothing else I could do but spend the rest of the night caressing both mother and child and soothing them with assurances that sounded improbable in my own ears.

✝

At dawn we woke after an hour's sleep, brought from our slumbers by the most malodorous stench. Florence had turned into a sewer. I cleaned the hearth, set and lit a new fire. Elena's colour had come back and she seemed recovered from the night's ordeal. The leather-worker returned with more money in his purse after a night's work than he would usually earn in a month. He gave the boat over to me, telling me that the price of passage had risen four-fold during the night, but it was not money I wanted, it was water. The Signoria, however, already had the matter in hand and had organised barrels of spring water to be collected in the hills and ferried into the city. Distribution points had been arranged in every piazza. This was a gleam of light, a sense of order in the midst of riot, and the citizens responded by organising help for neighbours, for the elderly and infirm, and starting the work of clearing up even before the flood had receded. Everywhere you looked, at every window, balcony and rooftop loggia, things were hanging out to dry. Heaven, too, responded and sent the sun to help the work.

I rowed to Ognissanti, where the flood was at its highest, and found Sandro Botticelli standing up to his armpits in freezing water, surveying the destruction. Four months' work had been lost; all his pigments were wet and useless; studies in silverpoint were floating in the lane outside. 'I am ruined!' he cried.

Filippino Lippi waded towards him, creating a wash in the studio. He grasped his master's hands. 'We still have these.' He took hold of Botticelli's head. 'We still have this. We still have our lives. Our talents have not been washed away. We can start again. Look, even now the level of water is lower than it was and the rain has stopped. And what is that in the sky if not the sun?'

'You infernal optimist,' Botticelli protested, but was mollified. He followed his journeyman to where the door had been before the flood had ripped it off its hinges and carried it away.

'Look, Sandro,' Filippino said, pointing to my little boat, 'you always did want to visit Venice. Come, Tommaso, give us a ride and I shall sing as we go.'

The two painters climbed into my craft and I rowed them through the streets of the district to witness the affliction of their neighbours. Serenading us like a Venetian ferryman, Filippino directed us into the canal that was the Via dei Fossi.

'Oh, Madonna!' cried Sandro. 'Look at Poliziano's house!'

The door had gone there, too, and now the house was regur-

251

gitating the little furniture that had been put in it. Among the wreckage was a loaf of bread which seemed fresh; I looked askance at the upper windows. There I saw an apparition of Angelo – him and yet not him. It was but a momentary vision before the shade withdrew.

'I thought the house was empty,' Botticelli said.

'No. Angelo gave it over to his cousin just before he left.'

'Was that his cousin at the window?'

'No, indeed it was not.'

'I saw the figure too,' said Filippino, 'and it seemed to be Poliziano himself, strangely altered – turned into a girl.' Filippino, who was not frightened by ghosts, even when he saw them himself, tied the boat to the horse-ring in the wall and jumped to the step. Botticelli followed more reluctantly. Knowing for certain that Angelo was in the Mugello, and believing Maso was away fighting, I wanted to stay in the boat but was hauled out by my friends. We entered a house where water lapped at walls as if at wharves. 'Who is there?' Filippino called. When no one replied, he began to climb the stairs.

'I shall wait for you here,' Botticelli said from the lowest step.

'And I.'

'Cowards!' Filippino shouted down to us. He walked on up to the next floor and went through a door. We heard him cry out just once, then it was silent.

'Pipo?' we called. 'What is it?'

There was no reply.

While Botticelli insisted on staying below to look after the boat, slowly and very hesitantly I climbed the stair, and as I turned a corner at the top, Maso Ambrogini was waiting for me. He took me by the throat from behind and my heart flipped over like a tumbler. I struggled wildly but could not make a sound except by drumming my heels, but it was not enough to bring Botticelli up to rescue us. Half-strangled and coughing I was pushed into a room alongside Filippino, who sat there dazed from a blow to his head. Maso, dagger in hand, interrogated us. Who were we? What was our business? If we had come here looting, there was nothing to steal.

As I was reminding Maso we had met before, suddenly the vision we had seen at the window entered through a far door, and I found myself looking at a girl the very image of her brother.

'Are you Angelo Poliziano's twin?' Filippino asked her. It was a stupid question, given how much younger she was, but the resemblance was unnerving. The girl blushed to be the centre of such fascinated attention. 'Am I like Angelo?' she asked her cousin.

'You have the same Ambrogini snout,' Maso said, 'of which I am mercifully free.'

I rubbed my throat, and looked critically about the house that had once been fine, if empty.

'A victim of war,' said Maso blithely, when I remarked on its ruin. 'And flood.'

☩

In the Mugello, Angelo paddled through the villa ankle deep in water, wondering how to dry the place out. He had spent the night working with the servants to salvage tapestries and carpets, rolling them up and storing them in attic rooms. The bishop and Malerba were also helping.

'Wooooh!' Piero came splashing towards him at a run. 'Let us make a raft!'

'This is no time for play.'

Lorenzo's eldest daughter, Lucrezina, entered holding her skirts up to her knees, claiming to have seen a fish. Piero waded towards her wanting to see it himself. Angelo said that they only thing they were likely to catch was cold, and they must go upstairs to the fire. He was told that all fires were out, all the fuel was soaked.

He sat down on a stair, his head in his hands. Clarice appeared on the landing above him.

'You were the one who was supposed to look after us, and see what you have brought down upon us, you and your gods!'

'Gods spare me,' he muttered, and did not bother to look up.

Epiphany was the most sacred festival for the Medici. It commemorated the coming of the Magi, the wise men of the East whom the Medici revered, seeing in those enigmatic figures followers of Zoroaster, the first of the line of the great sages of humanity. Within its compass fell the feast of Cosmos and Damian, the patron saints of the family on whose day Lorenzo had been born. In previous years, Epiphany had been spent in prolonged celebration. Not this year. The workers from the estate brought them dry wood, but it would take more than earthly fire to warm them.

As soon as the water had subsided, a courier arrived with a letter for Angelo from me. It told him of the damage to his house; it told him also of the visitors who were in it. As he read, Angelo groaned. His sister... hungry, in need, and in Florence, waiting for him.

'Maestro!' Piero called, doing cartwheels in the puddles and wanting attention.

Angelo stared at the boy, wondering where his loyalties lay – to his own kin, or to that of his patron. His head dipped back into his hands.

✠

Angelo wrote to Lorenzo: '*Magnifice mi patrone*. You ask me our news, and it is grave, though of course not as grave as yours. The children and Madonna are well. Monsignore still keeps to his room. Ser Malerba is in prayer all day long. The waters have receded now and I believe there is little damage done to the house and its contents.

I think it advisable that Madonna Clarice should come to the city to be delivered of her child. Here it is too dangerous. Let me know your opinion and that of the doctors. I commend myself to you, etc., Angelo Poliziano, at Cafaggiolo.'

After that he wrote to Francesco Sassetti, the manager of the Medici bank, to arrange for his accruing salary to be made available to his cousin and sister residing on the Via dei Fossi, and then to me, telling me of the arrangement, and asking me to liase between the family and the bank, to see that they wanted for nothing.

24

HAVING FOUND these entries in Maria's notebook, I have to add them to my account, even though sometimes it may seem vain to do so; even though sometimes the memories they engender open afresh the wounds of loss.

From my window I look out on a dying city. I have seen the smoke from pyres on the far bank of the river where the plague has ravished the people in the poorest quarter. I have seen soldiers parading along the Via dei Fossi; I have seen cut-purses at work and prostitutes looking for custom. But today all I can see is water. God has visited a flood upon us. Just to look at the reeking brown filth is to see, to know it as retribution for our sins. Everyone must think so. Not a Florentine could have lived through this night or awoken this morning without the realisation of God's wrath. Master Piero was right: I have not fled to safety but from it. For certain the flood will bring further disease and wretchedness. Shall I die here, alone but for a drunken cousin? Thinking such morbid thoughts, I watched boats passing to and fro on the Via dei Fossi, some of them bringing food supplies and filling the baskets that people dangle from the upper floors. I was about to go and wake Maso and tell him we need a basket and some stout rope when I noticed a boat stationery before our house. The newly risen sun, for sun there is this day, was so glinting on the water that I could not see the occupants clearly other than the forms of three men, who seemed, by the prickle on my skin, to be staring up at me. Our door gone, the boat passed through into our court-yard. I ran to Maso and shook him out of his stupor, telling him looters had arrived.

The first one up the stairs Maso clubbed on the back of the head and dragged into an unused room. The next one up the stairs he grabbed from behind by the throat and dragged him also into the room, but that one struggled and gasped, saying, 'Maso, it is me, Tommaso Maffei, Angelo's friend.' He let him go then, and the young man, rubbing his throat, called down to the third that it was safe to come up. Soon all three were gathered together and I stood before them as if on trial, feeling small and very vulnerable. The name of the young man with the sore head is Filippino, and he is the journeyman of the tall, older man called Sandro di Filipepi, the one they call Botticelli. Those two discussed me as if I were not there, asking Maso questions about me which he answered, and not always correctly. I must have been trembling because the young man called Tommaso, who so far had remained silent, laid his hand on my arm and told me not be frightened.

'I have known your brother for six years and worked as his scribe for many of them. Consider me your friend.'

He has a countenance as kind and gentle as his disposition; his words, and the touch of his hand on my arm, brought my soul to rest and made the interrogations of the other two not so hard to bear. I learnt that he is recently married to a daughter of the Pazzi family called Elena. She is the most fortunate of women, and the baby she carries will be the most fortunate of children, to be born to parents who love each other. He told me that he works for a priest who is a philosopher and scholar of Greek, and that as soon as he had taken his friends home he must row out of the city and return to his master.

'Your wife is alone?' I asked.

He looked at me then with his wide-open eyes, which are brown and flecked with light. Flecked also with anxiety. 'She is desperate for female companionship, and will be even more so when she enters her confinement,' he said. 'She has no mother, no aunt, no sister – all women of the Pazzi have been sent to the convent. There is no one to comfort and encourage her.' He came alive to the thought that was now flashing like a spark in my own mind. Tears of yearning hope sprang unbidden to my eyes.

'I have no knowledge myself of such things,' I said. 'But I do have some skill with herbs and simples.'

✢

I am writing this in Tommaso's house, in a cheerful room which Elena says I am to consider my own. She is as beautiful as she should be, married to such a man. Do I feel jealous? I did, for a glancing moment, but its fire was soon put out by my love of her.

On the way to this house we stopped at the bottega of Botticelli, where the painter and his journeyman disembarked. Much is ruined in their shop, but things on the upper floor remain safe. The painter was eager to show me some studies in silverpoint he has been making of the birth of Venus. At first I wondered why, and it was difficult not to blush at the nakedness of goddess who, standing on a scallop shell, was being wafted to shore by the breath of Zephyrs, but for the painter this was not a study of nudity for the sake of inspiring lustful thoughts. It was an image of Love that had been formed in his mind by my brother Angelo.

'He speaks paintings to me,' he said. 'He tells me the stories from the ancient poets, gives me images in words. He is a wonderful man, Maria – you will love him as we all do.'

Wafted to shore on a scallop shell. My dismal thoughts of the morning are quite gone. This is no flood but the very waters of creation. I have wafted ashore and stepped into the land where my brother lives. He receives me and covers my nakedness with a rose-coloured cloak. All shall be well.

25

Florence and environs, February 1479

BY THE END of January Monna Clarice was ready to go into confinement. Lorenzo's doctor, Stefano della Torre, arrived at the castello of Cafaggiolo to escort her to Florence. Angelo drew him aside for a private consultation: his voice had become husky and there was a perpetual constriction in his throat. Della Torre examined him peremptorily and declared that there was nothing wrong.

'There must be something wrong,' said Angelo hoarsely.

'But you say there is no pain?'

'None, but you only have to listen to my voice. I am short of breath. I feel suffocated.'

The doctor insisted that there was no physical cause. Angelo told the doctor that he was being poisoned, that he was under the curse of witches. Della Torre mocked him for irrational beliefs. 'So our Medici ladies are witches who wish you ill?'

'Oh, I speak metaphorically, Stefano. They are not really witches, merely women, women with incense and incantations and strange little poppy cakes who wish me dead.'

'You will be free of them tomorrow.

'God be praised.' Angelo croaked. 'Stefano, how long will she be in confinement?'

'She will be delivered in about a month, then she will have a month apart for purification, or more if it is a girl. And then she will be churched.'

'Lord, let it be a girl. Twin girls. Triplets.'

'Your levity does you no credit. The journey will be a terrible ordeal for her. The whole family must pray for her safety. I trust you will be joining the vigil tonight?'

'Of course, of course, I shall pray all night long. You misunderstand if you think I wish Monna Clarice harm.' Clarice had so impressed herself on his consciousness that she had become his first thought on waking in the morning and his last thought at night; the only thing that Angelo wished was that he did not have to think of her at all. He longed for her departure, even though she was going to take the lovely Iride with her. Indeed, since Iride was now also affecting his brain like a fever, he was almost glad to see her go, too.

Sure enough, as soon as the women had left he recovered his health. Even while the entourage was still in sight on the road, he was calling to Piero, 'Lessons in one hour, and bring Giovanni with you.'

'Maestro, Giovanni is with Ser Alberto Malerba,' Piero told him.

Angelo strode to the room of the priest and announced that he would be taking Giovanni away in one hour. The child clapped his hands in delight. Malerba objected, saying that he had strict instructions from Monna Clarice. Angelo said that he had even stricter instructions from Lorenzo, but omitted to say that it was several months since he had received them.

Before the boys arrived, he had the servants clean and air his room. Clarice was gone. As if by magic his nose and throat were unblocking. He could smell spring in the air.

✣

While busy with various councils and civic receptions of foreign ambassadors, Lorenzo was preoccupied with the need to find a midwife and a wet nurse. The midwife he had engaged for the previous births was unavailable, having fled the city like so many others, but he had engaged another in distant Bologna and she was due to arrive in a few days. He was having greater trouble finding a wet nurse. Cautious about having anyone from the city because of the plague, he had sent his servants out to Prato, the Mugello and the Casentino to find out a good and suitable woman. As one of the ambassadors spoke charmingly about the great affection his monarch held for the Medici and for Florence, Lorenzo was trying to recall what the architect, Leon Battista Alberti, had said about wet nurses in his wise manual on family life. He seemed to remember a passage where Alberti advised that a woman should be chosen for the qualities of her soul as much as her milk, for virtue, he said, is to be had at the nurse's breast. The father should give himself plenty of time to find the right woman, who should be honest, good and competent, not sick nor of immoral character. She must be free of all vices which corrupt the milk and blood. And her breasts must be small and well-shaped. Lorenzo wondered if Alberti had said that, or if he had learnt it from his mother. Was it something he had been told as a child, that his nose was flat because his nurse had had big breasts? Probably. It was the kind of tall tale his grandfather would have told him. So, a woman healthy in mind and body, not too fat, not too lean, with all the virtues, and producing milk at the time your child is born. 'Yet this sort of

259

person always seems to be unavailable just when you need her most.' Lorenzo remembered that line with clarity. He glanced up at the Portuguese ambassador and wanted to ask him if he was a father, but the man was now in full oratorical flight on the need to purge the Church of corruption and the lust for power.

The situation in the Chianti, where sickness and bad weather were decimating his encamped forces, was worsening. As soon as these embassies had passed on, Lorenzo must attend to these needs. And find a wet nurse. He rose and, on behalf of Florence, answered the ambassador with a long eulogy on the magnificence of the King of Portugal, and expressing his gratitude for the support the monarch had shown in sending such a fine ambassador to Rome to plead for peace. 'We await the outcome of your mission with great hope and pray to the saints that you will be successful. Be assured: it is not Florence who wishes this war.'

✝

On the night my wife came to the end of her term, I sent for a midwife. I was eighteen years old and all the arrogance of youth had fled, leaving me revealed as a grub under a stone, raw and ignorant. A midwife – what is that? Someone you call for when your wife is in labour. I knew no more, but as the hours progressed knowledge came upon me in tidal waves, that I should have arranged the matter earlier, should have spoken to people who know about such things, should have found a woman to be a mother to Elena and tell her what to expect and when. That Maria was with us helped, but she knew no more than we did. I soon discovered that the city was empty of midwives, as it was empty of anyone who was able to leave. Those few who remained were busy. I finally heard of one living in Antella and sent for her, leaving it to God to ensure that she did not come from a plague village. She came with her sister, both women wearing black cloaks with hoods drawn wimple-like over their faces. I looked into the baskets they were carrying which were filled with dried herbs such as rue, savory, chamomile and meliot, seeds such as flax and chickpeas, syrups, potions, laxatives and digestives, aromatics and other remedies, oils and bandages.

I longed for a real physician but I was told that no woman would allow a man near her at such a time..

'What is this?' I asked, pointing to a weed which, though desiccated, was still recognisable.

'Belladonna,' said one.

'For la bella donna,' laughed another.

'Poison!'

They expressed their indignation in a torrent of Tuscan as sharp as cheap wine. 'What do you know about these things? Everything has its use in right measure, even poison. What do you know, a scholar?'

One stuck out her tongue and pointed to it. 'This is how wisdom is passed on, by the tongue. Not by schools. All your bookish learning counts for nothing compared to what we know, what we've learnt from our mothers and mother's mothers.'

'Women, my fine young man,' said the other, 'do not murder each other, especially when they're in labour. Now take us to the lady.'

I ushered them into Elena's chamber. She was sitting up in bed and held out her hands to me, imploring me to enter, whatever custom might say. I closed the door gently. It would be my last sight of her until this ordeal was over.

Out in the antechamber I leant against a wall. Emotions were coming up in me like gushing springs, a sense of enormity, fear of death, belated grief at the loss of my own parents. I was useless. I had heard about this from other fathers, these swelling emotions, and how the company of other men soothes the time and makes it merry. But I was alone and little more than a child myself. I rolled up into a ball and wept in a deluge of fright and self pity. Every sound of my wife's travail I echoed with my own cries, echoes of agony. After a few hours had passed, I was feverish with prayer.

✠

My son was reluctant to come into the world. They tried to make me leave the house so that I would not hear Elena screaming, but I remained, distraught to hear such cries coming from the one I loved more than I loved my own life. I cannot write more of it. Even if I could penetrate the wall of oblivion I have built around the memory, there is not much I could say, for I was on the far side of the door while it happened. I could tell much of the door, about the fine grain of the wood, the solidity of oak, its resistance to pressure, the smell of its oil, the cocky impudence of its lock in keeping out the master of the house. But of what was happening on the other side of it... Maria has it all written down in her careful hand.

✝

Elena had her baby this night. To watch her agony made me resolve never to be a wife. Whatever I may long for in human love is not worth such pain. What I learnt in the convent about babies was a lie. No infant on straw here surrounded by an ox, an ass and three kings bearing gifts. No neat, starched Madonna quietly praying over him. What artist would dare paint a woman as she really looks when giving birth? Beautiful Elena was stripped of her beauty. Her lovely hair was tucked into a cap that was tied under her chin and made her look bald and ridiculous. They kept her dressed but her skirts were pulled up and her most private parts on view for all to see. She was wild on the birthing stool, screaming for the help of saints. The midwives consulted each other and decided the baby was breached. While one massaged Elena's abdomen with oil of violets (1 part essence to 2 parts almond oil, gently warmed) the other knelt down in front of Elena and with her hand (moistened with a decoction of flaxseed and chickpeas), reached in, lifted the baby's bottom out of the mother's pelvis and put it back in the right position. Elena's eyes started with outrage. I went from wall to wall like a trapped moth until the other midwife called for my help. She was making an infusion of coriander and singing an incantation over it.

'Fill the bowl with hot water from the fire, girl. Make yourself useful. And that cloth there – tear it into strips. You'll be learning how to swaddle within the hour.'

'Push!' cried her sister.

'I can't push!' Elena yelled. 'It will not come. Get a doctor!'

'A doctor?' cried the midwife. 'Do you want to die? He'd be at you with a knife before you could say one Hail Mary.'

'Save the child and lose the mother,' crooned her sister over her stirring. 'Save the mother and lose the child. Which is it to be? The tree or the fruit? The fruit or the tree?'

What a question! I stumbled towards the fire with my knees giving way under me. As I passed her, Elena's eyes opened to me, stared at me in horror, then her head jerked back, her body heaving and stretching in pain, agony in mortal waves running through her. A sound somewhere between scream and groan began deep and slow in the pit of her and came out as a roar. Then another pause while she panted for breath and re-focussed her eyes on me. From the far side of the door came the sound of Tommaso beating on it weakly, the sound of his sobbing. This was unbearable. Every little cosy dream I have ever had of love, marriage and motherhood – all blown away like dandelion seeds in a tempest. This! This visceral, malodorous, undignified torture. This is motherhood? I stepped forward on my shaky, drunken legs and fell on my knees beside Elena to begin praying like a wild anchoress. Then came another scream which shattered my prayers like glass and I began to cry uncontrollably, calling on the name of every saint I could think of.

The midwife pulled. 'Come on little one, come on my little pigwidgeon, my doll, my manikin. Come on my little man, my dapperling, my finger-ling, my dandiprat. Come! Ah!'

There was a rushing sound. Shlooop. And that was that.

Everything was quiet except for Elena's gasps and pantings. One mid-wife, ladle in the air, frozen. The other on the floor with this thing in her lap, frozen. He was blue, that tiny person in the image of his parents, blue, cold and lifeless, strangled by the umbilical cord. Oh! That foul, slimy thing – how did she clean it off him? How could she touch it? But she did, unwind-ing it, that gelatinous plait of a mother's making, bluey-white and pink, the colour of seafood. And at the end of it spongy stuff which has a name that is the sound of it as it hits the floor: pla-centa. It lay there like a dead octopus on a fishmonger's counter amidst blood, slime and mucous. I divided into two. Half of me swayed, about to faint. The other half said, How interesting! *That half vanquished the other.*

The midwives cleared up quickly, saying it was unlucky to stay, that they must take the placenta and bury it by the light of the moon or nothing would go well. As they unlocked the door to leave, Tommaso fell into the room. He took in the living and the dead in one glance and rushed towards the living. He wrapped his arms round Elena, pulled the bonnet off her and wept into her hair. I put the baby in the cradle Tommaso had had made for him and covered him with a sheet. Confined within her husband's arms, Elena began to thrash about and grow frantic. She had spent most of her pregnancy worrying about baptism. Under the interdict of the Pope, no baptism was allowed and, though the Florentine clergy ignored this and carried on as usual, Elena had continually fretted that the sacrament would not be sound in the hands of the excommunicated. Tommaso had laughed at her and called her superstitious, telling her that it was God who judged the hearts of men, not popes. Now she began to cry out about baptism. At first I thought she was raving until I understood what she was trying to say: her baby, dying unbaptised, was in limbo. We did our best to calm her down but failed since there was nothing to be said of any comfort.

Tommaso told me to look after things: he was going for help.

The day was pressing through the shutters, damp and dreary. I drew curtains over it and lit every candle and lamp I could find. I made constellations of light. I stoked the fire to a blaze and threw on twigs of pine and cone that crackled and spat forth their sweet resinous odour. I stripped Elena and bathed her, got her into bed and massaged her with juniper oil, pummelling warmth into her and getting the blood to flow again until she looked pink and healthy. Her poor breasts were full of milk that seeped out. What to do about this neither she nor I knew. We were alone together in ignorance at a time when mothers and grandmothers are indispensable. I hoped that Tommaso was able to find someone who would know what to do, since I believed I did not know. If I worked with the elements for the purpose of restoration, it was just to give myself something to do.

When Tommaso returned, he brought with him a man of about forty five, very short, with hair as golden as an angel's. As he entered the chamber, the air crackled, I swear it, and the look on Elena's face – how many painters *have tried to capture that look, of Mary greeting Gabriel. His name is Marsilio Ficino, Tommaso's master who is translating all the works of Plato and the Platonists. This scholar who is also a priest and a doctor is unlike any scholar, priest or doctor I have met. Scant few, I know, but those I have met have represented the common, and this man is decidedly uncommon. There is a luminous peace in his eyes, as if he is a keen observer of life but a reluctant participator. He looks and listens where others are mobbed by their thoughts. When we were introduced he held my gaze for a while, and, in that while, only he and I existed. Light began to shimmer in the air, the light of a truth I do not know, the light of a secret I will find out. No wonder Tommaso is so devoted to this man.*

He turned his attention to Elena and, sitting on her bed, held his hand on her brow and seemed to be listening to what his hand told him. Then, drawing in breath, he sat back. He looked across to me.

'Angelo's sister,' he said. 'You do well. The things you have done here are the right things. Where did you learn the art of healing?'

I felt like a raindrop being praised by Ocean for my liquidity. What I do, I told him, I do from instinct and not from knowledge. 'Daughter,' Ficino said, 'that is knowledge.' The firelight threw his shadow upon the wall and it towered over us, the shadow of a slightly hunched scholar in a cap, not his true form at all.

'A voice told me what to do, an inner voice, very calm and authoritative,' I told him. That it was silent on the matter of breast milk I was too embarrassed to say.

'A priestess in the temple of Asclepius.'

I wanted to ask who Asclepius was but it was not the time to pester this sage with questions.

Elena turned her head on the pillow and stared at the man who was her husband's master. Then she looked past him to the wooden crib where the little corpse lay shrouded, awaiting burial. 'Oh, my son, my son...'

'Limbus infantium,' said Ficino. 'A theory of the schoolmen, to assign unbaptised children to the edge of hell. Daughter, we have no way of knowing if it is true. The Platonists make no mention of it. Instead they teach of the transmigration of souls from one body to another. The soul is immortal, Elena. I cannot prove it to you; I hope it is enough to say that I,

myself, believe it. And within the soul, the divine spark, the pneuma, the spirit which is the true God. Your son was plucked back before birth. Perhaps to return to God, as light to Light, perhaps to seek another embodiment, for whatever reason beyond the ken of mortal man. Trust in the true God, Elena, and not the one who flings babies into hell. That divine spark that was the essence of your son is within your own heart. It lives. It cannot die. Rest in that, my daughter, and be well.'

There were those lights in the air again, subtle stars, harmonics of the dancing candle-flames. This was the secret truth, and everything within me woke up at once to that short phrase of redemption and resurrection: the soul is immortal.

Tears streamed down Elena's temples into the pillow. Her grief flowed and mingled with wonder.

I was staring at Ficino as if at the ineffable itself.

'What is it?' Ficino asked.

'You are visible,' I said in a whisper of wonder and relief, and knew as I said it that he would understand whom I was addressing. My invisible God – visible in men.

He did understand and smiled. In that smile, of acknowledgement and recognition, I disappeared. Only the light remained. Everything I presume to be me, body and mind, are but clouds obscuring the light. Light spoke to light, pneuma to pneuma. God to God. Invisible, yes, but also Present.

He rose, went to the crib that had become a coffin and laid his hands on the infant. Had the little boy started to breathe, I would not have been surprised. But he did not. Ficino said the rite of baptism over him, followed by a prayer for the soul of the baby, a prayer to sever connections with the body and speed the soul on its way. It was a sacred prayer but not a Christian one.

And then, and then… I tell you, my journal, what I can tell no man. I heard a tiny silver bell ringing and the voices of angels singing in the empyrean.

'His name!' I said urgently to Tommaso. 'What is your son's name?'

Tommaso could not think so quickly.

'Emmanuel,' said Elena.

266

There was, it seemed, a sigh in the room, and I knew the baby's soul was free.

Ficino leant forward across the crib. 'That was well done,' he said, 'Maria Poliziana.'

✢

Clarice screamed. Her eyes bulged, livid with rage, that she must endure this for love and duty. The midwife called on her to push. A guardadonna held a copy of the legend of St Margaret over her abdomen – St Margaret, the patron saint of childbirth, who had been swallowed by a dragon and, because of her piety, was regurgitated. Clarice tried to concentrate on St Margaret while an enormous force, within her but not of her, breathed on the baby and impelled it from the womb. Muscles in contraction and spasm. The agony which is the curse of Eve. And ye shall bring forth in sorrow. The room was full of women: her mother-in-law, her sisters-in-law, midwives, guardadonne, servants: some praying, some standing apart and talking amongst themselves, some heating water and preparing swaddling bands, some so close to her she could feel their breath on her face.

'Push,' the midwife was saying. 'Ninth, you say? Ninth is always the easiest. *Bello bambino*! Come on my lovely. One last gentle little push, Madonna.'

Clarice, who thought that one last little push was more than she could offer, clenched her rosary in one hand and the legend of St Margaret in the other and let out a roar to smite God in his heaven. It was as well that Lorenzo was not in the house to hear her. Nine times she had been through this, nine times! Everyone seemed to think that made it easier. 'It will come out as if it was greased,' the midwife had said. But now all her many attendants had disappeared in the fires of agony as she strained to free herself of this baby that was too big, too big. One more push and it would rip its way out of her, tearing through skin and muscle that was too small, too small. 'Push!' came the midwife's voice, commanding her as if her reluctance was wilfulness on her part. Anger flared up in her. She raised her head to shout at her. She opened her mouth to shout at her. She shouted, but the shout became one more scream. Then the rush and the flow and the ease. Cries of congratulation. A geyser of tears exploding within her. It was over.

Until the next time.

Clarice sat slumped, indifferent, on the birthing stool, supported by two guardadonne. The midwife was holding the baby until the moment it gave voice. It came, a long *aaaaaaaaaaah*. There was a new child in the world, a new Medici. The midwife said something.

'What are you saying?'

'I said, it is a boy, Madonna!'

Congratulations thrilled in the chamber.

'Oh.' Clarice closed her eyes.

'Would you like to hold him?'

'No.' Clarice wanted to be alone with herself, to heal herself, to be free of these people who were only interested in the fruit she bore.

✠

In Florence, during an audience with counsellors, Lorenzo received the news from a servant, whispered into his ear, that his wife had given birth and he had a third son. 'A boy!' he announced, prompting jubilation among his attendants and companions, and a great pouring of wine. 'And my wife?' he asked of the servant. 'Is she well? Was the birth easy or difficult?'

'Easy, Magnifico.'

'Thanks be to God.' Lorenzo settled to the celebrations.

✠

But in the Medici villa at Careggi all had become quiet. Servants moved softly about, not wishing to disturb Monna Clarice. Visitors were only allowed as far as the ante-chamber. There they left their gifts of water and linen, silver forks and spoons, marzipan cake. From Lorenzo there came a red surcoat, with damask for sleeves, and a silver cup. From Monna Lucrezia, a birth tray painted with a scene from the life of Ruth. Alone except for a few silent attendants, Clarice heard the distant sounds of the house like the sea in a shell. The growing light of a cold, grey dawn came through the shutters in horizontal bars, the day pushing its ways into the room, telling her to get up and make herself busy. The tides of pain that had swept through her had left her exhausted, but her mind was not still. Ignoring the concern of her attendants, she rose from her bed and crossed to the door; there she turned and went back to the bed. At the bed she turned and went back to the door, and so it continued: in a desperate attempt to quell this roar of energy, Clarice paced.

'Madonna, please!' said one of the women. 'Do not punish yourself like this!'

Taking no notice, Clarice walked to the door and back again. She lay down. She rose up. She walked to the door. The energy was relentless.

✢

Having left it so late, Lorenzo had had difficulty in finding a suitable woman to act as wet nurse, but one was found at last in a village near Prato. She arrived at Careggi in the morning and studied the baby in its cradle. She looked all round the richly decorated room; she looked at the lady surrounded by attendants; she looked again at the living baby, and felt stricken. Two lire a week was no compensation for having given birth herself to a dead infant. She could not feel gratitude, nor did she have the strength to be a pink-cheeked, ample-breasted, jolly fountain of milk. With eyes that could read souls, Clarice stared at the woman.

'Send her away,' she said firmly.

'Madonna! Your baby will starve!'

'Send the baby away with her, then.'

But the woman did not want the Medici baby and hurried from the house in tears.

Monna Lucrezia pleaded with Clarice to feed the baby herself.

269

'Myself?' said Clarice, shocked. It was inconceivable. 'I am an Orsini,' she said.

'You are a Medici!' her mother-in-law thundered, but it made no impression.

Monna Lucrezia took the midwife aside to try and determine what was troubling her daughter-in-law. 'It is an affront to creation for a mother to stand by and watch her baby starve,' she said.

The midwife had seen this sort of thing before and was frightened. 'Please, Madonna,' she said, 'never leave the mother alone with the child.'

The baby began to wail with hunger. Nurses did what they could with ewe's milk on a finger tip or in a bottle, but the hunger of the baby went deeper than for mere food. It knew with the instinct of nature that it had been abandoned by both mother and father.

✢

A servant of the Medici came to my house and knocked urgently on the door. 'Tommaso Maffei, is it true your wife has milk? Lorenzo would see you immediately.'

I found him at the palazzo on the Via Larga.

'Tommaso, I have heard your son was stillborn,' Lorenzo said. He had not summoned me to gush with compassion. 'Your wife has milk?'

'Elena,' I said, shocked, 'is a daughter of the Pazzi family. That family is now ruined, stripped of its arms and all its wealth, but those members who survive retain some pride, besides which she is married to a Maffei, who also has his pride. My wife is no one's wet nurse, Magnifico!'

'This is no ordinary request. I am desperate, Tommaso. My wife is ill with some sickness of the spirit. She has abandoned her own baby. He must be fed, and soon. Please, I beg you, plead with your wife for her help.'

'You would have your son nourished on Pazzi milk?'

Lorenzo flinched. 'Believe me, if I had an alternative, I would take it.'

'So would I,' I replied. We looked at each grimly.

'A Pazzi she may be,' Lorenzo said eventually, 'but she is a woman of virtue and good character. If she can feed my son with such qualities, there is hope for the future.'

My antagonism subsided. The agreement was sealed by an embrace. Then and only then did he remember to commiserate with me.

'All being well, we'll take the child. I shall send word,' I said.

'Take the child? No. It is too dangerous. I will not have my son sent out. Elena must come to us.'

'She is not fit to travel.'

'I will have her carried to Careggi by the most comfortable means.'

'Monna Lucrezia…'

'What of her?'

'I suspect, Magnifico, that your mother will not suffer to have my wife in the house, being of the Pazzi.'

'Then my mother will move here.'

I expected Elena to be furious and refuse. Instead she had a small chest packed and prepared to leave for Careggi.

'One baby is dead. It is enough. If I can be the means of life in another, it will help me, Tommaso, it will help.'

I sent word to Lorenzo.

✢

Clarice stared at the new wet nurse with eyes that can read souls, but she found no resentment there.

'You have lost your baby?' she asked.

Elena nodded.

'I have lost two. The pain never goes.'

'Madonna, if it were not for me you would have lost three. What ails you?'

Clarice leant forward, brought her face very close to Elena's and stared at her. 'Protect my children,' she said urgently.

'Whispering and conspiratorial,' Elena told me later, 'as if she did not want to be overheard by herself.'

That night as she slumbered by the cradle, Elena awoke to a soft noise and found Clarice bending over the baby. He was asleep. With his head lying sideways on the pillow, his profile was cherubic – a great sweep of podgy cheek dwarfing a snubbed nose. His fine eyelashes rested on his cheeks. His ears were tiny, and there were pink veins in his skin. He was new, unsullied and full of trust. Clarice was placing a crucifix on him.

'What is it, Madonna?' Elena asked.

'How dare you sleep?' said Clarice. 'Look after this child. Who knows what harm he will come to?'

After that, Elena took it in turns with Iride to stay up all night and every night.

✝

We buried Emmanuel in the cemetery for the unbaptised. With his son in such mournful ground and his wife at Careggi, Tommaso felt doubly bereft. I did what I could to comfort him but he just sat with his elbows on his knees and his face in his hands. At last he raised his head and stared at me, unshaven, bleary-eyed, hopeless.

'Maria, you are my only comfort. What I am about to say is going to take all my strength.'

'What is it?'

'You cannot stay here. Not alone with me. The law both divine and mundane forbids it.'

I began to shake with anger, for with him I am safe. 'What kind of law is it that would send me back to my cousin?'

'Maria, has Maso… offended you in any way?'

I was too embarrassed to tell him what had happened, but assured him that Maso behaves towards me as a brother. 'But I will not live with him, I will not! Please, find a convent that will take me in. Any will do.'

'Any will not do! Besides, I cannot take such action without Angelo's permission.'

He went to visit Lorenzo, to ask advice about me. I think he wanted me to join Elena in the service of Monna Clarice, but he came back with a different arrangement. I leave this evening to live at the Palazzo de'

Medici and act as a companion to Monna Lucrezia, Lorenzo's mother.

'She is a most marvellous lady,' Tommaso assures me, 'who loves your brother as her own son.'

✛

So, I am here, in a heaven built on earth: halls of marble and pillars of stone, tapestries in red and gold, vases of onyx, ancient statues and modern paintings. Vistas of courtyards and gardens open through doorways and arches. Such unimaginable riches! Coming into this palazzo of the Medici like a beggar girl I shrank into the nearest corner, terrified of such echoing spaces. I expected a servant to take me to Monna Lucrezia but, to my horror, Lorenzo il Magnifico came himself to meet me. He wore a fur-lined gown and a cap, expensive but not ostentatious. There is nothing ostentatious about Lorenzo. He looked at me, head to one side and quizzically, as all do who know Angelo. He seemed amused by my resemblance to his favourite companion. 'What a miracle of God,' he said, 'to send you to my house. You are most welcome, Maria, most welcome.' With that he led me himself to his mother's chamber.

Monna Lucrezia has an extraordinary face with heavily lidded eyes and shallow features, but those eyes! Anyone who tried to deceive her would be making a grave mistake. Her care is not expressed in cheap smiles and easy laughter. She has a solemn demeanour and listens very attentively to you: this is unsmiling love, love of the best kind. She tested me for what I know and, impressed by my skills in reading and writing, made me her secretary. The first letter she handed to me was from Angelo! It was a wonder to see the handwriting of my lost brother, a good hand, attractive if not beautiful (as Tommaso's is) with large and confident capitals. If one may read souls by handwriting, as some would hold, I would say that here was an open, honest man who loves wisdom and jokes in equal measure. He writes of his life at Cafaggiolo without Monna Clarice, saying he has established a republic in which all citizens are treated justly and are thriving.

'Lucrezina sews, sings and reads. Maddelena knocks her head against the wall without hurting herself. Louisa has discovered speech and Contessina has discovered noise,' he reported of Monna Lucrezia's grandchildren. Her eyes shone as I read it to her. 'And the boys?' she asked.

273

'He says that Piero has written his first letter to his father unaided.'

'Oh, Lorenzo will be so pleased with that.'

'And Giovanni, he says, has begun to spell.'

'To spell?' *Such was Monna Lucrezia's surprise that I nearly dropped the letter. I asked her how old the boy is.*

'He is three. Three and two months. To spell? Goodness! I am not sure which is the prodigy, the pupil or the master. What more does he say?'

I read on through the letter, which spoke of Angelo's concern for the welfare of Lorenzo and Florence.

'Yes, yes, that is all very well, but what does he say between the lines?' *she asked.*

'Madonna?'

'Your brother always has much to say between the lines.'

'I cannot read between lines, Madonna.'

'Useless girl. Give it to me.' *Monna Lucrezia took the letter and read between the lines.* 'Peace and justice reign in a world where I am king and Monna Clarice is absent, that is what he says. The children are benefiting from my brilliant tuition and, unfettered by religious superstition, are taking great strides in their studies.'

'Is there anything more?' *I asked, intrigued by her interpretation of white space.*

'Yes. He loves and misses me very much and is as frightened as a child about what the future holds for all of us. Dear Angelo… We must write a reply. Take up your pen.'

And so today I wrote to my brother Angelo, though he does not know it. Monna Lucrezia informed him that his sister was safe and ensconced in the house, but made no mention that it was I who was writing these words. But I tried, as hard as I could, to tell him between the lines.

Monna Clarice I have not met since she resides at the villa on Careggi, but apparently she and Angelo are at war over the education of the children. He would raise them on the ancient poets, and she would raise them on the Christian scriptures. It is Monna Lucrezia's opinion that both are right and that they should work together. I see the wisdom of this, but in my heart I root for Angelo, and so, clearly, does she. I like her very much.

Lorenzo walked in while we were at work, wishing to consult his mother alone on matters regarding Florence.

'What I want to know,' I heard her say as I was leaving the chamber, 'is when are you going to visit your wife?'

'Mother! I am trying to save this city!'

'Your new son is two days old and you have yet to see him.'

I closed the door softly on their wrangling and came to my room.

26

Careggi, March 1479

THE NEW Medici baby stared. Faces came and went. Walls. Edges of cradle. He was so swaddled that only his eyes could move, and his mouth: his nurse's breasts were generous with milk. Her face was kindly. The songs she sang to him were gentle and soothing. The room was warm. The cradle was snug. Yet something warned him that the world of appearances was a devious place and he cried endlessly. Only when a man with eyes full of love bent over his cradle did he stop crying, too occupied suddenly with wonder.

Lorenzo stared into his son's eyes to see if there was any recognition there, for Clarice had conceived two months after his brother's death. It was not impossible – unchristian, perhaps, but not impossible – that his son be the re-embodiment of Giuliano's transmigrated soul. Of course to see Giuliano he had only to look into the eyes of Giuliano's own son, but Lorenzo had put his bastard nephew out to nurse and had not seen him since. The wound was too raw. To have Giulio in the family would be to remind himself constantly that his brother had deceived him, had kept his marriage and his son secret. But on looking into his new son's eyes for the first time, Lorenzo saw what he hoped to see, and pronounced his name.

'Giuliano,' he said. 'He will be called Giuliano.'

Clarice gazed on her husband as if on a stranger. It was six months since she had last seen him and now he stood before her, as strong and striking in his reality as he had been the first time they had met. Was he a handsome man? Yes, he was. His handsomeness lay in his familiarity and his remoteness, in his power and his vulnerability, in his lovely dished nose and permanent frown. She wanted so much to embrace him, but her hands merely fluttered like a pair of doves. At last he was tangible, and she dare not touch him. But nothing could stop the scent of him reaching her, and as she breathed him in, her soul became stained with his colours, and when she spoke, her voice was pitched high, tremulous and apologetic, the sound of the Clarice who was married to Lorenzo de' Medici.

Lorenzo sat by his wife caressing her, running his hand over her shoulders and back as he would a pony that needed to be calmed. He found her strangely agitated. He spoke to her gently of the need for her to return to the safety of Cafaggiolo.

Although she longed to be with her children, Clarice refused.

'No,' she said. 'I will not go. Not while that man is there.'

'Clarice, please…'

She was adamant. She would not go. 'Please let me stay here until I am churched. Please. And you could stay with me. It is such a short ride to the city, you could stay here at Careggi and return to the palazzo each day. '

It was true, he could make the journey each day without trouble. If Lorenzo agreed, however, it was not to please Clarice, but because the strangely torpid atmosphere in the city was benumbing his mind. Here at Careggi he could think more easily. He had his room prepared but, as soon as he was there, his thoughts turned from the war to the woman who so often shared his Careggi bed. He needed comfort. He needed female companionship. As he could not sleep with his wife until after her purification and churching, he must sleep with his mistress, but could it be done with Clarice in the house? When on the following day Lucrezia Donati came to visit Clarice and see the new baby, Lorenzo drew her into his room. A few days later, she visited again, arriving at night and clearly not come to see the new baby.

'Madonna,' Marta whispered to Clarice. 'You should know, your husband has a guest.'

Any colour that may have been in Clarice's pale face drained from it.

'It was a blood letting,' Elena told me the next morning when I visited her on my way to Ficino's. 'She was cupped by the news. She sent everyone away but me. "You, girl," she said. "What do you know of the secret ways of this house?" I said I knew nothing but she would not believe me. In the end I confessed to knowing that there are secret ways, and that I had heard that one leads from the sala to the guardaroba and then on to Lorenzo's studiolo.'

I sucked air in through my teeth.

'Tommaso,' my wife said warningly. 'You must forgive me if I am weak under torture.'

'Torture? Of what kind?'

'Of the most subtle and terrible kind. Do not ask me to describe it. It is in her eyes: the pupils expand and one can do nothing but what one is asked to do. I told her very little – I know very little – only that there is a secret passage. She left me then.'

'Did she use it?'

'Oh, of course she used it. She must have found the studiolo and, I do not know how, but she was able to hear what was going on in Lorenzo's chamber without being seen. Can that be done?'

'Yes, it can be done. Did she tell you everything?'

'No, nothing. She returned some time later, as wan as the risen dead, and told me nothing of what had occurred. But as I was feeding the baby she suddenly asked, "Is it possible that a woman find pleasure in sleeping with a man? So much pleasure that she groans with it?" Imagine such a question, husband, imagine... What has it been like for her all these years?'

'Dutiful,' I replied, abstracted by a thought of the marble bust Lorenzo kept in his studiolo, the perfect likeness of Lucrezia Donati.

'Poor woman,' Elena sighed.

'Poor woman,' I agreed.

'Before my eyes something in her changed. I watched her face hardening, the muscles tensing themselves against the grief. First her mouth became still and taut, then the light gradually went out of her eyes, and I thought, she does not love him any more.'

'I am not sure she ever did.'

'Oh, Tommaso! Of course she did! How can you think otherwise?'

'Because she had no faith in him,' I replied. I was learning fast about the true nature of love. We had been married almost a year and were travelling a path as steep as any described by Dante in *Il Purgatorio*. Each day our hearts were a revelation to both of us. Love is not a feeling or a desire. It cannot be known or understood by the mind, only by the heart. What is Love? It is to think of another before yourself, to want the happiness of another and not your own (although you soon discover that the happiness of the beloved is your own). It is like water, soothing and dissolving all troubles. Elena and I did not live in a romance of happiness but often niggled and grumbled at each other as spouses do; such things, however, are but bubbles popping on the surface of the still pond which is Love. Sometimes we argued and fought, but even as the words of anger were leaving my mouth, Love stood back, watching it all, observing and commenting coolly that none of it was true; and I would know, even as I shouted, that the world had turned upside down but for a little while. Love would soon put it right again, and it did. The upsets and the conflicts were delusions: Love is the only reality. That Love, Ficino told me, is God.

Elena stroked my hair and awoke me from my reflections to tell me further news from the nursery.

'I was telling Iride how wrong Lorenzo is to keep a mistress, but she laughed and said what is wrong with a little harmless fun? She said that all men are the same, even the priests, and take your friend Angelo for an example.'

'What did she mean?'

'Apparently he has been trying to seduce her at Cafaggiolo.'

'That is ridiculous! It is a slave's fantasy! And not any slave, but that one.' Iride, who was not only literate but could dance like Salome, only faster, had been a gift from Lorenzo to his wife. How the two co-existed I could never imagine.

'She says it comes from being brought up on Catullus rather than the Christian scriptures, but apparently he cannot contain himself and is at her like a goat.'

My annoyance boiled over. I blamed womanhood for all the ills of mankind. 'Pandora and her box – the story is an allegory of woman and her mouth. She cannot keep it shut!'

My words hurt Elena but I would not change my mind. 'Gossip is a pernicious evil and I forbid you to indulge it while you are in the Medici household!'

She said she was only repeating what she had been told, and that I am usually happy enough to hear it. How true that was! I sat down with a thump on her bed and, as usual, I turned to Plato to unpick life's knots for me. 'It is all a matter of discrimination,' I told her, once I had thought it through. 'Reason is being able to distinguish the true from the false; what you have just told me was false, and I want you to be able to determine that for yourself.'

She told me that I think too much, that I am impossible to live with and hit me over the head with a pillow. The pillow, poorly made by her own dear hands, burst at the seams and snowed us with feathers.

✠

Ficino received a letter from Monna Lucrezia telling him that she had had reports of 'some mysterious and evil force' that had possessed her daughter-in-law. 'She has, I think, a malady that afflicts the souls of some women after birth, a deep melancholia.' Lucrezia, writing to Ficino as a 'doctor of souls', requested his help.

Ficino put aside his work and went to his astrological charts and ephemeris, unrolling them, studying them with absorption, tracing the heavens with his finger. His eyes became opaque, as they did whenever he was in deep consideration. I waited patiently, reminded of a line in Plato's *Symposium* regarding Socrates: *Let him alone. He has a way of going off sometimes by himself and standing still anywhere he happens to be. He will soon appear; therefore do not disturb him.* The atmosphere began to change, not so much in the room but in my mind. The fire was warmer, the light brighter; all the noisy hubbub of the mind's market place suddenly ceased, plunging me into a golden silence. Ficino considered; I waited.

At last he took a breath and spoke. 'Fetch me my priestly robe and my medical bag.'

While I did this he took various resins and powders from the apothecary jars he kept on a shelf. Frankincense, manna, storax – the oils and essences of fumigation – not the unguents of a physician but those of a theurgist. I helped him put them in phials and place them carefully in a box.

'What do the charts tell you?' I asked.

'They are strangely obscure. I must look within the patient herself to find out what is wrong. "As above, so below," as Hermes says. The macrocosm and the microcosm: one reflects the other. If the large is silent I must investigate the small.'

The philosopher who was a doctor put on his simple black cassock and transformed himself into a priest. Indeed, to the villagers, that is what he was, a local priest. And yet at his house he received letters from all parts of Christendom, from kings, cardinals and princes, asking questions of his wisdom. He gave all the credit to his own teachers – Plato, Socrates, Orpheus, Pythagoras, Hermes, Zoroaster, Plotinus. He spoke of the ancient philosophers as if they still lived, as they did – in him. Just walking beside him was to sense the presence of these great masters. I was convinced that what Clarice suffered from was an adulterous husband and a lack of love, but Ficino was content not to have an opinion before he saw the patient.

✣

At first Monna Clarice refused to receive him. We waited patiently in the antechamber for over an hour. Suddenly, and obviously aware of Ficino's continuing presence, she came out herself to demand to know what he wanted of her. What I saw was an angry and imperious woman; whatever Ficino saw made him recoil in alarm.

'Madonna,' he said, recovering himself. 'Your mother-in-law is concerned about your health and has asked me to see you.'

'There is nothing wrong with my health. Besides, I have my own physician.' Monna Clarice was staring at Ficino's black cassock and the crucifix hanging on his chest; she seemed confused by this image of a priest. Her eyes spoke to her in pictures; her mind spoke to her in words: the two conflicted.

'There is health of the body and health of the mind; for the latter there is nothing a physician can do. But I, a simple priest, may be able to help. You will not reject some prayers to the Lord for your well being?'

'Of course not,' she said doubtfully.

Ficino had trained in the great schools of medicine and was well versed in the apothecary's art, but he believed that the health of the body depends on the health of the mind. He could cure a headache by having a man change his thoughts. His healing arts went further, into realms of the soul, the health of which determined everything, and it was clear even to me that her disturbance was rooted there. He led her to the small chapel in the villa where they could pray together. In response to the instructions Ficino muttered to me, I brought out aromatic incense and the little burner and set light to the charcoal, thinking I was performing a rite of purification, nothing more.

She was still suspicious and wary of him despite the cassock, for here was the man who had taught her husband his heretical philosophy, but as soon as the ritual began she relaxed. She had seen it performed a hundred thousand times in chapel and church, and the scent of frankincense was the familiar one, the odour of sanctity and reassurance. She knelt together with Ficino as he recited prayers familiar to her, continuing at length until the tension had passed from her face and she looked serene. Then he gestured to me and I put storax into the burner and softly passed to him his lyre. Clarice – whose consciousness had sunk to the depths of her being – stirred a little as he began to play and her nose twitched at the unfamiliar odour now coming in clouds from the burner. Ficino sang a few psalms to reassure her, and then, when she was fully quiet again, he intoned a certain hymn in Greek which had a psalmodic metre. Without realising it, Clarice listened to an Orphic hymn addressed to Hera, and grew drowsy.

Kianeois kolpoisin enimein, aeromorfphi,
Era panvasileia, Thios sillektre makaira…
You are ensconsed in darksome hollows, and airy is your form,
O Hera, queen of all and blessed consort of Zeus.
You send soft breezes to mortals, such as nourish the soul, and
O mother of rains, you nurture the winds and give birth to all.
Without you there is neither life nor growth;
And, mixed as you are in the air we venerate, you partake of all,
And of all you are queen and mistress.
You toss and turn with the rushing wind.
May you, O blessed goddess and many-named queen of all,
Come with kindness and joy on your lovely face.

The smoke billowed round the altar and clouded the air of the chapel. Suddenly it was as if it caught fire with candlelight and grew increasingly radiant. I rubbed my eyes, thinking it was some optical trick, but the radiance became a presence in the room.

'Daughter of Saturn and wife of Jupiter,' Ficino said. 'Queen of the gods, mistress of heaven and earth, Hera to the Greeks, Juno to the Latins, what do you want with this woman?'

'She is mine, by virtue of her righteousness and piety.' The deep, sonorous voice came from the lips of Clarice.

'For what purpose?'

'I am forgotten and ignored. After centuries of neglect, men begin to revere the gods again, but whose names do I hear? – why, those of Minerva and Venus! Do you not recall what happened the last time I was passed over, by that incurious worm called Paris?

You mortals sing of it still, how I, the Mother of Mars, destroyed that fair city of Troy. Be warned, Florentine!'

'If we worship Minerva and Venus, it is because we value wisdom and love above mere majesty.'

'You dare, mortal, to say so to me?'

'I do so dare, being Man, and no mere mortal, but immortal and made in the image of God.' And so saying, the diminutive philosopher assumed his own true stature, which was pharaonic, colossal, and above the gods. 'Man,' he said, his own voice strong and resounding 'alone of all created things, is made in the image of the Father. Beasts will ever be beasts; gods will ever be gods; Man alone may ascend to unity with the Godhead.'

The goddess replied, 'I was betrayed by my adulterous husband Jupiter, tortured by him, suspended from heaven by a golden chain and weighted by a heavy anvil. As I suffered, so will you. Earthtreader! Transcend if you can. Be warned, Florentine.'

'Goddess, anger does you no honour.'

'It is the poets who do me no honour. Your poets revile me. Your painters and sculptors ignore me. Be warned, Florentine. I, who destroyed the fleet of Aeneas, who did all I could to prevent his arrival on these shores, will destroy him again, born once more in Lorenzo. I will destroy that faithless creature Aeneas!'

Such was my trembling I thought my very bones would fly apart. Juno! Ideas of Rome, the Pope, conspiracies: so much smoke of the imagination. Juno herself wanted to destroy Lorenzo. Incense was swirling in my brain and I swayed on my feet. Could this be true? How could it not be? It was as if a puppet theatre had been destroyed, leaving you face to face with the puppeteer. Worse, it was as if you could suddenly see the strings in your own being, and who was pulling them.

The conversation was coming to an end: the goddess was withdrawing. 'Your Majesty!' Ficino called to her. 'Promise me you will not harm the infant.'

'The child? It is not the child who is in danger,' said the fading voice.

Clarice's eyes fluttered open. For a moment she was herself, a simple woman, and beautiful in her way, clinging to the form which custom and tradition had forged for her, for without it she believed that she was nothing. On her was written her love of God and her devotion to her children. In her eyes, the scars of her husband's infidelity. But then her eyes grew dark and brilliant: Juno seemed to return.

'Who is in danger?' Ficino asked urgently.

The goddess did not reply. 'Father?' said Clarice, puzzled by the question.

'Forgive me, it was nothing,' he said.

We left the chapel and returned Monna Clarice to her chamber, where Ficino prescribed sedative herbs such as lettuce and lavender that are more gentle than poppy. Elena and I locked eyes, trying to communicate without words. In the end I just shrugged to indicate I would tell her all later. Unsatisfied with this, she came to me.

'You look very pale, husband.'

'Hush, I cannot speak.'

She went back to the cradle, throwing me a quizzical, concerned glance as she went. I determined there and then to find a replacement wet nurse for the child myself and take Elena from this house as soon as I could.

'According to Socrates, everyone has a daemon,' Ficino said as we returned to his house, 'a tutelary spirit as personal guide. Some of us have minor daemons, airy spirits of frantic colour; some of us have middle demons; a few of us have gods.' He was visibly shaken.

'Monna Clarice is possessed by a god?'

'By a goddess.'

'What may be done?'

'Only one action will cure this disease. Lorenzo must be persuaded to renounce his mistress.'

'Ha! Even Hercules could not perform that labour.'

'Nevertheless it must be done. Everything is at risk here. When a king and queen do not love each other, the very mortar of civilisation crumbles. For the sake of this city and this country Lorenzo must heal his marriage.'

27

WHILE THE ARMIES of Rome and Naples rested for the winter, Florence was busy clearing up sludge and drying out houses; by the time the war began again we were exhausted. When at last the cherry and almond trees were snowy with blossom, and the north wind gave way to the west, all over Tuscany camps sprang up like meadow flowers. Running streams of melt-water became horse troughs and baths. Pine forests were cut down to fuel cooking fires, make siege ladders and engines. Everywhere the call of mating birds was drowned out by the sound of drums and soldiers' curses. With the renewal of hostilities, panic took Florence in the form of a peculiar languor. No one had the energy or motivation for work; soon the masters of the wool and silk factories began to lock out their workers.

Lorenzo knew. No amount of self-confidence or public bravado could hide the truth; he was losing; this renewal of the war would be the last one. He sent ambassadors to Milan and Venice begging for more help but none came and in March our stronghold of Poggio Imperiale fell. The soldiers had become careless; after successfully storming the Sienese town of Casole, they fastened on the spoils like carrion crows, only to become themselves easy prey for eagles: the Neapolitans rushed on the fortress and took it without a fight. Now all that stood between Florence and the Dukes of Calabria and Urbino were sixteen miles and the demoralised remnants of a defeated army.

Monna Clarice spent the two months of confinement at the villa on Careggi. Lorenzo changed his mind about living at the villa and returned to his house in Florence. That he was not pursued by a flow of letters encouraging him to visit was not something he noticed: his attention was wholly on the war. There was a brief reversal of fortune when one of our captains – a mere count – went into the territory of Perugia and utterly routed the Papal troops. The next easy, obvious step was to break up the forces of the Neapolitan army led by the Duke of Calabria and Prince Federigo. But Ercole d' Este, our grand Duke of Ferrara, insisted the task was his and promptly took no action. Thus our victory turned out to be but a gleam of sunlight in an otherwise leaden sky.

✝

Monna Clarice returned to Cafaggiolo, taking her possessions, her servants and my Elena. I had tried to see Lorenzo, to ask him if he would allow me to find a new wet nurse but had been told il Magnifico was too busy to see me. With Ficino's permission, I accompanied the party on its journey, for Angelo needed to be warned of the nature of his opponent, and it was not something I chose to do by letter.

✝

Sitting on the flowery lawn of the garden and hugging their knees, Lorenzo's children listened to the master tell his tales of old, stories of the gods and the heroes, of battles and of glory. Told first in the surging rhythm of Latin verse, and then in Tuscan rhymes, the stories danced in the air and filled their minds with pictures. The green hills and soft valleys, the burbling streams, the river nymphs and tree spirits, the sound of distant pipes, the rustle of oaks in the breeze: this Arcadia, this land of shepherds more ancient than the moon, this kingdom of Pan, seemed to be the true land-scape of the mind in which the children ran. Angelo realised that the places he had visited in his boyhood dreams were still there, and that his pupils were now running through those same sweet glades, a quiver of arrows across their backs, bows gripped in their strong young hands. The Golden Age. For a moment he thought he could hear the pipes himself. But then the sweet, distant music was overcome by disturbance in the house. They could hear the portcullis creaking; voices shouting; servants running.

The children opened their eyes and stared at the tutor, as if for a moment they did not know where they were. Then suddenly it dawned on them what was happening and they rushed into the house, to the courtyard, the older ones scooping up the younger ones to run with them. Their enthusiasm evaporated in the sight of their mother. The girls stood demurely in her presence while Piero drew back and stood in the shadows of the arcade. Only Giovanni toddled forwards, arms outstretched in greeting.

'Please, take me to my room,' Monna Clarice said wearily to the chief servant who had come out from the house. Giovanni toddled after her.

'Stay,' Clarice told him, as if he were a dog. 'Children, you may visit your mother later. For now she is very tired.'

As she passed Angelo, he bowed briefly and hoped Madonna had had a safe journey. She ignored his question. He turned and, registering my presence, and then Elena's, came over swiftly to help my wife down from the wagon.

'This is not good,' he said to me privately. 'Take your wife home at once.'

'If only I could.'

While the children gathered round Elena to see their new brother, Angelo drew me out to the garden, an apron of land that had been carved from ebullient nature and tamed. Against a back-drop of wild forest there were six square beds edged with box and separated by gravel paths. Here herbs were thrusting into new life, rose bushes were in bud and bees were droning among the orange and lemon trees in huge terracotta pots that had been brought out from the orangery. A strong scent of pine wafted across from the forest and wood-smoke from the monastery was curling above the trees in a single, spiralling column. The monastery bell began to toll for vespers.

'It is the wood of the imagination, is it not?' he said, staring at the mixture of dark pines and trees in fresh, bright leaf. 'One almost expects the Green Knight to come trotting out at any time, to fling down his gauntlet and demand a joust. The Christian imagination – an overgrown tangle full of beasts and strange men. I prefer the pagan world and its Arcadia of grazed upland meadows, but do not tell Madonna.'

'I think she already knows, Angelo.'

We both laughed then.

'Oh, it is so good to have your company. Now tell me everything, but first, if I may be selfish, tell me about my sister. Is she happy with Monna Lucrezia? Of course she must be. Monna Lucrezia's secretary has changed. Is it my sister's own hand I am reading? Tell me how she looks, and of her character. It is strange to have close kin whose face I cannot even imagine.'

'Look in a mirror.'

'That close?'

'You would be twins if years did not separate you.'

'Why has Monna Lucrezia taken her in? What happened to Maso?'

'We took care of Maria during the flood, but I was not happy to return her to your cousin.'

'Why not?'

'Something happened, Maria will not say what, but Elena believes she was attacked.'

'By *Maso?*'

'No, I think not. He may be a barbarian, as Lorenzo says, but with regard to his family and your sister he seems to behave well enough. But Angelo, he is an arms dealer, a brawler and a drunkard. Do you want your sister to live with him?'

'We must find her a new convent as soon as we can.'

'Or a husband.'

'Ha! How could I afford a dowry? Even the state fund cannot help, since Lorenzo has drained it dry. But tell me more about her.'

And so, as we walked in the garden, treading gravel and camomile underfoot, I described his sister to him, her lack of feminine beauty, her lack of feminine grace, her very unfeminine intelligence and her altogether masculine courage.

'You paint a very monster!'

'I have no skills in portraiture. But of all the people in the world, she is one of the few I am happy to have beneath my roof. She is intriguing, stimulating, challenging company. Her presence during Elena's travail saved us from insanity. And when she met Ficino…'

Angelo looked startled at the thought of one of his kin meeting Ficino.

'It would be too strong to say like to like. But think of Diotima and Socrates: the wise woman meeting the wise man. Or Sheba and Solomon. Not the same, but exceedingly complementary.'

'Maria is a wise woman?'

'No, of course not. She is only sixteen and as green as this season. But she loves learning. It is my belief that neither the cloistered nor the marital life is right for her.'

'What other option is there? Unless it be living as a sibyl in a cave with scorpions.'

'Apart from the scorpions, I think that would be her preferred choice,' I said, and left it at that. We moved on to discuss Lorenzo, his exhaustion and apparent loss of heart. I told Angelo about the floods, the famine, the plague which is forever flaring up and dying down but never disappearing. Worst of all, Lorenzo's enemies within Florence were beginning to emerge like the armed men that grew from the dragon's teeth sown by Cadmus, rival families who welcomed the war if it meant a fall of the Medici.

'This throws my problems into deep perspective. Imagine converging lines drawn by Brunelleschi or Alberti and, do you see there in the distance, that little blob close to the vanishing point? That is the size of my concerns when compared to those of Lorenzo depicted in the foreground.'

'Some painters put the crucifixion of Christ into the background.'

He laughed merrily. 'Thank you for being a true friend, but it is not that bad!'

'Angelo, your troubles are worse than even you suppose.'

I told him, as carefully as I could, of what Ficino had discovered in his examination of the soul of Monna Clarice. Poor Angelo Poliziano. He looked as stricken and hopeless as any hero of Greek drama who knows his fate.

'Is this true?' he asked.

'As true as anything one must take on faith. You believe Ficino as we all do when he instructs us in the ways of Truth. Believe him now.'

Angelo paced up and down, reflecting on what I had told him. 'The goddess is right – we do neglect her. I cannot remember mentioning her once in my poetry. What is to be done?'

'Ficino says you must be exceptionally vigilant, that your morals must be above reproach, for she is the goddess of purity.'

'My morals? What else can my morals be in a place such as this? It would be easier to sin in a hermitage.'

I told him then of a rumour about himself and Iride, the slave, and his reaction was such that I was convinced that it was false.

'Where have you heard such things?' he demanded.

'It is the gossip of the nursery, Angelo, a very hotbed of rumour and speculation. Elena of course is party to it all now.'

He shuddered. 'Have you come here to realise my worst fears?'

I apologised. 'With regard to the goddess, Ficino advises you not to struggle. He says the battle is between the husband and the wife and you should not get in the way.'

He gripped my arm. 'You are not going to leave me here alone, are you?'

'I must.'

'At least stay the night!'

'One night only.'

We returned to the house. Monna Clarice was in her room and seemed content to keep her distance from Poliziano. Discovering that he had been tutoring little Giovanni in her absence, she merely sent Ser Alberto Malerba with a message to say that, though she was grateful to Poliziano for his care of her children, she would be instructing Giovanni from now on.

'Whatever you wish, goddess,' Angelo muttered.

I congratulated him on his surrender.

✢

That evening Clarice took the children through the rosary. They knelt on the hard floor of the chapel as their mother clicked the beads, saying together five Paternosters, ten Hail Marys, the Five Sorrowful Mysteries, another decade of Hail Marys followed by the Five Joyful Mysteries, followed by ten more Hail Marys. When, after an interminable time, Clarice came to that wonderful bead that was the last bead, to the horror of her children she began again. Maddelena began to weep from the pain in her knees; at the next recital of the Five Sorrowful Mysteries, Lucrezina swooned.

Elena told me the story later. 'I was in the nursery when Iride came in with this sad troop of children. We had such trouble getting them to bed, and when Angelo stepped in to say goodnight, Piero flung himself into his arms and wept. It was the most pathetic sight. Angelo was very angry and wanted to know why religion uses truth as a mace.'

'Quite. Good question.'

'Those poor little cubs. What is wrong with Monna Clarice? You know something you haven't told me.'

I told her that the mistress was beset by a Saturnine humour of the blood. Elena said that her ability to distinguish between the true and the false was improving with practice, and that I was lying. 'And I know I am not to repeat gossip, but this is something I saw for myself rather than heard from another: when Angelo left the nursery, the gaze he exchanged with Iride was not, well, not indifferent.'

'Elena! Stop this! It is not true. She means nothing to him.'

I got out of bed to close the shutters, for the moon was very bright and in my eyes. Below in the garden I saw two figures

291

walking together, light of step and playful. She was circling him, laughing and teasing him. I closed the shutters with a power of discrimination I did not know I possessed. Whatever was occurring between Angelo and Iride was none of our business. I apologised to my wife and said perhaps things were happening that deserved blind eyes.

Early the next morning Angelo sought me out. I asked him if he had slept well – a natural enquiry, one I always make – and he said he had barely slept at all. 'I got to bed rather late – reading, as usual – and fell asleep at once. But then the moon moved across my window and turned my dreams silver. And in my dreams came a voice, telling me to open my eyes very carefully, for there was someone in my room. And it was true. There was.'

'Iride came to your room?' I gasped.

'Iride? No. Madonna Clarice! I opened my eyes slightly and there she stood staring at me with white eyeballs. The desire, the need, to cover my nakedness was almost impossible to overcome, but I knew I must not move, that I must feign sleep the best I could. And then she started whispering like a ghost.'

This was the man who had taught me not to be frivolous in my figures of speech; the least I could do was remind him of the lesson. 'Since ghosts do not exist, they cannot be said to whisper.'

'She whispered like a demoness, then, or a witch, whispered to herself, asking God to forgive my sins. She whispered. It was the most dreadful sound, Tommaso. Outside an owl was hooting, and a wolf howled in the distance, but in my room there was this rustling, sibilant speech of a woman praying for my soul, and I don't think I have ever been so scared. And then, and then…'

'There is more?' I began to wonder if this were one of Angelo's jokes, being spun out in response to my banal enquiry as to his night's repose.

'I was sprawled on my bed. My limbs, you have to understand, were in a very happy and abandoned state of relaxation…'

'That relaxed and blissful condition that is a consequence of reading late?'

'Exactly so.'

'No wonder you love study.'

He cuffed me. 'Do you want to hear this or not? Listen. My arms were flung wide across the mattress like this, and she touched me, here, stroked my arm.'

'This is a joke, Angelo!'

'It is not, I swear it. She stroked my arm and hand, and she repeated my name over and over again, only – and this is the strangest part – it was not my name, it was Lorenzo's. Lorenzo, she said, Lorenzo, Lorenzo, Lorenzo. Have I not been a good wife to you, my lord? she asked. Have I not borne you sons? Have I not risked the pain of death nine times to bring your children into the world? And is this how you reward me – with infidelity? You, a Christian by your own reckoning, breaking the commandment: Thou shalt not commit adultery. Those are the words of our Lord, and you break them nightly under our roof. Lorenzo! LORENZO! Everything that befalls us happens because of you and your sin!'

I was already jumping like a cricket when Angelo delivered the denouement. 'She was asleep. Throughout it all, she was asleep. Her eyes quite rolled up in her head. God knows how she found her way through the house in that condition.'

'You are lying!' I cried. 'By all my powers of discrimination, this is one of your jokes, and quite the worst I have ever heard!'

I told Elena the fantastic story that Angelo Poliziano had told me, and what a wonderful storyteller he was.

'That was no story,' she said. 'It was true. It is well known that Clarice is walking in her sleep.'

I was agitated and alarmed. Like Bishop Gentile before me, I suddenly considered war and plague to be preferable to being in this place. At least in Florence one had some chance of survival. However, when I told Elena we were leaving, as soon as I had found a replacement wet nurse, she persuaded me I had nothing to fear on her behalf.

'There is something I have not told you,' she said. 'It pleases me to feed little Giuliano. Without him I would have known only despair these past months. The smell of a baby, Tommaso… I know he is not my own, but it is so much better than nothing. Besides, his mother will not touch him and he needs me.'

The next morning, when I took leave of my wife, I clung overlong to her, burying my face in her hair, breathing her in, impressing the image of her warmth and scent on my soul.

28

Cafaggiolo, May 1479

ANGELO'S RESOLVE not to battle with Monna Clarice did not, could not last. In the months of her absence, Giovanni's progress had been rapid; he had taken strides in language that seemed impossible for such a small child, and was able to identify all the letters, pronounce all the syllables and read quite a few words by himself. Angelo became desperate to encourage reason in the woman of faith. If only Clarice would listen to her son reciting a few lines of Latin, and hear how the language of Cicero sounds on the tongue of infants, how ripe, how full-bodied vowels are in young mouths, surely her own heart would leap with delight and she would understand. After a few weeks had passed, he went to see her, resolved to attempt calm discussion. But he entered her chamber to find Giovanni, his little prodigy, reading aloud from the Psalter, struggling over holy words in a debased tongue and clearly miserable, not because of the words but because of the lack of enthusiasm and intelligence in Malerba, who was reading with him. All Angelo's prior rehearsals in diplomatic, not to say sycophantic persuasion, vanished. He walked into her chamber, took one look at Giovanni and said, 'Stop this torture of a child. I do not approve!'

'Of the Psalter?' cried Monna Clarice, aghast.

'Of course not! You misunderstand… You need to know about

this translation. It will geld the boy, cauterize his enthusiasm, castrate his love of language.'

'Get out! Get out of my room! Apostate! Heretic!'

Elena said that Piero, who had come in with his tutor, burst into tears. Ser Alberto Malerba scratched the spots on his face nervously and began to intone a prayer for the tutor's soul, that he be forgiven for his blasphemy.

'Religion is in the deed and not in the word, Madonna!' Angelo shouted. Piero's wailing grew louder. 'It is my duty and intention to educate your sons, and I mean to do it, to raise them to be men, but you obstruct me at every step. You throw yourself between Man and God and the shadows of ignorance lengthen because of you. You obliterate the sun of knowledge. You, you stupid woman, create misery and unhappiness wherever you go. And do you wonder your husband does not love you?'

At this she began to scream to drown out his words. Piero and the other children began to scream with her.

'Get out of this house!' she yelled. 'Get out, get out, get out! I cannot *bear* to have you here. You proud, conceited slug! You are the source of all that is wrong. You have corrupted my husband, turned him against me. You are jealous, envious, you want him entirely for yourself, you snatch his attention, you beguile him. You catamite! You foul, disgusting, aberration of nature!'

Angelo took a step back in shock and laughed nervously. 'Is that what you believe? Then you are lost to all reason. Lost. You poor, pathetic creature.'

'*Get out!*'

'You do not have that power.'

'*Power?*' Clarice screamed. 'You are speaking to an Orsini!'.

'What, would you wield your name? To frighten me? A mere name? That is your real objection to me, isn't it? That I am an Ambrogini, a family with no titles and no wealth. That your husband favours me, an orphan and a beggar, is beyond your comprehension. And so you would destroy me, because I offend you.'

And then, Elena wrote, Clarice lifted her head, straightened her back and grew in height. She began to speak thunderously in a voice which, deep and sonorous, demanded obedience. 'She commanded him to leave the room, commanded him in such a way he could only obey and creep out backwards like a beaten dog. Queenly? She was magnificent! She certainly showed him the difference between noble and commoner. The rest of us present began to tremble violently, as if we had been the ones to be reminded of our baseness. Piero tried to run after his master but Malerba scooped him up. The boy struggled like a squealing piglet but soon enough he tired and slumped into moody acquiescence. It is the children I fear for most in all this, husband. They are being torn apart by people claiming to care for them.'

Thus she wrote to me, adding as a postscript, 'Come as quickly as you can, on any pretext, to this dreadful house.' The letter came with the morning courier and I was at Cafaggiolo by nightfall. Everyone had already retired by the time I arrived. I found Elena in her room and she told me that during the day there had been peace of a kind. She apologised for frightening me and making me ride over the mountains for no reason. Glad of her mistake, and needing no apologies, I took her to bed. Just to be beside her brought me an infinite peace that no amount of Plato study could bring. Accuse me of being uxorious if you will, but I happened to find a repose of the soul in the company of my wife. Was it so strange, therefore, that I wished always to be with her? She completed me. Without her I was, I am, a shadow man, a man without substance, a homunculus in a bottle. Elena made me realise my own stature; Elena fulfilled me. I forgot about the house and its troubles and thanked the Lord for this opportunity to be with my beloved. We stayed awake most of the night, but just as I was sinking into blissful sleep there came a scream that could pierce chain mail. Elena and I sat upright as one.

'It is the Madonna!'

How quick is the mind, and how communal. Before our hearts had taken another beat we had both presumed Clarice was being murdered and that it was Angelo doing the deed.

'Oh God! Oh God!' Elena cried, running round the room and doing foolish things like putting on my hat. Equally incapable of doing anything as straightforward as dressing, I ran out as I was, with my shoes in my hands for some reason, shouting to her to remain in the room.

Other servants were coming from their beds, the bravest running, the majority hanging back. As I followed the ear-splitting sounds, I became aware that I was not running towards the Madonna's room but away from it, to the far side of the house, to Angelo's room. I careered past maids and serving girls huddled in curious groups, turned corners, cannoned into frozen attendants. I was the first into his room, but before I could close the door enough servants had squeezed in behind me to ensure a scandal.

The moon large in the window illuminated everything: the Madonna, holding the bed sheet and screaming because she could not help it, because she could not stop, pulling on her son's arms, dragging him from the bed of a man who was making just as much noise, only roaring in protest, hollering incoherently as he scrabbled for his clothes, as frantic as a grub under a lifted stone. I took hold of Monna Clarice and tried to calm her down. She was all sinew and tension – in shock and beyond speech, and yet communicating. How often she had tried to warn us, and we had not listened.

What I saw when I entered the room was near enough what Clarice had seen: her son in bed with the tutor. That is what everyone saw who came into the room. The physician attending the Madonna pushed his way through the crowd, expressed outrage and bundled his patient away. Half awake, stunned and trembling, Piero stood weeping in a warm puddle of his own urine. I stooped down to comfort the boy the best I could.

'Bring him!' Monna Clarice cried behind her. 'Bring my son away!'

I gave him to one of the servants and ordered everyone back to their beds. Marta, who was the last of them to leave, turned and spat at Angelo, a dismissive expulsion of saliva that a galley-slave would have admired. Which left me with Angelo. My face must have betrayed my feelings.

'Well?' he said, staring at me. 'What do you think happened here?'

'I do not know,' I said curtly. 'It is between you and God and not for me to pass judgement.'

'I thought I could trust you at least.'

'So what did happen?'

'I do not know! I woke up like everyone else to the shrieks of that Maenad. Dear God, that sound will go with me to my grave. Piero was in bed with me. That is what happened.'

'For what reason?'

'Ask *him!*' Angelo shouted. 'I was oblivious to it until I woke up!'

I told him to get dressed and wait for me; I would be back presently.

Returning to Elena, I laid out everything that had happened as if it were a puzzle for her to solve.

'But I am only the novice in discrimination,' she protested. 'You are the expert, being a man. You tell me if he is guilty or innocent.'

'I cannot! I do not know! But you know – you can make these judgements without knowing.'

'Yes I can – and that is the difference between male and female reason.'

'So? Is he guilty or innocent?"

Elena reflected a while then said, 'If I were a little boy and scared at night, I know where I would go for comfort: to the one who stands in my father's place. It is obvious. But everyone else is going with the evidence of their eyes and the accusations of Monna Clarice. And you? You are thinking the same way as the crowd.'

'It is the middle of the night. I do not know what to think.'

'Well a pox on you and your reasoning. You fail him as a friend. Get back to him. Right away. Go. Now, Tommaso! Why do you hesitate?'

'They are going to throw him out. If I take this step, I shall be thrown out with him and most likely lose the favour of the Medici.'

'How do you have time for such considerations? Go!'

'What about you?'

'I shall pack your bag.'

'Only I am to be expelled then?'

'They have no argument with me, they need me, and at least one of us is going to have to earn some money.'

When women think, they certainly think quickly. I felt several paces behind events as I retraced my steps. I found Angelo arguing with the chief steward, saying he was very willing to leave, but not until morning.

'It is morning, near enough,' I said. 'Come, I shall go with you.'

'What made you change you mind?' he asked bitterly, stuffing clothes into a travelling chest.

'The truth, once I could see it for what it was. I am sorry, I was blinded by my senses.'

I went to fetch his books and papers from the library but a guard at the door turned me away, saying that no one was to enter by order of Monna Clarice. 'The witch has her revenge,' I thought. Angelo's fury, when I told him, was such that I had to restrain him from going to Clarice's chamber.

'But my work!' he shouted. 'How can she possibly confiscate my own work? My poetry! My translations! This is madness, insanity!'

'We shall have everything sent on later,' I assured him, 'when things are calmer here.'

While he packed the few meagre possessions he happened to have in his room, I went to say my farewell to Elena before meeting him in the courtyard. The house was alive with whispers and what servants I met stared at me with knowing eyes. Wherever I went I interrupted conversations and the echo of whispers hung in the air until I had passed. Then came the sound of Angelo shouting in the courtyard, so violent, so amplified by the walls, that it silenced the crowing of cocks. By the time I got there, dawn was fingering its way over the garden and into the house but there was no chorus of birds that morning. All nature was listening. There were two men in the courtyard and one horse, which was mine. The factor was standing, arms crossed, implacable in the face of Angelo's rage.

'Those are my orders,' he said, and obviously not for the first time.

'She cannot possibly claim to own my own horse!'

'The Madonna says *all* your possessions belong to the Medici.'

'But not including my horse! My notebooks! Here, will you take my clothes? Take my clothes why don't you? Take my skin, flesh and bone. You have my heart – you may as well take the rest, since everything I possess belongs to the Medici! How do you expect me to live?'

I mounted my horse and held out a hand to him. 'Come on. You cannot reason with unreason. Come with me.'

His rage collapsing into hopeless resignation, he mounted pillion behind me. We crossed the drawbridge and before we reached the road the heavy oak doors of the gate were closed. Angelo, reliving his expulsion from Montepulciano at the age of nine, laid his head heavily on my back. I rode on steadily, saying nothing. The sun was rising on fields brilliant with green corn and scarlet poppies. Larks were singing in the sky. The wayside verges were full of white campion and cowparsley. But Angelo Poliziano was blind to such beauty, one fearful question so dominant that it blotted out the sun of his intellect: which of the two was Lorenzo going to believe, his friend or his wife?

29

Careggi, May 1479

IN FEAR OF the answer to that question, Angelo could not return to Florence; we went instead to the villa at Careggi where Monna Lucrezia was now resident, for in this world of surrogate parents, she was his mother more certainly than his own. Hearing that Angelo Poliziano had arrived unexpectedly and awaited her in the courtyard below, Monna Lucrezia hurried from her room. From the gallery she looked down on a man come back from battle, his head bowed, his spirit broken, his flame snuffed out. 'Oh!' her hands flew to her mouth. 'Angelo?' The noble, aloof mother of Lorenzo flung all reserve aside. Her boy was hurt; her feet were winged; she ran down the stairs.

'What is it? What has happened? Who has done this to you?' She gave a volley of orders: bath to be filled, barber to be called for, fresh clothes of Lorenzo's to be laid out, hot food to be taken to Lorenzo's room, which was to be prepared for Master Angelo.

Angelo protested. 'Please – do not be so generous, not until you have heard me and believed my story. I could not bear it.'

She took him travel-stained and unshaven to her own chamber.

'When Lorenzo and Giuliano were little boys,' he said, as soon as they were settled, 'did they ever sleep with you?'

'Of course.'

'It is a natural thing for children to do, especially when scared?'

'More natural for them to be with their nurse, but yes, of course it is natural.'

'And if my position at Cafaggiolo was as another Lorenzo, would it still be natural?'

'What are you saying? Dear God! Was it Lucrezina? Maddelena? Oh God! What are you trying to tell me?"

'It was Piero. I woke up, and there he was. Unfortunately it was his mother that woke me. She tours the house each night under the guise of sleep walking.' Angelo took Monna Lucrezia's hands in his own. She flinched but did not withdraw them. 'If ever I have spoken the truth to you, Madonna, I speak it now. If I love Piero, it is as my own son and in no other way. He is very scared and upset by his mother's strange moods, and I suppose it seemed to him a natural thing to do, to come to my bed and curl up by my side. The cat does it. Why shouldn't he? Perhaps he could not sleep in his own bed, and in the middle of the night the idea seemed to him a good one. Please, help me. Speak to Lorenzo. Tell him the truth of what has happened.'

'You must tell him yourself, and face to face, as soon as you can. A letter from Clarice will be with him already.'

'Will you secure me an interview with him?'

'I shall write to him at once. And so shall you.' Monna Lucrezia turned to a servant and asked for her secretary. Maria came to the call.

✝

What a deceiver is the imagination! All my life I have dreamt of him, my older brother, as lithe, tanned, invincible in the face of the world. My hero and protector. There was noise in the courtyard this morning but I did not know who it was until I was called to Monna Lucrezia. There he sat, myself in a man's form, haggard and broken. His eyes, seeing me, filled with shame and horror that we should be meeting now. The reason why he has been expelled from his position they would not tell me, but I did not need to be told, for I know that the root of it is Monna Clarice and her hatred. Oh, how I have dreamed of this meeting! Always the same dream. I would fling myself into his arms, sobbing with relief, and feel the returning pressure of his own embrace. Broken bonds would retie into a pretty bow. In reality? He was so frozen and embarrassed it was for me to offer him reassurance. His embarrassment became my own and we stood either side of a gulf. The presence of dear Tommaso helped, for he encouraged me with his eyes and gave a gentle nod as if to say, 'Step over the divide. It is for you to do it. He needs you.'

So I did. I crossed the marble floor to where he sat and put my hand on his bowed head. He grasped hold of me and buried his head in me. He was as a shuddering sparrow in my hands. What could I do but kiss him on the head? Love that is deeper than any filial affection flowed out of me and into him and soothed his trembling away. He came to himself with a sigh and looked up at me. I held his face, which is my own face.

'Two peas from the same pod,' said Monna Lucrezia. Our laughter broke the spell of the moment and, as Angelo drew me down to sit on his knees, I became his little sister. We considered each other in wonder.

'You need a shave,' I told him.

'Come, Maria,' said my mistress. 'There is work to do, letters to write, truth to be told.'

30

Careggi, May 1479

THE FOLLOWING morning I was deputed to deliver the letters to Lorenzo in person, but first I went to see Ficino. There was a cold north wind that morning. Ficino's villa was strangely quiet, not with the sweet silence that usually emanated from the place, but with the dusty silence of abandonment. The door was open. On the desk was a page from Plato, half-written in Ficino's own hand, the quill left on the parchment where he had set it down. Dregs of wine in the bottom of a glass were dry and caked: there had been no one here for at least two days. Ficino's mother lived in the house, an aged woman we rarely saw, but who kept to her room with a servant as companion. I knocked on her door; there was no reply. Becoming agitated and fearful, I started to run through the house calling Ficino's name. There was no one to be found any-where. At last I flew out of the place crying, as if God had gone missing from his heaven. The gardener found me and shook me back to myself. I gulped air and laughed, thinking my fears had been misplaced as usual, but the gardener looked sombre. 'He has been arrested,' he said.

'For what reason? With what is he charged?'

'The murder of Giuliano de' Medici.'

✝

Lorenzo was in the Grand Sala of the Palazzo della Signoria, sitting in conference with the red-gowned priors under huge wall paintings of the state's glorious victories in battle. To look at the walls one would think war a noble fight for justice, aided by divine powers and heavenly signs. Lorenzo was grey with tiredness. Everyone had advice to offer. Messengers arrived in a stream with news and letters. Unable to get near him, I had to be content with his secretary, Niccolò Michelozzi, who told me that the anticipated onslaught had not come. The sixteen miles between the enemy and Florence remained untraversed, and the Duke of Calabria, having as little will as the Duke of Ferrara to bring such a profitable a war to an end, had set up a siege at Colle. The Florentines had sent the Duke of Ferrara to meet him, but 'we may as well have sent a tortoise.' Dancing behind the drum and pipe, Este's men were making their colourful way through Tuscan valleys that did not lead to Colle. All was as expected, but then, to everyone's surprise, and quite contrary to the rules of modern warfare, the people of Colle, under the leadership of a Venetian captain, had begun to defend themselves and spiritedly. Again and again the forces of Rome and Naples threw themselves against the walls only to be repulsed. Goliath beaten by a boy even smaller than David. The name 'Colle' had become a rallying call to the Florentines. Without doubt the place would be glorified in a fresco in time to come. By Lorenzo's side was Bartolommeo Scala, informing him of military progress, giving practical advice for the support of troops and relief of towns. Lorenzo seemed to depend on him entirely.

I learnt from Niccolò Michelozzi that Ficino was attending a secular inquisition, set up by Scala to discover who in Florence had been involved in the conspiracy of the Pazzi.

'They cannot possibly suspect him!'

'At least three of the murderers were friends of his, ex-pupils and fellow Platonists. How can they not suspect him? The Duke of Milan was murdered by the disciples of a teacher. Seen through certain eyes, this case is not so different.'

'It is utterly different and you know it.'

'Tommaso, Lorenzo has to be seen to be fair. It is for form's sake only that Scala has called Ficino in, as so many have been called

304

before him. Have you lost your trust in Lorenzo in so short a time?'

'To trust anything in this world is to place your faith in quicksand. Where is Ficino being questioned?'

'Here in the Palazzo della Signoria, downstairs.'

'Niccolò,' I said, 'can you see Lorenzo gets these letters from his mother and Poliziano? They are very urgent.'

'His mother. Poliziano. I shall put them with the several from his wife that arrived earlier,' he said, making a great display of the fullness of the satchel he wore over his shoulder. 'What is going on at Cafaggiolo. Has something happened?'

Now if there is a community more prone to gossip and rumour than a nursery, it is that of the companions of a lord. As soon as Lorenzo's brigata got wind of Angelo's humiliation, they would be baying.

'Nothing,' I lied to Niccolò Michelozzi. 'Nothing has happened.' I tried to retrieve the letters, wanting to deliver them myself into the hands of Lorenzo, but Niccolò would not let me have them.

My imagination in chaos, I ran downstairs to the dungeons in the basement, expecting to hear Ficino screaming as they turned the wheel of the rack. What I found instead was my master leaving his cell walking unaided and obviously unhurt, having been moderately questioned by a tribunal of judges. But his face, his face – I had never seen it set so hard with anger. He brushed past me. Not so easily dismissed, I fell into step with him, keeping silent. As we came into the large and marble-blazoned courtyard of the Palazzo della Signoria, we met Lorenzo and his entourage coming towards us.

'Marsilio!' said Lorenzo, but was cut dead by the glaring, hostile eyes of his erstwhile tutor.

'Marsilio…' he said, placatingly.

'Do not speak to me!'

Lorenzo looked like a beekeeper swarmed by his own hive.

I wanted to shout, 'Do not fight each other! It is what the enemy wants!' but it was not my place to do so. I ran after Ficino, determined to stay with him no matter how hard he tried to shake me off.

'I believed in him, believed in him,' he said at last, as we approached his town house. 'I raised him!' In this house, in the district of Santa Maria Nuova, was his mother, along with his servants. 'He was my pupil. I raised him up to be a man, a good man, a philosopher and a poet. And now this! He throws me into gaol, accusing me of murder.'

'It was just a tribunal, Father, to gather information.'

'How could he suspect me?'

'How could he not? Archbishop Salviati was your patron, the Pazzi your friends.'

'They were his friends, too. But does he interrogate himself?'

It is easy with hindsight to see the villains; at the time they were faces in a confusion of friends, or men pretending to be friends. How could we tell? I was as guilty as anyone for colluding with the enemy, more so since I was a brother of the one who had tried to murder Lorenzo, and I had suffered my own arrest and examination the day after the attack. That I live is entirely due to Lorenzo de' Medici who, in his generosity, put the Maffei under his protection. If I had ever loved him before, it was never as much as I loved him then, and no one, not even Marsilio Ficino, could turn my heart against him now. I stood firm and would not be swayed even as Ficino continued to vent his anger.

'Whatever you think,' I told him, 'Lorenzo is still a good man, and it is all due to the power of your teaching and example.'

'Then why is he acting like this?'

'The order was Scala's,' I said, 'not Lorenzo's. Listen Father, Angelo has met the trouble you anticipated.'

'What has happened?'

I could not say. 'Please, Lorenzo must know first. Forgive me.'

Ficino nodded, and thanked me somewhat ruefully for bringing him back to himself. I ran off blushing: the world was truly upside down. Catching up with Lorenzo as he settled himself at his desk in the Palazzo de' Medici, I coincided with a messenger from

Germany with yet more letters. Lorenzo took both his and Michelozzi's packets at once, to shuffle through international and domestic news together.

'Where is Riario?' he asked absently of those advisers who crowded round him. 'No one mentioned him in the council.' There was no answer. He looked up. 'Well? Where is the Count of Imola?'

Girolamo Riario, so-called nephew of the Pope, and the man behind the plot to kill the Medici, was the one Lorenzo feared most. No one knew where he was. The Roman army that he captained had disappeared.

'What do you mean, disappeared?'

It was thought the army was somewhere in the mountains.

'Which mountains?' Lorenzo snapped, opening a letter from his wife pressed upon him by Niccolò Michelozzi. Written by Ser Malerba, it was two pages of inarticulate emotion expressed in turgid prose. I was astonished and most relieved to see him screw the letter up and throw it on the fire behind him. 'Which mountains?' he repeated, his voice growing harsh. But there were many mountains between Florence and the enemy, not just those in which his family nestled, and it was thought that Riario was near Borgo Sansepolcro, somewhere in the mountains of Umbria.

I moved forward as Michelozzi presented him with the letters I had carried.

'From your mother, Magnifico, and Angelo Poliziano. Most urgent,' I said.

Lorenzo glanced up at me. 'How is Ficino?' he asked.

'Practising forgiveness.'

'I should have warned him it was to happen, then he would have been prepared, but I did not have the opportunity. Please make my apologies to him. You have come from Cafaggiolo? How is the family? And how is our Angelo?' he asked, as he opened the letter. I allowed him to find out for himself that Angelo was not writing from Cafaggiolo, but from Careggi, and watched the colour drain from his face as he read.

'What is it?' he asked. 'What has happened?'

'Please, it is for Angelo to tell you himself. When can you see him?'

Lorenzo swung round to the fire, where his wife's letter was now but a molten ball.

'What did she have to say?' he asked.

'I do not know. Can I tell Angelo to come to you?'

'Here? No! I shall see him at Careggi.'

'Is he welcome to stay in your villa?'

'Of course, without question. Why should he not be?' Lorenzo's eyes narrowed momentarily, then he dismissed any suspicion I was breeding in him. 'Of course he is welcome to stay in my villa.'

I stood in awe of him then. With men all around plucking at his attention, with the weight of such terrible problems upon him, he was loyal to his friend. And to me, his friend's friend.

'Where is your wife?' he asked.

'She remains with yours at Cafaggiolo.'

'I shall look for a replacement so that she may return to you as soon as possible.'

Bowing low, I promised to serve him in whatever way I could, then left.

Outside the sala I was surrounded by members of the brigata, wanting to know details. Oh, if only we could harness the energy of Rumour and Gossip – what speed we should have in communication.

'Is it true Angelo was caught in bed with Clarice's maid?' Matteo Franco asked.

Niccolò Michelozzi said it was impossible to believe and called on me to tell him it was not true. Bartolommeo Scala joined us wearing the look of a man suddenly convinced of divine justice, and insisted on hearing the details of 'our angel's dizzying fall.' He offered his gratitude to the gods, that he had been so wonderfully vindicated by events, whatever the events might be.

'He should never have corrected that letter,' he exclaimed. 'I said he would live to regret it.'

I looked at him amazed. 'You think he has lost his dignity, his position and his pupil because he once changed an *a* to an *e* in one of your letters? Even the God of the Old Testament was never that harsh!'

'Has he lost his position?' Niccolò Michelozzi asked. 'Does that mean Lorenzo is looking for another tutor? My brother Bernardo would be interested.'

'Oh blessed justice, sweet revenge!' Scala cried in a very spasm of pleasure.

'You parasites!' I snapped. 'I thought you were his friends!'

Baccio Ugolini, whom I had unjustly included in this accusation simply because he was there, led me away to impart to me the skills of an ambassador, the first rule of which is never to betray your true feelings.

'Since I am not destined to be an ambassador, your lessons are wasted on me.'

'How do you know what you are destined for? I am serious, Tommaso. Do not cross men like Scala.'

'You mean I might lose everything in sudden misfortune? What is that man? A devil?'

'Close enough, I fear.'

'Why can't Lorenzo see it? Why does he keep him?'

Baccio told me that, contrary to my belief, Lorenzo was neither perfect nor superhuman.

'He has faults and weaknesses,' he said, 'and one of them is his reliance on Scala. Scala does the work Lorenzo cannot bear to do: the work that is tedious, the work that is dull, and the work that is unpleasant but necessary.'

✝

Still angry about the interrogation, Ficino returned to his Careggi villa. I joined him there and was just completing a rare day's uninterrupted labour when Poliziano arrived. Ficino rose from his desk to embrace him.

'I am awaiting a summons from Lorenzo and cannot settle to

anything,' Angelo explained. Picking up Ficino's zucchetto he fingered the little cap nervously. 'When you became a priest, was it for expedience only, to secure yourself a living?'

'No! How dare you even think it? Why is it that, just because I play the lyre of Orpheus and sing to Apollo, men believe my soul to be beyond redemption? Faith,' said Ficino earnestly, 'is a matter for the heart, not for discussion. It cannot be acquired, nor given, nor implanted: it can only grow from seed through nurture. You were given that seed at baptism, and nurture is the role and purpose of the priesthood and the Church.'

Angelo spoke then of the local church of his boyhood, the smell of its incense, the way the candle-smoke got into the throat if you did not use the snuffer with care, the sound of the liturgy, the sense of continuity. 'It was all broken. Destroyed by a knife. Severed. How could I love the God who took my father away?' He had attended mass at least once a week ever since, and had never been there – always lost in thought and dream, going through the rites of his religion because he had to.

'All things are God,' Ficino said.

'I know, I know. That at least I fully believe.'

'Do you?'

'Of course.'

'Even when all things include the man who murdered your father? Or Monna Clarice de' Medici?'

Angelo stood with his eyes downcast and said nothing.

'You did not come here to discuss the Christian faith with me. What is it?'

'Piero...' he said, inhaling deeply and trying to steady himself. 'The task that you vested in me, the education of Piero. Our philosopher-king. I have failed, Marsilio. Failed! It is almost inconceivable, to believe in something so much, to want it so much, and to fail in it.'

'Perhaps we vest too much in our pupils,' said Ficino, his own disappointment in Lorenzo still fresh. 'Perhaps we do not need kings, nor philosopher-kings, but priests, and philosopher-priests.

A true priesthood, Angelo, to pray and care for all these troubled souls. That is what we need.'

'I am almost a priest.'

'You cannot be almost a priest. That is like being almost a man. You either are or you are not, and Holy Orders, when they come, come from God. You are here for my advice? This is it: Hold fast to the One who is not moved. Do not in any way trust in the position and power of men. Mighty edifices fall most heavily.'

Angelo felt a cold hand on his spine. 'Trust in God, not in Man: this is your recurring message to me.'

'When will you heed it?'

'Is it Lorenzo? Do you mean Lorenzo?'

'That which you love in Lorenzo is God. Trust in the divine essence when you cannot trust in the man.'

Angelo started to breathe again. His gaze turned to the room itself, and a fresco on one wall that depicted the sphere of the world flanked by two Greek philosophers: on one side Democritus was laughing at the folly of Man while on the other side Heraclitus wept for his misery. Under the cornice that circled the room ran a frieze of letters, gold on dark blue, so beautifully proportioned and executed that these simple letters did more for the soul than a painting could. The words said: ALL THINGS ARE DIRECTED FROM THE GOOD TO THE GOOD. REJOICE IN THE PRESENT. SET NO VALUE ON PROPERTY. SEEK NO HONOURS. AVOID EXCESS. AVOID DISTURBANCE. REJOICE IN THE PRESENT.

'By that definition,' Angelo said, 'I see I am no philosopher, since property is all that stands between me and a lifetime's dependence on faith and miracles. Honours – they are surely the very backbone of a man's standing. As for the rest of the injunctions, I concur with them, happy as I am to avoid excess and exertion and to rejoice in the present.'

'Then you understand nothing, you who exert yourself in study, are excessive in learning and rejoice in the past.' Ficino, who believed that scholars should be good rather than learned, gazed at his friend searchingly. Since they had last met, Angelo had lost the down of his youth. His features had hardened and were growing more pronounced. At the same time, and despite this, a certain beauty was becoming detectable, the beauty of a man living to his full potential, the beauty of virtue: *gentilezza*. This was the butterfly within the grub, the grub that had to die.

We turned at the sound of an approaching rider and I opened the door to a messenger on a white horse, ghostly in the twilight. The man, hooded by a black cloak, called out that Angelo Poliziano was required at the Casa Medici in Florence. He was to come at once.

'The Grand Inquisitor calls,' said Ficino grimly. 'God go with you, my friend.'

'But in case He doesn't, I shall,' I said, rising from my labours.

31

Florence, May 1479

'I TRUST YOU know the way well,' Angelo said to the messenger ahead of us, 'for it is getting very dark and there is no moon tonight.'

'There will be, in an hour or less, but my old mare she knows every stone and pebble 'tween here and the Porta San Gallo. Put your trust in her, sir, and in the Lord.'

Although it was a short journey and the stars were bright, it was too dark to risk anything faster than a walking pace. Angelo wanted to dwell on the conversation he was about to have with Lorenzo but the messenger was of the kind who wishes to make conversation; and, like so many messengers who enjoy conversing, his grammar and diction were appalling.

'Note the man's peculiarities of speech,' Angelo said quietly to me. 'Here is an excellent example of a rustic pretending to be a townsman. It is a fine night!' he observed.

'Tsfine alright if you're alive. These days taint nothing else but death. Florence is finished. The great city is dying.'

'I cannot believe it, not while Lorenzo lives.'

To that the messenger gave a great sigh, and said that he was loyal to Lorenzo, and would remain so until his own death, but it seemed these days that he was the only one. Angelo protested.

'Well, if you don't mind my saying so, sir, you too have betrayed him. You of all people.'

'Monstrous! How dare you?' Angelo demanded from behind.

'Ah, pardon me, sir, but I'm only repeating the rumours, and you might as well know it, as you will have to face them soon enough. I'm doing you a favour, telling you the truth. They say as how you violated his wife's maidservant.'

Angelo laughed sourly. 'Is that what Rumour says? Does Lorenzo believe it?'

'How should I know? But what I do know is this, him who makes free with other men's property will never tolerate anyone making free with his own, if you see what I mean, sir. Personally I don't know how a good Christian can live with such contra-dictions, but, there you are. That's how it is, in't it, sir? Life's not fair.'

'What do you mean?'

'I mean, sir, that Lorenzo is an adulterer himself. Perhaps not a ravisher like you, I mean he doesn't have to force himself on any-one, except perhaps his wife. Ha ha!'

'You vulgar ape!'

'Nevertheless,' the messenger continued unabashed, 'he has little right to accuse you of this kind of crime, but he will, won't he?'

'I think he must.'

'Well I don't know about you, sir, but that sort of hypocrisy makes me mad. Don't get me wrong. I love Lorenzo as I love butter, but that sort of thing makes me wild. Hypocrisy, that's what it is. That's the name for it. Hypocrisy. Greek, they tell me, for saying one thing and doing another.'

'Perhaps, but whatever his faults, Lorenzo has an ear for

truth. I trust him more than the Lord and your mare put together.'

'So what is the truth?' asked the hooded messenger.

'That is private, my good man.'

'As you like. Only I thought you might like to make use of me, in my hermetic capacity.'

'Hermetic capacity?' Angelo laughed. 'And what would that be?'

'Why, to spread the news. Hermes was the messenger of the gods, wasn't he? So I'll be the messenger of men. The only weapon against words is words. So tell me the truth and I will broadcast it in the taverns. They all listen to me, being as how I'm a Medici courier an' all.'

'Ah, I think Rumour will defeat even you, my Mercurial friend. She always wins, being so much more richly adorned than plain Truth.'

Angelo asked me in Latin if I could see wings at the man's heels. Such a close student of Homer, he believed that eccentricity must hide a god. Fully suspicious now of the identity of his companion, he tried to ride alongside to see if a god was indeed hiding beneath that cloak, but the messenger always kept a horse head's distance in front of us, as spirits do in folktales. Defeated, Angelo fell back. 'Your idea has some appeal. Please, O wing-footed one, let it be known that Angelo Poliziano has been unjustly accused. He is innocent. Heavy-handed Nature has a habit of throwing him out, and she has done it once again.'

We rode on in silence for a while. The moon began to rise, huge and full over the black hills. The shapes of trees emerged, and they were familiar, local; our blood began to tingle with an awareness of Florence. The cathedral's dome could be seen against the sky, as well as the hill of San Miniato beyond. The scent of the Arno, though not fragrant by any means, was yet dear to us, for it was the odour of our city.

'This must be how it is for an exile to come home,' Angelo said to me.

Rousing from his own reveries, the messenger said, 'The war's going badly.'

'How does it proceed?'

'Badly.'

'Yes, but how badly? In what way?'

The messenger told him how the stalwart town of Colle was under siege, and that its loyal citizens were fighting to the death.

'A throwback to past times, ain't they? All alone they are, and fighting, while those multi-coloured codpieces of Ferrara strut about like silly capons under the hooves of the Apocalyptic riders. Between you and me, sir, Lorenzo made a mistake choosing the Duke of Ferrara – but for the love of God, never tell him I said so. I suppose this is all news to you, being how's you've been removed from it all, as if you was a precious treasure.'

Being how's you've been, Angelo repeated to himself, memorising this convoluted verbal phrase.

'Not interested in martial matters, are we sir?'

'Hmm? What? Oh, yes I am, of course I am. The best stories come from war, expressed in quatrains and fine pieces of literature. War is a great spur to civilization. It provides wounds to exercise the skill of doctors and physicians. Then again, it challenges the ingenuity of those who like to invent stratagems; even artists may become fully engaged in designing the machinery of destruction, inventing truly creative methods of maiming and killing. And some would say that there is nothing like a good scorching of the countryside to renew the virility of the land. All these things are undoubtedly true, but sometimes when I hear the name war, I cannot help but think of the kind of pain that can make a man lose his senses, and then my interest recedes. Some men accuse me of an overactive imagination, but why is it overacting to imagine yourself in the place of another and suffering unspeakable agony? I think of it as a miracle of the mind, though not one I wish to exercise too often.'

As an experiment, and inspired by his mood at Cafaggiolo, in the winter Angelo had composed some verses as if written by a doctor in the last stage of a mortal pox, describing in graphic detail what happens to a body as it dies. Even though most of the

315

gruesome details of his tearing at his irritated skin had been of Angelo's own invention, inspired by some fleas bestowed upon him by his cat, they had been so convincing that he, the poet, had made his readers – and himself – feel very ill and deeply disturbed. But it had to be faced, especially in a time of plague, that the body of man, the human form, so beautiful in life, is repulsive in death and, once the spirit is fled, immediately subject to slimy, visceral, maggoty decay.

Dwelling on composition and decomposition, and wondering what the difference was, since the difference was the answer to all things, I suddenly saw, as if superimposed on the dark city, the image of a man perfect in form, the image of a man drawn geometrically, harmoniously, the image of a man that is the image of God. I wished Ficino were with us, so that I could ask him, What is it that brings the order, the beauty, the harmony to living forms? What is the difference between composition and decomposition? What is the principle of organisation, and whose design is it? What is the Sacred Law? I remembered a passage I had copied out from his translation of the great sage, Hermes Trismegistus:

What happiness, my son, to behold Him who is unmoved moving in all that moves, and Him who is hidden made manifest through his works! Such is the order of the universe. But if you wish to see Him through mortal creatures also, both those on earth and those in the depths of the sea, think, my son, how man is fashioned in the womb; investigate with care the skill shown in that work, and find out what craftsman it is that makes this fair and godlike image. Who is it that has traced the circles of the eyes, that has pierced the orifices of the nostrils and the ears, and made the opening of the mouth? Who is it that has stretched the sinews out and tied them fast, and dug out the channels of the veins? Who is it that has made the bones hard, and covered the flesh with skin? See how many crafts have been employed on one material, and how many works of art are enclosed within one compass! All are beautiful, all true to measure, yet all are diverse one from another. Who produced all these? What mother, or what father? Who but the hidden God, who has wrought all things by his own will? No one says that a statue or a portrait has come into being without a sculptor or a painter; and has such a work as this come into being without a Maker? How blind men are! How impious, how obtuse! Never, my son, deprive the things made of their Maker…

'Stop!' came a shout from the militia camped at the base of the city walls. 'Who are you? What is your business?'

'I bring a visitor to Lorenzo de' Medici,' called the messenger. 'Here is a letter. Let us in.'

'Who is the visitor?'

'Angelo Poliziano.'

'Angelo Poliziano?' A crossbow-man snatched up a burning brand from the fire to light his way and came towards us curiously.

'Ha! What brings you to this place? We have no comforts here for you.'

'Maso!' Angelo jumped from his horse to embrace his cousin. 'Are you with the militia? How do you fare? How is my house?'

'Lorenzo awaits you,' said our hermetic messenger crossly.

'Lorenzo awaits you,' Maso mimicked him. 'So you must go, lap dog, puppy. Go. Woof woof. Go to your master, you slave.'

'He is my cousin,' Angelo appealed to the messenger.

'He is scum,' the messenger replied without hesitation.

Maso leapt at the man, trying to pull him off his horse, but only succeeded in pulling off the man's cloak, and with it the hood, revealing a face more familiar than our own.

'Oh God!' cried Angelo, trying to remember everything he had said on the ride. He had overshot the mark when he had suspected our companion of being a god. 'Lorenzo!' he snapped, angry to have been so easily deceived.

'Scum, am I?' Maso was shouting. 'Let me ask you something.' He faced Lorenzo with a courage Lorenzo was not used to. 'When it comes to it, which of us is going to die for this city, you or me?'

Lorenzo was taken aback by the question.

Maso continued. 'Scum I may be, but it is me at the walls all night every night, protecting mighty Florence. Me who the tax-payers have armed with a breastplate and a crossbow. Me, I am the one. The rest of you – Angelo Poliziano, Lorenzo de' Medici, chancellors, priests, all of your sort – it is all talk. Do you hear? All talk.'

'That is enough! If I suffer your insolence at all it is because of your relation to him. How many times have I saved your mean little life, Maso? Each time it was for his sake, because he begged me to, even at the risk of my displeasure. If anyone should be showing a little gratitude, it is you. Now leave go of my horse. I have spent more than enough time on you.'

Maso lifted his shirt. 'See that?' he pointed to a scar in his ribs near the heart. 'That is what I got trying to save his father's life. I am pocked all over with scars, but our Angelo, there is not a mark on him. I ask you again, who is going to be the last man to tumble from the walls with an arrow in his neck? It could be me, but it certainly won't be you. We're dying for you, Lorenzo, dying for you, and all you can say is, "Let me go, I've had enough."'

Lorenzo spurred his horse forward. Angelo, horrified by his cousin's choice of moment to vent his anger, leapt into his saddle and caught up with Lorenzo to ride with him into the city.

'You were born into the wrong family,' Lorenzo told him. 'You should have been born into mine.'

'My soul was born into yours. Thank you for your long sufferance of the Ambrogini, and for taking in Maria.'

'What really happened with my wife?' Lorenzo demanded. 'Why did she throw you out?'

Angelo could not tell him, not yet. We rode through the empty streets that were silent except for, here and there, within dark houses, the keening of the bereaved. Streets of the infected were barricaded off. The reeking stench of sulphur fumigation masked the smell from the ordure of horse, pig and dog that lay in piles everywhere. Rubbish collected in corners and blocked gutters and drains. Beggars held out their hands in supplication, many of them only children orphaned by the plague. What is composition? It is the spirit of life and the will to live. The seed of order when nurtured and cultivated grows into civilisation. What is decomposition? It is the loss of the binding factor and the separation,

318

disintegration, of the whole into parts. Florence was no longer a city: it was a collection of individuals reduced to surviving as best they could, and no one caring for another. The city was indeed dying.

We followed our patron into the palazzo, where Angelo was reunited with his friends. 'You will need a drink,' Lorenzo said, 'being as how you've come a long way.' The sound of him laughing at his own joke bounced around the courtyard and amazed the household, for they had not heard such a sound for nearly a year. The two of them disappeared into Lorenzo's chamber. I waited outside. Angelo was not long, and when he came out, he looked more cheerful than I had seen him since the war had begun. I stared at him, amazed. 'What did Lorenzo say?'

'He listened to me carefully, and then asked why I was trembling. I told him I was scared that he was not going to believe me. "Ah," he said, "if only you had as much faith in me as I have in you." Then he apologised for the suffering his wife had caused by her false accusations and promised to restore Piero to me as soon as he could.'

We went to the chamber we were to share with other members of the brigata.

'To hear Lorenzo laugh – it was like hearing rain in Calabria,' said Matteo Franco.

'It was like theeing David come home with Jonathan,' said Baccio Ugolini, a length of catgut held in his teeth while he restrung his lira da braccio. 'All is wight with the world again now.'

'Well,' said Angelo, throwing himself on the bed. 'How is everyone?'

'Oh, how blessed you are,' said Matteo, falling on the bed beside him and nudging him like a conspirator. 'So, tell us about the delights of our Iride.'

Angelo struck out at him.

'When this man was a boy,' said Niccolò Michelozzi, 'he was very ticklish.'

'No!' Angelo shouted.

Together the *brigata laurenziana* set upon him to tickle a confession out of him. The other residents of the house heard the noise raining down from the eaves and wondered if there could be any sleep for them on this night, now that Master Angelo was back in the house and the brigata were playing like bullocks. We talked and sang and joked half way through the night, as we used to so often, before the war forced maturity upon us. For the night we shared the campfire of jocularity, and kept the dark at bay.

32

Fiesole, May 1479

FROM POVERTY to plenty, from loneliness to family, from winter to spring: everything has changed as if overnight. My brother is blessed by strange good fortune that, once again in this time of war, Lorenzo has given him peace. We have come to Fiesole, the conical hill above Florence, and to the Villa Medici here, which Lorenzo says Angelo is to treat as his own. The journey itself was a joy. In leaving the city we left the horror of death behind: in the countryside of Fiesole it is as if there is no war, no plague. We set out from the city early in the morning, accompanied by Lorenzo himself who is on his way to visit his wife at Cafaggiolo. To see her, comfort her, reacquaint himself with his children? No. He is going himself to do what no other man is able to do, which is to wrest Angelo's books from her, and since that is the cause of his going, his mood was not a good one. However, as we rode up this hill, even Lorenzo's anger could not survive the onslaught of beauty.

Each little house we passed on the road had a tiny wicker cage hanging outside its window. Lorenzo told me that tonight is the 'Feast of the Crickets' when the little creatures, caught in the grass by children, will chirrup all night in the cages. He promises me they will be freed tomorrow. Apart from this short conversation with me, Lorenzo rode alone with Angelo, the two of them greedy for each other's company. I wanted to join them, to discuss Virgil and Dante with them, but it was obvious that my place was a horse-length behind, trailing along on a mule like a piece of baggage. I have been charged by Lorenzo to look after my brother and act as his house-keeper. Of course I am very content with this, given that it puts me in his company, but if Angelo thinks I shall spend all my days walking about with the keys to cupboards and doors, looking out for tasks for the servants, overseeing their work, planning meals and sewing his shirts, well, he is in need of education. I shall speak to him tonight on the matter. But for now I am content to drink in the wine that is Fiesole.

This hill and its marvellous perfection of shape, as pure a cone as a pile of sand poured on the ground, was surely the model of Dante's Paradise. Its terraces stand one atop another like stairs to heaven. The two men rode side-by-side, leaning towards each other and talking animatedly, growing ever more unconscious of me. Lorenzo on a white horse, a red cloak draped round him, a scarlet cappuccio hat hanging behind his right shoulder, stood out like a brilliant flag against the lush greenery of the countryside in May. Beside him Angelo, dressed in brown jerkin and hose, his red cap jaunty on the back of his head, his feet hanging free of the stirrups like a palio rider. It seemed that being on this hill demands a less formal relation to life than the city, and a closer harmony with nature.

The nasty north wind of the last few days has dropped and this morning the breeze was easterly. Some snatches of their conversation came to me, and I thought they must be discussing the change that has come into Angelo's life, the responsibility that has settled on him with my arrival. Lorenzo was advising him, perhaps. The horses climbed the hill without haste. I looked about me in wonder. Fiesole, which must be beautiful in any month, surpasses beauty in May. Bird-cheep is everywhere, filling the air as new plant-life fills the land. Abundance and lushness and so many kinds of green! The silver green of new grass, the golden green of vines, the black green of cypresses. Here and there the red tiled roofs of villas, the grey of stone walls.

'You think philosophy is a matter for the brain,' I heard Lorenzo say, 'but you are wrong. When you see this beauty as separate from the objects, then you will have begun on the path.'

Without their noticing, I caught up with them.

'I was trained in the Studio under Argyropoulos and Ficino. I have read all Plato, all Aristotle and all their pestiferous commentators. And you say I have not yet begun? It is my experience that philosophers have a precious way of thinking themselves superior to everyone else. Perhaps I do not want to begin. Poetry is my art, and Calliope my Muse.'

'Poetry and philosophy – the one without the other makes no sense. I have asked you to catalogue my library. If Filosofia comes to meet you in the course of the work, welcome her. That is all I am asking.' And so they continued, speaking of learning and libraries, and as we passed the road that leads to the Badia of Fiesole, Angelo looked down it with bright intent.

'While I am cataloguing your library, I could do the Badia's at the same time.' He inhaled as a man in bliss, filling his lungs with the sweet, fennel-laden air. 'I cannot believe this is my fate in a time of war. Oh, my Maecenas, I will do anything you ask. And more. Whatever you need that I can do, I will do. But Lorenzo...' His tone became serious. 'About Piero. Nothing compensates for losing him.'

'I understand,' Lorenzo said, 'but I must keep my wife happy.'

'I have been reading in Pliny the story of Apelles, the painter of Alexander the Great. His most perfect picture was of Venus Anadyomene, but death prevented him from completing it. I feel like the dying Apelles – frustrated beyond all measure. Beyond all measure. My heart pounds with rage against God, to be snatched from the project at such a moment. Lorenzo, your son is our unfinished work of art. Restore him to me.'

Lorenzo sighed, equally frustrated. 'My lady is adamant.'

'And she is wrong.'

'When you are married, you will understand how this feels.'

I twitched as if stung by a horsefly.

'Hopes of marriage recede like the tide, leaving a very dry bed,' Angelo gazed on his friend. To lighten the moment, he played with the metaphor, extending it beyond grace. 'As dry as sand, where little worms plunge down their holes, seaweed pops in the arid heat, and small silvery fish flip-flop in their death throes...'

'Stop it!' Lorenzo laughed and pushed at him. 'Your figure of speech runs away with you.'

Though they were smiling, they regarded each other with serious eyes. I could see their pleasure and their pain, for this brief time they were spending together was coming swiftly to its end. We turned the last bend in the

322

winding road and entered into the grounds of the villa. At its front is a grace-ful loggia with a view of the city that the Olympian gods must surely envy; we gathered there while the servants prepared the house to greet us, Lorenzo pointing out the features of Florence as if he owned them. The air was full of bees and the scent of lemon balm. I was afflicted by a mixture of pain and pleasure, as if the opposites of the world were being held in a gentle balance. Here in the midst of the most profound beauty we looked down at a city facing destruction. Though he had gained a new position of librarian, Angelo was suffering the loss of his pupil and imminent separation from Lorenzo. Lorenzo himself was enjoying only a brief respite from hell. I looked out on the gentle Arno valley and felt such simultaneity of gain and loss that I could not find words for my feelings, only a sudden gush of tears.

☩

This evening I dined alone with Angelo and told him everything of my life, of the convent, of Montepulciano, of the family. His mood changed colours like a chameleon: sombre brown when I spoke of his brother and sisters; the green-blue of grief when I spoke of our father; the flame red of anger when I spoke of our mother.

'Have you met her?' he asked.

'No.'

'She is best forgotten.'

I tried to tell him it was not her fault that she abandoned us, that she had no choice, but he would not listen. Instead, so as to get my point across, I dwelt long on the fate of our sister Lucrezia.

'She is living with Saracina,' I said.

'No. I have had a letter. She is living with Derio who has returned from Siena. Derio is demanding money and if I do not send him any, he will send Lucrezia to me.'

'And the boys?'

'What of them?'

'It is not right, Angelo! All these foundling hospitals of which Florence is so proud are not for foundlings at all, but for fatherless children. If only custom allowed children to remain with their mothers, we would not need these hospitals.'

He got up from table and paced about, calculating, estimating, weighing up the matter.

I pressed my point. 'You know what it feels like to be abandoned. Do you want your nephews to suffer the same?'

Angelo is a poet. Only half of him is male, the other half, female, in that he can feel, can put himself in the place of another and experience the pain.

'Look at us,' I said. 'We are living in luxury, free from want.'

'But I have so little money of my own. I have already sent to Derio what I can afford.'

'Bring Lucrezia and the boys here.'

'Here? This is no more than a weighing station where my soul is in the balance! There is nothing permanent here. Here is where I have been placed while Lorenzo considers what to do with me.'

'We are your flesh and blood. As the eldest, you are our father. Angelo, our family was broken up and scattered like Osiris. It is for you to gather the pieces.'

'How do you know about Osiris?' he asked, desperate to jump into another field of discussion. I did not reply but waited for his answer.

'Very well,' he said suddenly, collapsing into his chair. 'I shall ask Maso to go and fetch them. The Chiana valley is clear of fighting at the moment: everything is centred on Colle.'

My brother is a good man, full of love. I am resolved to do everything I can to make his life pleasant. I shall skin rabbits, sew shirts, whatever it takes to please him.

✝

This morning we toured our new home, going from room to room, all of them Medici rooms, none of them truly ours. Angelo gave me keys to doors and cupboards and vested in me the duty of keeping the house. Turning and turning, I went giddy to see the paintings, the fine cornices, the decorated ceilings. He made me sit in the loggia to experience its peace and its high, square view of Florence and the terraced garden. 'This is where Monna Lucrezia does her sewing when it is fine,' he said. If he was making a point, I missed it.

'Where is the library?'

324

'We passed it awhile ago.'

'But we did not look in, and I do not have its key.'

'I have it.'

'How then shall I enter?'

'You shall not enter. No woman is allowed in.'

I stared at him, unable to fathom what he was saying. 'Then you must bring some books out to me,' I said.

'Why? What for?'

'To read! What is life if not for reading?'

'Sister,' he admonished me. 'If you wish to return to a convent you have only to say so. But in my house you will conduct yourself as a woman.'

I flinched and shrank back, thinking he was about to hit me. He apologised quickly if he had sounded harsh, but I ran away to my room.

'A plague on women!' he shouted after me, his voice echoing in the peaceful halls of the villa; doors banged as he went to the library. 'They are all the same!' he cried in the distance. A door banged. His voice was closer. 'Why do they not listen to me?' Then further away again. 'Will anyone tell me how to subdue a woman and make her do my will?'

I got up and banged my own door to shut out his wandering voice.

If I am stabbing my nib at you, dear journal, you will understand.

✢

It was morbidly quiet at the midday table but Angelo has spent too long in his own company, as indeed have I, to bear this silence for long. He cleared his throat and asked me about my reading and what I know of language. I told him that I have Latin and would like to learn Greek. That this caused him to choke on an olive gave me great pleasure.

'Does the name Epictetus mean anything to you?'

I said that it did not.

'I found a text this morning written in Greek on parchment which I estimate to date to the fourth century.'

It was my turn to find difficulty in swallowing. The only books I have ever handled have been copies made in our own time. 'Here?'

'Lorenzo's collection is beyond value. It was begun by his grandfather, Cosimo, who spent a king's ransom on books. The Medici have agents around the world, with eyes as keen for literature as for gems and antiquities. All these rare texts are piled up in the library and only a fraction of them have been read. It is the same at the Badia down the hill – the library there also houses part of the Medici collection. All unread, uncatalogued, a very mountain of learning that no one has scaled.' Enthusiasm was making him forget our row.

'Who was Epictetus?' I asked.

'A Stoic philosopher of the first century. His manual is full of wisdom, a gospel of inner freedom which appeals to me greatly. It even teaches you how to love your enemies.'

I was expecting him to offer to read it to me. But no, he was merely stating his intention of spending a philosophical afternoon under the almond tree. There he sat on the grass, the book on his knees, reading instructions on how to order his life so as to distance himself from its pain and troubles. The sun moved round and warmed the back of his head. His chin dipped down to his chest. He dozed.

I found him there, stretched out with his back against the almond tree. Sunlight playing through the leaves had shadows dancing all over him. Instead of waking him up, I paused to consider him, this stranger who was of my own blood, my own soul, my own image. I wished I could have known him earlier, for here was the one who could have taught me to ride, to dance, to play the lute, to add up, to read and write in Latin, to hawk with falcons. Given that he would have wanted to, that is.

I pushed against his foot with mine.

He awoke, as if alert even when asleep, and squinted at me. 'What is it, Maria?'

'What are you doing?'

'I am studying Epictetus.'

'With your eyes closed?'

'It is called contemplation.'

'It is called sleep!'

He looked rueful. 'Must you argue about everything?'

'That depends on what you say.' I sat down beside him and took the book from his chest.

'You cannot read that, it is in Greek.'

'Then translate it for me.'

He did as asked and began to read out loud. He translated in the air, bringing the Greek into Tuscan without a moment's pause or hesitation, and after a while and without thinking, I was leaning against him, transported by his learning.

'God has entrusted me with myself. He has made my will subject to myself alone and given me rules for the right use thereof.'

I frowned, not quite comprehending. Angelo read on, paraphrasing, explaining this doctrine of liberation: 'God tells Epictetus that his body is not his own, but is merely clay, and that the power he has to desire and decline, to pursue and avoid, that power is from God, and if Epictetus exercises it, then shall he be free from lamentation.'

A grasshopper sprang on to his arm. I brushed it away.

'You know yourself what you are worth in your own eyes, and at what price you will sell yourself. For men sell themselves at various prices.'

If he paused there, it was not because of any difficulty with the language.

'Do you think that is true?' I asked.

'Not for me. I would not sell myself at any price.'

'Nor I.' I ran my hand through my hair, as long as his by now, and crossed my legs at the ankles, same as him. 'Is this what you call philosophy?'

'Yes.'

'I heard you say to Lorenzo that you loathe philosophy.'

'This is stoic philosophy: practical wisdom – recipes for a good and happy life. What I loathe is men arguing over abstractions. I had one professor at the Studio who asked me what I meant by the word "meaning". Dry, arid, useless stuff. The same with theology. But once you get to the texts themselves, there is much life in the subject.'

He picked up the book.

'If a man could only know that he is sprung from God, and that God is the Father of men as well as of Gods, he could never think anything ignoble or base of himself.'

He read the line again, thoughtfully, and his thoughts were clear to me.

'She hurt you very much, didn't she, Lorenzo's wife?'

'Anyone who causes a man to lose his reputation, his virtù, *is guilty of*

murder. Yes, she hurt me very much, but not half as much as she has hurt herself. Listen, little boy-sister, I have to tell you, the happiness of women depends entirely on the happiness of men, and the happiness of men depends entirely on the obedience of women. I am sorry I shouted at you earlier, but if you do not do as I say, you will destroy the harmony of this household, fragile as it is.'

I stared at him, breathing hard. I had never been spoken to in such a way, and to have these words delivered so calmly! – I fumed like a dragon.

'It is not always easy to distinguish right from wrong, and we must not let our emotions guide us. Reason is the proper guide, but he sleeps. That is why we need books like this one, to wake him up.'

If he wanted reason, he could have it. 'Would you say,' I asked innocently, as if very dim, 'that it is the reading of such books that awakens reason?'

'Of course, I have just said it.'

'Would you say that in women reason sleeps more deeply than in men?'

'By the bruises of experience, I would say yes, most emphatically.'

'So women have greater need of books than men?'

I watched his mind stumble, and gave it no time to recover its step. 'So why do men keep us from books?'

'What is it you want, Maria?' he asked appreciatively. 'You say you will not marry. Do you want, then, to return to the conventual life?'

'No!'

'I could find one here in Florence that has some integrity, say at Santa Maria Novella, near my church.'

'No!'

'What then? What do you want? Wife or nun?'

'Am I constrained by only two choices? What I want is neither of these things. What I want is to visit Lorenzo's library, and do what you do.'

'You cannot. It is contrary to custom. A female scholar? The world would laugh at us.'

'Our family has been destroyed by custom,' I said. 'How long must we suffer custom's tyranny? What is custom, anyway? Is it a divine law, revealed to Moses? No, it is of more earthly origin, it is the habit of the group, and being so, is more prone to sleep than student philosophers! No one asks

328

questions of it. Custom dictates, and that is that. It is how we do things, have always done them, since an earlier time, when there was another set of customs. Why should I not read, just because custom forbids? Happily for Socrates, Diotima, his teacher in divine love, did not spend her time sewing.'

My brother stared at me. 'Come, then,' he said decisively, pulling me up to my feet. 'Let us see what you can do.'

The library is on the north side of the house, away from the glare of the sun, cool, the light filtering through alabaster windows. I crossed the threshold forbidden to Medici women to smell frankincense in the air, as well as the odour of parchment and vellum. A few volumes are piled on shelves, but most of the books are so valuable that they are locked away in great chests. Angelo held the keys and turned them in the heavy locks one by one, to open lids on the world's knowledge. There is much here to be expected: the works of Augustine, Clement and other fathers of the Church; the books of Aquinas and Duns Scotus; the plays of Terence and Euripides; works of science and astronomy, medicine and music; anthologies of Greek epigrams, poems in Arabic, bestiaries and herbals. There are many books that no one knows what they are, and these are Angelo's special interest, but I was drawn to the chest of philosophy, beguiled by the very names: the Poimandres of Hermes Trismegistus, the Chaldean Oracles, the Orphic Hymns, the Dialogues of Plato, the Enneads of Plotinus, the book on angels of Dionysus the Areopagite, the works of magic by Iamblichus. I could have climbed into that chest and pulled its lid down on me, entombing myself with these lovely, mysterious names, and been entirely happy, except that almost all of it is written in the Greek language.

'They are being translated,' Angelo said, kneeling down beside me to empty the chest of its contents, 'by Marsilio Ficino. He began on the Dialogues of Plato about twenty years ago, but Cosimo de' Medici made him stop when the Poimandres was discovered. Since that pre-dates every-thing, Cosimo said it must be translated first. And so he did.' He pointed to a shelf above, where the modern works were piled, and I stood up to reach for Ficino's manuscript of the work of Hermes. I gasped as I opened the cover, for the writings of the mysterious Hermes Trismegistus have not only been translated into Latin, but set in borders the colour of precious stones, and written in a hand of surpassing beauty.

'Did your Tommaso write this?'

'No. It is by Sansovino, a master who torments my friend with perfection. Tommaso is a workhorse, as am I, and if you think it is hard for you not to be a man, I tell you that for men it is just as hard not to be other, better men.' He held out his hand for the book, but I would not relinquish it.

My eye roved round the gold and scarlet brocade of the border in which little cherubs bore the shield of the Medici. Angelo identified for me the ancient philosophers portrayed in roundels, and explained some of the emblems for reflection and interpretation. Then I began to read out loud in Latin: 'Once, when mind had become intent on things which are, and my understanding was raised to a great height, while my bodily senses were withdrawn, as in sleep, when men are weighed down by too much food or by the fatigue of the body, it seemed that someone immensely great, of infinite dimensions, happened to call my name, and said to me, "What do you wish to hear and behold, and having beheld, what do you wish to learn and know?"'

Oh…!

Angelo praised my competence in reading and asked me to translate into Tuscan. Though my eyes were swimming with tears to read this account of someone who had met the invisible God, I did so without faltering.

'Read on,' he said, impressed.

'When he had thus spoken, he changed in form and forthwith, upon the instant, all things opened up before me. And I beheld a boundless view. All had become light, a gentle and joyous light. And I was filled with longing when I saw it.'

He took the book from me, brushed the tears from my cheeks and said I can come back to the library whenever I wish. He keeps the keys on his bedpost.

✣

Tommaso joined us this evening, restless and jumpy. Elena is expected home and I believe he only came to us because time had got stuck in the hourglass and would not flow. We sat together in the loggia, where Angelo read Epictetus to us. Afterwards Angelo leant back in his chair and stretched out his legs. The evening was settling on Fiesole like a blush of fine silk. He had the company of a good friend and a glass of Lorenzo's finest wine to hand.

He wanted only music, and this he could supply himself on his lute. So he picked it up, tuned it, and began to play a song of Lorenzo's composition. Lorenzo's songs are bittersweet and make your heart melt. The notes began to dance with the gnats and sing with the blackbirds, and Tommaso, his heart settled by the music, sang the words in a fine tenor.

Into this scene of utmost tranquillity rode Lorenzo himself, returning from Cafaggiolo. He had sent his retinue on to the city and was alone, it seemed, except for a servant and a train of three donkeys laden with Angelo's books. Although the evening was not chill, he seemed to be quite swathed about by his cloak.

'You bring my books yourself?' Angelo asked, deeply flattered.

'They are trophies of war, won at great cost. My pride demands I present them myself, for I desire the glory. But now that I am here, I have to ask, why do you want them – Plato, Demosthenes and Cicero? You must have read them a dozen times. They are only of use when you are tutoring.'

'You know what it is that I hope and pray for. What is this hump at your back?' Angelo asked, jabbing his finger into Lorenzo's cloak. There came a merry squeal from within.

'The answer to your prayers,' Lorenzo said, pulling aside his ample cloak to reveal his son sitting on the croup of his horse.

Piero slipped off the horse and into his tutor's arms, throwing his arms round him possessively. With a shout of triumph, Angelo swung him about in the air. 'How did you do this?' he asked Lorenzo. 'By what trick of conjuration?'

'I kidnapped him,' Lorenzo said lightly, dismounting and giving his horse to a waiting servant. 'I did not ask my wife's permission. Bernardo Michelozzi is a good tutor, but Piero is now accustomed to brilliance and will not suffer anything less. Any chance of supper in my own house?'

Tommaso was hopping from foot to foot, wanting news of his wife.

'Why are you here?' Lorenzo asked. 'She returned with the main party and will be home by now.'

Tommaso leaped on his horse and sped off, hardly pausing to shout farewell. Lorenzo watched him go and you could read in his eyes that story of the prince who envied the pauper. Then, with a sigh, he returned his gaze to us. 'Well,' he said, rubbing his hands. 'What is to eat?'

33

*MY SISTER Lucrezia and the boys arrived yesterday evening with Maso.
The widow has been returned to her kin, a common enough occurrence, but
this is not common. Not here the head of the Ambrogini family established
in the house of his ancestors, all his alliances and familial bonds in place, his
position in his contrada and city well-defined and secure. Not here the
bustle of wife, children, aunts, servants. Here instead a bachelor in a
magnificent villa not his own. Looking round the house, Maso whistled
appreciatively and laughed at Angelo's good fortune.*

*'Thrown out of the fire into a feather bed,' he said and went to choose a
room for himself.*

*'Maso! You already have my house in the city!' Angelo called after him.
'And the city has the plague,' Maso flung back. 'I shall be quite comfortable here. After all my exertions on your behalf, it's the least I deserve.'*

*Lucrezia became ridiculously bashful in the presence of her brother, whom
she has not seen for fifteen years, and refused to look up and meet his eye.
Her boys clung to her skirts, burying their heads in the fabric when their
uncle stooped to greet them. When Piero de' Medici came into the room, they
sought to hide themselves completely, two little rabbits sensing the presence of
a lion. Piero, recognising competition for Angelo's attention, became imperious and wanted to know who all these people were in his house.*

*'It is my family,' Angelo told him. 'The Ambrogini are being re-
assembled.'*

✝

*I hope he has no regrets. His pastoral retreat has turned into an inn. No
doubt we seem like mules and donkeys to him, when he is used to the silent,
noble company of thoroughbreds. Certainly we seem so to Piero, who stands
in silent disapproval of the boys who, over-excited by their new surround-
ings, run round the villa squealing and screaming. Lucrezia has a thunderous voice on her when it comes to instructing servants. Maso sings soldier*

songs, no matter that ladies are within earshot, no matter that he cannot sing in tune. Angelo has taken himself and Piero off to the Badia for the day. He has renewed his ban on my entering the library, though he will bring me out whatever book I desire. To my surprise, my sister also enjoys reading, but in Tuscan only. Perhaps I made a mistake in persuading Angelo to let Maso stay with us here when he is not on duty, but Maso is family and families should be together.

✚

The monks of the Badia have done their best to care for the books that Lorenzo's grandfather, Cosimo, bequeathed to them, but they are over-whelmed by too many incomprehensible titles, and too many books with no titles at all. Angelo separates the ancients from the moderns, the Greeks from the Latins, but each book he handles is a new wonder to him, opening up a multitude of thoughts and ideas – so many books, by so many learned men! And yet these texts are as subject to corruption as the parchment they are written on, worm-holed by the ignorance of scribes who have transmitted error and multiplied it over the ages, until now, he says, people take plain idiocies as scripture.

Though he does not claim to be a philosopher, my brother loves Truth, he loves her fiercely, protectively, and is her champion. His Truth is called logos *by the Greeks, which means the Word, and it also means reason. My brother loves clear thinking, beautifully expressed. He does not love scribes, especially careless ones who copy for money and pay no attention to what they are doing. Though he abhors ignorance, he loves chaos, because it gives him the opportunity to reveal order (he has taught me to say 'reveal' and not 'impose', since order is the natural state of things and not something laid on top). He revels in these two libraries, the one here at the villa and the one at the Badia: they give him every opportunity to indulge his loves and hates. One moment he is reading wisdom with humility, another he is stabbing 'at those puff-balls of learned opinion that grow up in the damp ground of the universities.' He intends single-handedly to clear the ancient texts of all error. He is resolved to make spelling uniform. He is devising methods for tracing and establish-ing the lineage of manuscripts so as to find the earliest, which, being the earliest, must be the truest. Truth, to Angelo Poliziano, is the definitive text.*

He goes out at dawn each day to the Badia and returns at dusk, and after he has eaten he goes to the house library to lock himself up with books. I have told him that so much reading is bad for him, for his eyes and his health and his mind, but he says he has to do it while the opportunity is here. 'Who knows what tomorrow will bring?'

'I do! It will bring madness!'

His reading is so universal and all-embracing. He reads everything, because, he says, how can he choose what to read without knowing what the choice is? And so he reads it all: philosophy, theology, literature, geography; patristic fathers, astronomy, herbals; Greek tragedies and bestiaries; metaphysics and lyric poetry. Daily he offers the kindly abbot miscellanies of assorted facts. The abbot, whose own thoughts revolve on the effects of the excommunication upon his soul and that of his brethren, finds himself enraptured by the story of the Nemean lion from a remote Greek source, or the origin of the term panic, or a riddle from the works of Varro, or the story of how purple dye was discovered in the shell of the murex snail. The abbot begins to look on life in wonder, seeing it as a manifestation of the limitless invention of the Creator, but when he tries to repeat these stories to others, they lose their magic.

'I am beguiled by the teacher,' he says, 'who vividly colours everything with his enthusiasm.'

Although it is true that these miscellaneous scraps of knowledge are unified only by the spirit of their discoverer, and – like his jokes – only amusing when he tells them, I think it important that they be collected and written down. As Angelo does not have the time to do it himself, I do it for him. And it is my advice that he keeps sane amongst these starfields of knowledge by concentrating on one constellation: Epictetus. Thus he has begun a translation of the Manual.

When asked one's country, never answer, 'I am an Athenian or a Corinthian,' but do as Socrates did and say, 'I am a citizen of the world.'

A citizen of the world Angelo may be, but his tenure is precarious. As soon as Lorenzo needs this villa back, he will take it, and we shall have to move on. I feel an urgent need to send a tap root into the earth, to anchor us all and keep us still. Lucrezia is making friends among the wives of the rich merchants who summer on the hill, and she has learnt a piece of news that seems to have come from heaven: the Provost of Fiesole is dying. Is it really sinful of me to think that he dies so that we may live?

Whenever I visit Angelo at work, I am careful to knock so as to draw him out gently from his studies or else incur his anger; but when I heard this news today I ran down to the library at the Badia in uncontrollable excitement. My sister followed more slowly, dragging our nephews along by the hand.

'Come out, Angelo! Come out!'

'What is it?'

'The provost of Fiesole is dying!' I did not mean to sound so pleased about it, but I have been praying ever since we arrived at Fiesole that we need never leave again, and now it seems my prayers are answered.

Angelo blinked. 'Oh?' he said, not quite with us in present time. 'Poor fellow.'

'Poor fellow? Fortunate us! Do you not see? – his office will become vacant any day. It is in the gift of Lorenzo, so it could so easily become yours. Think! You could be provost of Fiesole!'

'Maria! This is unseemly if the man is not dead. Are you a carrion crow, hopping around, impatient to peck out the eyes of the dying?'

'No I am not, but others are. We have to be quick, or they will get to Lorenzo first. Brother Angelo, this job was made for you in heaven! You would enjoy it, because there is nothing to do. It is just a title, but with it comes a beautiful house, a lot of land – two farms, I believe – and all for a name: provost. Angelo Poliziano, Prior of San Paolo and Provost of Fiesole. Does it not have a certain ring?'

'It is certainly alliterative. If the pattern of the recurring P continues, who knows, one day I may be pope. Papa Poliziano il Primo.'

'Be serious! Think, we could live on Fiesole forever, all of us together in your own house, secure at last, and dependent no more on any man but yourself.'

'Get thee from me, siren.'

As provosts cannot marry they must have housekeepers. In the moment of hearing about the illness of the present incumbent, I had been to the end of my life and back, seen it all and approved. By this means, angelic in its timing, I will be able to lead a virtuous life outside the nunnery with my celibate brother the provost. He shall read books all day, every day. I shall learn Greek and help him in translations.

'What do you think, Lucrezia?' Angelo asked our sister. To my horror, Lucrezia said that Angelo asks Lorenzo for too much, that he has received more than enough already, and must not now ask him for this. 'If he gives it to you of his own volition, well and good, but please, please, ask him for nothing more.'

How stupid can she be? 'Lucrezia!' I stamped my foot angrily. 'This is a gift from God – he must not reject it.'

Angelo looked bemused.

'Well?' I demanded of him. 'What do you want?'

He scratched his head under his cap, sighed loudly and then leapt to retrieve one particularly grubby nephew who had slipped into the library and was making for a copy of The Lives of the Caesars, *possibly the oldest copy in all the world.*

'What do I want? I wish you both gone to husbands as soon as can be, taking these monkeys with you!'

We stood there, paralysed, thinking he meant it. As soon as he saw our faces, he was remorseful and apologised. He stooped down before the boys and asked them if they had heard of the Emperor Domitian.

'It is said that he spent most of his days catching flies and killing them with a bodkin. Apparently when someone asked if anyone was with the emperor, he was told no one, not even a fly.' Both he and our nephews found this extremely funny.

'Why do men have such a puerile sense of humour?' I demanded angrily. 'You should spend your time on something more worthwhile than this trivia.'

Angelo's eyes flashed. 'When I want the opinion of a female, I shall ask for it.'

In sudden rage I accused him of denying our nephews any hope of a future. We are all going to starve and perish, and it will be his fault.

Angelo clamped his hands over his ears and cried for peace.

'Well?' I demanded.

'Do you know what you are asking?' he stormed. 'Not only would I have

to plead with Lorenzo – a degrading activity at the best of times – but I would also have to take holy orders.'

'Just so. Become a priest. What could be better?'

'Fatherhood could be better. I want to have sons, Maria.'

His confession stunned me into silence, then everything in me rushed to the surface in tears.

'What will happen to us if you marry?' I wailed. 'You will lose us again.'

'Maria, Maria. Whether I become a father or a provost is not in my power to determine,' he said, 'according to Epictetus.'

This could not be denied. 'It is in God's power,' I agreed. 'But what you can do is to ask him.'

'Who, God or Lorenzo?'

'Both, stupid!'

He groaned, the anguish of a poet disturbed from his labours by petty affairs. I felt guilty, but was adamant. Such gifts from Almighty God must be accepted as they soon as they are offered, and not left for another day. I saddled his horse for him, it was the least I could do. When he rode off, however, it was not to Florence but down the lane leading to Careggi.

'Lorenzo must be in his Careggi villa,' I said.

My sister disagreed. 'I think he is going to see Marsilio Ficino, to ask how a man may keep his patience in the face of a demanding sister.'

'Nonsense. Lorenzo is in Florence, but Angelo is going to the Medici Villa to see Monna Lucrezia and put his request to her. How wise of him. She will be like the Virgin Mary, will listen to him, know the sincerity of his heart, and will present his petition to her son in due course. And then Lorenzo will endow him with the provostship and we shall all live here happily ever after.'

Lucrezia smiled at my fantasy. 'You must know that Angelo is busy arranging a new marriage for me. Saracina's husband is searching Montepulciano for someone suitable. My days here shall be few.'

'Is that what you want?'

'No. Not if it means losing the boys.'

'We will keep them. One way or another, we will keep them.'

'He is looking for a husband for you, too.'

Though a breeze rustled in leaves of trees, the day was hot and we walked slowly. Suddenly it was very much hotter. 'No, I could not bear it.'

'I think that is why he has gone to see Monna Lucrezia. He cannot afford your dowry. The state fund has been drained by the war. Monna Lucrezia feels guilty about it – yes, I have no doubt, she will provide your dowry herself.'

'No! I shall never be married. It is sewn into my fate. I have been put on this earth to be a helpmeet to my brother, and to keep him well-directed. This I mean to do, no matter how much he resists. I shall never marry – he shall never marry. A wife and children would be a terrible distraction from his work.'

The boys ran ahead playing at Turks and Christians amidst the drone of bees and the sighing of tall grass. As we came from the lane to the main road leading down to Florence we heard the sounds of trundling carts and the clink of military. A procession of wagons carrying produce, escorted by soldiers, was being taken down to the city. The food is meagre, for what is grown here is now kept on the farms for the use of the landowners. Little gets to market, but what does has to be protected. Fine soldiers in shining breastplates rode proudly in front and behind wagons piled with cabbages and carrots. The apple trees in the gardens are bare, their fruit picked early. We eat well at the Medici villa, but sometimes it is difficult to swallow when the thought of the suffering of others enters the mind.

✝

When Angelo returned to the villa, I was ready to challenge him to tell me the truth about his plans, for I am all a-boil and a-bubble with anxiety about my future, but his arrival coincided with that of a visitor, a youth about my own age riding in with a splendid entourage, all reds and golds and white horses.

'My lord is not at home,' said Angelo, shielding his eyes, for the young man on the white horse had the sun behind him.

'Are you Angelo Poliziano? Lorenzo said I should present myself to you. I am Giovanni Pico, brother of the Count of Mirandola.'

He is tall, slender, with unkempt hair the colour of wheat falling past his shoulders. He has eyes the colour of dawn. I wanted to know why he had

338

come but Angelo kept sending me off on errands. 'Maria, organise refreshment for our guest.' 'Maria, see that the servants of our guest are well looked after.' 'Maria, why are you loitering? Go about your duties.'

When I had done all I had been sent to do, and returned, Giovanni Pico looked at me and smiled. I smiled back.

'Maria!' said Angelo. 'I have a guest. Go.'

There is a window into the loggia where they were talking together. Listening there, I learnt that Giovanni Pico is by title a protonotary, but that it is an empty title. In truth he is a student travelling Italy and Europe to study at the most ancient and renowned universities. He can speak ten languages and says he wants to know everything there is to be known.

'But there is much to know that is beyond the curricula of the schools. That is why I am here. You independent men of Florence with your Greek manuscripts… you hold the key.'

Without any trace of pride, he described his noble birth in the castello of Mirandola, telling Angelo that it had been attended by fiery flames and other divine portents.

Angelo said that he too had enjoyed a miraculous birth. 'Mysterious letters appeared in the headboard of my cradle.'

'Yes?' said Pico eagerly. 'What did they say?'

'Property of the Medici.'

Pico laughed and began to relax. Continuing with his story, he said he was studying theology and philosophy at the schools of Paris, Bologna and Ferrara.

'You are destined for the Church, then?'

'It is a narrow mind which confines itself to a single porch,' Pico replied. 'I want the life of contemplation, but without the monastery.'

'Oh!' I thought. 'This man is the brother of my soul.'

'How will you live?' Angelo was asking him.

'I have my own fortune, and require no patron. It is a very crime,' Pico said suddenly and brazenly, 'that you are not in the same happy position.'

It was all I could do not to launch myself out of the window shouting that it was not for the want of trying on my part.

'But I am,' Angelo said. 'Look at me – living in this beautiful house, wanting for nothing, with much of my time devoted to study. Come and see the library.' So saying, he led Pico out of earshot.

After an hour, I took some refreshment to them, a bowl of fruit and some wine. The library door was open and I saw Pico stretched out on the floor in a sea of open books, his head propped on his hand, listening to Angelo, who, also laid on his stomach, was reading a text out loud from a huge tome. 'It is Lorenzo's opinion,' Angelo was saying, 'that Eurydice represents Platonic wisdom.'

'But how does that interpretation work?' Pico asked, glancing up and blinding me with another one of those generous, brotherly smiles. I entered to offer him some fruit. He took the plate gratefully and laid it on the floor without taking anything from it.

'At a symposium the ancient Greeks would eat,' I said.

Pico looked bemused.

'Forgive my sister – she knows too much for a girl.' Angelo reached out and took some grapes himself, enjoying the thought that, indeed, Greek symposia had been just like this: a feast of intellectual ideas exchanged by men propped up on one elbow. 'You are out of bounds, Maria.'

I went out and returned with cushions. 'If you are going to be Greek philosophers,' I said, 'you may as well be comfortable.' When Pico smiles, it has a strange effect on my knees. Why should that be? What is the connection between a male rictus and female knee joints? The only contact and communication is through the eyes. Do my eyes talk to my knees? What a mystery.

I handed them the cushions. 'Eurydice,' I told them, 'represents a woman murdered by neglect.'

They were so absorbed they did not hear me. I went outside to sit alone, frustrated and cross. It was another hour before they emerged, these privileged men, and they would have ignored me had I not leapt up like a cricket and joined them. Pico is eight years junior to my brother and taller by a head, but in those hours they had spent together in the library they had become equal. Angelo was not a cobbler's apprentice walking beside a nobleman; Pico was not a raw youth walking beside someone senior in years and learning. They walked as friends, and if they did not mind my being with them, it was because they were oblivious to me.

340

They had so much to say! You would think all of the past and all of the future had to be contained in the few hours they spent together. They discussed the Greek language and its authors, Homer, Plato, Hesiod, Herodotus, Aristotle, Euripides, Xenocrates, Epictetus, Plotinus, Hippocrates. They did not mention Sappho or Hypatia or Diotima. My heroines did not figure in their expansive history of literature. They discussed philosophy, poetry, history, theology, astronomy, medicine. They agreed that the world stands on the horizon of a new age under the rising light of ancient wisdom, returned to illuminate men – only men? – and bring reason to our – their – metaphysical speculations. Too much superstition and nonsense in the catholic faith, they agreed, and not enough good scholarship. Why, some people – mostly women – believe the world is flat and yet here we are, surrounded by all this literature telling us truths known long before the birth of Christ, all to be ignored since it is not Christian.

'We need to expand our studies beyond the confines of Christianity,' Pico said. 'Once I have mastered Greek I shall turn to Arabic and then ancient Chaldean and Aramaic, Hebrew, too, if I can.'

Angelo blew through his cheeks like a zephyr and wished he were sixteen and had all hours of the day available to his studies. 'I have wasted so much time.'

'We could work together. My knowledge – your judgement. A chariot pulled by two such horses would fly straight to the sun.'

Angelo gazed on him with such a look of longing. That look – it seeded something in my heart, an anxiety deeper than anything else I have experienced today. In Pico Angelo has found a friend who is not a Medici. His visit was an epiphany of Mercury, a wing-footed god, free and independent, asking my brother, 'Why are you so bound?'

Giovanni Pico della Mirandola is dangerous.

I stood with Angelo to bid farewell to this princeling and watch him ride away with his men. Angelo sighed to see him depart, and stood overlong watching the party disappear. He turned back to the house at last, looking dejected.

'I thought for one wild moment that I had found you a husband,' my brother said. 'But he told me he has no intention of marrying.'

341

'Nor I,' I said at once. 'I shall remain here with you, sister of the Provost of Fiesole.'

'I went to see Monna Lucrezia. The position, when it comes vacant, is reserved for another.'

The disappointment hung on my heart like a lead weight and dragged it down. Since I could hardly feel worse, I decided to learn the whole truth.

'Are you looking for a husband for me? Lucrezia says that you went to see Monna Lucrezia to ask for help with my dowry.'

'There is a limit to how many favours I can ask for.'

I said nothing, but began to breathe again with hope.

He stood hesitantly, not knowing where to go, whether to his room or the library. 'Do you remember the story of the Cumean sibyl in the sixth book of the Aeneid? She sits in her cave writing all the wisdom of the world on thin leaves, but when Aeneas enters the draught sends everything whirling into the air like ash or snowflakes. I suppose I had better go and collect them up and see what I can make of them. But, oh, how grey the day is.'

The sun, I pointed out to him, was falling on us like hot metal out of a blue sky.

'The sun? It is but a shadow compared to the light of intelligence. Perhaps I should go and visit Ficino.'

'Only because you think you'll find Pico there.'

'He made me feel as if I am sailing oceans in search of spices to pepper food, while he, this boy, dives to the ocean's floor in a daring quest for pearls. I was telling you how I find theology and philosophy abstruse and abstract. All that careful employment of words to describe the ineffable, the indescribable, the invisible. Pico loves it, feeds on it. He made me feel almost enthusiastic myself.'

He returned to the library, muttering his intention to seek out some pearls.

✝

Left to myself I roamed the hill above the villa. Invisible deities rustled about me and, like lizards, attracted my eye with their darting movements. They laughed, these happy gods of Fiesole, disporting in the sun-baked grass, which grows ever drier as the summer heightens. With everything in seed it seems there are as many different kinds of grass as there are words in the bible. The provostship will go to another, and it seems that Angelo's tenure of the villa on the hill will be brief, transitory. I do not know what the future holds, and I long to know. I long for permanence and stability. Meanwhile I must content myself with the bliss of these months, with Lucrezia happy in her sewing and sonnets, Angelo happy in his studies, the boys flourishing under his care and tuition. Even Maso seems to have acquired a little grace from the time he has spent in Lorenzo's house. I try to be happy myself, but the harder I try, the more difficult it becomes.

When Piero de' Medici is with us, I join him in his lessons. I am learning to ride with him, and I share in his studies of Virgil, memorising selected passages. Alone on the hill late this afternoon, I settled down to practise what we are learning from the ninth book of the Aeneid, working through word by word, trying to remember sentences, trying to make sense… my eyelids grew heavy… the sun was on my back… I awoke to a clear voice speaking.

'So you do not want me as your comrade on this great expedition, and I am to let you go alone into dangers like this? This is not how I was brought up by my father during the Greek terror and our sufferings at Troy.'

I snapped awake, wondering who had spoken, but I was alone; there was no one there; it had been a dream. I stared up into a blue sky where white clouds sailed slowly in a della Robbia sky, and felt grief immeasurable. Tears ran warm from my eyes to cool on my temples, and run into the grass. The sobs rose up within me, for a grief that was not mine. Life and everything in it – all so agonisingly transient, passing like the clouds which change shape as they go.

34

Fiesole, August 5th, 1479

ANGELO HAS BEEN in correspondence with the husband of our sister Saracina: arrangements are now in place for Lucrezia to be married to one Paolo di Papi of Montepulciano. He told us this morning and awaited our ecstatic response. He waited in vain.

'Well? Are you not pleased?'

Lucrezia stared at him with her mouth open. I spoke for her.

'Pleased? We do not know this man. Who is he?'

'He has a moderate amount of wealth, is a good man, a widower.'

'But does he smell? How are his teeth? Is he fat? Does he sweat? Have you asked these questions, Angelo?'

'Of course not.'

'But you would send our sister to his bed? How could you!'

He raised his hands, palms forward, and silenced us. 'Paolo di Papi,' he announced, 'will accept the boys. You may keep your sons, Lucrezia. What more do you want of him? Of me?'

'Nothing,' she said, and ran to embrace her brother.

✛

August 15th, 1479

We prepare for Lucrezia's departure.

'Perhaps,' she said to me, 'once everything is settled, and I know this new husband better, perhaps you can come and live with us.'

'Oh no,' I said at once. 'My place is here, taming this beast who thinks he knows so much,' and I smiled at my startled brother.

'I shall find her a husband,' Angelo assured Lucrezia.

'No you will not,' I replied. Then I threw myself on my sister and we both wept copious tears, that the family is being separated once again.

✛

August 19th, 1479

Once again we must be grateful to Maso, who is accompanying Lucrezia to Montepulciano. He will stay in the south, having been assigned to the army fighting near Colle. Now that only Angelo and I remain, I am allowed once more into the libraries.

He is searching the bestiaries in the Badia collection for some reference to the 'crocodiles' he has found mentioned by Quintilian. He is also busy with comparative readings of the Orpheus myth in the works of many poets. Orpheus is a strange, elusive figure. According to Ficino, he had historical existence and is one of the line of sages who have passed on the tradition of

344

what he calls 'The Hermetic Wisdom'. Angelo says this aspect of Orpheus as a magus is to be found only in the works of the Platonists, that in the works of the poets Orpheus is a mythic figure, a Thracian poet born of the muse Calliope with perhaps Apollo as his father. The story of the death of his wife Eurydice; how Orpheus charmed the god of the underworld with his music to regain her; how Pluto warned him not to look back; how Orpheus did look back and lost Eurydice forever – this is common amongst the poets. The death of Orpheus, ripped apart by the female followers of Bacchus called 'Maenads', is also common, and how the pieces of his body were collected together and buried under Mount Olympus, except for his head, which was thrown into the river Hebrus and floated – singing all the way – to Lesbos. Although details vary from poet to poet, the main thread of the story is the same. But Angelo, remembering that Orpheus was said to be one of the Argonauts, has been reading the stories of Jason and the Golden Fleece, since a commentary scribbled into the margin of one book by a scholar of the twelfth century remarked that Orpheus, inherently a coward and no hero, was included in the adventure simply as a musician. Irritated by this, Angelo has scoured the works of Ovid and Diodorus Siculus and discovered that the Argonauts were saved from destruction by the sirens only when Orpheus began to sing. This night, as we ate a simple meal under the vine arbour, serenaded by frogs and crickets, we were speculating on what kind of sound a poet could make that would quell sirens, a speculation that led Angelo into a discourse on harmony and the theories of the Platonists on the subject of number. In passing he told me about Orphism and Orphic hymns.

I grow plump and healthy on such food. Sitting together later on the loggia, listening beyond the insect noise of earth to the silent song of heaven, looking down on Florence visible by starlight, I seemed able to soak up Platonism without reference to anything but the elements around me. It was most curious. I had never heard of this philosophy until this summer, a philosophy which Angelo says was fused with Christianity in the early days but then became severed and outlawed. From the very air I pluck names such as Origen and St John Chrysostom and find them as sweet morsels in a hungry mouth. These men, these early Church fathers, asked questions of the Invisible God that are my questions. These are men for whom it was not enough to believe, they had to know. It seems that all my questions may be *answered in the obscure books in this library and I long for the day when I am able to read the Enneads of Plotinus, the Life of Pythagoras by Iamblichus, the works of Porphyry, for myself. Angelo says that will take me forever, but that I am free to read the translations made by Ficino and copied out by Tommaso, as and when they are finished; that meanwhile I should read Plato.*

Of course, the Platonist who interests me most is Hypatia.

'Ah, the only woman to head the Platonic Academy.'

'Daughter of Theon the Mathematician, author of works on algebra, murdered by Christian fanatics.'

'How do you know about her?' he asked.

'I must have read it somewhere.' These names come up like memories and are nothing new to me.

Our eyes met; suddenly I communicated myself to him, and he understood my desire. Women had once been members of the ancient Academy. Why not now? In its rebirth in Florence, why did the Academy keep its doors closed to women? Suddenly he felt my need as if it were his own.

'If you would obtain intelligent children, you should be educating the mothers,' I told him.

He nodded. 'Quintilian says as much.'

'Angelo, why do you rely so heavily on ancient authority? I could have told you that before I had even heard of Quintilian.'

✝

August 28th, 1479

In this summer, spent sitting out the war like a god on Olympus, Angelo is restored to his muse-mother, Calliope. He has only to walk in the garden or in the lanes for images to work themselves naturally into lines. The old alchemy is back, and once again he is the crucible in which the mundane is mixed with high language and made eternal. The gold that has come from base metal is his song for Giuliano, wrought now in a new measure and exquisite in its beauty. Each time I hear it, I stop breathing, my heart slows, I weep. A song for lost beauty.

Sometimes I pass by the library or his study and see him at his desk with his head on one side and I know that he is listening, that writing is

346

listening, and that he is in private communion with his Muse. Then I tip-
toe away to the kitchen and arrange for him a tray of refreshment, as I always
do, usurping the servants in this duty, and put a flower there, a marigold or
a lily, as my own offering to Calliope.

Other times Angelo will be grumbling and annoyed, claiming that life is
three parts banality mixed with two parts insecurity: a tedium relieved only
by thought of inevitable death. Then I fetch his pen and notebook and encour-
age him to write, for life was ever thus, I tell him. It was thus even for the
ancient Greeks and Romans; if it seems through books to have been more
colourful, more brave, nobler in the past, it is only because of the language
of poets. Now, as Virgil had done for Rome, he, Poliziano, must do for
Florence.

Such was my song, with idle thought
In Fiesole's cool grottoes wrought,
Where from the Medici's retreat
On that famed mount, beneath my feet
The Tuscan city I survey,
The Arno winding far away.

September, 1479

A tempest! Just as a clear sky can turn thunderous, and heavy claps boom
through the mountains, and downpours soak the ground, so can the mood of
my brother change, especially if Bartolommeo Scala is about. This morning
he was sunny and cloudless, for he finished his translation of Epictetus
yesterday evening and performed that miraculous thing for Poliziano, which
is to bring some one thing to completion. Out of the scatter of leaves, a book
of wisdom. He went straight off to Florence and the bookshop of Vespasiano
da Bisticci, hoping to find an audience. Despite war, despite plague, the
famous bookshop still attracted several customers, among them Bartolommeo
Scala. Being in charge of the entire corps of soldiers in the war, Scala was
not someone Angelo had expected to meet in a bookshop, but, as Scala
announced to the company present, even though he was busy day and night
in the defence of Florence, he still found time to maintain his scholarly
pursuits.

Vespasiano asked Scala how he accomplished so many great things and still found time to read.

'My secret is the night. I do not sleep. No more than three hours at a stretch. In my opinion, sleep is a great waste of time.'

There were murmurings of admiration throughout the shop, but Angelo had forgotten Scala on the instant when he saw a certain pair of grey eyes watching him. Giovanni Pico della Mirandola, passing once again through Florence on his way back home, had called into this bookshop, as famous for its customers as for its books. It was in itself an academy, attracting scholars and poets with an hour to spare for conversation. Angelo went to him and told him that his translation was finished. Pico silenced the chattering customers and called for their attention. He announced the completion of Poliziano's translation of Epictetus and called for a reading from the author. Angelo complied, went to a reading lectern and began to recite the tenets of stoicism, thrilling to the power of the words.

'Clearly the thrill was lost on the audience,' he told me. 'It was not long before I was reading for Pico alone, for he alone can appreciate the thought of Epictetus in its profundity.'

When he came to the end of the Manual, he invited comment.

Scala expostulated 'like a bursting bubble of sulphur, a hot splut of noisome mud.' The prior denounced Epictetus, saying that his precepts were not only so obscure as to be impenetrable, but that they were also false.

'How do you know they are false if, as you admit, you cannot understand them?' Pico asked, colouring as he spoke, as bashful as he was brave. Emboldened and encouraged, Angelo flashed a smile of gratitude at his champion before rounding on Scala and telling him that, if it was a literary battle he wanted, he would be very pleased to meet him in the field.

Scala's eyes narrowed. He was not used to being challenged, and he had still not forgiven Poliziano for humiliating him over his error in Latin. He twitched angrily, but the presence of the mysterious youth was giving his enemy subtle strength. 'I agree, this is best fought out in writing,' he declared. 'I shall state my objections in a letter.'

'Well, if you are sure I will understand what you have to say…'

'Aaaarh!' Scala cried, as if shot by an arrow. 'You upstart shoemaker! You pagan! I will so refute you and your heathen stoical philosophy as to have

348

you chased from this city. Aye, and your pretty friend with you!' He strode from the bookshop.

Vespasiano the bookseller was concerned on Angelo's behalf. 'I have no doubt that you will win the argument, but at what cost? It is an unwise man who makes an enemy of Bartolommeo Scala,' he said.

Giovanni Pico told them that, in the north, in the ancient universities, men lived to contend. 'Logical disputation, or dialectic, is the most profitable exercise for the intellect, since what survives any argument is that which is true, and truth is what matters. Men's feelings are of no consequence.'

'But even if they are,' Angelo said, 'then disputation is still to be recommended, for such battles, according to Homer, bring much glory and renown. The Greeks called it kudianeira.'

'And most of them died young,' the bookseller said pertly.

But with that belief in immortality which is the prerogative of youth, Angelo expressed his willingness to accept Scala's challenge, especially if he had Giovanni Pico as his squire. Others present warned them both against youthful rashness.

'Please do not forget,' said Angelo, 'who started this. Only moments ago Scala was, in front of you all, denouncing the great Epictetus. I mean only to defend, not attack. I myself have gained nothing but profit from this little book. Scala is utterly mistaken to say it is not true.'

By the time he was home, however, his brilliant self-confidence had become a storm of fury against all philistines, especially those in high places, and he has been booming and crashing about the villa ever since. I shall go and persuade him to sing a few lauds with me, for it is impossible for a man to sing and be angry at the same time.

35

Florence, September, 1479

THE SUMMER SWELLS *towards autumn and mosquitoes are born of stagnant ponds. Peasants eating bean bread and blighted wheat are having visions of saints before they die. St Michael rises in flames above Tuscan hills,* and circles of angels appear in the sky like a funnel to heaven. Even as they die starving and with the words of Revelation pounding in their ears, it does not occur to any of these honest Tuscans that the evil which has befallen them is because of their own pride. They are too proud for that. Instead, to the end and in their death throes, they curse the Pope and his evil brood, and commit their blood and bone to the nourishment of their native soil.

Angelo has told me a story he heard from Lorenzo. Phillipe de Commynes, the amabassador of France, went to Rome to tell the Pope that, with Turkish advances in Greece and Bosnia, and with Turkish threats to the borders of Hungary and Poland, now was not the time to be in a feud with a Christian brother. The Pope sent the embassy away. So the Holy Roman Emperor, Frederick III, sent a mission to Rome, calling for a General Council to debate the infidel threat to Christendom. The Pope rejected the authority of the Council and sent the emissaries of the Emperor away. So the King of England sent a deputation to Rome to plead for peace. 'Good God, man,' the English ambassador shouted at the Pope, temporarily forgetting himself. 'Have you lost your wits?' The Pope, graciously choosing to honour the custom whereby ambassadors enjoy freedom and protection in hostile courts, sent the Englishman away with his bowels intact. But the Englishman's words rankled Sixtus until finally – when confronted by the joint embassy of Florence, Milan, Venice, France and the Holy Roman Empire – he consented to a truce with Florence.

'But,' he thundered, rising before the ambassadors like a mountainous island erupting from the sea, 'I demand that the Florentine Republic – in the person of Lorenzo de' Medici – do humble itself before me, beg forgiveness for her transgressions, and make reparation to us for our losses in the war.'

The two Florentine representatives snorted contemptuously. Although they resumed their ambassadorial masks at once, and looked like innocent angels kneeling on the sacred ground of St Peter's, the Pope had heard their scorn and glared at them with undiluted hatred. He sent them back to Florence to present his terms to Lorenzo.

Lorenzo found himself unable to accept those terms.

'So he is not going to humble himself and beg forgiveness?' I asked Angelo.

'Of course not!'

'What will it take to end this war?'

'Intelligence. We have never supposed we could match the brawn of Rome and Naples combined, at least, not since we discovered the friendship of the King of France is made of gossamer. David slew Goliath with a little stone and a sling.'

'What is our little stone?'

'A word. The right word in the right ear at the right time. Lorenzo will talk his way out of this war. He has the gift of speech like no other.'

My doubt must have been expressed on my face, for suddenly it was reflected in Angelo's and he pushed his plate away and could eat no more. He sat at table with his head in his hands.

We can no longer ignore the war, pretend that it is not happening, that it does not affect us.

'Angelo,' I whispered. 'We must speak about it. Behind all the false, incoherent accusations, the matter is simple: Rome wants Florence. Rome will have Florence. Florence without the Medici.'

He nodded without looking up, his head still in his hands.

'Without the Medici means without us.'

He nodded again.

'Angelo, have you any plans?'

His hidden head turned from side to side within his hands.

'In a poem we would give ourselves up to death, but this is not a poem, it is life. We need plans.'

He looked up then, his face white. 'Maria, I have no plans, can have no plans since without Lorenzo I cannot exist. Do you not understand? I, depending as I do on patronage, am a parasite who cannot survive the death of the host.'

'What will happen to them, Lorenzo and his family?'

Angelo rose up abruptly, saying he did not want to discuss the matter. He left the room. He was back at once. 'You,' he said, 'are returning to Montepulciano.'

'No! Never! I shall never leave you!'

'Death will force the issue.'

'Then we shall die together!

✝

351

This evening Angelo dined alone with his patron, trying to divert Lorenzo with various precepts of Epictetus which show that Man is spirit and not matter. Lorenzo appreciated the attempt, but suddenly he, the philosopher, did not want to be told that this world was the realm of shadows and dreams; he had Ficino to tell him that. He wanted solid things, not abstractions, something to hold on to.

'I hear you are taunting my Scala and making him look a fool.'

'He does not need my help to look a fool. He is arguing against Epictetus by ignoring the whole first book of the Manual, which is like taking the centre out of a circle and then saying it is not a circle. Without that first book nothing else remains coherent, and of course now he accuses Epictetus of incoherence. Lorenzo, I was raised to wear no sword, and I abhor violence, but there are times when I want to take Scala by the throat and press my thumbs into his windpipe. Not because I hate him, but because I consider his ignorance an offence to Almighty God.'

'If that is so, leave God to do the choking.'

'If God acts through agencies, who is to say I am not His agent?'

They were interrupted by the sudden, alarmed entry of a servant who was trembling as he told Lorenzo that he was required to attend a meeting of the Council of War.

'What has happened?'

'Our fortress at Poggibonsi – it has fallen to the Duke of Calabria.'

Poggibonsi, situated at a great meeting of roads, was our last stronghold. All that remains now between us and disaster is the little town of Colle.

Lorenzo stood up at once. 'Happily Bartolommeo Scala lives,' he said tartly as he left, 'or else who could I turn to now?'

Angelo came back to Fiesole, disturbed by what Lorenzo had said. He would not speak to me at first, nor tell me why he was wearing the aspect of Zeus. He went directly to the library and set to revising his latest response to Scala refuting the man's feeble arguments. Intellectually my brother could dance round the prior as Odysseus round the blinded Cyclops, but he was not enjoying it.

'It is done,' he said, re-emerging late, his gown spattered with ink and candlewax, brandishing a letter. 'The matter is settled. Scala will not be able to answer this, and I shall provoke him no further.'

He read to me his burning defence of a stoic philosopher long dead and the accompanying letter that ended, 'We must struggle against the turmoil of these times, Scala, defending ourselves as far as we are able by studying literature and philosophy.' He put the letter down and gazed at me, asking me what I thought. 'Is it true? Is literature a proper study for such times as these? Or will Scala shower me with further scorn?'

My poor brother. Raised by a pacifist father, he yet dreams of being Patroclus. While Maso is on duty at the camp at San Casciano, Angelo is living the life of a pampered eunuch. He wants to fight, but fate and nature have not equipped him. Therefore he has created his own battlefield, but to fight by studying literature and philosophy? A man such as Scala will take much convincing.

I asked Angelo how he had felt as he wrote it, and he described having the power of Poesia coursing through him, 'as if I spoke for all poets and all philosophers of all ages, and I know I wrote the truth. But you do not believe it.'

'It is difficult to think, with the enemy almost upon us, that the reading of books is any defence.'

'That is because you believe the enemy is the Roman and Neapolitan armies.'

'Who then?'

'Remember the myth of Orpheus. The Maenads wanted to rip him apart, but while he was singing their weapons were powerless. They had to overcome his song and they succeeded by creating such a clamour, such screaming and screeching, that he was drowned out. And then they killed him. Who is the real enemy? Look into your mind, Maria. What are the Maenads doing but screaming, creating such fear that we doubt ourselves and our God? It is not the armies that will win this war, but Fear and Doubt. Therefore we read our books and keep singing. Keep singing. The song must be sung. The song of beauty, harmony, justice. It is our only defence.'

As he spoke these words, tears welled in his eyes.

✠

Bartolommeo Scala was not there to receive Angelo's letter. The Council of War wished to send someone to rally the Florentine allies in support of Colle.

Lorenzo offered to go himself, but was told it was too dangerous. The loyal Scala went in his stead.

October, 1479

The autumn weather is beautiful, the sun bright, the air cool and scented, the skin prickling with anticipation, but of what? It seems strange that autumn should lead to winter. It should lead not to death but to transformation of a more sublime kind, a liberation from earthly bondage which is not death. Olives hang on the trees like tears. Dew drops hang on spiders' webs like tears. There is a solemn hush in the air until, every now and again, the wind sobs. All nature seems to be at a funeral. The beauty of it makes the pain intense.

We get little news up here on our hill of purgatory. Lorenzo is too busy to see Angelo. Rumour and Gossip have as their favourite topic one Bartolommeo Scala. When he left Florence he went first to San Casciano, where the various forces of the league were camped, and tried to get them to move to San Gimignano, closer to Colle. He toured the whole region, organising the troops and ensuring good supplies not only for the soldiers but for the inhabitants of town and country. He was tireless, he was efficient, he was ruthless. Having done all he could, he returned to Florence to take up his pen and vanquish that arrogant poet, Angelo Poliziano, but in this tournament of philosophy he did not have the command of Latin grammar required to control the lance of his intellect: he could not say what he meant, and with every exchange of letter, Poliziano unhorsed him. People accused Angelo of troubling our hero of the war.

Scala was recalled last week from the groves of the academy to the field of battle and returned once more to the league camp at San Casciano, but still he cannot persuade the captains to move to San Gimignano. Having arranged all the other forces to take the enemy's rear, Scala wants Colle to mount an attack.

'Who are you to make the strategies?' demands Ercole d' Este, the Duke of Ferrara and the commander of our forces.

'A secretary of the Republic, my lord, and one of the Council of War. We want action. We want this matter resolved. The time for dallying is over. You have bled us dry with your demands, and now we want the goods we have

bought. We want action and we want victory!' (Florence cheers at this reported speech.)

'You do not know the first thing about war,' thunders Duke Ercole. 'I do not answer to secretaries. Leave these matters to soldiers!'

Scala leaves the duke's striped tent in a blaze of indignation. He walks through the camp, criticising everyone in his path. He comes across a man asleep in a tangle of armour.

'Look at you, sluggard!' Scala said, kicking the thigh of Maso Ambrogini.

Maso opens his eyes slowly and gazes at him. 'You must be Bartolommeo Scala. Your reputation precedes you.'

'Do you know how much we pay you to sleep?'

'Precious little. And certainly not enough to die for.'

'I have had lesser men than you whipped for insubordination.'

'Whip me and you will have Lorenzo de' Medici to answer to. He is almost my kinsman.'

'In what way?'

Maso announces that he is the cousin of Angelo Poliziano. Scala orders his immediate lashing.

'What is my crime?' Maso shouts as he is dragged to the stake to be tied there.

'The sin of your fathers is visited upon you,' Scala says drily, wielding the whip himself until his arm aches. He leaves the young man alive but barely, and wishes that it was the man's cousin who is sagging in the thongs, weeping in his agony.

☩

Arriving at San Gimignano, the walled hilltop town in sight of Colle, Scala finds the captain of the local force asleep in his tent. 'Still in your bed at dawn?' he cries. 'We are at war, man. Rise up at once!' He cracks his whip across the soles of the man's naked feet.

Even before the captain has recovered, Scala is out of the tent and rousing the militia, having them assemble on the hillside outside the town, where their burnished armour would catch the rising sun and be visible to the Neapolitans camped outside Colle. 'Today,' he declares, 'Colle is to give the battle signal, and I want the enemy to know we are here.'

355

A shivering man is brought to him, a Neapolitan spy, it is said. Scala himself attends the interrogation and hears the man's confession, brought from him only by extreme torture.

'What shall we do?' the captain asks.

'Send his statement back to Florence.'

'No, I mean with him.'

Scala does not even glance at the panting, bleeding man staring up at him with the eyes of a beaten dog.

'Hang him,' he says, and leaves the room.

As he continues his inspection of the town, he makes lists of supplies required by the soldiers and the people, and listens carefully to all petitions. A member of the infantry, who has the misfortune to be both a foreigner and a coward, is brought before him and accused of avoiding duty. Scala has the man given over to the children of the town to be kicked to death.

'If what we need to win this war is sluggards,' he writes to Lorenzo, 'we shall be victorious everywhere.'

By the end of that day, however, there are no sluggards left in San Gimignano.

Battle has commenced on the distant hill, clouds of dust can be seen, and fires starting, but no other detail is visible. Scala continues in his efforts, having bread and flour brought into the famished town. 'First fortifications are the hearts of the inhabitants,' he tells his men. But try as he might, even Bartolommeo Scala cannot get the league camp to move to San Gimignano and come to the aid of Colle. The brave people of that town fight alone to defend themselves.

This is the story going round Fiesole, and people call out the name of Bartolommeo Scala in joy and say this is the way to win a war. Angelo sits alone with the letter that has come from Maso, written for him by a camp scribe, a letter crumpled up in his fist, and says to himself, 'Peace does not come from superior strength. Peace comes from Love and Reason. Love, not war. Love, not war. Heavenly Venus, subdue your livid lover Mars. Protect us, Venus, protect us.'

36

WHILE BARTOLOMMEO SCALA was still in the south, Lorenzo was visiting his family, preparing them for yet another winter in the Mugello, although this time in the tower of Trebbio. He was putting his castello at Cafaggiolo up for sale. Although the term of office for members of the Council of War was at an end, and elections were due for the next council, neither he nor Scala expected any change in its members. Why should they? The Council did nothing without their approval. But in the absence of its two dominant members, the Council met and discussed the abject fortunes of the city, the course of the war, the demands of the Pope, the needs of the people. In the absence of Scala and Lorenzo, they grew brave and acted on a wild initiative. They re-elected a Council where every single member, including themselves, was replaced.

Lorenzo received the news on his return. He stood staring at Niccolò Michelozzi unable to absorb the message. He laughed. 'What do you mean, I am not elected?' It was incomprehensible that Florence could do anything without him, that his city might be independent, might indeed be the republic it called itself.

'None of the original magistrates have been reappointed, Magnifico,' said Niccolò Michelozzi. 'It is the city's choice.'

Lorenzo stared at his secretary. 'What is the message beneath the message, Niccolò? What are they telling me?'

Niccolò dared not hazard a guess. It took a supreme effort for him to tell Lorenzo the other news, that after spending all summer hiding in Appenine valleys, the army of Girolamo Riario was now on the move, coming towards Florence on the Mugello road which would take it past Cafaggiolo and Trebbio. 'Do not be concerned! It flows as slow as lava and we have about a fortnight before they come anywhere near the villa. We can go and get the family before they arrive.'

'Send for them at once. Do not delay!'

Lorenzo stared at the crucifix on the wall. Carved by a master such as Donatello, a piece of limewood had been invested with sorrow, the body of Christ a very human body twisted in mortal agony. He stared at it for a long time, and in that time became broken himself and dispirited. He went to his mother's chamber.

'Mother,' he said, taking hold of her hand. 'Everything has fallen away from me. The city wants me no longer, and without the city I am nothing. I have spent a year and a half inflated, held up by the confidence of Florence. Without that confidence, I am nothing.' He looked into her troubled face, seeking wisdom there. 'What counsel have you for me now?'

Monna Lucrezia went to speak but all she produced was juddering breath. 'Lorenzo,' she whispered at last, 'I do not know what to say, but if you lose faith then so do I.'

'I have spent all this time shored up, animated by the belief that I am right and the Pope is wrong.'

'How can you doubt that? He killed your brother!'

'Lately a thought has entered as a worm. What if I have been wrong? What if it is true, that I am culpable and sacrilegious? What then?'

'But it is not true. This war is founded on the accusation that you murdered the archbishop. But he was the murderer and his death was a just punishment. What are you saying?'

'The Pope's accusation is false in that respect, but what of others? Am I free of sin? Ha! I am riddled with it. But it is not that. For three generations the Medici have played patron to a new philosophy and a new learning in the belief that by such means Man may find God. But the Church says that it is hubris to seek to know God, that we may only approach Him by faith. A man who would know is a heretic.'

'Your wife would think so.'

'Aye, Clarice. And what if she is right and I am wrong? If we would know the Will of God, we have only to look at what is in front of us. What faces me now is hatred. The hatred of the Pope

I can explain and justify, but the hatred of my Florentines I cannot. In their faces I see the will of God. He does not love his Medici, and there is nothing I can do to win back His love. It is finished.'

'No! No, Lorenzo!' Tears started to Monna Lucrezia's eyes and ran unchecked down her face. There was nothing she could say. She had reached the end of her counsel and advice. It was all with God now.

God and Ficino. Monna Lucrezia sent a message begging for Marsilio's help.

'My son,' she wrote, 'believes that all these ill omens have one clear message: that God is displeased with him and wants him dead. His mind is a contagion of doubt and he believes he is in error. One of you must surrender his pride, and Lorenzo cannot do it. You have been abused by us, Father Marsilio, and on my son's behalf I apologise. Please help us, Father, please.'

Ficino went to see Lorenzo in his chamber and, walking in unannounced, found him alone, stripped naked to the waist and in his hand a flail of five leather thongs tipped with iron.

'Give me that,' Ficino said. 'Do not abase yourself this way. This is arrogance, this is false humility, this is a crime against God.'

Lorenzo cracked the whip in the air angrily, making the philosopher start. 'I have listened to you for too long. Believed in your Divine Providence too long. A crime against God? What care I about God? He is my God no longer,' said Lorenzo. 'He is my enemy. For all His Omnipotence, He has judged me and found me guilty. And He is wrong. He does not know my heart. He is a false god. With a false church!'

Ficino took a step backwards, repelled by such blasphemy.

'He took my brother. What kind of god is that?' Lorenzo raised the flail above his head again, but when he brought it down this time it was neither in the air nor on himself. He threw all his weight, all his fury behind it and cracked it hard against the image of Christ crucified, with such force that Donatello's wood carving exploded in fragments and fell in a shower of wall plaster. Ficino stood there aghast. Lorenzo snatched up the figure of the dying God and hurled it against the wall.

'What is this religion, that has murderers for popes?' he shouted. 'What is this Holy Spirit that always elects the wrong man?'

'Lorenzo!'

'This is superstition, all of it, and I will believe no longer!'

'Lorenzo! One more step on this road and you are lost. Go no further, you are at the edge of the abyss.'

'What brings you here? Have I not killed your friendship with suspicion? What brings you here now?'

'The hope for reconciliation,' Ficino said simply. He bent down and picked up the fragments of the cross, carried them to a table and tried to piece them together. 'It is just as well that neither God nor his Love are made of wood.'

In the face of Ficino's wry humour, Lorenzo's fury could only subside.

Ficino smiled. 'Admit it. You do not believe one word you have spoken.'

'But I should believe it. The alternative is too terrible: that I am the one in the wrong.' Lorenzo sighed. 'Father, I was your pupil once. I am your pupil still. Tell me what is absolutely good.'

Ficino sat down, Lorenzo did likewise, sitting with Ficino as he had when he was a boy, listening to him speak in a prophetic vein.

'God is loving light in which there are no shadows. God is shining love in which there is no hatred. He who stays in this loving light and shining love abides in God and God in him. Your soul is immortal, Lorenzo. This God you deny pervades you. Without him you are not.'

'What is His will?' Lorenzo asked angrily, 'that He torments me like this?'

'Ask your self such questions. What is your will? Why do you torment yourself? These will bring you more practical answers. Is it your will to live or die?'

'To live, of course.'

'Are you sure?'

'What man is unsure of it? Tell me, what must I do to end this war?'

'That much at least is obvious.'

'To whom?'

'To anyone who is not Lorenzo de' Medici. You must surrender yourself to the enemy.'

Lorenzo jumped to his feet in anguish. 'I would rather die!'

'I thought as much.' Ficino regarded him with that familiar twinkle in his eye that Lorenzo both loved and loathed.

'You think it is easy, do you, to prostrate yourself in front of one such as Sixtus IV?'

'Impossibly difficult,' said the philosopher, still smarting from the memory of his own inquisition. 'Therefore it is my advice that you do not go to Rome, but to Naples. The King bears no personal animosity against you. Talk to him. Speak to him of truth and poetry. Enchant him. Draw him to you.'

'The King of Naples eats people.'

'Fables. Besides you will have God with you, and you will not be eaten.'

'How can you be so sure? I am not a child any more. I am a man, and am grown sceptical with age. I cannot believe you just because you tell me to.'

'Who is speaking? Where is my poet? Where is the man who wrote those sublime verses on The Supreme Good? Where is the man who is in communion with Dante? Lorenzo!'

'He is dead! The poet in me has died – he had to. He could not sit in endless councils of war and survive!'

'Lorenzo,' Ficino's voice entered him, commanding. 'Stop this arrogance now, this assumption that the war is not only your fault, but yours for the winning or losing. You cannot do anything but enact God's will, or not – that is your only choice. The winning or losing is for Providence alone.'

'How may I enchant the King of Naples?'

'By being yourself, who enchants us all. What is the source of this doubt?'

361

'Experience.'

'Experience of what?'

'Human nature.'

'But humanity is your greatest love, your *gentilezza*, your beautiful lady. Do you toss her aside, believing in false accusations made against her? Love her, Lorenzo, serve her, you are her knight and champion. And listen to me – I am convinced that you must go to King Ferrante and speak to him in person. He is a good man who has forgotten goodness. Appeal to his soul.'

Lorenzo expressed doubt that King Ferrante had a soul.

'Undoubtedly he is ruthless,' Ficino replied, 'but even cruel men have souls. And as souls are bestial or angelic according to that by which they are nourished, so you must go to your enemy and feed his soul with truth. As you are no longer a member of the Council, you may go not as a statesman but as a private citizen and a poet. When you find the opportunity, gently remind him of the qualities of his father, Alfonso the Magnanimous. He will listen. And Lorenzo,' the philosopher concluded, 'never forget your own soul, which is undoubtedly angelic and divine in origin.'

Lorenzo asked him if success were possible; Ficino said that it may not be. 'Let there be no mistake. What is being asked of you is that you sacrifice yourself. One life in return for so many – it is a small price, if it must be paid.'

'Ha! Easy for you to think so.'

'Easy indeed, given that I believe in the soul's immortality. And so do you. This is the Will of God: to live by that which you know to be true, and be prepared to die for it.'

✝

What Lorenzo did not know, but I knew, was how many letters Ficino had been writing, letters of prophecy and inspiration, calling on all the players of the play to recognise the truth and goodness of themselves, letters to the Pope, to the King of Naples, to cardinals. Extraordinary letters. Mirrors for souls to gaze upon themselves. For the past eighteen months he had worked with other philosophers of the inner circle of the Platonic Academy, had studied the planets, had read and understood the power of Mars and Saturn over us at this time, had forseen war, famine and pestilence – had seen further, and knew that a false prophet was to come, and that Italy would be swamped by foreigners. But he had not told Lorenzo because he had wanted Lorenzo to realise for himself what was necessary, that he lay down his pride, and his life if necessary.

✢

Lorenzo picked up the splinters of Christ where Ficino had arranged them. A knee. A hand, its palm pierced by a nail. A face of pain. A crown of thorns. Reviled. A piece of inscription: *This is Jesus, the King of the Jews.*

Lorenzo went to his knees then prostrated himself on the floor. 'Dear Lord my God, hear my prayer. Whatever you will for me, that will I do. Guide me in every step, and open my ears to your guidance. I will lay myself down for you. If it is your will that Florence be saved by my death, so be it.'

Even as Lorenzo ended his prayer and came to his feet, Niccolò Michelozzi knocked and entered. 'The King of Naples has sent a messenger demanding that you surrender in person to Alfonso, Duke of Calabria.'

Lorenzo nodded, quiescent. 'Let it be.'

Michelozzi stared at him in horror.

'In Naples,' Lorenzo said.

'My lord?'

'I will surrender in Naples, to the King himself. Make arrangements, Niccolò. And let it be known that I am acting as a private citizen and not as a representative of Florence. Tell the Signoria I shall stop this war with my life.'

Michelozzi froze in shock.

'I trust you will regain your powers of speech and movement soon, for I am in a hurry.'

'My lord.' Michelozzi bowed. 'Who will you take with you?'

'Only my most trusted of friends.'

'My lord.'

'Are you one of them, Niccolò?'

'My lord.'

'Is there nothing else you can say, man?'

Poor Michelozzi, who did not want to die, could think of nothing. 'No, my lord. Except – I hope my courage may match my loyalty, for I am your friend. My lord.'

Lorenzo left him to discover in himself how deep his friendship lay.

Matteo Franco approached him excitedly with another message.

'We have just had word, Magnifico. The Mugello is under snow. Riario's army has turned back. The family is safe.'

37

Florence and Fiesole, December 1479

I FOUND ANGELO and Maria at the hearth in the master chamber of the Medici villa on Fiesole, wrapped in fur-lined cloaks against the icy draught. The hills are for summer, not winter, and the cool breeze that is so pleasant in August is a torment in December. The whole air in the house was bitter and damp, except in the pool of the fire. I joined them at its hearth to listen to Angelo's story-telling. He was recounting the myth of the golden apple.

'It was at the marriage of Peleus and Thetis. The goddess of discord, who had not been included among the guests, arrived and took her vengeance by throwing into the assembly of the gods a golden apple on which were written the words *For the Fairest*. All the goddesses claimed it as their own but in the ensuing contention the competitors were soon reduced to three: Juno, Venus and Minerva. The gods were wise enough not to be the judge of the matter and they elected Paris, son of King Priam of Troy, to arbitrate. Poor Paris! The goddesses appeared before him naked and unadorned. *Poor* Paris! Juno offered him a kingdom; Minerva offered him military victory; Venus offered him the most beautiful woman in the world.'

'Fool!' said Maria. 'He chose Venus!'

'Indeed. The most beautiful woman in the world was Helen, wife of Menelaus of Sparta, and her abduction by Paris led to the battle of Troy. Which goddess do you think Paris should have chosen?'

'Juno,' said Maria.

'Why?'

'Because she offered him a kingdom! Better that than a mortal woman, no matter how beautiful.'

'Minerva,' said I.

'Why Minerva?'

'It is one thing to win a kingdom, another to keep it against your enemies.'

'Indeed,' said Angelo, satisfied. 'Minerva is the right choice.'

Maria tossed her head imperiously on behalf of the rejected goddess. Since the night of the birth, I had come to view her differently. She was no longer a stranger, no longer Angelo's sister, but my own. We enjoyed an easy affection now when we three were alone as on this night. She could *harrumph* and pull faces or argue to the death without any need to assume formal behaviour or affect demureness.

I had come via Fiesole on my way home from Careggi because I wanted to know if Angelo was aware of Lorenzo's plans. To look at him contented before the fire with Maria was to know the answer: he was oblivious to them. When Maria went to arrange for some refreshment, I asked him, 'Have you heard the news?'

'Yes,' he said. 'Lorenzo is going to Pisa.'

'Pisa?'

We stared at each other.

'What is it?' he said.

'Angelo, he is going to surrender himself – and himself alone, not the city – to the enemy.'

The blood drained from his face.

How could he not have known, he, the one man who would follow Lorenzo to hell? While each of Lorenzo's friends in the city prevaricated and tried to find an excuse not to go, this one, the one who would have gone without question, did not even know about the plan. I said a mistake had obviously been made, that a letter from Lorenzo must have gone astray.

He agreed, that must be the reason. We both knew it was not.

I was a friend of his, as were others such as Ficino and Pico della Mirandola, but we were in a lower heaven of friendship. In the empyrean there was only Lorenzo. As there was nothing I could do to heal the hurt I had inadvertently delivered, I rose from my chair.

'Apologise to Maria for me but I shall not want refreshment. I need to get home to Elena.'

He nodded.

I could not leave fast enough.

✢

I told Ficino that Lorenzo had not asked Angelo to go with him; Ficino told Lorenzo that he had forgotten someone. Lorenzo said he had not forgotten. He had not chosen his companions yet, was still sounding men out, and did not feel the need to sound out Angelo Poliziano at all. 'Since his constancy is beyond question. I will of course, but not until I see him in person on Sunday. I trust he has not heard of the plan in advance?'

'No,' said Ficino to Lorenzo. 'No,' said I to Ficino.

✢

When the sturdy city of Colle fell to the Duke of Calabria, all the bells of Florence tolled as if for a funeral. Although the armies had retired for the winter, everyone believed that all that stood between us and disaster was time. With the spring would come our doom, and there was nothing we could do but wait.

Maso returned to the Medici villa on Fiesole. At once the

cousins began to argue. Maso saw no reason not to sue for peace, while Angelo reminded him that the Pope's terms demanded that Florence offer up Lorenzo.

'So?' Maso shrugged. 'Let us do it.'

Loyalty being the measure of his friendship, Angelo said nothing of Lorenzo's plans; instead he rushed to Lorenzo's defence, rounded on his cousin for speaking such words in Lorenzo's own villa, and expelled him, sending him back to his house on the Via dei Fossi.

'That place stinks!' Maso protested.

'Then it will be a good place for you to rot.'

'Go to hell!'

Thus, with their usual expressions of endearment, the cousins parted.

Maso spent one night in the house on the Via dei Fossi before volunteering for the civic militia. He said he would rather sleep under the stars in December than endure another night in that decrepit building. In between spells of duty patrolling the battlements, he passed the time on the city walls by playing knucklebones and dice while getting drunk. With every passing day, the militia grew increasingly uncaring. Death loped back and forth outside the walls, watching them, waiting for them, tongue lolling, slavering; there was little to be done but try and outstare him, taunt him, dare him to come for them. Cheap wine in leather bottles was passed round, rough wine which could rob a man of his balance in no time at all. In response to a comment about his birthplace, Maso Ambrogini drew his dagger, and because of a sneering use of the word 'poliziano' a man fell from the walls and into the jaws of Death. Maso was dragged off to the city gaol, protesting all the time that he was no ordinary soldier but one who lived in the house of the Medici.

Lorenzo, in the midst of preparation for a new set of ambassadorial robes, surrounded by tailors with mouthfuls of pins, was approached by a civic magistrate and asked if he had any knowledge of one called Maso Ambrogini – for the man was in the gaol and claiming a connection with the Medici. Within the hour Maso was brought to Lorenzo's presence. Heavy pressure on his shoulders by the guard sent him to his knees.

'You have come to beg forgiveness?' Lorenzo asked.

'Not at all. Kill me if you like. What do I care? My life means nothing to me. But I hear that you are about to surrender.'

'How did you hear that?'

Maso had heard it in the prison. 'I am very impressed. I had not expected this of you. Will you be taking my cousin with you?'

'My arrangements are no business of yours.'

'If they touch on my cousin they are. Who will look after his sister if he dies and I am in gaol?' For the sake of the family, Maso was prepared to demolish the honour of its head, and he continued: 'Not that his death is likely, mind, since I do not suppose he has agreed to go with you. Angelo is a coward. I know it. You know it. His father was murdered in front of him and he did nothing about it. He is feeble and a coward. You cannot depend on him: he will let you down. You want a hero? Then take me in his stead. I will go to the enemy with you. I'd be glad to. This war is so dull that just to think about it is to fall asleep on your feet. Take me. If you want a hero, Magnifico, I am your man.'

'I do not need fighters. I need men who will face death with dignity. You are not my man.'

'Then neither is Angelo Poliziano. Face death with dignity? Ha! He cannot even face a headache with dignity. He does not want to die.'

'He is my most loyal servant and trusted friend. I have no doubt that what he wants is to be with me at all times, whatever the circumstances.'

'What my cousin wants is his independence but he is too cowardly to tell you so. There, it is out. But it is true. He has confessed himself to me. He wants to be free of the Medici.'

'That is a lie!' Lorenzo shouted. 'You are lying, you scoundrel. You cannot open your mouth without lying. This matter is private and I shall not discuss it with you.'

'And what of his sister? Whose business is she?'

'Being his sister she is my business.'

'Do you possess him so utterly? Let me tell you, Magnifico, she is my uncle's daughter. She belongs to her kin. If Angelo cannot look after her, she must be returned to Montepulciano. And who will safely escort her if not me?'

Lorenzo glared at him. Irritated, he called a secretary to him and had a letter written requesting Maso's release, dated, 'the day of my departure.' He gave the letter to Maso and then, with a nod of his head to the guard, had him escorted back to the gaol.

'And give him ten lashes for his impudence.'

Maso cursed Lorenzo hotly as he was pushed out of the room and wished him an evil fate. 'As you deserve!' he shouted. 'This is all your fault, Lorenzo! Everything that is happening! How many have died for you, you despicable tyrant?'

'Twenty lashes,' Lorenzo called.

Outside the door Maso shook off his guards. 'I can walk without your aid,' he spat at them. Coming up the stairs was a figure horribly familiar. Maso placed himself in front of Bartolommeo Scala and would not get out of his way. 'Never rest,' he whispered. 'Never close your eyes at night, not while I live.'

The sweat jumped out on Scala's brow.

'Snakes and scorpions – something small with sharp, poisonous teeth, in your bed or in your shoe when you least expect it. Never rest.'

'Who are you? Why are you threatening me? I have never seen you before!'

'I think you are more familiar with my back than my face. I am the cousin of Poliziano. We met at San Casciano.'

'Where are you taking this man?' Scala demanded of the guard.

'Back to the gaol.'

Scala ran up the stairs to see Lorenzo and implore him to have the key to Maso's cell thrown away.

‡

On Sunday Angelo went to the city to find out for himself what was happening. As he walked into the palazzo on the Via Larga, one of Lorenzo's bodyguards stepped forward and intercepted him, made him state his name and explain who he was.

'Francesco!' Angelo called, seeing one of the secretaries in the gallery above. 'Tell this fool who I am. And where is Lorenzo? Where will I find him?'

'If you want to see him you must make an appointment.'

'What?'

But Francesco did not have time to linger. Angelo found Niccolò Michelozzi and had it confirmed: he did indeed need an appointment.

'Even you. God Himself could not get to see Lorenzo today,' Niccolò said.

Angelo remounted and rode to Careggi to find Monna Lucrezia.

'Something is happening, is being arranged,' he said without preamble. 'What is it? Lorenzo is planning to leave and I must go with him. He must not leave me out of it. Madonna... I could not live. Matters are too serious now for me to play at being a poet or librarian. If we are facing death, then I will die at my friend's side. Oh, I know I am no hero, that I am only Patroclus in my dreams. But Orpheus sailed with Jason and the Argonauts, and I would sail with Lorenzo.'

Monna Lucrezia studied him closely. 'Are you truly willing to die?'

'Without question, since there would be no point in living without him.'

'I do not mean poetically, Angelo, or ideally, or heroically. But perhaps protractedly, under torture, in agony. There will be no glory in this death, only shame. Will you do that for your friend?'

'Tell me what is being planned! Is he going to Rome?'

'I will not tell you until I have your answer.'

Angelo had read too much Homer and Virgil. Across his mind raced images of pierced throats, gouts of blood, spilt brains, a severed hand groping for its sword. Young lives lost for no reason.

No reason. But in this war there were no battles and no glory. Death when it came would come by flaying in a public square, or by a beheading. The most Angelo could hope for was that they would kneel together at the same block, two necks severed by one blade. Together in death and everlasting fame.

'Well?' Monna Lucrezia interrupted his thoughts.

'Would I die for and with Lorenzo? Yes, of course, he is my friend, my brother, my self. There is no question of it. Why do you keep asking?'

'Because men have a tendency to think of glory, while women think only of pain. Have you understood the question?'

He looked her full in the eye, told her that when it came to death, his imagination was better than any woman's, and that nevertheless he meant to go. His voice was grave and sincere, his eye honest. Monna Lucrezia reached out and touched him affectionately. 'I shall tell him. For now, return to Fiesole and make your preparations. Word will be sent in due course, but there may not be much notice so have your clothes packed and ready.'

'Where are we to go?'

'I cannot say.'

'What of Maria?'

'I shall take her. She may come here.'

✝

Angelo came back from Careggi looking pale and strained. He went to his room and only after an hour did he call me to him, to tell me that Lorenzo is going to surrender himself to the enemy, and that Angelo is going with him.

No! I threw myself on him, clung to him begging. He is me and I him. We cannot be parted. I will die and so will he. 'Do not send me away! Do not leave! Let us stay here on Fiesole forever. Oh why did you not become the provost? Now do you see? You should have listened to me!' The words came out back to front and upside down and made their own kind of sense. 'Take me with you. Look, I can cut my hair again. I shall be your page.

No one will know. Or your brother. Let me be your brother. You cannot leave me. I will not go!'

He prised my hands off his jacket. I felt the world going cold and the sky above us freezing over. 'Don't go. Don't leave me. Angelo, please, don't go! What about your books? Your work? What shall I do with it all? All those books – what shall I do?' I fluttered and struggled like a bird caught in nets.

'You are breaking my heart, little sister. Be quiet and trust in God. I am called to go, and go I must. I have made arrangements for you to take refuge with Monna Lucrezia at Careggi. Maria, she needs you as much as you need her. You will be collected this afternoon.'

'When are you going?'

'Now.'

'Now? You will need to pack clothes, surely?'

But he had done that himself already, before speaking to me. I went to the courtyard on legs that could barely support me and watched him mount his horse. A mule was brought out and loaded up with a travelling chest and some leather bags. I stood and cried, for all that I have hoped for is vanished like smoke. I kept my face in my hands. He did not say farewell. There was the clopping of hooves on the courtyard stone, words exchanged with servants, the sound of a gate opening. And closing.

Now I have no hope and no vision of the future. My prophetic heart is silent, plunging into a void both profound and terrible.

✝

On his way to the Palazzo Medici, Angelo went to the gaol to see Maso, to tell him what was happening. Maso was lying face down on a pallet, his back scored and bloodied by iron-tipped thongs.

'What has happened to you?'

'Lorenzo ordered it,' said Maso, painfully rising up.

'*Lorenzo?*'

'It is what tyrants do, especially when you tell them the truth about themselves. Why are you so surprised? So, you are going with him. You are going to throw your life away and not trouble about your family. A pox on you.'

'Maso, this is no time to argue. About Maria…'

372

'I will look after her. Rely on me.'

'There is no need. I have arranged accommodation for her with Monna Lucrezia.'

'Lorenzo has appointed me to be her guardian.'

'What? You liar! When was that arranged? And how can you look after her, locked up as you are?'

'As soon as Lorenzo departs I am to be released. He has given me his word.' Maso held his cousin's eye steadily. 'Maria is an Ambrogini, not a Medici. She must come back to us. For the honour of the family she should be married or in a convent, and Derio and I will arrange it, since you are so reluctant to act. Lorenzo agrees.'

'I do not believe you! He would not arrange my affairs without speaking to me.'

'When are you going to learn to trust your kin and not your powerful patron? You should know where your loyalties lie.'

Angelo glared at his cousin, not knowing what to believe. Maso showed him the document Lorenzo had signed. Then Angelo believed. Then he acted. He went from the gaol to the Palazzo Medici like a bolt from a crossbow. He did not make an appointment to see Lorenzo; passing through guards and waspish secretaries as if on an open road, he made straight for his chamber.

'Ah, you have heard,' Lorenzo said. 'I'm sorry if…'

'Who gave you the right to interfere with my family? Who do you think you are? You treat me like a pawn on your chequerboard. You want me to lay down my life for you, and yet you cannot be bothered to ask me yourself. You treat me like a woman! You treat me like a slave! I am not your possession!'

Lorenzo rose up in fury, but Angelo was the more furious. 'I thought I was your servant by my own free will, but you bought my soul in the market all those years ago, and I have lived here as your slave ever since. You have deflected me, altered the track of my life so that it runs through your lands. It was not enough to possess me, you wanted control of my soul. Where is my work on Homer? Abandoned! All my writing now is in Tuscan, what writing I do, which is precious little, so busy am I chasing after your children, suffering the abuse of your wife, the rudeness – the violence – of your servants. You call me your friend, and yet you send me away, you do not write to me, do not speak to me, you sweep past me like the Holy Roman Emperor and I have to make appointments to see you. You chain me up with your books, alone on the hill, one more bauble to impress visitors. "Look!" you tell them, "Among my treasures there is an angel with three tongues, the mighty Poliziano, see how neatly he tidies my bookshelves." Thus you say, such is your wealth, your power, your overweening arrogance!'

Lorenzo gazed at him with hooded eyes. 'Get out,' he said.

✞

I came across my friend standing in the gallery outside Lorenzo's room, gazing down distractedly at the activity in the courtyard below. As I joined him, the door was opened from the inside by a page and a visitor ushered out; Angelo strained to catch a glimpse of Lorenzo within but failed.

'We have had a row,' he said. 'I need to apologise.'

Niccolò Michelozzi hurried towards the chamber. 'Niccolò, stop! Give a message to Lorenzo. Tell him I am sorry. I take back everything I said. It was but the heat of the moment. I have had time to think, to cool down. A misunderstanding lies at the heart of all this, I am certain. Nothing here is ringing true. Tell him, Niccolò, tell him I apologise.'

In a distant room, Baccio Ugolini was playing upon a lute, that Orphic sound that could draw souls – but on this day it failed to work its magic on Angelo Poliziano. Bartolommeo Scala swept past, glancing at his enemy with a puzzled frown. 'Why are you skulking out here like a dog in disgrace? Tell me, your cousin – is he still in gaol?'

'Yes, why do you ask?'

Looking relieved, Scala said nothing but went inside the chamber, not requiring an appointment himself.

Angelo turned back to me. 'What have you heard about Lorenzo's destination? Is it Rome? Everyone says he is going to Pisa. I know that is not true. It is Rome, is it not?'

'It is Naples.'

He blinked, that I should know something he did not. 'Naples,' he repeated. He glanced several at times at the door, then exclaimed that he could wait no longer, not at the risk of meeting Scala again. 'I have to go to the tailor's. I am having new robes made, fit for an ambassador. This will all blow over by nightfall,' he said unconvincingly. 'But if you see Lorenzo, tell him it was a misunderstanding, I am certain of it. Maso has a clever trick in bending other men's words to new shapes.'

I slipped into Lorenzo's room to deliver a letter from Ficino. 'You must listen to our counsel,' Scala was saying to him, 'and not your mother's. She loves Poliziano like a son and is blind to his faults.'

'As I have been,' said Lorenzo.

'You love him. It is understandable, but for love's sake, leave him behind. I will go with you, Magnifico, even to death. Take me.'

'I need you here,' said Lorenzo, convinced of that much at least. 'To leave the city at such an hour as this is to leave it to my enemies. I need you here.'

'His pride will undo you. Two lashes from his tongue and he has the city's most learned men flinching in terror. He cannot curb his enthusiasm for verbal rectitude.'

'Verbal rectitude?'

'A man has only to open his mouth and Poliziano is half way down his throat finding error in his pronunciation or syntax. This is not a diplomat, Lorenzo. This is a grammarian. I beg you, do not indulge yourself by taking him with you. One small sneer from him in the presence of the King and it is farewell to your head.'

I left the letter from Ficino with Michelozzi and then ran from the palazzo to catch Angelo at the tailor's. I watched him being fitted for extravagant robes he did not know if he would use or not.

I did not like his humour. It was too bright, too fragile, so I stayed with him the rest of the day.

When we returned to the palazzo, however, he was told that Lorenzo wanted to see him. His doubt evaporated like mist in the sun. We were ushered through the twin doors leading into the sala. The large reception room was filled with men, many of whom we did not recognize: ambassadors, priests, bankers, members of the Signoria, a sea captain – men from the unpoetic side of Lorenzo's life. Everyone hurrying by had an enviable air of purpose. They knew who they were and what their place was in the great scheme of things. Angelo fell into conversation with anyone he met but his eyes followed Lorenzo everywhere. Lorenzo himself, surrounded by advisers, was oblivious to his presence. Hours passed, a whole afternoon given to pointless conversations. In the evening, when we went to table to dine, Angelo strained to get near to Lorenzo, but Niccolò Michelozzi drew him away, wishing to discuss details about his finances, and, by the time he got to the table, he was a dozen or more places distant from his lord. Councillors and bankers and ambassadors and captains: who were these people to come between them, between souls joined to each other, who knew the deepest desires of each other so well? How was it that Poliziano was at one end of the table and Lorenzo at the other? And why did Lorenzo never look up?

✠

Following a renewed outbreak of plague, all prisoners were freed from the gaol. Maso went to the Via dei Fossi, but could not sleep. Angelo's house was too cold and damp. He felt ill. He had already used the furniture as firewood and now there was nothing left. A lonely soldier needs warmth at night. He thought about going to Fiesole but it was too far and he was too tired. So he went instead in the other direction and sought out his shoemaker cousin in the Santo Spirito district. Crossing the Santa Trinità bridge, he stumbled suddenly and was forced to rest there a moment before moving on, determined to reach his destination even though his head was now swimming with fever. He looked into the Arno as if into a flow of black ink and images came to him from childhood stories, of red-horned devils with iron pincers, and rivers of forgetfulness.

✤

Seated between the Cavalcanti brothers, Angelo let them converse with each other across him without paying much attention, but then Stefano Cavalcanti asked him, 'Are you coming with us?'

Angelo nodded.

'I thought it was only men-at-arms who were to go.'

'Orpheus sailed with the Argonauts.'

'Did he? I never knew that. A fit image, sailing. Orpheus sailing to Naples.'

Angelo stared at his plate without appetite. Naples! The Pope and his whelps were an enemy that he could understand, men like himself, only corrupt. But King Ferrante and his sons stirred up atavistic fears. Whilst ostensibly champions of the new learning, scholarship and the arts, they yet resembled lords of a bygone age. Stories abounded which were doubtless only stories, but they put a man off his food.

'I have heard,' said Stefano Cavalcanti told him, 'that the wife of Ferrante once took a lover. When the affair was discovered, the king had the lover murdered and cooked in a pie that was then served up to the queen, and she ate it, thinking it to contain pork.'

'And then there was that ambassador who annoyed the king,' said his brother, 'and was boiled alive in a cauldron.'

'These are tales made up to scare children,' Angelo protested. 'According to the annals, in the 1460s an ambassador sent to Naples insulted the king and was killed. That was all.'

'That was all? He went under safe conduct, and he had more claim to Ferrante's favour than Lorenzo does, but he was thrown into a dungeon and afterwards murdered in secret.'

Ferrante had sons, all of them bred on battlefields. Of the whole evil brood only Prince Federico had a human heart. Angelo thought about the book in the library, Lorenzo's collection of the Tuscan poets made for the prince. Had Lorenzo remembered it himself? Was it already packed along with other numerous gifts? He must find out, make sure – the book must not be left behind. Slowly, guardedly, Angelo looked up towards that central seat of the table and Lorenzo.

If Lorenzo looked exhausted and beaten, it was because his vision, his belief in *gentilezza*, was under siege. The barbarians were at the wall; those to whom beauty and grace and virtue are repugnant. It seemed incredible, unnatural, that Lorenzo, champion of Truth, must surrender to the enemy. If Angelo had felt humiliated earlier, it was nothing to what Lorenzo must endure when he came to prostrate himself before King Ferrante and beg for his city to be spared.

Angelo sat staring at his friend and patron, his food left uneaten on his plate, his eyes growing darker and darker. At the moment I realised he was on the point of tears, he stood up so quickly that his stool fell backwards with a crash.

I heard him running down the stairs and out across the court-yard. A door banged. Lorenzo summoned a secretary and conferred with him. Most men at the table continued with the meal without knowing anything was happening, but I watched, trying to understand as secretary went to secretary, and then to Scala, with much whispering in the ears. Lorenzo's party of companions was clearly being rearranged: a gap was being filled. I wanted to leap from my seat and shout at Lorenzo that he had misunderstood. Angelo had not run away. He was outside, clearing his heart of grief, and would return. But I did not. Such a passionate outburst – I would have felt a fool to draw so much attention. Such was my self-concern, I who considered myself a friend.

Angelo had gone along the Via Larga towards that pool of quiet which is the San Marco monastery. The run in itself dealt with the pressure of the emotion, and he soon found himself in the square before the monastery, the outline of the building and its proud cross visible against the moonlit sky. He leant against the wall that bordered the garden Lorenzo had bought as a site for a school of sculpture. He had told Angelo his plans as they occurred to him, had taken him with him to the lawyer on the day the land was purchased. 'The art that Donatello rediscovered, of how to make figures of stone or metal stand on their own legs, free of support – it has all but died with the master; but one old man remains alive who trained with him: Bertoldo. I am going to commission him to teach and find him students. We must salvage what we can while we can. A world without art is not fit to live in. I want you to help. I want you to teach the sculptors poetry, to raise them up from being rough artisans to fine men, educated in all the arts.'

Angelo turned to gaze at the cross that stood out black against the sky. What was this humanity they served? A mass of selfish brutes. But that truth and goodness are reviled does not diminish truth and goodness. It was time to fight, for both his lord temporal and his Lord divine. Filling his lungs with the cool night air, he brushed wall dust off his clothes and turned back towards the Palazzo Medici and his duty. There were three hours to go until midnight, at which time, it was said, Lorenzo would depart. Any doubt or vacillation he had suffered passed away: his mind was firm. He was going to Naples with Lorenzo to die. Protractedly, perhaps, and in agony, but to die, for a life without Lorenzo was a life without *gentilezza*, and a life without *gentilezza* is not worth living.

But as Angelo turned into the gate he almost collided with a party of men riding out. The expressions on their faces were stern, almost brutal, and Lorenzo was at their centre. They rode off towards the Cathedral. Forgetful now of everything, and willing to surrender even his dignity, Angelo ran after them crying Lorenzo's name. But Francesco the secretary, who had walked out behind the party, pulled him back.

'We thought you had fled. Your place has been taken by someone else.'

A silent crowd was spilling out from the house and neighbours opened windows to find out what was going on. I made my way through to Angelo who stood there not knowing what to do or say. This humiliation was too public: there were too many of his enemies here ready to enjoy themselves at his expense. But there was one in the gathering crowd as distraught as himself. Lucrezia Donati, whom Lorenzo had suddenly abandoned without explanation after the recent birth of his son, stood wrapped in a cloak, looking as harrowed as the Magdalen. It seemed to her that Lorenzo had gone to his death without saying farewell. She and Angelo, facing each other for a moment, reached out and clasped each other's hands in wordless and mutual grief, but then I pulled on him, wanting to hurry him away to safety and privacy, away from the mob. We left Lucrezia Donati to her tears.

I did not know why he steered me back inside the house or why Angelo was hurrying towards the library. He seemed possessed by an idea. He threw himself inside and found the lectern empty that had displayed the *Raccolta Aragonese*.

'Yes, thank God, he has taken it,' he said. 'He has taken our book of beauty with him.'

He laid his hand on the lectern then, as if the soul were being ripped out of him, he roared to heaven, the sound of Christ on the cross, abandoned by his Father.

38

Florence, December 8th, 1479

THE BELL in the campanile of the Cathedral tolled the hour of midnight, reverberating deeply through the city, but the Florentines were used to its clamour and were not disturbed in their sleep. Nor did they stir at the sound of a party of horsemen trotting towards the road to Pisa. Florence slept while her first citizen, without word to the Signoria, departed to undertake the journey south by sea to offer his life for that of these citizens who were, at this moment, unconscious in their beds.

The following morning Florence awoke to the news. Copies of a letter from Lorenzo, explaining his actions, had been posted at all churches. Emotion ran in waves through the city. Many prayed for Lorenzo's deliverance: services in chapels ran all day long. Even some of Lorenzo's detractors fell on their knees in contrition, although not many; most looked triumphant at the news. No work was done: everyone talked, in the piazze, on street corners, from window to window. The news separated people as curds from whey. Some flew heavenward and turned to prayer for Lorenzo's salvation; others plunged into the hell of cynicism and made plans for a new government. When the news had become exhausted by repetition and the people needed a new sensation, they woke up to something else: the realisation that Lorenzo had left someone behind.

Angelo Poliziano, it was said, had refused to go, for he was a coward and a traitor.

✥

I waited and waited for someone to come and collect me. I stayed up all night. By the candlelight winking visibly through distant shutters, so did others on Fiesole. I should not have gone to the piazza, but there was no one here to stop me, and I could not bear to be alone in the house, suffocated by the weight of not-knowing. So I went to the piazza and was not the only woman there, though I was the only one alone. Extraordinary times create extraordinary events. We heard soon after midnight that Lorenzo had left the city. A moan went through the crowd, a sorrowing that was shared by all. Can it be true? Is he so magnificent that he has given up his life for us? The monks came out of the monastery of San Francesco and performed Prime in the open air, followed by a mass. The night was frosty, the stars a scatter of scintillating diamonds on black velvet. Christmas-tide approaches and the baby Jesus is cradled in our hearts. A baby being visited by three wise men, one of them the young Lorenzo de' Medici. I saw the scene so vividly in my mind, Lorenzo bearing his treasure to the King of Kings. But what was this analogy? Did it not equate King Ferrante with Jesus? Blasphemy! But there was more to this image, more… at first I could not see its message but as the Mass proceeded, I understood. No matter how evil a man be, no matter how thick and impenetrable his own self-regard, everyone, even King Ferrante and Pope Sixtus, has the Lord cradled in his own heart. And it is to that that Lorenzo, the Magus-Medici, journeys. Lorenzo has one hope: to find the spark of humanity in his enemy. And as I realised this truth, tears welled and flooded in me, and the presence of the invisible God permeated me body and soul. God is good. God is love. God loves Lorenzo. Lorenzo will win. Who could not weep at such a torrent of love? And that Angelo should be with him at this time: my soul swelled as if to burst with the waters of love.

✢

Thus I spent the night, but this morning two riders came; one, Tommaso, I recognised at once, but the other: who was this broken wretch? Angelo, my hero of the night reduced to something less than even a man.

'Lorenzo went without him,' Tommaso said simply.

My stringless brother, a puppet abandoned by the puppeteer, left lifeless on the floor of the puppet theatre. I looked to intuition to know what to do to help and heal: it was silent. No herb, no simple, no syrup, no unguent on earth can help him. He is in his room. I have left him there, but his presence has turned the place into a grave.

Tommaso lingered after we had helped Angelo to his bed. 'Remember,' he said, 'that contractually he remains in the pay of the Medici and can do nothing without Lorenzo's permission. Whatever he thinks or plans, he should do nothing. Maria, this is a test of patience. Help him remain quiet in the face of the storm. Have faith.'

'In whom? God or Lorenzo?'

'Both.'

✢

He has kept to his room for a day and and will not speak to me of what has happened. This afternoon, however, he emerged and took a little light food. I asked him if he would like me to read from Epictetus and he said he would, but he was not listening as I spoke the words. Still, life returned to him little by little, and I began to hope that he would soon recover by Nature's own efforts, but then we had a visitor. Ser Bartolommeo Scala called on his way to his own villa. I went out to meet him alone. He affected concern at Poliziano's well-being, 'given the rumours flying about that he is a coward.'

I told him my brother was studying.

'Life as usual, eh? Well, I am not sure that that is appropriate now, or how long he may remain here. I shall have to consult Monna Clarice on the matter. As for you, young lady, it is not seemly for a woman to live with her unmarried brother and the sooner he arranges for your return to the conventual life the better. May I speak with him?'

'He does not wish to be disturbed.'

Scala smiled maliciously. 'Must I make an appointment?'

'I am sure you understand, Signore, that life is not as usual here, and that my brother's wish to be left alone could be honoured for a day at least.'

Angelo came out. 'What is it you want, Bartolommeo?'

'Madonna Clarice,' said Scala, 'asks to know by what right you remain in this house.'

'I suppose it would be too much for you to tell me how the children fare and what their condition is?'

'They are not your concern. I want to know how you have the bald face to remain here.'

'It is my duty,' said Angelo woodenly.

'Remain then, but find your own accommodation and do not venture into the city. The streets resound to the glory of il Magnifico Lorenzo. You, who have deserted him, would be torn limb from limb. The Florentines hate you, boy.'

'You know that I did not desert him.'

'I may know it. They do not. To them, your fellow citizens, you are contumacious and disloyal. Your reputation is destroyed, your fame has lost its lustre, your renown is in tatters. You are a broken, despised thing. In their eyes. I shall call tomorrow and expect to find you gone.'

'Gone? Gone where?'

'Into exile.'

'That would be the act of a traitor. My duty, as a servant of the Medici, is to continue in my post here.'

'I have come as a friend, my Angelo, to warn you. Heed the warning. If the people ever loved Lorenzo, they love him now, and they know where you are.'

After Scala had gone, violent tremors ran through my brother as if a fever were starting, but it was a sickness in his soul worse than any mortal disease.

'If you listen to that man you are mad,' I said firmly. 'You know your duty. That much is clear. You will stay here. The Florentines will forgive and forget in time. Do your duty. Lorenzo is alone, too, and needs your faith and your prayers.'

'According to Scala, Lorenzo considers me contumacious and disloyal.'

'Contumacious – a Scala word if ever I heard it. Lorenzo would never use such a word.'

Angelo rubbed his arms to warm himself.

'Come to the fire.'

'Of all the men on this earth, I trusted Lorenzo. I placed him higher in my affections than my own kin. But who is here when he is gone? Why, my little sister.'

'Do not solve one error by making another. You cannot trust me, either, for I am human and like all humans, protean.'

'Protean! – a Maria word if ever I heard one.'

I smiled mischievously. 'Maria words are choice, well-considered words, based on serious study. Protean, I say, and like Proteus subject to changing form. Nothing human may be relied upon. Trust no one but yourself, Angelo.'

'Ah, such a confident pronouncement would sound fine from Ficino, but not from you.' He took his place by the hearth. 'A woman who knows too much is a monstrous creature.'

I have a trick of throwing dried leaves on the flames for dramatic effect. I did so now with twigs of pine and Angelo jerked in surprise as a sudden, explosive sheet of flame roared up and filled the air with an aromatic scent.

He smiled. 'Where did you learn that trick from, you witch?'

Together we stared into the brief wall of fire looking for angels. His suffering was beyond my experience. He has neither slept nor eaten for two days and there are deep brown shadows beneath his eyes. Sitting on the floor *beside his chair, I leant against his knees, wishing I were him, and he me, and stared into the flames. Since his return I have felt strangely quiet inside, the condition, I am told, of one who is about to die. Let us call it resignation. To resign, to unseal and to cancel. Surrender. Give up. The hollow necessity in the pit of the being. The hand of Sheba in Solomon's. This is wrong, this life we are leading, wrong and unlawful. I have got what I wanted, and now I must give it up.*

'*Angelo.*'

'*Mmm?*' *He was staring into the fire as if looking upon the Tyrrhenian Sea for a certain galley.*

'*If the only way to relieve this pain is through flight, then do it.*'

He gazed down at me. 'A moment ago you were telling me it is my duty to remain.'

'*See how protean I am. A moment ago I was not thinking how it might feel to be you. But in the fire I see your enemies everywhere. How can you stay? If you must go, then go. I believe I would be happier to know that, wherever you are, you are holding your head high. I cannot bear to see you like this. It is not right. Maso will take me back to Montepulciano.*'

'*If I leave this city I may as well be dead. Exile? It is worse than death. Better to be the faithful, beaten servant.*'

'*Indeed it is not!*' *I threw on more twigs and watched them being consumed. 'In his commentary on his sonnets Lorenzo writes wisely on mystic death, how one must die to this life to be born anew.*'

Although he was no longer astonished by my intellectual activity, Angelo wanted to know how I had come by this work.

'*It is here in the library. All Lorenzo's poems are stored in the same chest as yours.*'

'*Have you been reading our poems?*'

'*All of them.*'

There was the slightest pause and then the inevitable question. 'So?'

'*So?*'

'*Which of us is the best poet?*' *He tried to sound carefree, as if this were a question with too obvious an answer. What could I say?*

'*You are the most fluent poet I have ever read, whether ancient or* modern. Such sensuous imagery, such an exquisite feeling for beauty, such lovely, tender words.'

'But?'

But… What could I say, that would not cause him to throw me out of his life and heart forever? But if only you would engage with God, if only you would stop living life at arm's length and start to penetrate the mysteries, then you would be a great poet, as Lorenzo is a great poet, even though he does not have your genius for expression. Lorenzo is in dialogue with God, but you – Man, not God, is your subject, and perhaps your true vocation lies elsewhere. How could I say such things?

'Lorenzo's Commentary is a very mysterious work,' I said. 'But this much is clear, that to live one must die. And you are already dead, Angelo, so what do you have to fear? I am convinced you cannot find new life in this place. You must go.'

'Lorenzo too is dead.'

'Forget Lorenzo, forget me. Go. Can you not feel the force of it? The contraction of it? You are being expelled from here, so go. Do not linger.'

He looked into the dark beyond the fire. 'Where shall I go? What shall I do?'

'Follow truth. Do you really believe you are Lorenzo's creature, that without him you are nothing? You are wrong! Find yourself, my brother, find your true self. If you put your trust in God, there is nothing to fear.'

'I shall send to Monna Lucrezia and see how things lie with her, whether I still have her love or no. I shall ask her to give you refuge.'

✢

A brief message has come from Careggi, saying, 'Love that wavers is not love. Maria may come to me. I shall send someone to collect her. Farewell, my adopted son, and God speed your return.'

✢

Since Angelo had not unpacked the chest he had made ready for Lorenzo's departure, this evening he put it back on the mule. He took his farewell and so we parted once more, but this time, in place of the chittering, selfish monkey was a young woman full of noble conviction. Protean indeed. I kissed

him on both cheeks. He mounted his horse and, under cover of darkness,
rode into Florence.

✝

Angelo went to the Via dei Fossi to find Maso, to tell him of his arrangements. Although Maso, he knew, had been freed from the gaol, the house was empty. Angelo left a letter with a neighbour and went on to Santo Spirito, to his cousin, the shoemaker. On the way, crossing the river at Santa Trinità, he passed the Compagnia della Misericordia, who used the hours of darkness for their voluntary work of collecting corpses. The river was illuminated by their torches as they came over the bridge in a macabre procession following a trundling cart. Led by a priest singing *Veni Creator Spiritus*, they looked like a flock of crows in their black hoods and beaked masks. Angelo covered his nose and mouth with a piece of linen and meant to spur his horse, but could not help but stare at the cart and its horrible contents. A pile of bodies, brittle as twigs, unconsumed kindling found in the ash of a dead fire. Anyone else would have fled then, but Angelo was already dead and had nothing more to fear or lose. He went on into the poisonous alleys of Santo Spirito and found Maso alone in the shoemaker's house, lying on the sordid rushes of the floor, as grey as river mist. Maso struggled to rise. He glared at his cousin, but there was no more fight left in him, and his face collapsed in pain.

'What are you doing here? Go away! I have the pest and could kill you with my breath.'

'What can I do for you?'

'There is nothing.'

'Have you seen a priest?'

Maso began to weep. 'There is no time and it would be no use. All my sins await me.' He looked up at his cousin, an idea dawning in his eyes. 'Could you…? Would you…? Angelo, absolve me.'

'I cannot. I have only taken minor orders.'

'Break the rules. Throw yourself on the mercy of God for my sake. Sweet Mary, absolve me!'

387

'Then confess,' Angelo said, hesitating no longer.

Maso did not have enough breath to be anything but efficient. 'Father, I have sinned. I have murdered once in revenge and twice in anger. I have raped eight or nine times, and sired children out of wedlock, five or six of them. I have abandoned my lawful wife and children. I have stolen many things, not least from my cousin Angelo – I have milked him for everything I could get. I had him repay a debt three times more than was owed. I have betrayed him, destroyed his friendship with Lorenzo, so that he would be left behind and not go to his death in Naples. And now I beg forgiveness of you, my Lord Jesus Christ, and I beg forgiveness of him, and if you both forgive me, my soul has hope of purgatory.'

Angelo stared at his cousin, his heart beating fast, wanting to damn him to hell. But the function is greater than the man, and he felt a power of forgiveness coursing through him which, since he did not possess it himself, could only have been divine in origin. As a priest, as an agency of the Lord, he raised his hand and made the sign of the cross over his cousin as he recited the prayer of absolution in a strong voice. When it was done, he pulled Maso up into his arms and wept over him.

'Do not come so close! The miasma…'

'You may not have the plague. It could be something else. I shall take you to the hospital at Santa Maria Nuova. We shall get you well, Maso, and start again. You and I, we shall start again. Maso?' But his cousin had become heavy in his arms. 'Maso!' he cried.

'Has he gone?' asked the shoemaker, looking round the door.

'Where have you been?'

'Keeping my distance. Get him out of my house.'

Maso had lost so much weight that it was easy for Angelo to pick him up and carry him out alone. He put him on his horse and took him back over the river towards San Paolino where he could have him buried. The Arno was milky in the light of stars, and Venus was bright in the sky. The men of the Compagnia della

Miseracordia were returning over the bridge, their dreadful cart having been emptied on the pyre outside the city.

'Where are you taking that corpse?' they asked him.

'To burial at San Paolino.'

'It is forbidden. Give it to us.'

Angelo laid the body of his cousin in the cart that was clearing the city of its dead like so much rubbish.

✣

The guards at the gate were not interested in departures, only entries. They let him out without question and the heavy, iron-furnished doors of Florence closed behind him. The pyre was in a ditch beyond the gate, with the faggots piled up and a man waiting with a flaring torch. Taking the Bologna road across a frosty landscape visible in the light of stars and the rising moon, Angelo rode past without any idea of where he was going. The way could have led to the realm of Dis for all he cared. Everything he had worked for was lost; his best friend was lost; position and reputation all gone. His cousin Maso, given absolution by an excommunicated Florentine in minor orders, must be burning in hell fire. Alone in the night, Angelo threw back his head and let out a cry of anguish he had been storing for sixteen years. The cry came back to him, like an echo from the cosmos, as if the whole world cried for the one who is lost.

✣

With my thoughts so absorbed by the troubles of my brother, I did not realise what I was coming to when I came to Careggi. I thought it would be as before, when I stayed with Monna Lucrezia in the palazzo in the city. In my imagination nothing had changed except for the location. I found our beloved Madonna busy writing letters in her own hand, but sitting in the same room was a lady who I knew at once to be Monna Clarice, the Medusa wife of Lorenzo. When I entered the chamber, her hand flew to her mouth and she gave a little cry, as if she were seeing the object of her hatred in a new form. A raw feeling of anger boiled in me then, that feeling which is the seed of all war. Here she was, the abominable daughter of the Orsini who has caused my brother so much unnecessary pain, regarding me as if I had just crawled out of a ditch.

Monna Lucrezia took us both in with a single glance. 'I will have no enmity between you two, no enmity in this house. You must learn to love one another, as Our Lord commands. We have work to do, of a subtle kind, and it is based on love. So we begin here, we begin now. Kiss!'

We stared at her.

'Clarice, this is Maria. Maria, this is Clarice. Kiss each other.'

One does not disobey Monna Lucrezia. I stepped forward and proffered my cheek to the odious Clarice, she to the odious me.

The Fourth Book

ORPHIC JOURNEYS

39

*L*UCREZIA DE' MEDICI *writes letters until my arm aches, to the
duchess of this state and the countess of that, to the Queen of France
or the wife of the Holy Roman Emperor. Wherever there is a
man with power to influence events, she writes to his wife. Last week she
wrote to the Duchess of Calabria, the wife of Alfonso the Duke, a fine
woman who was a friend of Lorenzo's in his childhood. The daughter of
Sforza of Milan, she is a lonely Italian in the court of the Spanish King
Ferrante. Speaking woman to woman and in affection, Monna Lucrezia
asked the duchess to look after her son Lorenzo on his arrival in Naples.
The reply from the duchess arrived this morning, saying how willing she
was to help, and that she awaited Lorenzo's arrival with great anticipation.
I sat wondering at the speed of couriers, that they could get to Naples
and back before Lorenzo arrived. We sent these heroes galloping all over
Europe.*

*Such extraordinary letters are only in addition to Monna Lucrezia's usual
correspondence. Another letter this morning came from the wife of the
manager of the Medici bank in Venice, offering friendship and support to
Monna Lucrezia 'in these harsh times.' She went on to give a vivid description of a form of 'weaving in air' she had seen done by the peasant women
of the Veneto. 'It makes a kind of net,' she said, 'but the delicacy of the results
depends, of course, on the kind of thread used and the bobbins.' She described
a hard pillow, a pattern, the pins and the bobbins which carry the thread.
She also described the women singing, inspired by the rhythm of the work
as they make this material called lace.*

*Monna Lucrezia read the letter out to me to see if it generated a spark of
interest. When I am not acting as her secretary, I sit and stare out of windows, with not only my linen embroidery lying neglected in the basket by
my feet, but my book also. I can concentrate on nothing. My brother is like*

a swimmer who dives into a lake and does not come up again, while I stand on the bank hoping, praying for the best. The hours pass like snails as I wait for news. Each clattering entry of a messenger in the courtyard has me calling from a window, 'What is it? What news?' And each time I return with a satchel of letters for Monna Lucrezia and a heart full of disappointment for myself. News about the entire world comes to the Medici villa on Careggi, but about Angelo Poliziano, nothing. The days crawl painfully into weeks and I gaze at the still, unbroken surface of the lake which is Italy and begin to believe him drowned.

Monna Lucrezia tries to coax me to ply a needle, to make chains of golden thread to decorate a jacket, or sew beads and fine jewels on to velvet, saying it will bring me happiness, but I resist. I feign enthusiasm, but say that my fingers are too thick for such delicate work, that they would be best employed spinning from the distaff. I say this knowing that Monna Lucrezia would not countenance her ladies doing anything that would make their hands greasy. The others, her married daughters who visit each day, her daughter-in-law, and her granddaughters, stitch pearls delicately, obediently. They look at me with compassion, as if to say, if only you would obey, how much easier life would be for you.

'Maria, come here you useless girl. Have you heard of lace? Listen to this. "It is a twisting of thread, in which the whole pattern is the fabric, and the fabric is the pattern. Such is the concentration it requires, and such the rhythm of the work, that it ennobles the mind, and laps it in delightful emotions." And this: "Makers of lace take their pleasure in ancient paradises, and the poetical past becomes their reality, while the dullness of present life becomes but a dream. By this art we may overcome any malady of the soul, for lace is beauty, and beauty, like contemplation, has the effect of evoking the light of the mind." Now what of that, my dead head rose?'

'But will it bring back a lost brother?' I wondered in silence

'Lace,' she repeated.

'What of it, Madonna?'

'Would that not interest you?'

'It certainly sounds intriguing,' I said without enthusiasm.

'You disappoint me,' she said severely. 'It is within the power of a woman to weave peace, but to do so she must be at peace herself. You are not at peace.

Look at you. You have given way to your fears. You are useless to him in this state – useless.'

Monna Clarice stared at me with bovine eyes which seemed to say nothing.

A messenger clattered into the courtyard. I went to the window in a desultory fashion. 'What news?' I called.

'I have a letter from Angelo Poliziano for his sister. Is she here?'

Sobbing, I ran down stairs to collect it. Sobbing, I ran back up again, to stand there with it crumpled in my hand, completely lost to a watery confluence of grief and relief.

Monna Lucrezia prised it from me and smoothed it out. 'Carissima Maria,' she read, 'I am in a monastery not far from Florence, where I have stayed these past two weeks, alone in a bare cell, to see if I had been infected with the plague. Have you heard what happened to Maso? He is dead, Maria. He caught the pest in Santo Spirito, or perhaps in the gaol, and died while I was with him. Though he caused me much pain and difficulty in his lifetime, his loss aches in me. Will you write to his wife in Volterra? Send her money if you can. I will repay you. I had hoped to find the solace of contemplation here, but instead I am going mad with my own repetitive thoughts, which buzz in this white room like blow-flies. Now I know that I am clean, I shall travel on to Bologna today and perhaps find a position in the university by which to rebuild my life. More anon. Your loving brother, Angelo.'

I took it back from her and sobbed over it, making the ink run.

'Bologna…' said Monna Lucrezia thoughtfully. Tapping me on the head quite hard with a straight-edge rule, hard enough for pain to cauterise my tears, she told me to prepare myself for dictation. 'I must write to the wife of Bentivoglio. At once. At once. Come along, girlie.'

'He quarantined himself,' I cried. 'How noble of him.'

'Ha!' said Clarice.

I glared at her. We are having much trouble obeying the commandment of Our Lord.

Monna Lucrezia summoned me to the desk and there dictated a letter to Ginevra Bentivoglio of Bologna, advising her of a certain young man arriving in her city, who would grace her court with the most beautiful poetry *if only she could find him and take him in. 'Please look after him,' she wrote. 'He is like a son to me.'*

Then she wrote another letter, this time to the Medici bank in Venice, requesting they find a maid for her, one who was adept in the new art of making lace.

✠

The girl from Venice has arrived and brought with her several skills in the art of lacemaking. She can weave in the air by means of a frame, she can make patterns of fine thread on a cushion using bobbins, and she is learning Greek lace, made with a needle. This last is very beautiful – its geometric designs would have pleased Plato himself – but it is the pillow lace that attracts me, bewitching me not so much by its results as by its music. The 'pillow' is not one you would ever wish to sleep on, being stuffed hard with hemp. The girl gave us a demonstration, talking excitedly in a dialect that none of us can understand. We stood in a ring about her, Monna Lucrezia, Nanina and Bianca, Clarice, her daughters and I.

At first Clarice gazed on this activity as if on a fisherman mending his smelly nets, but even she became fascinated as the girl began to weave the bobbins, the repetitive clicking sound exerting its charm. As the first lines of lace appeared on top of the pattern, the girl started to sing to the rhythm of the work; hearing in the sounds the very metres of poetry, I was captivated.

I gestured to her that I wanted to try it myself. Although my first attempts were risible, I caught the trick of it quicker than any of the others and soon led the way.

'Do not think, you must not think,' I schooled Monna Lucrezia, whose own attempts resulted in knots and unravellings. 'Listen to it, do not look.'

Not wishing to be entirely humiliated, Monna Lucrezia is taking it upon herself to be the experimental lacemaker and tries all the methods. I am concentrating on the pillow, keeping the bobbins flying round each other, braiding and knotting, twisting and weaving, to the sound demanded by the drawn pattern. The very mathematics of it, the relationship of sound and pattern, take possession of me. Long after the other ladies have tired of the novelty and gone back to their embroidery, I continue to perform thread poetry and am making a strip on a fourteen line pattern.

✢

Today, while Monna Lucrezia was absent on business in the city, we had a visitor. At the request of Monna Clarice, Elena Maffei came. Clarice grew fond of her while Elena was nursing little Giuliano but, since Monna Lucrezia cannot be reconciled to any member of the Pazzi family, they can only meet in secret. It was wonderful to see Elena again with her beauty quite restored, and so utterly self-possessed as to be a lesson to us all. I threw my arms around her and asked after Tommaso.

'He is still at work with Ficino,' said Elena, 'writing out the Plato from dawn to dusk.'

'Are you alone all day?'

She shrugged, as if to say it did not matter, and came to look at my lace pillow.

'What are you making?'

'A Petrarchan sonnet,' I replied. This is the kind of response that is giving me a reputation for lunacy in this house, but Elena accepted it as fact. She counted down the edge of the lace and said, 'Ah yes, a b b a a b b a,' identifying my pattern correctly.

'Fourteen lines of eleven syllables each,' I said.

'And in cotton – how wonderful!'

'You know Petrarch's sonnets?'

'I have them by heart, along with those of Dante. They keep me bright in my solitude.'

'You must stay with us here,' I said at once, but with no right to do so.

'Monna Lucrezia would never allow it,' Elena said simply. The children were brought in from the nursery; Elena, reunited with them, and little Giuliano in particular, went to sit with their mother and play with them. Lucrezina, the eldest, came to watch my lacemaking. Her head bent over the work, she was silent and absorbed, hearing the pattern in the click of the bobbins. Her breathing was soft, warm and even. I became as aware of her as I was of the lace; aware also of the others in the room, the toddlings and the fallings, the little parades of infant vanity.

'I can wead!' Giovanni was telling Elena.

'I can jump a three foot hurdle,' claimed Piero.

'I can wun too. Look!'

'Not here,' said his mother, 'not now.' But Giovanni was already half-way across the room before a maid caught him and brought him back.

For a moment I could see that all events, small and large, take place in the lap of peace. I fell quiet, absorbed by wonder. We think peace is something that has to be found and established by us, but it is already here. We just drown it out. We listen to the sound and not the silence. Peace is the silence behind the sound.

✝

With the introduction of lace making, Monna Lucrezia has achieved her aim: a room full of Medici ladies working quietly (except that I keep muttering the sonnets of Petrarch), weaving and stitching peace. Even Clarice, usually so haughty, is beginning to relax in this company and to speak to the others about the children, their achievements, their little ailments, their likes and dislikes in food. Under Monna Lucrezia's dominion, the speech of the women weaves rhythmically like my bobbins; under her gentle direction, the concerns of the group begin to broaden, to encompass the troubles of the city and beyond. And while her various daughters converse and sew, Monna Lucrezia writes her letters.

We have learnt how Angelo fared in the court of Giovanni II Bentivoglio. Ginevra Bentivoglio had him tracked to a lodging house near the university, where he was found rejected and in misery. She told him robustly that he was too good for the university and invited him to the court. 'He is lauded and celebrated here, with everyone desiring his company, but he does not flourish,' she writes. 'I am encouraging him to go on to Mirandola where my sister-in-law Constanza lives. Perhaps there he will find his happiness.'

We have heard from Lorenzo in Naples, and it was Monna Lucrezia's turn to sob with relief, though I did not rap her over the head with a ruler to cure her of it.

Lorenzo has been to Naples once before, on a diplomatic mission when he was a youth. When his galley turned into the Gulf of Gaeta, he saw the bay of Naples just as he remembered it, as a vision of pure beauty. The white city, clinging to the terraces of a steep hill-side behind the harbour, rose like Venus out of a Mediterranean sea the colour of lapis lazuli. Remembering Plato's words, that where beauty is, there is God, Lorenzo was encouraged. He disembarked on the long jetty to be received by his friend Prince Federico, with whom (Monna Lucrezia now tells us) he had planned this venture, and was led with much pomp to the Castello Nuovo to meet the King. At the harbour he purchased the freedom of the slaves who had rowed the two galleys King Ferrante had sent to collect him, and bought each one of them a new pair of green breeches. 'Such magnanimity,' the duchess reported enthusiastically in her own account of the arrival.

'My villa at Cafaggiolo!' cried Monna Lucrezia, for Lorenzo used the proceeds from the villa to pay for this voyage. But he had been right to do so: the King would surely be impressed by such largesse from one supposedly ruined by the war.

The King was waiting for him outside the Castello, a huge man who surely must have been winched on to the back of his suffering horse. Though born in Italy, King Ferrante was Spanish both in his looks and his mien, and though he could trace his lineage back to the Emperor Theodosius, not every drop of blood in him was royal. He wore the collar of the Order of the Lily, a golden griffon on a pendant, and his white horse was draped with the colours of his five kingdoms: Aragon, Catalonia, Sicily, Sardinia, Valencia and Majorca.

The entry into the castle was between two massive battlemented towers, a gap that has been filled with a tall, slender arch in the Roman style, and a pair of bronze doors. Though Lorenzo had seen the triumphal arch on his previous visit, the doors were more recent and he made much of them. 'Your Majesty,' he said, sweeping in a low bow. 'What art!' he exclaimed, as he straightened up. 'The last time we met, these were just plans. But now! What a triumph of bronze working!'

On the white arch are parades of figures celebrating the triumph of the King's father, Alfonso of Aragon. The man had been a truly great king, and if anyone deserved to be immortalised like Trajan or Hadrian, it was Alfonso. He had known the bible by heart; had attended Mass three times each day without fail, had fasted every Friday and had clearly made his Christian faith a practical reality. Tales abound of his mercy and magnanimity. But his son is of a different order.

'Here I am,' Ferrante said to Lorenzo, pointing out a newer relief panel. 'This is me. Was I here the last time you came?' Lorenzo gazed upon a depiction in stone of a slim-waisted knight in armour, surrounded by his companions, celebrating the victory over the barons in 1462. 'Made by a pupil of your Donatello,' said the rotund king. 'Come along, come and see my other treasures.'

'But let us pause at the doors, your Majesty!'

'Oh yes, the doors. Bronze, like your Baptistry doors. I will confess it to you, since it is so obvious anyway, that we rather imitated the Florentine model. These are our Gates of Paradise.'

But rather than show the scenes of the Old and New Testaments as do those in Florence, they depict the battles of Alfonso with Duke Rene d'Anjou of France, reminding Lorenzo that Naples was now, as it had always been, an object of desire fought over by Spain and France. He had tried to arouse King Louis to assert his claims; now he stood with the man who opposed those claims, who must surely resent Lorenzo's efforts. But chivalry demands a certain code of behaviour, and if King Ferrante intends to kill Lorenzo, he would not do it immediately on his own doorstep. He must fatten him first.

The King, either forgetting Lorenzo had been before, or locked into a description of his own treasures that was invariable, showed his guest every-thing as if for the first time.

'You will find all our sculpture to be either Florentine-made or Florentine-inspired. My father took your Donatello to his heart. As for our paintings,' he said, casting his arm round the halls they walked through, 'they are mostly Flemish, as are our musicians. We try and foster native talent, but the only way to do that is to import the best from elsewhere. There, look, a Van Eyck – St George and the Dragon. We have two by the great master – the greatest, even you will admit, I think. An Adoration of the Magi is upstairs. And there – Rogier van der Weyden.' The tour took two hours. Before Lorenzo was rested or refreshed from his journey, he had to see again all the treasures of Naples, and wonder at them, which he did without

effort, for there were many additions to what he had seen last time, not least in the library.

'Cicero, Livy, Caesar, Seneca, Aristotle,' intoned the King wearily as they walked in. 'Please, use my window seat overlooking the bay – any time, any day. Make the place your own. Look, here is the Codex of Livy that was a presented to my father by your grandfather. I was a boy when it came, but I remember it vividly because my father refused to accept it until it had been examined by the royal physicians.'

Lorenzo wondered madly if the book was sick after its long voyage.

'We thought it was poisoned,' the King explained. 'A magnificent man your grandfather, but only a fool would trust him.'

Lorenzo smiled a Florentine smile, a smile that forgives everything in the cause of greater profit. The King, for all his learning, seemed disposed to believe in fairytales. Then, when Lorenzo's nerves were already tuned to a high pitch through exhaustion and fear, the King picked up a golden reliquary in the shape of an arm and handed it to him with the most solemn expression. 'This,' he said, 'is the arm of Livy. The right arm. His writing arm.'

Lorenzo fought to restrain laughter since it was not honest laughter, but maniacal, suicidal howling. Should he let it out, the King would run him through at once with the sword he wore.

'You honour your poets,' he said, most carefully. 'You treat them like saints. I would that the Florentines were so reverential of literature.'

His sigh would have filled sails. The King looked askance at him.

'You are tired and I am only wearying you,' he said. 'I will have you escorted to your chamber to rest and relax.'

The Duchess of Calabria stepped forward from the crowd that attended the King.

'My lady!' said Lorenzo, recognising his childhood friend for the first time.

'I shall show you the way myself,' she said.

Unlike her husband, the cruel Duke of Calabria, the duchess is alive to all that is fine in life, and both loves and practises learning with great sincerity of heart. She writes to Monna Lucrezia that she has adopted Lorenzo as her 'brother in humanity' and that she walks with him often through the palace gardens, 'which are budding in February, and from where we have a fine view of the sea.'

I glanced at Clarice as these words were read to us. I think she has never walked anywhere with Lorenzo, or ever seen the sea, but she seemed to have been carved from marble and no expression was visible on her face.

'Also,' Monna Lucrezia reported to us, 'Lorenzo has, on the suggestion of Prince Federico, presented that beautiful book on the Tuscan poets to the King. He says that in Federico is a noble heart and that all he has to do is to find in the father the virtue which is in the son. His book, he says, will help him do it.'

✝

Lucrezia has written to the Duchess of Milan, expressing sorrow at her dreadful plight of losing power to her husband's brother, offering her prayers and what help she could. She has written to the niece of the King of France, encouraging her literary studies. She has written to Eleanor of Aragon – the Duchess of Ferrara and wife of Ercole d' Este – and praised her daughters, Isobella and Beatrice, the beauty of whom, it is said, is matched only by their skills in music. 'There is approaching your city,' she told the duchess, 'a young man who is as a son to me. Please look after him.' She has written to Barbara of Brandenburg, the German mother of the Marquess of Mantua, and commiserated with the loss of her husband Ludovico. She has written to a young woman in Venice called Cassandra Fidelis, whose reputation for learning has spread to Florence. And so Monna Lucrezia weaves her webs of peace, interlacing all women in a sisterhood that begins to stretch across many lands, so that, with a word in the ear of the Kings of France or England, a favour granted to the Holy Roman Emperor, a sweet reward promised to the papal nuncio, they do what Monna Lucrezia de' Medici wants them to do, which is to protect the lives of her son and his friend and so bring peace and unity to Christendom.

✝

Angelus Politianus Tommaso Maffeo suo S.D.
I journey as a knight of old in a dark wood, with ladies appearing at the well or fountain as if they were expecting me. In Bologna I

tried to find a position in the university but was rejected, only to be taken in as a guest by the wife of Giovanni Bentivoglio. I lodged for some weeks in the court, but could not rest, and my lady encouraged me to go on to Mirandola. If I went, it was in the hope of meeting once again Giovanni Pico, but I only met Constanza, wife of his brother and sister of Bentivoglio. She is a mysterious and wonderful woman, but Mirandola is the size of a boot and, without Giovanni, there was nothing to keep me there, so I went on to Ferrara. There I tried to find employment in the university: once again I was rejected. But then a messenger came to my lodging house from Eleanor d' Este, the Duchess of Ferrara. It seemed that she was expecting me and she invited me to stay at the ducal palace. She made a great fuss of me despite my no longer having any connection with the Medici. Is it possible that one day I may stand up on my own, like a sculpture by Donatello, without any visible sign of support? I yearn for that day. Meanwhile, however, I cannot rest.

From Ferrara I went to Padua. There I tried to find employment in the university. You may guess the outcome. My skills in languages and in poetry count as nothing in the formal institutions. These are the centres of medicine, of theology and philosophy, the great, weighty topics, where poetry is considered a pastime for idle minds. But what do they know of eloquence and literature? Nothing. Universities – what are they but sealed communities of celibates who loathe each other? It is only in the courts that I am prized.

So now I am in Venice, which in its wisdom has neither university nor court, and it will come as no surprise to you to learn that a fine bed awaited me in the Palazzo Bembo on the Grand Canal close to the Rialto Bridge, its sheets already turned down as if I had been expected. Is it my reputation that precedes me, or is it witchcraft?

Another wonder: the further I journey from the Platonic Academy, the closer I come to it. Everywhere I go I hear myself praising philosophy and the Platonic discipline with a conviction

I did not know I possessed, and yet I am sincerity itself, and no one is more convinced by my words than I am. Perhaps, having lived so close to Ficino for so long, I had lost perspective and the extraordinary had become commonplace. But now, from this distance, I can see the Academy for what it is: a divine grace that has settled upon Florence, a banquet of the gods.

Bernardo Bembo, the Venetian ambassador to Florence, is the astrological twin of Ficino, born on the same day at the same hour, and a true friend of Lorenzo. Even so, and despite my fall from grace, he has taken me into his house and settled me into Venetian society, introducing me to every scholar he knows – which is all of them.

One such is an intense young man of the Barbaro family called Ermolao, as passionate an Aristotelian as Bembo is a Platonist, yet the two – despite this division which sunders the universities into irreconcilable camps – remain particularly fond of each other and love to debate their differences. I, like the democratic man described by Plato in the Republic, find myself agreeing with both and having no point of view of my own. A Platonist who appreciates Aristotle, I am a strange, composite creature, rather like a camelopard. What strikes me as hybrid and unnatural, however, appeals to Ermolao Barbaro: that a man may inhabit Plato's ideal reality while remaining an interested participant in the realm of the senses; that a man partakes of both worlds, divine and mundane. It is an attractive idea, if something of a philosophic centaur. However, if we can pursue this thesis, and prove it true, we shall succeed where all the schoolmen fail: we shall reconcile Plato and Aristotle. I spend my time reading the texts of both philosophers in Greek with Ermolao, working with him to discover the errors that have been made in transcription over the ages, to clear away the dross of commentators, and to find out what those giants really did say. In the view of our friends and companions, this is dry, dull work, yet after every session of study we emerge from the library radiant with visions of intellectual beauty.

Another wonder: the wife of Bernardo Bembo seems to know

more about me than I know about myself – even down to details such as what foods I like. How is that possible? Does she have second sight? She wants me to meet a freak of nature called Cassandra Fidelis; a monster since she is a woman who reads and writes in both Latin and Greek. I find excuses to avoid this pleasure, since I can see in the Signora's eyes a certain keenness to find a husband for her unnatural friend. Having Maria for my sister, however, I see no call to add further curiosities to my life.

All these magical coincidences are but marsh gas enchanting a child. They make me forget my troubles. But sometimes I wake in the middle of the night in yet another strange bed, and feel like a tree that produces leaf even though it is hollow in its trunk. What news, Tommaso? What news of Lorenzo?

Vale. Angelo on the Grand Canal.'

40

Venice and Naples, February-March, 1480

IF ANGELO STAYED longer in Venice than he had intended, it was because Venice had ensnared him with her watery charms. He moved from the Palazzo Bembo to the Palazzo Barbaro, to work closer with his friend Ermolao of that family. This brought him closer to San Marco square and the open lagoon, and every day he wandered the island as an explorer, dazzled by the reflections of a thousand canals. The Venetian dialect intrigued him. Being host to numerous colonies of foreigners, the city state had developed an idiosyncratic vernacular, at its thickest amongst the artisans and sailors. While its vocabulary borrowed heavily from Greek and Arabic, its grammar came with German inflections, and there was a queer tendency to drop the last syllable on proper names. More often than not he heard himself referred to as Anzel rather than Angelo.

Though the population had been badly depleted by a plague six years earlier, the narrow streets between canals were home to Jews, Greeks, Germans, Swiss, Armenians, Moors and Africans. East-facing Venice is the centre of the trading world; it is also the axis between the Byzantine east and the Latin west, the route by which ideas are exchanged between the two. Anzel found himself able to sit by wharves, to speak ancient Greek and be understood by Cretan seafarers as if the past thousand years had not happened.

Amidst this life of nations strolled the patricians, sombre in their long black mantles, dignified, grave, and yet open-minded. It was among such men that Anzel found his friends and by such men that he was entertained in various houses, apparently valued and held in high esteem. Their wives made much of him. Their children importuned him, wanting both his attention and his stories. His translations of Homer and his unfinished epic verse on the Joust of Giuliano had long been known and loved here. Whenever they could, the Venetians persuaded him to recite his new poem about Giuliano, and began to refer to it as 'The Golden Song'. Not one man among his friends suggested that he might work at anything but his studies. Everything he needed was made available to him – shelter, food, clothing. And women.

The Venetian courtesans were high-bosomed, chalk-faced ladies with bleached hair dragged up into topknots, ladies of leisure who received their visitors with polished grace. Angelo pretended not to know what he was supposed to do with them other than converse. As soon as he discovered in each new companion the intellect of a lap dog, he would rise, bid her good day and leave, much preferring to spend his time reading Aristotle in Greek with Ermolao. One day during Carnival, Ermolao himself broached the subject as they travelled in a gondola to Bembo's house. 'Do you have no taste for women, Anzel?'

'All things in right measure,' Angelo replied. 'Often the mere pinch of a woman is enough to spice the dish of life.' He laughed, but the echo of it off the palaces bordering the Grand Canal was hollow. He stopped being facetious and turned on his friend. 'They *smell*, Ermolao, these beautiful women of yours, they smell stale, and no amount of pomanders and perfumes will mask it.' He wrinkled his nose in distaste. 'Like the stench of this canal. And they cannot read. I get better conversation off their greyhounds.'

'You are not supposed to talk to them,' Barbaro said.

'Then what are you supposed to do?' Angelo hoped to silence his friend by embarrassment.

'Perhaps we have been serving you the wrong kind of dish.'

'I do not want boys, if that is your meaning,' said Angelo sharply.

Barbaro shook his head. 'No. I have someone else in mind. I will arrange for you to meet Cassandra Fidelis. She is rather special, a woman of great learning. You are not to harbour any base desires; our Cassandra, as pure as a vestal virgin, is for the delight of the mind only.'

Angelo trailed his hand in the water and disturbed the pink reflections of palaces.

'Forty thousand died in 1474,' Ermolao said.

'So I heard. God take their souls.'

'Our island cemetery could not cope.'

'No. What? Then where…?'

'We pitched them into the canals. With such quantities there was nothing else to be done.'

Angelo withdrew his hand quickly, looking aghast into the water as if seeing dead faces floating there. The beauty of Venice seemed like heat haze, suddenly, a beguiling phantasm, nothing more.

✢

'Oh! Who broke the thread?' I cried, taking the linen cover off my work. The cover was undisturbed, but the thread had broken clean through. I stood staring at it. The Venetian maid showed me how to join the thread, but suddenly I lost all interest in my Petrarchan sonnet, pulled out the pins and threw the cotton away.

It was an act of childish petulance and I was justly punished by Monna

Lucrezia, who would not allow me to start a new piece until I had apologised to God. I sat in a corner in black silence, not prepared to apologise to God for something that was His fault. My silence lasted so long that the rest of the ladies forgot about me and carried on with their work as if I were not there.

With the passing of the weeks on Careggi, a little colour has begun to return to the cheeks of Clarice. Back in her rightful place, which is in the shade of Monna Lucrezia, she has abandoned her attempt to be her mother-in-law's equal. It seems as if harmony and balance have been restored to life; things are as they should be, with Monna Lucrezia doing all the thinking and deciding and instructing. Being here, in the very heart of the Medici family, with her sisters-in-law visiting often, and so many healthy children under everyone's feet, Clarice almost looks happy. But there stays a canker in her heart, a viper yet to be plucked out.

'How fares Monna Lucrezia Donati?' she asked her mother-in-law stiffly this morning.

'As with any mistress,' said Monna Lucrezia, 'she suffers.' She leant forward. 'Clarice, do you have any idea how she envies you?'

The blood rushed to Clarice's cheeks.

'The wife has all the support of heaven,' Monna Lucrezia said, 'the mistress none. She must bear the grief of these times alone. Pity her.'

Clarice said nothing but I could read the thoughts on her face.

A courier arrived with letters from Naples, including one from Lorenzo.

Magnifica Domina mea, – *Last night I had an audience with King Ferrante and Prince Federico alone. We read poetry together and I explained to the King the great human aspirations of the poets of the* dolce stil nuovo. *Federico said later that as I spoke I became animated by a fine light, that he understood whilst listening to me what 'enthusiasm' really means: to be taken by a god. The King is one of the most selfish, cruellest men alive, but even he became affected by whatever divinity was present. He sighed and said that he, too, once had such aspirations when he was a boy. Under the influence of his father, he had believed in goodness. He grew reflective, casting his mind back over the past and seeing, no doubt, an ugly and crapuscular vision of himself. Who knows what choice, what decision once taken puts a man on* a path away from the light, but the King has at least the faculty of memory and can remember a time when his own heart sang the Orphic song. I seized the moment and confessed my ambition to create a unified Italy of independent states tied by alliance, an Italy free of petty wars.

'To what end, my Florentine? An increase in profitable trade?'

'When a man has to battle for survival, he cannot raise his snout out of the mud. All his waking thoughts must be given to food, shelter and defence. Only in a city that is well governed and peaceful, where tasks are shared and goods exchanged for coin, not barter, may a man rise up and consider the heavens, the earth, his place between. The ascent of the soul is the journey from coarse to fine, from matter to spirit. Not everyone can make the full journey, but if a man but turn himself in the direction of heaven then his life will be sweeter and the benefit will be shared by many.'

'And this is the vision you are prepared to die for?'

I went down on one knee before him. 'Your Majesty, the Pope is demanding that you send me to Rome where I shall undoubtedly be executed. If you follow such a course, you will be free of me and free of the Pope's displeasure, but…'

'I would be left with my snout in the mud.' The King was quiet and thoughtful for a moment, then said, 'But if I were to sign your treaty, I would be turning my eyes towards heaven.'

I thought my heartbeat must surely echo in the great hall.

Eventually the King nodded. 'You have won me to your cause,' he said, 'but I will not sign your treaty. Though in my heart I wish to support Florence, it would be no simple matter to desert Rome. My son, the Duke of Calabria, would be too disappointed, since he intends to claim your territory as his own. Besides which, our alliance with Rome rests on the payment of tribute. The simple truth is we cannot afford to break it. I am not insensible to the virtue of your plan of an alliance of four states to resist the Turks, yet I cannot sign. Lorenzo, rise up. You are a young David, whistling the sling of reason round and round my head, and I need no further convincing.'

'But you will not sign.'

'I cannot.'

I awoke this morning with the taste of fear rather than triumph. With *each passing day my fears grow, not about what may happen here, but about what is happening at home. Our enemies are coming out of the shadows, I hear, and beginning to speak out against me in the squares. Mother, do everything that is necessary to protect the family. I shall return as soon as I may, but I must have that treaty, or else this will all have been for nothing. Commend me to my wife and children. Your Lorenzo.*

✝

I glanced at Clarice, whose own letter from her husband was the usual perfunctory three-liner telling her to look after herself. She looked vacant.

Each day we hear news of the advantage our local enemies are taking of Lorenzo's absence, with rival families moving their pieces rapidly on the board to promote themselves and block his return. It is difficult to keep a sense of urgency out of our prayers, but all the time Monna Lucrezia counsels peace, peace, peace, and we ply our needles and bobbins as if weaving Penelope's web, awaiting the return of our Odysseus with faith.

As I sat in my black humour, lines began to spin out in my mind, lines from hymns. I had heard Angelo sing them, the Orphic hymns which Ficino has translated from the Greek into Latin, hymns to the gods of the ancient times. Angelo likes to sing them in both languages, early in the morning while the dew is still on the grass. He says they work magic. I used to tease him, observing soberly that absolutely nothing had changed with his singing, except that all the birds were flying upside down. He could never resist looking, no matter how preposterous my lie. He used to laugh, and tell me how little I understood, that magic is not conjuring tricks but the transformation of the soul. 'Well, you are not transformed,' I told him. 'You are just as bossy as ever.' He would tell me off then, accusing me of being facetious. Now as the hymns begin to sing themselves in my mind I take them very seriously, for they are lovely and I remember how their music used to greet the day on Fiesole. Angelo was right: they do have transformative powers. As I concentrated on them this morning, so my pitchy humour began to dissolve and, forgetting why I was in the corner, I rose up and returned to my work, trying to remember as many lines as I could, to piece the fragments of memory together in a new pattern of lace.

'Have you apologised to God, Maria?' Monna Lucrezia asked.

'I am singing hymns to Him in my mind, Madonna.'

'Very well,' she said, and smiled at me benignly.

✛

Tommaso de' Maffei has just visited, arriving in a tempest of concern and barely remembering to observe the niceties. But he did remember and fell on one knee belatedly before imploring Monna Lucrezia for help.

'Marsilio Ficino is leaving,' he said.

Silence fell in the room. As far as any of us knew, Ficino had never left Florence before in his life.

'Leaving?' Monna Lucrezia was astonished. 'To go where?'

'To the villa of his friend Cavalcanti at Regnano.'

'Leaving?' Monna Lucrezia repeated. 'Why?'

'He says he cannot hear. The blast of war has severed his communication with the muses and the angels. He says he is deafened and must retreat. It is a subtle noise, you understand, but he can no longer concentrate on his work and must go away.'

'He is leaving?'

'I have to go with him. The Plato is not quite finished. Madonna,' he said, turning his cap nervously in his hands. 'I know what it means to you, I know how much I am asking, but you are a lady of great heart and goodness. Madonna, will you take my wife in? I dare not leave her alone. The enemies of Lorenzo…'

'She has no fear of them, being a Pazzi.'

'She is the wife of Lorenzo's loyal servant, Madonna,' Tommaso retorted.

Monna Lucrezia stared at him. Her bosom rose and fell, rose and fell. We all willed her to speak, Clarice and I for once in complete accord. Monna Lucrezia raised her eyes to stare into space.

'No,' she said, her voice strained. 'You ask too much, Tommaso. She is a Pazzi. I cannot.'

'Madonna!' Tommaso protested. 'Not one drop of Giuliano's blood is on Elena's hand, not one shadow of the sin of her father on her soul. Else would I have married her? Did I not love Giuliano too? She is innocent, Madonna, innocent!'

411

'No, Tommaso. I cannot. You ask too much. You must find a refuge for her somewhere else.'

Tommaso's face died. As all hope expired, his features expressed nothing and, rising from his seat, he left us without saying anythng further. When he was out of earshot, Clarice and I spoke at once to our lady mother, begging her to change her mind.

'It is a fault,' she said. 'I know it is a fault, like a blackness over my heart. But I cannot forgive what her family did to ours. I will never be able to forgive.' Tears began to course down her face. 'My son, my son, oh Giuliano, my son!'

I ran out and caught up with Tommaso, finding it so hard to believe that Ficino was leaving.

'Was it stupid of me?' I asked. 'I thought he would help us. I thought he would make magic for us, that he would cast up his hands against a stormy sky and make the angels put everything right again.'

'It was very stupid of you,' he said. 'And stupid of me to think that, like the Virgin Mary, Monna Lucrezia would listen and respond to my plea. How very, very stupid we are, Maria.'

'What will you do?'

'I do not know. Love or duty? I do not know. There is nowhere to go or to turn. Elena has no kin, mine are in Rome, and I can hardly send her there. But she insists I go with Ficino.'

'I will go to your house and stay with her,' I said decisively. But Tommaso was adamant that I should not.

'At the moment she is only in danger from the enemies of Lorenzo who, though strong, are few. If you were to be with her, she would also be in danger from the friends of Lorenzo, who are many.'

I cried out. 'What do you mean? Why would Lorenzo's friends harm me?'

'Do you not know? Angelo is reviled as a traitor. Bartolommeo Scala makes much of it. So for you to come to my house would only be bait to them. I do not know what to do.'

'What does Ficino say?'

'He says what he always says: "Do your duty and trust in God." But how can I? I do not have the strength.'

I promised him that I would work on Monna Lucrezia, that, somehow, we would get Elena into the household. 'Have Ficino write to Monna Lucrezia, begging her to do this thing. Elena can stay in the palazzo in the city – she would not have to be here at Careggi. Now go and be at peace,' I told him.

He bent forward and kissed my cheek. I gazed into his troubled eyes.

'We are all in danger, Maria,' he said. 'Whatever may be the outcome of this war, we still have the Turks to face. They say they are advancing through Bosnia and gathering a fleet at the coast.' He embraced me, gripping me hard. 'I pray God we meet again.'

✣

Homeless bands of freelance soldiers like wolves were driven closer to the city by the February chill. A small band made a camp on Montevecchio, above Careggi, warming themselves at a fire and feeding themselves by raiding local farms. One party came across a courier bearing letters for the Medici, and its members amused themselves reading correspondence meant for the mother of Lorenzo, who seemed to receive letters from all over the Christian world. One local letter, to Monna Lucrezia from Marsilio Ficino, got dropped in a ditch along with the rest that were of no interest.

✣

For a month the King of Naples has prevaricated and continues to delay. There was a fall of snow yesterday which delighted me, but today it has melted and everywhere flowering bulbs proclaim the spring. The spring. As the birds sing and the hares leap, it cannot be denied it is spring, and the soldiers will be returning to their camps. As the soil warms, so does the blood heat, and nature's regeneration must mean war for men.

There is news from the city: the enemies of Lorenzo are waxing powerful. Bartolommeo Scala is tireless in generating support for the Medici, but every day his strength weakens. If Lorenzo does not come home soon, he will have no home to return to.

'Mother,' he said in his most recent letter, 'I fear the worst. There is a rumour that the Roman army is on its way here to trap me, that I am to be

betrayed by the King, and yet what can I do but continue to talk to him, to hope, to pray that he will sign a treaty? To leave without the treaty signed will be defeat; to remain and be trapped by the papal forces will also be defeat. I pray for miracles.'

Monna Lucrezia looked gravely on us all. 'Tonight,' she said, 'we keep vigil. We have done what we can by our own efforts. We have prayed, but not really prayed. We offer lip service to God, but do not speak to Him. We tell each other to trust Him, but do not practise our own wisdom. Such is our arrogance. Tonight we keep vigil. Tonight we lay down before God. Tonight we abandon all hope and throw ourselves on His mercy.'

Perhaps after such a night I may approach her on the subject of Elena. I have visited her often in Florence, and she keeps well, but the anarchy on the streets scares me and I must bring her here. I must. Oh, why does Ficino not write? Only he can make Monna Lucrezia change her mind. Still, after a night of prayer, I must do what I can.

✢

On this sleepless night I recited psalms and found unexpected comfort and rest in them. I sang until my voice and the words were one, until I was both the singer and the listener, and my voice grew strong with confidence. The other ladies were in the sala, reading from scripture together. I went alone to the chapel to sing and make the air rain with harmonics. To sing thus is to invoke angels.

Towards midnight the door opened and Clarice entered, wrapped in a heavy blanket and carrying a candle before her. 'Is that you, Maria, who is singing?'

I felt embarrassed to be caught in this rapture of my own making, conducting a seraphic choir.

Clarice put her candle on the altar. 'It sounded like a multitude. Was it only you? What do you sing?'

'Psalms, Madonna. Will you join me?'

'I find the Latin so hard to remember. I came to pray.'

'For Lorenzo?' I asked boldly.

Clarice sighed. She knelt down beside me in front of the altar. 'What do you know of love? Nothing but your own imaginings. If you were to sing in here and there was no echo – that is how it feels to love with no return.

*Do not ask me to pray for him – it is too much to ask. I pray for myself and
my children.'*

*'Come,' I said, making room for her at the altar. 'As our lady mother has
asked us to do, let us concentrate on God, direct our prayers to Him, beg
Him for His guidance.'*

*Clarice looked at me cautiously but then closed her eyes and brought her
hands together in front of her face. I composed my own prayer, which came
in the* ottavo rima *I had been patterning on the lace cushion, and I called
on God to show us how to love without an object to that love, without hope
of return, to love, loving love for love's sake, not to possess or to claim anything as one's own, to love as if to suffer pain, unable to love enough. The
words seemed to be pulled out of me, as if they came unravelling from the
distaff of the heart. 'Dear God,' I said at last, folded over myself and
rocking on my knees, 'protect our menfolk and bring them home.' When
I was done, I fell quiet and stayed where I was, rocking silently; then came
a sound of ice breaking on a frozen lake – the echoing sound of Clarice, of
her denied love forcing its way out from her.*

*'I love him so much,' she cried, her freed voice rebounding off the walls.
'Oh, God, so much! The pain is too great to bear. I have lost him!' Her
grief was overpowering. I held her tightly as if to hold her together and could
feel the grief surging up inside her, a pent-up force now released and rushing like floodwater. With a wild cry from the pit of her, Clarice threw her
head back.* 'Oh God!' *she cried, her voice resounding in the small chapel.*
'Save my Lorenzo!'

*The angels took her words, made fluttering banners of them and danced
in a circle in the empyrean.*

✠

Unable to sleep, Lorenzo walked alone on the royal terraces above
the gardens of Chiaia. The moon was full and played on the waters
of the sea, dappling the world with its reflected light. Though it
was February, the air was mild and fresh, full of the suck and draw
of the waves. It was all so utterly beautiful. What damage men do
with their greedy desires, to themselves and to others, he thought.
Life is so short, and we fill it with the blast of war, robbing

ourselves of what little awareness we have of the peace of God. Strangely he did not feel alone, nor despairing. He felt instead a part of the world and ready to acquiesce to fate. *Let it be, let it be, let it be,* he thought, *whatever is to come.* For whatever it was, it could have no effect on the beauty. That was eternal. That was God's own. And with that thought, Beauty herself seemed to rise off the sea, to be detached from it, and to fill the starry universe. Lorenzo stood staring at a vision of the true Venus, who has no form, and his face was transfixed with awe.

Then he heard his name spoken in a voice he recognised as that of his wife, so clearly that he looked about him but saw no one. 'Lorenzo,' said the voice. 'Leave Naples at once, and do not go by sea!'

Angels, Ficino had once told him, take the form of the familiar, or of the stranger, but he with the ears to hear will recognise them. Lorenzo did not hesitate, but returned indoors to rouse his companions.

✠

Each night as the sun sets on the city, Lorenzo's enemies go about their business, visiting people still loyal to the Medici, persuading them otherwise, tempting them with the promise of rewards or threatening them with violence. We do not know why Elena was riding to Careggi, we can only imagine that on this night, the night of our vigil, such men went to Tommaso's house, that Elena heard them coming, that, alone and scared, her horse already saddled, she slipped out by a side door and escaped.

It was the night of the full moon, the chaste moon, the golden orb of Artemis. Elena rode up the hill to Careggi to throw herself on the mercy of Monna Lucrezia and beg for refuge.

✠

The marble floor, green, pink and cream, was cold. The moonlight coming in through a high window fell upon the altar and made its plate gleam. The candle flames were gold set in a sea of silver. The occasional hoot of owls only made the stillness of the night more profound. Somewhere far off a horse whinnied in alarm. The sound ran through my own silence like a tremor, a sudden ripple in the ether. Was it a scream of a human or a fox? There are only two choices of emotion these days: deep peace or acute alarm. Peace, peace, peace, *I said to my heart to calm it down.*

We are waiting for our doom, for the riders who will come in the night to rid the world of the Medici pups. The armed men at our gate are too few, too easily bought off. It is only a matter of time, but Monna Lucrezia makes us spend the time wisely, and we pray.

I heard noises in the courtyard, the gate being opened, the sound of someone running up the stairs. It was only one man, but my heartbeat deafened my ears. I opened my eyes and found the other ladies as pricked up as hares. The door opened tentatively and Matteo Franco, who was praying with us, went to speak to the servant standing there. He came back and whispered in the ear of Monna Lucrezia. Her intake of breath ruptured the stillness. All concentration was gone and we rose to our feet.

'*Where is she?*' *Monna Lucrezia said.*

'*On the road, Madonna, not far from here. Her horse is lame. It must have stumbled in the dark and pitched her off.*'

I knew before the words had been said, could feel the meaning in the cold air.

Oh, no… *Elena, Elena, Elena…*

'*Maria, stay here with Clarice,*' *Monna Lucrezia ordered me. But Clarice could stay no more than I. We all went to the courtyard. Servants of the house carried her in on a litter, shrouded by her cloak. I went to her and lifted the cloak off her face. There was blood on her head but not much, not enough to warrant death. I clutched at this, to the hope that she was not dead at all but in a coma. I laid my hand on her throat but it was as cold as the tomb. Women were screaming about me, as women scream. Monna Lucrezia, her face contorted by an agony of guilt, fainted into the arms of her daughters.*

Matteo Franco gave orders for the body to be taken to the chapel, to be washed and laid out. Left alone, I stood in vacancy, feeling nothing. Then a thought bloomed in my mind, a picture of Tommaso, and I dropped to my knees, felled by grief. The tears that came were not for Elena but for Tommaso. How brief is human love. Such transience in this world. I cried

417

for all dead things, for Emmanuel, for two trees I saw lopped down in the autumn. I cried for everything, but not for Elena, and not for myself.

✣

Tommaso is here. He came with the man we sent to fetch him and arrived mid-morning. His dear face is swollen and puffy and he keeps it lowered to hide from us the nakedness of his soul. Matteo Franco took him to the chapel and has spent the afternoon with him. Every now and again there echoes through the house the sound of a man keening and everyone here who was present after the murder of Giuliano at once cries at that dread and familiar sound. Monna Lucrezia has shut herself up in her chamber, but sometimes we hear the same sound coming from her. It is a knife to tear the belly of heaven, to have God undo what is done, but time cannot be set back and the dead must remain dead.

The household is dissolving into chaos. We await the arrival of one of Lorenzo's uncles, Giovanni Tornabuoni or Tommaso Soderini, to see what we should do, but no one comes. The city, it is said, is in the same condition of hopelessness. It will not be long now before the Duke of Calabria rides in to occupy it.

The only one of us to have retained any peace from the vigil of last night is Monna Clarice. I found her gathering irises in the garden to take as an offering to Elena. She alone has colour in her cheeks and a lightness to her body.

'You must leave!' I told her. 'You cannot spend another night here. Let us take the children and fly to the Mugello.'

'No,' she said quietly.

'Please, Madonna! Little Piero must be protected, in case, in case…'

'There is no need, Maria. Have faith.'

For once her words had some weight in them. She meant what she said. I stared at her and met eyes that were clear and tranquil.

She smiled, as only Monna Clarice can smile, that is, with no alteration to her features, only an increase in the light; she has a smile like the dawn. 'There is nothing to fear,' she said. 'My husband is coming home.'

'How do you know that?'

'We are of one flesh. How could I not know it? He is already on the road.'

418

'You mean on the sea.'

'I mean the road! Must you be as tiresome as your brother and argue with everything I say?' But as she spoke, she smiled.

'Without Monna Lucrezia to guide us, the servants are at a loss.'

'Then let us go to the kitchen and arrange dinner.'

'Who can eat at such an hour?'

'We must arrange dinner,' she said quietly, 'even if it remains uneaten.'

41

Naples and Mantua, March, 1480

LORENZO BROUGHT the Cavalcanti brothers and Niccolò Michelozzi gently to wakefulness. 'Have our things packed and be ready to leave in an hour or less,' he whispered. Leaving his chamber, he slipped past the dozing guard to seek an audience with the King.

Ferrante was awake and sitting up in his bed, his egg-shaped head kept warm by a velvet cap braided in gold.

'Something is afoot,' Lorenzo told the bemused monarch. 'You may not know it yourself, but danger is approaching. I shall be leaving within the hour.'

Ferrante was amazed. Who had told Lorenzo that a papal emissary from Rome had arrived? How came this man to have such intelligence? Having been informed by the emissary that a Roman army was marching on Naples, the King had decided to let events take their course and not interfere; now he heard himself insisting that Lorenzo escape at once, and by sea. 'The Romans are coming by road. Take a galley from the port. There is one there in readiness.'

Lorenzo shook his head; it was too slow to go by sea. 'I must leave now, at once and by land. Is there another road I can take?'

Ferrante, his amazement increasing, nodded, offered him the

best horses in his stable as a gift and told him the route by which he may avoid trouble. Lorenzo bowed gratefully. It was with some concern that Ferrante sat in his silken bed and watched him go. He sat there and thought the thoughts that had occupied him for so long, thoughts of earth and heaven. Well, it was all out of his hands now. Lorenzo was leaving – Rome was on its way. He fell back on his pillows and closed his eyes. As he did so, he re-entered the dream from which he had awoken earlier with a start. A vision of his father Alfonso appeared. Just that. A vision. It did not speak. It did not have to. The picture itself was enough to haunt the son with the memory of his father's virtue. 'What do you want of me?' Ferrante cried out. The answer was so obvious and so easy – what made it difficult? It seemed to him that his heart had become like a shell that never opens, sealed and encrusted with barnacles.

'Damn you!' shouted the King, rising from his bed. 'Damn you, my saintly sire. Will you never let me sleep?'

He called for a servant. 'Send a rider after Lorenzo de' Medici. Bring him back here. He has left without his treaty,' he shouted. 'Tell him I will sign.'

Lorenzo was intercepted and persuaded to return; the treaty was signed; he left the court for the second time in the hour, in that dawn hour which saw a ghostly fleet of Roman galleys moving silently across the bay of Naples, to form a blockade to catch for the Pope his heart's desire, but Lorenzo had gone. And by road.

✝

Cassandra Fidelis wrote to the wife of Bernardo Bembo saying that she had heard that Poliziano was in Venice, but that she had been indisposed and unable to attend the banquet at the Palazzo Barbaro. She wanted now to receive him in her home, hoping that they might converse on literature, if he did not find that too strange a desire in a woman. She had heard much about this famous Florentine scholar and longed to meet him.

'Alas we have received your letter too late,' Bembo's wife responded. 'Our poet left us early this morning, moved by who knows what prompting of his

420

heart. He has been restless and ill-humoured, did not attend the banquet himself and has refused all social invitations.'

Cassandra Fidelis wrote to me. 'Your unhappy brother has gone to Mantua, the city of death.'

I took the letter with me when I went to visit Monna Lucrezia in her chamber.

'Madonna,' I said, sitting on her bed and holding her hand in my lap. 'If you do not forgive yourself, you will destroy us all.'

'Why should I forgive myself, since I cannot forgive others? I should forgive myself last of all. I must begin with the Pazzi.'

'Stop this torment. Only you can help Tommaso.'

Monna Lucrezia moved her head slowly side to side. 'I could not. Where is he?'

'At Ficino's villa. He has stayed there alone since the funeral and receives no one.'

Monna Lucrezia shook her head again. 'No, I could not face him. Not yet. Not yet,' she said. 'What news of Angelo?'

'He is on his way to Mantua.'

'Good,' she said quietly.

'How is it good, Madonna?'

'Mantua is much closer to Florence than Venice.'

'But it is the city of death!'

'The plague has done its work there and passed on. I know your brother better than you do. Our Angelo is on his way home.' She smiled, but it was such a feeble effort. 'Maria,' she said. 'Get pen and paper. I must write a letter to my German friend.'

✝

Angelo made his way south by way of Vicenza and Verona and arrived at last in Mantua, the city embraced by lakes and reedy rivers. Flat, marshy, the home to frogs and pestilence, this was sacred ground to him, being the birthplace of Virgil. Following the loss of Ludovico Gonzaga to the plague, along with 18,000 others from Mantuan territory, the empty city was now recovering under the benign government of the good and pious Marchese Federico, a man who favoured art, culture and the new learning. This is what Angelo told himself as he crossed the bridge at the Castello San Giorgio. That one could reach Florence in a few days from Mantua – one day if God and the horse were willing – had nothing to do with his decision. He presented himself at the gate and was surprised to be told that he was expected by the mother of the Marchese, Barbara of Brandenburg.

He was received, however, by her son. A model of courtesy, the Marchese was a hunchback, suffering from the affliction which had been in the family for two generations. It had arrived with the grandmother, who had also brought a true taste for civility and art to the court, so that, for Mantuans, hunched backs and high culture were inextricably associated. 'The gods themselves have led you to my house,' declared the Marchese. 'To have you here… well, Lorenzo's loss is truly my gain.'

Feeling he was being watched, Angelo glanced up at the ceiling of the audience chamber. He flinched. Several ladies were staring down at him in amused fascination. Gonzaga laughed heartily at his expression.

'My painting deceived you! You thought it was real, yes?'

'Indeed, yes,' Angelo replied, annoyed. Without doubt the paintings of the audience chamber, where various members of the Gonzaga family formed a life-sized parade around the walls, were the most realistic he had ever seen. Glancing up at the disconcerting ceiling again, he allowed himself a grudging smile. The effect of realism was such that he wished to meet the artist, and he said so.

The Marchese was accompanied everywhere by a dwarf. This fellow now pulled on Angelo's robe to gain his attention and, wagging his finger at him, said, 'No one who is sane *wants* to meet Andrea Mantegna.'

And as if to convince Angelo of the need to take to his heels and not to commit himself to this court, Marchese Federico Gonzaga broached the subject of his salary. 'I am afraid there can be none. The plague has decimated the workers on my estates, and those that remain are so few that they can demand what wages they like;

and then this war, in which I support your Florentine cause and fight against the Neapolitans in Tuscany, has all but drained my treasury. My coffers are empty. When Lorenzo de' Medici repays me, I can pay you.'

Angelo stared at him, stunned by the irony: that here in Mantua he was again dependent on Lorenzo.

'I can offer you the status of perpetual guest,' Gonzaga went on. 'You will have good accommodation and may sit at my table, but additional income… I am sorry but it is not possible, not at the moment.'

With nowhere else to go, Angelo was forced to accept, but he had one question. 'Shall I be free to spend my days as I choose, in study and writing?'

'Of course,' Gonzaga was surprised even to be asked.

'You will not require me to repay your hospitality with my services as a tutor or secretary?'

'*You?* Of course not!'

Angelo smiled. 'Then I accept your generous offer.'

Gonzaga was staggered. 'Are you telling me that there are patrons who harness fine steeds to carts?'

'There are patrons who, working hard themselves, ask their friends to share their burdens.'

'I am not one of them. Poets should sing, not groan.'

Suddenly bells began to ring, throughout the court and beyond the walls in the city itself.

'What news?' the Marchese said as a secretary hurried towards him.

'A messenger has arrived from the south. Naples has signed a peace treaty with Florence. The war is over. Lorenzo de' Medici is on his way home!'

The Marchese shouted with triumph. He called for celebrations. He called for letters to be written. When he had calmed a little, and remembered the man beside him, he turned to Angelo. 'All our negotiations have been in vain since you will be returning home now, I presume?'

'It changes nothing. I have no home,' Angelo said. 'I was hoping to find one here.'

✣

He went about the court, familiarising himself with its many buildings and multitude of inhabitants. The castle itself was a military fortress but it led to squares of pleasure palaces and apartments. Peacocks perched on walls, and pet monkeys chained to balconies threw down nuts on the heads of those passing below. A giant, resident in the court, was constantly employed giving rides to children upon his back; dwarf-buffoons somersaulted as soon as anyone so much as glanced their way, as if driven by a vicious fate that says he who is born small must amuse others. Odd, then, that they should seem content; indeed, everyone seemed content, even the scholars, who did not resent Poliziano's arrival among them. But then these were no ordinary scholars, no petty-minded, shrunken-souled, shrivel-hearted university men, but the heirs and disciples of the school of Vittorino da Feltre.

Vittorino, the tutor of Gonzaga children when the Marchese had himself been one of them, had seen each child as unique and had educated him in totality. He made thin children fill out and fat children slim down; he made soldiers out of scholars and scholars out of soldiers; he taught girls as well as boys; he matched every child of the wealthy with a poor child who was to be taught at the wealthy man's expense: Vittorino da Feltre was a potter at the wheel of humanity who had shaped crude souls into exceptional men and women. The protégé of that lady who had brought hump backs and a lasting vision of beauty to the Gonzaga, Vittorino had achieved godlike status in the memory of those he left behind. Once, long ago, on their visit to Mantua together, Lorenzo de' Medici had turned to Angelo Poliziano in the schoolroom and said, 'This is how I want my children raised, in the full light of reason and the humanities.'

The schoolroom, called La Casa Giocosa, the House of Joy, was decorated with scenes of children at play. Standing within these

424

walls again, Angelo stood staring, his mouth hard, his eyes cynical. 'A dream,' he muttered, 'all a dream.' He did not hear someone enter and join him.

Andrea Mantegna, seeing in the face of this new arrival a bitterness that he understood, was moved to display kinder traits than were usual in him. Thus Angelo's introduction to Andrea Mantegna – Palatine Count, Knight of the Gilded Militia and curmudgeon of Mantua – was as to a brother, one who believed himself equal to all, who shared his passion for the antique world.

Mantegna took it upon himself to be the younger man's friend and guide and they spent days walking from one end of the court to another, through squares decorated with the spread-winged imperial eagles and other accoutrements of Empire brought to the family by German wives. They went beyond the court into the narrow streets of Mantua to see the workshops where Lombards practised the art of Flemish weaving. They trod the newly paved streets and marvelled at the town clock which struck the hours. In the Marchese's library, Mantegna showed Poliziano the architectural plans for the house he was designing for himself. 'It is a work of art, no?'

Angelo was deeply envious. It was not over large, nor ostentatious, nor ornate, but simply a glowing fruition of the architectural principles of ancient Rome. 'You must have been reading the books of Leon Battista Alberti.'

Mantegna said he had given Alberti's books on architecture a passing glance, but had found that there was nothing in them he had not already discovered for himself. He peered at Angelo. 'Do you find me rude and overbearing?'

Reeling from the dismissal of his hero Alberti, Angelo nodded in silence.

'Then judge me on these…' Mantegna thrust a notebook at him. Inside Angelo found page after page of studies of such consummate artistry that they took his breath away. Here was a man with the skill of Leonardo da Vinci, and yet, where Leonardo was beautiful and gracious in himself, Mantegna was ugly.

'What do you think of them?'

'Only love can produce art like this. Am I right to think that, in these pages, the real Andrea Mantegna is to be found?'

'You are.'

'Then why all these pretences of greatness – chilvaric orders, titles and other such gilded fripperies – when you are great already?'

'At your age, I was a painter's apprentice, a humble artisan and in love with my art. I was like an instrument being played by some divine power, and, as its servant, I dedicated myself to that power. I soon came to the notice of patrons. Patrons! Rich men who look for those of talent to glorify their houses and amuse them like tumblers or jesters. They wanted my power for their own use. They wanted me bowed before them in servitude. They commissioned paintings and thought they had the right to dictate changes at whim. Since the time of the great Cimabue and Giotto, we artists have ceased to be anonymous; these days we can put our names to our work; but still we are treated like artisans. When I became a master, I thought, why am I not worthy of a loftier station in society? After all, is it seemly for a priest of the Muse to grovel for his bread?'

Angelo winced. 'You touch an open wound in my soul.'

'I know. That is why I sought you out. What are you doing freeing yourself from the Medici only to attach yourself to the Gonzaga?'

'But the Gonzaga family has looked after you well these past twenty years.'

Mantegna laughed sourly. 'Gonzaga looked after me while he could afford to. Now his ruin is my own. It is very unlikely that this house of Mantegna shall ever be built. The last time I had any money from him was by suing him for letting his cows stray in my fields.'

'The Marchese has admitted his poverty to me, but says he will provide accommodation and the freedom to pursue my own studies. I ask no more.'

'And you believe him? Let me tell you about my current

426

project. It is the design of a vase. My last project? – the design of a vase. My next project? – the design of a vase. Do you think it is me who wants all these vases? And listen, the man in the workshop outside the court who makes the vases – do you think he does it for nothing? Of course not. He is a humble artisan and must live. Unlike me, he gets paid. I have been wondering, I thought I might ask you, do you think Lorenzo de' Medici would be interested in taking me into his household?'

Angelo told Mantegna that Florence also treated the artist as an artisan, that even one such as Sandro Botticelli lived in a workshop with a carpenter on one side and a fletcher on the other, and was neither more nor less than his neighbours. A house such as the one Mantegna had designed for himself, with its Roman atrium and circular courtyard, would be unthinkable for an artist in Florence.

'It is unthinkable here, too, while your Botticelli at least receives payment for his work. No, I will go to Florence.' Mantegna questioned him about Leonardo da Vinci, but Angelo told him that Leonardo, war-weary and harassed by the demands of commissioners, was threatening to quit Florence for the more attractive Milan. 'If you want land, farms, titles, follow him north. Do not go to Florence.'

Mantegna looked at the plans for his house and shrugged. He declared that he would exchange all his worldly goods for the opportunity to paint one great picture. 'A triumph. Filled with soldiers, banners, horses. A subject fit only for Lorenzo de' Medici.'

'Lorenzo, too, is ruined,' said Angelo. Opening up a book lying close to hand he found it to be a volume on the animals of the earth by Pietro Candido Decembrio. He went through it methodically, looking for a camelopard, but did not find one. He did, however, discover the crocodile.

'Exist? Of course they exist,' Mantegna replied to Angelo's question. 'We have a dried one hanging in Santa Maria della Grazie.'

427

In the same book they found a one-horned, armour-plated monster called a rhinoceros, which Angelo took for a portrait of a remote ancestor of Andrea Mantegna.

42

Florence, March 1480

NOT WISHING TO enter Florence travel-stained and exhausted, Lorenzo went with his entourage to the house of a friend near Grassina, south of the city. There they rested, bathed and changed into their ambassadorial finery. Lorenzo sent word into the city of his imminent arrival. He came, he said, bearing a peace treaty he had signed with Ferrante, King of Naples. When the transformation was made, and twenty tired riders were turned into a hero and his escort, then, announced by trumpets, Lorenzo entered the city he had saved. His enemies were cowed, his friends were triumphant. The city erupted in jubilation. The whistles, shouts and screams of the Florentines sent pigeons up from squares in clouds of fright. Caps were flung so high in the air that they never came down again. The war was over, Goliath defeated, and here was their David, their Lorenzo, returning back through the gates in glory. The gods in heaven, wearing Florentine caps, looked down and were satisfied.

Lorenzo stood in his stirrups to address the swelling crowd, but he found himself being pulled from his horse and set up on a litter like a statue of the Madonna, to be borne to his house on the shoulders of the citizens of a free republic. It was a turbulent ride and as he was carried swaying over the heads of the people he concentrated on keeping his balance. Perhaps it was that shakiness, but for a moment he thought he saw a familiar face amongst the press of citizens. Angelo? He stared hard into the crowd but the insubstantial ghost had vanished.

At the palazzo he was met by his mother, his wife, his sisters, his cousins and all the children. The impossible had been achieved: the Medici family had survived and were reunited. To see his city in such a delirium of relief almost made sense of everything.

✣

Clarice watched him arrive, her husband, being carried to her as if he were a gift from God. She saw him perhaps for the first time, watching his eye glance over his family and pass her by, but she continued to gaze at him, willing him to look again. Cautiously Lorenzo's haunted gaze returned and settled on hers. She smiled then, radiant and clear. He descended from the litter and embraced the children who threw themselves at him. He embraced his tearful mother, who seemed to have aged ten years. He thanked his uncles and cousins for their support. To his wife he said nothing, but as he passed his hand brushed hers accidentally, and suddenly, instinctively, those two hands clasped each other, like two friends divided by war, reaching out to each other in silence, as if to say, 'Love is here but cannot be acknowledged. Not yet. In time, all in good time…'

✣

In Mantua, Angelo wrote a poem about Lorenzo's triumphal return, as if he had been a bystander at the scene; indeed, so vividly did the pictures play in his mind, he believed he was there and seeing Lorenzo being carried aloft by the people. Opening his eyes to Mantua jolted him. He sent the poem to Florence, along with a letter that tried to explain his actions, but neither earned a response from Lorenzo.

The longer he stayed with the Gonzaga, the more convinced he grew that the system of patronage was an evil; each time he wrote a letter to Lorenzo de' Medici begging to be reconciled, he felt as if he were murdering his own dignity. Lorenzo's silence threw his words back at him and deepened his sense of self-disgust. Finally he stopped writing letters and left Lorenzo to enjoy his triumph alone.

Caro amico Tommaso, – Why do you not write? Is all Florence under an interdict not to communicate with me? Nevertheless, I shall write to you, in the presumption that our friendship survives, no matter what the reason for your silence. The Marchese's brother, Cardinal Francesco, arrived here yesterday to be honoured by a great banquet held in the court. The Marchese, who believes that I am an *improvissatore*, that I can bow the strings of a lira da braccio and sing as moved by the gods, asked me to perform. As you know, I have never been taken by the gods to sing verses that come fully formed to my lips, at least, not in public. Whenever I try, the only result is a dumb poet bowing away on a lira. The man the Marchese wants is our Baccio Ugolini, but I need this position, and I know how to feign divine frenzy. When it came to the time for me to perform, I sang some songs of recent composition, rolling my eyes and twitching as imposters do, but when I realised that no one was paying any attention, I sang as usual my own verses. I am facile enough on the lira da braccio, but not happy. Playing one line of melody and singing another takes all my attention and leads to a wooden performance. This parody of entertainment might have continued, except that a god did intervene. A youth with long, wheaten hair stepped lightly on to the dais and, without saying anything, took the instrument from me and began to play, leaving me free to unite with my song and let the words soar. Did you meet Giovanni Pico when he was in Florence? I have travelled the flat lands of the north looking for him, but in the end he has found me.

While we entertained them, the Cardinal and the Marchese were in conversation. In that conversation, the Cardinal was expressing an interest in my talents, and the Marchese was presenting me to him as a gift. By the time our song had finished, I had been given away like some exotic beast and am become a creature of the Cardinal and his menagerie. If it had not been for the presence of

Giovanni Pico, I would have acquiesced, for slaves can have no desires. But on my behalf Pico asked the Gonazaga what my function would be. We were told that the Cardinal needs a chaplain. 'It is a paid position and not too onerous,' the Cardinal assured me. 'It should leave you very free to write.' This was enough for me, but not for Pico.

'But surely he cannot be graced with such a position without taking holy orders?'

'That is nothing to be concerned about. We can arrange a quick, simple ceremony,' said the Cardinal.

And so I write to you, my silent friend, at midnight, to tell you that, by this time next week, indeed, on Sunday at the third hour, I shall have been received into Holy Mother Church. Pico is furious. He accused the Gonzaga of castrating poets. The Cardinal found this very amusing, and said that it is entirely up to me whether I keep my vows or not. As for the tonsure, it is very small and the hair soon grows back. The secular priesthood, he said, is not taken seriously by anybody these days. So, in exchange for a little hole in my hair, I can have whatever I want and I am happy to acquiesce. Pico is horrified and keeps shaking me, telling me it means I can never marry. But I have no wish to marry, now or ever. And should I change my mind later, one can always annul such vows, given sufficient funds. Since I want only to study, this seems an excellent plan – the first rung on a mighty ladder. Who knows where it may lead? Pope Angelo has a certain ring to it, do you not think? It is better by far than becoming an anonymous shade in some infernal university. *Vale.* Angelo. In the birthplace of Virgil.

✠

A letter arrived in Mantua sealed with the Medici stamp. His heart thudding, his hand shaking, Angelo opened it carefully. It was very short. In a few lines, and in the hand of Bartolommeo Scala, Lorenzo thanked him for all his letters and wished him good fortune in finding another patron.

✠

I unpicked my lace. Something had gone wrong with the pattern: the metre had changed. I went back a few lines, singing to myself to catch the rhythm again, and began once more to twist and plait the future with bobbins. On Sunday Tommaso called for me to visit. I went up to Ficino's villa. Ficino himself has returned and is at home, performing rites of natural magic to restore Tommaso's soul, but Tommaso is far from cured, is haggard and wears the beard of a hermit. He greeted me affectionately, but his eyes made the smile of his mouth seem insincere. He wore two expressions, and I knew which one was the real one. He handed Angelo's letter to me and I read it.

'Maria, I have not written to him because I cannot. You understand? Please, write to him on my behalf. Tell him what happened.'

I agreed abstractedly, too astonished by the letter's contents to pay full attention.

'He is taking Holy Orders? Today? What is the hour now?'

'It is the hour,' he said. 'That is why I called you here.'

With Ficino and Tommaso I knelt down to pray, to be with my brother, soul with soul, in this sacred moment.

✝

Dressed in a robe of coarse white wool girdled by rope, and following the instruction of the liturgy of ordination, Angelo went first to his knees before the two bishops and the cardinal, and then face down on the floor, his arms outstretched in the ultimate posture of surrender. It was simple enough. It meant nothing. It was the act of an ambitious, desperate man, making a decision that was only skin deep. He could get out of this any time: a word in the right ear, money in the right hand. Nothing binding in this.

But as he went down God came to meet him, and suddenly, with the smell of the floor in his nose, he knew he was making a vow in his soul that could never be undone.

He lifted his head in sudden breathless panic. He expected to see Giovanni Pico scowling with disapproval but saw instead that his friend was deep in prayer. Angelo struggled, desperate to jump up and flee, but a tremendous force was pinning him to the ground while the words of the liturgy were intoned over him. The antiquity of the rite poured through the chapel as the sun through the window that was burnishing Pico's hair. Pico was kneeling on the marble floor like a marble knight, his praying hands held under his chin, his closed eyes upturned towards the shafting light, his lips moving to his own silent liturgy. A vision of true piety; without doubt Giovanni Pico della Mirandola loved God. Angelo lowered his forehead to the floor, smelt dust, and surrendered himself. There was nothing else he could do, no more fight left in him. He would follow the model of his friend and submit.

'I don't know who you are or what you are,' he said to himself, 'but this is for you. For you. And for my sister. This is her desire. Please God, look after her.' A few moments later, he was a priest. 'For you, Maria,' he thought. 'This is what you wanted. Let it be.' He rose up.

'Father Angelo!' said the Cardinal, coming forward to greet him.

☩

Carissimo amico, – So now I understand your silence, what can I say? I dare not speak, for these days I cannot open my mouth without hearing the sound of a hypocrite. Forgive me for not being good enough as a friend. I would tell you that she is in heaven, or has become a new star in the sky, but of what use are such poetic conceits in the face of immeasurable grief? Endure, Tommaso. Your Angelo, at Mantua.

43

Mantua, July 1480

PICO LEFT MANTUA the next day but in the summer, when the university at Padua had closed, he returned. Because of the preponderance of dwarves at court, along with numerous clerics of Rome – all of whom had an ear to gossip and detail – most of the conversations between Poliziano and Pico took place on one of the three lakes which circled the city. In the evenings they hired a small boat with two oars from a local fisherman on the pretext of wanting to fish, but no one on the bank saw those two cast the net. Oblivious to fish they rowed the water discussing scholastic and Platonic philosophy; the nature of truth; the virtues of the Tuscan language; the elegant use of Latin; the existence of camelopards; the need to know Hebrew to understand the significance of the Old Testament; Orphic rituals; the methods of summoning angels; the evils of patronage. Pulling on an oar each they rowed together in such harmony that it was as if they were one man.

One evening they discussed the revival of theatre. Angelo, seated behind Giovanni, told him how theatre had begun with the Festival of Dionysus – or Bacchus as he is known to the Romans – and the wonderful processions held annually in Greece; how the first actors had been the chorus in masks, but then the great playwrights, Sophocles, Euripides and Aeschylus, had made two, then three, step forward to recite dialogue. 'Plato hated theatre, but borrowed its form,' he remarked wryly. 'And that theatre, those plays, held out of doors in great fan-shaped spaces like the Campo in Siena – they were the drama of Man. They were religious events, not entertainments, but it was a religion of Man.' He was so caught up in his subject that his oar was idle and Giovanni had to work hard to stop them turning in circles.

'What do you mean?'

'I mean the whole of Man, bestial and divine. In those plays they dragged out the worst and the best, the passion, the glory: all great emotions being called forth from the audience. If you saw a murder on stage in Greece, they said, you would not perform one in the streets. That is what *catharsis* means – a purgation of those wild emotions not suited to a civilised man. Where is my oar?'

Giovanni paddled the boat back to where it floated on the water.

'Their self knowledge was incredible,' said Angelo, reaching out to retrieve it. 'They knew that the gods are within us. Ficino has

434

rediscovered that, but they knew it then, all those centuries ago. And what have we done with our Christianity but cover such knowledge over? Did you know that Tacitus considered Christianity a "pernicious superstition"? It all comes down to point of view in the end.'

'It does not. The Christian faith is true!'

'Oh, well, perhaps, but Christian drama is not. It is halt and lame. Lorenzo and I read the Roman playwrights together.' (In the fervour of argument, Angelo mentioned Lorenzo's name easily.) 'There is a copy of Terence at Fiesole – did I show it to you? We tried to write a miracle play based on ancient principles but it did not work. Ancient drama must have ancient themes. And I can't explain those themes. I wish I could. The great raging emotions that end in death. We Christians find it very hard to comprehend. We like our justice to be served on us from above, and sometime in the future, rather than from within and immediately.'

The Cardinal had mentioned the need for 'some entertainment' in a series of forthcoming celebrations. These two words had metamorphosed in Angelo's mind as 'the need for ancient theatre to be revived, here in Mantua.'

'I don't know how you expect to write a play in two days, let alone revive ancient theatre,' Pico said, watching a pair of swans pass, the male bird chasing off some geese.

'It must have an ancient theme – and what is more ancient, or more appropriate, than the drama of Orpheus? Orpheus, destroyed by the followers of Dionysus.' Angelo opened the leather bag he had brought with him and drew out a book.

'What is that?'

'The Marchese's copy of Ovid.'

'Here, in the middle of a lake? A book of that value?'

'Sssh. Keep your voice down. I don't trust those swans – they could be spies. Let us put up our oars and read.' He passed the book to Giovanni. 'It is in book ten of Metamorphoses.'

Giovanni found the place and began to read. In his powerful voice Ovidian Latin boomed out over the lake. The blades of the resting oars hung dripping in the air; the boat bobbed like a moorhen on the breeze-ruffled water.

Pico kept interrupting to question his friend on matters of interpretation. What was the meaning of Eurydice and the hero's loss of her? If all the gods are within us, where is hell and who is Pluto? What is the significance of the second death of Eurydice? They discussed these things avidly, Angelo drawing on Lorenzo's ideas to interpret the poem according to the four levels of meaning, in which Pico was particularly adept. 'Read on,' he said at last.

And so Pico read from the book, telling how three times the sun reached the sign of Pisces, that marks the end of year, and in that time Orpheus rejected the many nymphs who vied for his attention. Whether it was because of his loss of Eurydice or whether because he had taken a vow, he repulsed them all, to their fury. *'Orpheus preferred to centre his affections on boys of tender years, and to enjoy the brief spring and early flowering of their youth. He was the first to introduce this custom among the people of Thrace.'*

Silently Pico read the text again to himself and then began to question whether this was overt homosexuality or a cipher for some other meaning, but Angelo was not listening. Taken by anger, he was staring into the lake. It was as if he had swallowed a capsule of poison months ago and only now had it burst inside him. In truth, he had forgotten this was how the Ovidian version ended, but it was too late now to do anything about it. He stared into the lake and what he saw was Lorenzo taken from him by Clarice and her false accusations. The rumours had followed him round Italy: he knew their source. In Bologna he had been taken aside by one man and offered boys 'very cheap'. In Venice, he had been asked to procure boys in exchange for an ancient text of Cicero. In Padua he had been warned not to try and find a post as tutor. On each occasion he had taken refuge in his innocence and ignored the provocation. But now he was angry. He imagined Clarice in the audience for his play and tried to picture her response to this ending. A particularly vicious few lines of poetry started to evolve in his mind.

'I think you should avoid this ending,' Giovanni said.

'Why?'

'Plato banned the poets not because the poets were bad, but because people took them literally. You put this on your stage and you will be out of this palace and state before the following morning. Besides, I have no wish to be implicated, and there are rumours starting.'

'What rumours?'

'About us. We spend too much time together.' Pico had long since ceased to blush in Angelo's presence – indeed, Angelo marked the establishment of their friendship as that moment when Pico first said something without changing colour – but now his cheeks were reddening.

'You and I know what it means, that what Orpheus brought to Greece was not unnatural sex but the mystery religion, and that the love of boys represents the Higher Venus – non-reproductive, celibate love. Divine Love, which, as Ficino so often says, must be chaste. We know that. But Nature hates chastity and will attack Orpheus, all claws. Uh.' Despite the heat of the evening, he shivered. 'It grows late – the wind is getting up.'

'While we are on this subject, and in full understanding of its meaning, there is something I want to tell you.' It was Angelo's turn to blush. 'You are the companion of my soul. I trust you. I love you. You are my dearest friend.'

Pico regarded him in complete and abandoned wonder, but then shook his head, saying, 'I am not the one you love, not with the love that hurts, that tears you apart.'

'And I thank God for it. Who wants that kind of love?'

'We suffer it whether we would or no.'

'I despise it. I prefer this. I want your company alone. I have never felt so equal to any man. The eight years between us, they are irrelevant. That you are a noble and I a republican – irrelevant. That you are trained in the theology of the schools and I a student of literature – irrelevant. Together, we are strong. When I am with you, I fear no one. Do not tell me I do not love you. It is not true.'

'Nevertheless I cannot replace Lorenzo de' Medici in your affections,' said Giovanni, softly. 'If you could see your face when you mention his name, which you do all too often, you would know what I mean. He is your Jove, and while you float on this lake, attracting the birds and the trees with sublime poetry, you are denying your true love.'

'Ridiculous! I am my own man. I need him no longer.'

'You are the one always recommending Orphic rites,' Giovanni continued. 'Only yesterday you were saying that one has only to become in tune with the gods for right action to be facilitated, and that this is called *spiritus influxus*, to be filled with beneficent power. Well, you should practise it. Better that than this morose abjection. Perform an Orphic rite. Tell the gods your deepest desire and lay yourself at their mercy. If you truly believe it works, then practise it.'

'I have no time. I have a play to write in two days!'

Giovanni was quiet for a while and then said, 'I need to go to Paris.'

'*No!*'

'You could come with me, enrol at the university. I would pay for you.'

'To do what?'

'Study philosophy.'

'The philosophy of the schools is stagnant, based on ignorance! How many times must I tell you that? When I was at the Florentine Studio, I laboured over the works of doctors of philosophy and rhetoric. Some of them proved to be so ignorant of Greek and Latin that they sullied the purity of Aristotle. A flood of nonsense spilled from their benighted minds. Sometimes they made me laugh; mostly they made me ill. Day after day I went through this torture, and there was nothing they could teach me which I had not already learnt.'

'That was Florence. It is different in Paris.'

'It is worse in Paris!' Angelo thumped his oar on the water, sending the boat rocking and the ducks flapping away. 'Men of the universities: aloe-hearted, gall-mouthed, wormwood-minded, sloe-spirited churls!'

Giovanni sighed.

'These philosophers of the obscure – braying donkeys each and every one of them!'

Giovanni sighed again.

'Weasels!'

'Yes.'

'Muckworms…'

Seeing that his friend's ire was almost spent, Giovanni began his opposition. 'You can only find the Truth through disputing the untruth,' he said; before Angelo could object, he went on to cite a staggering range of authors. He asked why he should accept Plato as being greater than Aristotle, or Saint Augustine, or Origen, or William of Okham, Thomas Aquinas or any other philosopher? Truth, he said, was not the property of any one man, but was available to all in some degree. Angelo was confounded by this intelligence. He did not know enough. He could not argue with this precocious youth. Simple repetition of what he had heard in the Platonic Academy would not satisfy Giovanni Pico della Mirandola. Realising the shallowness of his own studies, he floundered.

'I think in Paris I may find doctors of learning who will help me develop these ideas,' Giovanni said.

'I think perhaps you will,' said Angelo moodily. 'I certainly cannot. To think I came out here today because I wanted to tell you how Orpheus came by his lyre.'

'I know the story already.'

'Of course you do!' Angelo snapped.

Giovanni ignored his friend's anger, for he understood its source. 'Hermes met a tortoise. He spoke to it, called it his darling, and said, "You are the best medicine against black magic while you are alive, but you will make wonderful music when you are dead." So saying, he took a knife, stabbed out its life and scooped out its marrow. Then he made a lyre from it and said that a new animal had been born.'

'I always feel sorry for the tortoise.'

'Hardly a wonder since you are its kin. If only you would give up this marrow of your own self-concern, you could become the instrument of divine music.'

'Is that what the myth means?'

As one man they began to ply the oars again, each following his own train of thought, and the little boat splashed rhythmically across the water. The sun began to sink, marbling the lake with the colours of rust and indigo. Their oars plucked at the water while moorhens preened themselves at the lake's reedy edge and bathed their wings in the water.

'What I dislike most about philosophy,' said Angelo at last, gazing at the scene with open wonder, 'is that it seeks to convince me that this world is not real.'

'You are confusing beauty with the object. This scene will be dead in a few seconds; the sun will set, the birds will sleep, the beauty will seem to vanish in the darkness. This world you love is transient. It cannot fulfil your desires. It can only create longing and frustration. But the beauty – that is eternal.'

'And love, what of that?'

'Like beauty, that too is eternal, but again we confuse it with the object.'

Angelo stared at the young man who was becoming his teacher. At last he had understood, but still he protested. 'I am a poet and grammarian. The deepest desire of my heart is to clear literature of error. Words. The Logos. That is what I love, that is my bliss.'

'And philosophy is mine, but the bliss is the same.'

✠

Florence, July, 1480

The war is not fully over yet. Siena, that perfidious city, having invited in the Duke of Calabria, cannot now be rid of him, but so pressing is the Turkish threat that Lorenzo can do nothing about Siena. His attention now is not on Tuscany but on Italy and all Christendom with it. If he is lonely it is of his own volition. Sometimes I see him passing by, deep in grave thought, sometimes sporting with the children, but always with this chill air to him. His resolution not to see Lucrezia Donati is a self-denial which seems to bring no reward other than deeper emptiness.

The children provide some diversion; though he may have his mind on saving the Christian world, Lorenzo still finds time for them. One party of ambassadors from Poland were surprised when two little Medici ran into the audience chamber to show their father a bird's nest with eggs in it. Lorenzo fell to one knee to share his children's wonder, and then to remonstrate with them for taking eggs, as he himself had once been told off by Poliziano. When the ambassadors complained about the interruption, Lorenzo promptly dismissed them, adjourning the meeting for a day so that he could go with his children to the place where they had found the nest to see it restored.

Clarice, rejected, stays in her own rooms. Lorenzo does not come to the bed of his wife. When they meet, he avoids her eyes. As for the rest of the household, if they display a new deference to their lord, it is not because of an increase in his stature, but because he frightens them. He has grown harsh, unloving and short of temper. Some say it is a result of the death of his brother. Others say that it is because he has been betrayed in friendship.

His son, Piero, wears the same forlorn air, and probably for the same reason. Whenever either of them come upon me, their surprised eyes widen in pleasure and then cloud over as they realise who I am – and who I am not. I miss him too, my lost brother, and wander the house listlessly, my prayers abandoned on the lace pillow.

Lorenzo's reputation throughout Christendom is soaring; he is courted by kings and princes; with regard to the defence of Italy from the Turks, everyone is looking to him to provide leadership. So why is it that, at such a time of triumph and ascendancy, he spends his leisure time alone with his books?

His return has drawn Monna Lucrezia out of her seclusion but she is quiet these days and lacks her confidence and authority. She is just a mother who fusses over her son until he grows irritable. She looks critically at Clarice, as though to say that it should be the wife, not the mother,

441

ministering to the man, that Clarice should emulate her instead of retreating to her chamber or to the nursery. Despite all that has happened, this is still a divided house.

Lack of forgiveness. What I find wanting in Monna Lucrezia is also found wanting in me. I keep blaming her for the death of Elena and cannot forgive. She knows that and shuns my company. It is all reflecting mirrors: blame and retribution bouncing among us and becoming magnified. I feel as if I am here on sufferance. Lorenzo does not want to see me because I remind him of Angelo; his mother does not want to see me because I remind her of Elena. Sometimes, in passing, Lorenzo says, 'We must work out what to do with you, my lady.' It is only partly because of this that I choose to retreat to Monna Clarice. If I am honest, if I truly bare my soul, I shall confess it: I like her. Yes, pasty-faced, swan-necked, bovine-eyed Clarice is becoming my friend. On the subject of my brother I must remain mute, but on all other subjects we speak freely to each other.

She asked me this morning, her attempt to sound indifferent a clear fraud, what I know about Lucrezia Donati.

'So far as I know, Madonna, your husband abandoned her a year ago.'

'Is it true?'

'When your little Giuliano was born.'

'Then why…?' she began but could not finish.

'Why does he still neglect you?'

'Oh, Maria…'

'Lorenzo is in deep misery,' I said.

'But why?'

In her heart she knows the cause. She alone has the power to relieve his sorrow, but she does not want to.

'Come, Madonna,' I said, 'let's to the lace.'

As I returned to weaving my webs of hope and prayer, a package came from Marsilio Ficino to Clarice, the accompanying letter written in Tuscan.

'And why should the Father of the Platonic Academy write to me?' she wondered. 'Shall I bother to read it?'

'Of course you shall!'

'Has not this heresy caused all our woes? When shall it end? When

shall my husband return to the true faith? Only then, only then will he be happy.'

I was looking inside the package and drawing out a book. 'Oh, Madonna!'

'What is it?'

'Read the letter.'

She read through it quickly and at once held out her hand for the book. It is a copy of the Psalter, beautifully written and illuminated, a jewel, but that is not its value. Ficino has translated it into Tuscan. Her face began to clear in wonder as word after word opened its meaning to her. In her hands she was holding a copy of the sacred book in a language she can understand. The words, those impenetrable hieroglyphs, are now doors to meaning she can walk through. Ficino has opened the way for her to understand, to penetrate her own religion. I shared her wonder to see scripture in our own language, familiar and relevant.

To be alone with the book, we went to the chapel. It is a magnificently distracting place, all four walls depicting the return of the Magi in a huge crowd of men and kings – almost all of them recognisable. One cannot look at these astonishing walls and think of holy things: the mind bounds about like an excited puppy, yapping at everyone it knows. Clarice would not relinquish her book and insisted on reading out loud from it herself alone. I smiled at her childlike possessiveness and she returned the smile, looking naughty and delighted.

I sat in one of the stalls and listened to the psalms recited in her slightly lisping voice, heard the songs of ancient Hebrews, their sorrows, their vindictiveness against their enemies, their soaring praises of God. Tears welled that made my eyes swim and the figures on the walls seemed to move. There is one young man, a squire in attendance on the golden-haired king called Gaspar, who looks so much like Angelo my eyes keep returning to him. It is impossible, of course: these walls were painted when Lorenzo was about ten years old. Still, my eyes return often to the young squire, and today, looking through water, he was animated. The tears began to overspill and fall in sheets down my face.

Oh, Angelo, brother Angelo, Father Angelo: where are you? How long must we remain apart? When, where will you settle so that I may join you?

443

I was brought from my reverie by the arms of Clarice embracing me gently. Then I sobbed into her kind, warm shoulder.

'What can I do to help?' she asked.

'You know, Madonna.'

Her breathing quickened. 'What? Admit that I have been wrong? I cannot.'

'You must, or nothing will heal. All the wounds will remain open. Help me, help us all. Only you have the power.'

Now she was gasping for breath, her hands crossed over her heart, colours scudding over her face. I thought she was going to faint.

'Madonna, do it.'

She stumbled towards the altar, fell to her knees, gazed up at a painting of the Madonna in adoration of the Child. I confess I have not noticed this painting before; so overwhelming are the chapel walls that it would be like noticing a reclusive hermit in a street procession during Carnival. With her own hands steepled in prayer in the very same attitude as the Madonna's, Clarice went alone into the dark forest of her soul, the forest of the painting. For in this strange Adoration there is no stable, nor ox nor ass, neither shepherd nor king, no Joseph. In the clearing in a pine forest, Mary is alone with her Emmanuel, who lies amidst garden flowers on the forest floor. St John the Baptist is there, and a praying saint. Above all, over all, resplendent and visible: God the Father. Below him, God the Holy Spirit, in the form of a dove. This is a picture of the Trinity! I have never seen God portrayed before, and here He is, most beautiful, most benign, most loving, on the altar of the Medici. Overseeing everything.

The door must have opened behind us, for we were joined by Monna Lucrezia. She knelt beside us quietly, forming us into our own trinity at the altar steps. She said a prayer behind her hands but kept glancing at Clarice with the furrowed brow of concern. Clarice had gone so deep, was being pulled down to hell by her inability to speak. The spell had to be broken.

'Who is the saint?' I asked Monna Lucrezia.

'The holy Saint Romauld. Have you heard of Camaldoli, Maria? It is a hermitage and monastery high in the Appenines, above the Casentino Valley, and the Order of Camaldoli was founded by Romauld. For him, as for St Francis, our faith is a matter of simplicity. The soul is a forest which

must be cleared by discipline, and in the clearing is planted the garden of the soul. First one must cut down the trees of pride, then uproot the stumps and brambles of deceit and falsehood. Next the garden must be fenced by good company and a guardian appointed for the gate – only then will the flowers of a good life spring up.'

'Who is the guardian?'

'I think at first it must be a spiritual master, whether priest, abbot or philosopher, but ultimately it must be our own power of reason. As Romauld taught, so he lived, and in the fir forests of Camaldoli each monk has a clearing and a garden where he lives in solitude. It is the most beautiful place. I used to go often with my husband, taking Lorenzo, Giuliano and the girls with us, and in those retreats we practised our faith as a family. There is more to Camaldoli. Under the auspices of the good abbot Ambrogio Traversari, the Platonic Academy was founded there. It was there that Ficino learnt Greek; there that he was raised in Platonic Wisdom.'

Clarice turned, and her expression was one of slow-blinking, open-mouthed, horrified astonishment.

'You never asked,' said Monna Lucrezia. 'Always assumed. But yes, it was there at Camaldoli, in one of the few places on earth where Christianity is as it should be, that the Platonic Academy was born. There is nothing heretical about it, my daughter. If you want heresy, look to the war-mongering Pope, who murders in the name of the Lord and practises nothing but greed and self-aggrandisement. There is your heresy.'

I looked again at the perfect painting, its rocks, its standing trees and felled trees, its garden floor, and the Christ Child.

'In the little garden of the soul, tended with devotion, and with meditation, He may be born again in our hearts,' said Lucrezia. '"For whosoever shall do the will of my Father which is in heaven, the same is my brother, and sister, and mother."'

Clarice fell forwards, arms outstretched on the floor, fully penitent, her sin pulled like a thorn from her heart.

I have discovered from Matteo Franco that it was Lorenzo himself who commissioned Ficino to translate the Psalter for Clarice. He has taken advantage of his excommunication to break the rule of the Church that scripture must not be translated into the vulgar tongue. Now that it is in her possession, he waits for her. We all seem to be waiting – for something, some impulse from heaven that will make everything come right.

At supper tonight as we all gathered, Lorenzo said, 'Where is my wife?'

'In her room,' said his mother. 'She wishes to be alone.'

Such was Lorenzo's ill humour that Francesco the secretary approached cautiously to tell him that a letter has arrived from the Gonzaga of Mantua. 'There are to be two betrothals: that of Chiara Gonzaga to Gilbert de Montpensier, and that of the Marchese's son to Isabella d' Este of Ferrara.'

Monna Lucrezia heard the news as one with an interest in the results of stock breeding; Lorenzo heard it as a change to the political map. While Lucrezia wondered if the cross-fertilization between Ferrara and Mantua would help remove the hump from the Gonzaga line, Lorenzo saw what the Marchese intended. 'He is making northern alliances!'

'You are invited to the celebrations,' Francesco informed him.

Lorenzo's mouth tightened in a bitter line. 'Inform the Marchese that I cannot come, I am too busy trying to save our country from the infidel Turk. Tell him that in a covert way; bury that truth in some florid paragraphs of congratulation, will you? And tell Baccio Ugolini that he is to go in my place. Gonzaga has a discriminating taste in poetry and music; he will appreciate the quality of my substitute.'

Baccio approached Lorenzo to receive his instructions. Lorenzo told him who to speak to and who to be wary of, what information he needed, and how he wanted the Gonzaga and Este families to help in the coming trial that Italy must suffer.

'I hear that our Angelo is in Mantua,' said Baccio lightly. 'Is there any message for him?'

'Is he in Mantua?' Lorenzo said, disingenuously.

'He has become the chaplain of Cardinal Gonzaga.'

Lorenzo grunted. 'No doubt even as we speak he is pressing his patron for benefices and bishoprics. Convey my condolences to the Cardinal; tell him that he has been beguiled by a lonely-looking poet who in fact heads an insatiable family of ingrates. Tell him he has my deepest sympathies, and if he requires a loan to finance his chaplain's demands, my bank is at his service, with a favourable rate of interest.'

How did I remain in my seat? How did I not fly at him like a cat, all teeth and outraged fur?

'Bitterness does you no honour, Magnifico,' said Baccio with some courage.

Lorenzo raised a warning finger to him. *'You go too far, but I forgive you, as usual. Ugolini, remember you are a visitor to Mantua. Refuse any offers the Gonzaga make to have you remain with them. I promise you, if you leave me to adorn their court, you will become very ill very quickly. You come back here, do you understand? I have lost quite enough to Mantua already, and am not in the mood to lose any more.'*

44

Mantua, July 1480

GIOVANNI PICO looked askance at Angelo's weary face. 'Did you sleep well last night?'

'Yes, very.'

'And Mass this morning? Did you remember everything?'

'It went very well. I have had the liturgy off by heart since childhood.'

'Am I disturbing you?'

'Yes.'

Nothing more was said for an hour. One man read while the other wrote, fast and furiously. A servant entered the room with a letter for Angelo, forwarded by Bernardo Bembo in Venice.

Marsilio Ficino to Angelo Poliziano, his fellow philosopher: greetings.

'If I now say, Poliziano, that I admire in no small measure the subtlety and eloquence of your writings, perhaps someone will think me too full of admiration, for while it is usual for that which is new to arouse admiration in others, I for one seem to admire in Poliziano the qualities which have been familiar to me for a long time. Yet the truth is that I am now marvelling not at those qualities long manifest in you, but at those that have newly flowered. For in a very short time my Poliziano has grown so naturally that with his changing stature I see him as a new and different man. And so that man who pleased me not a little as a boy, and greatly as a youth, the same pleases me most of all as a grown man.

As his stature has grown from day to day, so has his grace. This is all the more delightful, as I often foretold that it would be so. Therefore, I beg you, continue as you have begun: make yourself divine and so make me a diviner at the same time.

The others join me in showering you with innumerable good wishes.'

✝

Angelo read the last line several times over.

'What others?' Giovanni asked.

'My friends in Florence, I suppose,' Angelo said, moved beyond measure. 'But why does he call me "fellow philosopher"?'

'He is aware of the work you began in Venice with Barbaro.'

'But I have done nothing on it since.'

Giovanni Pico shrugged. 'As he says, Ficino is a diviner.'

✝

Angelo was only half way through his play when Mantegna told him that it must be set to music.

'Of course.'

'No, not just some of the songs – all of it. I am convinced this is how Greek theatre was, sung from beginning to end.'

'Chanted perhaps by the chorus, but not sung.'

'No, sung.'

Angelo laughed nervously. 'There is only a day left before rehearsal begins! You want it all set to music?'

Mantegna thought that it would be simple enough, since Angelo wrote to lyrical rhythms for which much music already existed. It just needed to be collected, adapted and arranged. He went to find a court musician to do the work.

Angelo paced the room, translating Ovid's Latin into Tuscan canzone, composing little songs for various actors, none of whom had been engaged yet, to sing to music which had not been found yet. He thought he had been asked to write a play, but it seemed he must do everything himself, even engage and rehearse the actors. He appealed to Giovanni Pico. 'Put aside your studies and help me.'

'You want me to leave holy philosophy to help you entertain wedding guests? You were the one to throw yourself into this servile position without thought, Father Angelo. Do not drag me down with you.'

'For the love of God, the sake of friendship – and the revival of theatre!'

Giovanni put aside his book with a loud sigh. 'I shall find the actors, so that you may concentrate on the words.'

'Words which no one will listen to.'

'I will listen to your words.'

✝

Lifting the Orpheus story out of *The Metamorphosis*, Angelo translated it into a Tuscan verse form. There was no time for rewriting the myth; besides, Ovid could hardly be improved upon, except for that ending, and Angelo deferred that problem by concentrating on the beginning and middle.

Giovanni Pico cast some of the parts among the court musicians and singers, and some among the Gonzaga family. He himself took on the part of Aristaeus, the youth who tried to steal Eurydice from Orpheus, 'for no one else will agree to playing the villain,' he said. And he cast Angelo in the part of the young shepherd with the awful task of informing Orpheus of the death of his wife – a piece of unaccompanied singing for the voice of a man who has known grief. But no one he could think of, no one in all Mantua, had the right combination of beauty and voice to play Orpheus. The finest tenor in the city was an ugly man, and Pico was beginning to think that they would have to use him dressed in a mask when the Florentine embassy arrived in court, with Baccio Ugolini at its head. Pico watched the party arrive, and surprised Marchese Federico by approaching the ambassador directly and asking the striking looking man if he could sing.

'Indeed,' said the Marchese, coming between them. 'Baccio Ugolini is an *improvissatore*, and one of finest musicians in Florence. I am hoping I may tempt him to stay with us.'

But Pico was not listening. He hurried away to tell Angelo that Orpheus had been found.

✢

While Angelo laboured to finish the play in time, Giovanni Pico sat outside in the cloister courtyard where they stayed, now reading Hermes Trismegistus to himself, now reflecting on the beauty of the child Isabella d'Este of Ferrara. At other times he provided the bridge between the author and the musicians, running between the two with messages.

Angelo's fingers worried his hair into ringlets. There was stubble on his chin and dark shadows under his eyes. He battled alone inside his cell, making a short, shallow entertainment out of Ovid's melting images. He read:

Yet the sweetness of Orpheus's songs would have rendered the weapons harmless saving that the growing clamour, the Phrygian flutes and beating drums, the Bacchic howlings and hand-clappings, drowned the music of the lyre. At last the stones reddened with the blood of the poet, whose voice they could no longer hear.

He wrote:

> *Ho! Sisters! Up! Alive!*
> *See him who doth our sex deride!*
> *Hunt him to death, the slave!*

His hope that Lorenzo might come to Mantua for the nuptials had been dashed, and he was grim-faced as he wrote, his pen dashing over the paper, line after line after line of Tuscan verse. Tuscan. Lorenzo's language.

> *Thou snatch the thyrsus! Thou this oak-tree rive!*
> *Cast down this doeskin and that hide!*
> *We'll wreak our fury on the knave!*
> *Yea, he shall feel our wrath, the knave!*
> *He shall yield up his hide*
> *Torn as woodmen pine-trees rive!*
> *No power his life can save;*
> *Since women he hath dare deride!*
> *Ho! To him, sisters! Ho! Alive!*

He read and re-read the lines in Book XI, how the first efforts of the Maenads to kill Orpheus were thwarted by the power of his song; how their weapons slaughtered the animals gathered round the poet, but not the poet himself; how it was only by drowning out his voice with their bacchic howlings that they succeeded in striking him. Could he include the graphic imagery of live oxen being pulled apart by bare, female hands? Of course he could not.

He was tired. It was too hot. This play had to come to an end, and it had to conform to the ancient principles of theatre. Therefore he must ignore the blood and pathos of the murder and write a stage direction: *Orpheus is chased off the scene and slain.*

Angelo threw down his pen.

The music of the lyre: he and Lorenzo had written it, played it, sung it, for the sake of Man, to raise him up, to remind him of his dignity, his divinity, his grace. The music of the lyre, the harmony and order of the world, may be drowned out by the howlings of the mob. It is destructible. Even as Florence quelled the noise from Rome, it was to face the clamour of janissary bands: the Turks were on their way, with their clashing cymbals and clanking crescent moons, their sabres, the chain mail that rattled as they marched.

Giovanni swung round as Angelo flew out of his cell like a wild man from the forest.

'The music of the lyre is destructible! Harmony, even divine harmony, can be destroyed, can be howled down by ignorance. And this is what is happening. We have to sing, Giovanni, sing as loud as we can, of truth and beauty and God, or we shall be destroyed.'

Giovanni, startled, presumed his friend was ill and feverish. He caught hold of him and made him sit down.

'Is this your play?'

'No, it is not my play. My play is a trifle. I am ashamed of it before I have even finished. But how can I do Ovid – or literature – justice in two days? It is not possible. These Gonzaga and their demands – what are they but part of the mob? What do they know of real beauty or divine grace? Nothing. They want a bauble. God forgive me, I have written a bauble.'

✢

Rehearsals began while the set was still being built. Behind locked doors, musicians began to fit Poliziano's words to music. On the stage Susanna Gonzaga, who was to play Eurydice, practised dying from snakebite. Angelo interrupted the rehearsal of the shepherds to tell Eurydice that, according to ancient principles, she must die off stage. Carpenters and joiners hammered and chiselled to create the entrance to Hades. The shepherd Mopsus wanted to bring in a real lamb for the sake of authenticity, but was told that he was the shepherd of cattle, not sheep, and that the cattle would be beyond the brow of the hill now under construction and therefore out of sight. Angelo was beginning to lose his voice.

Baccio came in to await his turn to rehearse. He sat beside Pico to watch the Cardinal's chaplain ordering everyone about. 'I barely recognise him,' he said.

'He is very tired.'

'He is also considerably more mature and confident. And yet...' Baccio leant forward to study his friend more closely. 'There is something wrong, some bitter note. Is he playing a sympathetic string to Lorenzo's discords?'

'What will it take to reconcile them?'

'Divine intervention, nothing less,' was Baccio's opinion.

☩

The night before the play, there was a banquet. Exhausted and overwhelmed by all that was yet to be done, Angelo had to be forced to attend. While he felt incapable of anything but falling face down in his soup, he had to bear Giovanni Pico's eulogies in praise of the girl Isabella. Finally and grudgingly Angelo allowed his weary head to be turned in her direction.

She sat beside the Marchese, who was not destined to become her father-in-law for some years, for this betrothal was being made far in advance of the marriage. Her face was pale and grave, her blue eyes watchful. An abundance of curly chestnut hair was caught up and interwoven with chains of pearls, a metaphor for the girl's own spirit, which was wild yet controlled by good behaviour. She was seven years old and about to be formally claimed by a gangly hunchback.

'How is it that one as beautiful as this has sprung from the loins of Duke Ercole d' Este?' Angelo asked Giovanni.

'Obviously the seed was from the mother.'

'Our doctors of learning insist that the seed comes only from the father.'

Giovanni Pico shrugged. 'They are wrong.'

'Ah, so you, too, have read Galen?'

Pico nodded.

Angelo turned his gaze upon Isabella's mother, Eleanor of Aragon, the daughter of the King of Naples, and the very model of beauty. To his surprise, he found the lady's eyes were on him, as if she were watching him. He blinked nervously and turned his attention to his food.

Between courses, Baccio Ugolini was invited to sing to the company, and the song he sang was in praise of Lorenzo de' Medici, line after line of inferior verse.

'This man is my friend,' Angelo said to Giovanni Pico, 'but his poetry is execrable. His lines scrape across the floor so much they are giving me a headache. I can endure no more. I think I shall retire.'

'Headache!' said Giovanni Pico. 'O man of self-possession: one small breeze and your boat sinks. If you leave now, everyone will know why. There is nothing wrong with his lines – it is his subject you cannot tolerate. We all know the lie that you are living. That you are a free, independent, transformed man – it is a lie, and everyone knows it.'

Angelo, breathing heavily, waited until the next course was being served and then left. He went to the courtyard where the play was to be performed on the following afternoon.

The place seemed to whisper with the echoes of the day. The frenzy of activity remained as a movement in the air. The half-built set of a meadow with a cave to the left and a hill to the right was empty of god or shepherd; yet it was not empty. He could hear the echo of voices, if not the words spoken. The image of a nymph painted on a curtain was animated by a draught. The musicians had left some of their instruments in a pile on the floor and he picked up a lute to hold it lightly, thoughtfully, knowing what it was that he wanted to sing, and not daring to begin. But as he lifted up the instrument and rested it against him, it was as if Calliope were with him, in him, taking him over, as if he could hear spring water trickling into the basin of a fountain half hidden by evergreen ivy. He straightened and touched the strings with the plectrum. The notes played; the song followed. He listened to it even as he sang the words forming in his mind. The rhythm of the lute was different from that of the song, and the two rhythms, being played simultaneously by one man, set up between them harmonic intervals which were palpable. Angelo Poliziano died. His consciousness of himself sank as if into sleep, withdrew into the innermost centre of him. The Orphic hymn took over.

He sang a song of heaven in a mode he had never heard before. The intervals of concord and discord drew aside the curtains of reality and the words flowed out of him. He sang of the sadness

454

of joy, of the sweetness of pain and the torment of love. The cry, that rose from the pit of him, that translated into lamentation, was not his own. It was of creation itself. It was universal. It was the cry of Man for his lost God. And for Angelo Poliziano at that moment, the face of his God was Lorenzo's. He was ready to surrender everything – fame, fortune, independence, pride – if he could only look once more on that beloved face and serve his chosen, earthly god to the end.

45

Florence, July 1480

I WORK ALONE at the lace pillow. The Turks, they say, are about to land at Otranto in the south. I tell myself there is no point to this work, that it will be destroyed soon, and myself sold in slavery to some cruel pasha. But I work on, steady and sure, equally certain that the work must be done if only for the work's sake. The hymn I have been making is almost complete. It is time to start drawing in the threads.

Clarice despises cosmetics – indeed, her husband will not allow her to wear them – but that lovely inner beauty that has been in her all day since we were in the chapel demands enhancement, so I braid her hair in a new way, freer and less severe. And I persuade her to wear some perfume, an attar of roses that one of Lorenzo's agents brought from the Persia. In her reflection in the mirror, she is ox-eyed and white-armed, truly a Juno that Jupiter will not be able to resist. Once we are done, I whisper in her ear, 'Call for him.'

Her skin trembles like a silk sheet. 'Very well, yes,' she said.

'Shall I send a servant?'

'Yes.'

She is reading to the children from her Psalter when Lorenzo enters.

'You sent for me,' he says coldly.

'I thought you might like to hear the children reading. They can all

read now. Little Giovanni, and the girls too. This book that Father Marsilio sent me is in Tuscan. So they can not only read, but understand as well.'

Lorenzo arranges himself in a chair. 'Let me hear.'

Clarice gathers the family round the book, resting on a lectern, and one by one they all read a few lines each from Psalm 88.

Lorenzo softens. 'And you, wife. Do you read?'

'I do.' She brings her eyes close to the book and reads slowly.

Then thou spoke in vision to thy holy one, and saidst, I have laid help upon one that is mighty; I have exalted one chosen out of the people. I have found David my servant; and with my holy oil have I anointed him: With whom my hand shall be established: mine arm also shall strengthen him. The enemy shall not exact upon him; nor the son of wickedness afflict him. And I will beat down his foes before his face, and plague them that hate him. But my faithfulness and my mercy shall be with him: and in my name shall his harp be exalted. I will set his hand also in the sea, and his right hand in the rivers. And he shall cry unto me, Thou art my father, my God, and the rock of my salvation.

She raises her head from the text. Her husband sits staring at his family as a leper stares through a stone squint at the holy sanctuary. Emotion is moving under the surface which he strives to contain.

'Lorenzo?' she says, 'What is it?' Clarice steps towards him, reaches out and touches him. 'What is it?' she repeats softly.

He catches hold of her and pulls her to him, as if to hide his face in her body. His words are muffled: 'Would that God loved me as he loved David!'

'But He does!'

He sits back a little, his face upturned to her. She takes it between her hands, runs her fingers through his hair. 'Lorenzo, Lorenzo, forgive me. I doubted you, and I was wrong. I was wrong. I believed that everything befalling us was your fault. I usurped your place in the family, but when I fed my children it was on shells and not on meat. I had no knowledge. Lorenzo, I love you so much. Please forgive me.'

'The fault is not yours.'

'Perhaps, but the pride is mine alone.' Clarice kneels before him. She

456

takes his hands in hers and lays her cheek against them. 'Call him back,'
she whispers.

Lorenzo leans forward. 'What did you say?'

'I said, call him back.'

'Who are you speaking about?'

'You know well enough.'

'Use his name.'

'I want you to recall Angelo Poliziano. I need his forgiveness almost more
than I need yours, for I tortured him cruelly. I was so jealous.'

'Of Angelo?'

Lorenzo holds his hand above her head, as if in benediction; it hovers
there like a dove, and then comes gently to rest on her hair. The softness
of his touch releases her tears, but his voice remains harsh and therefore
contradicts the message of his hand. 'My argument with him is my own.'

'Then let me plead on his behalf. Forgive him, my Lord, and call him
back. If I was jealous it was because you loved him as I would have you love
me. And you still love him. Call him back.'

'There are many charges for him to answer.'

'There are none! He is innocent.'

'It was his decision to leave Florence and the service of this family.'

'He did not leave straight away but remained in the villa as a loyal
servant, until it became impossible for him. Scala drove him out. I could
have stopped the spiteful rumours, but I did not. I encouraged them. Forgive
me. He left in search of dignity and independence, and he has found it.
But he misses you as you miss him, and what he desires above all things is
to be your friend of his own volition. Therefore, call him back, but not to
employment in this household. Only if Messer Angelo is free, can he freely
be your friend and most loyal companion.'

'And the accusation regarding Piero?'

Clarice gazes into his eyes. Suddenly it is as if she stands outside the
worlds; all the limits of her being drop away as her soul joins with that of
this man, her husband, Lorenzo.

'The accusation was false.'

'Do you believe that?'

'Without doubt. Our son was not touched. Piero told me that himself, but

I thought the master had threatened him in some way. I believed what I wanted to believe; now I believe the truth. Your friend is innocent.'

46

Mantua, July 1480

MUSICIANS, WHO had been playing a gentle piece of music while the audience settled itself, now stopped playing and waited until the ensuing silence had spread through the assembly. When the silence was complete, a drum was struck. Doom-laden, it resounded through the hall and a helmeted boy with winged feet jumped on the stage to announce the fable of Orpheus. A chorus of girls walked across the stage holding a long garland between them and singing, 'Be still and listen!' They went on to tell of a shepherd, a son of Apollo, who was in love with the wife of Orpheus, and how, as Eurydice had flown from his pursuit, she had been bitten by a snake and died. Susanna Gonzaga ran across the stage, pursued by Giovanni Pico dressed as a shepherd. Young men now entered and joined their voices to the chorus to tell the rest of the story.

The guests, enchanted by the music and the poetry, gave themselves up to the play. Angelo sat behind the scenery, listening for the first time to the music and finding that by its addition his trivial, hurried work had been made momentous. Themes set by himself were taken up by viols and voices and by the end of the first act the author was, like the audience, captivated. No one stirred as scenery was changed and an intermezzo played. The drum was struck again, a reminder of ever-present Hades in this Arcadia.

Baccio arrived on stage as Orpheus wearing a laurel wreath on his head. In his perfect tenor he sang a panegyric to Cardinal Francesco Gonzaga – a piece of customary sycophancy which

Angelo had suggested to his patron in the vain hope that the Cardinal would tell him to dispense with such flattery. The music of his accompaniment on the lira was slow and melodic. The voices of the chorus joined in and carried the audience like leaves on a river of sound. The drum being struck to mark each verse was the heartbeat of the earth itself. Verse followed long verse and ended with one that likened the river of Mantua to that of the sacred Muses. By the end there was not a person present who was not convinced that, by coming to the Cardinal's house, he had come to a very temple of the liberal arts.

The Cardinal's initial pride, however, eventually transformed into disgruntlement: to be so praised put a deal of responsibility on him. Were this song to become well-known, there would be no end to the largesse expected of him. He must either turn his purse into a cornucopia of patronage, or else be deemed undeserving of his reputation. The Cardinal did not know whether to applaud Poliziano or curse him. But the lilting music took its effect even on him and at the end of the eulogy, resigned to his fate, he stood and cheered with the rest when, dressed as a shepherd, the poet himself ran on to the stage. Angelo accepted the ovation and then signalled for silence, making a mental note that he had put the eulogy in the wrong place. Now he had to get the audience back into the mood of the play before he could sing the sad tidings of the death of Eurydice. The music itself did the work, its sad refrains so heightening the emotions of the audience that, when Orpheus came on stage to sing his lament, and the torches in the hall were snuffed out one by one, tears filled the eyes of the ladies present and then began to spill over. Angelo, watching from the side, was gratified.

As the meadows gave way to the underworld, so tenors gave way to basses. A dwarf juggler playing the part of Ixion turned a wheel of flaming torches, the only illumination of the scene. Sisyphus pushed on a huge boulder while thirsty Tantalus stood up to his chin in a pool of water he could not drink. These three permanent inhabitants of Hades enacted their tortures in silence.

Then from a distance came the melodious strains of Orpheus; as he approached, the torments of the sufferers ceased, but the yapping three-headed dog, Cerberus, being played by over-excited dwarves tied together beneath a fur cape, had to be silenced with a surreptitious kick. Pluto appeared, terrifying in the dancing light of hand-held torches which caught the gold and silver of his robes. The God of the Underworld thumped out his song, demanding to know the identity of the intruder who had so distracted his realm with the music of his lyre. Orpheus made his request of the god, but it took the intercession of Pluto's queen, Proserpina, to effect a change to the immutable laws of death: Pluto agreed to restore Eurydice to life, but made the condition that Orpheus must not look back to see her until he had left Hades.

Orpheus began his journey back to the upper world, singing in triumph. But he could not hear his wife behind him and was not sure she was there. As the light of the upper world dawned, he could not resist looking over his shoulder. Eurydice had been there, but now she was drawn quickly backwards, plucked at by shades of the dead. Orpheus struggled to reach her but the Furies intercepted him.

The final act opened. Angelo grew hot and lost his nerve. He wanted to jump up and explain to everyone the hidden significance of the myth, but nothing he could say would explain his bitter poetry, since it only had one meaning, and that was literal. In the act of composition, the only audience he had considered was the scholarly one; he had striven for accuracy and interest, for impressive turns of phrase, for innovative forms of lyric metre. Now he sat in front of an audience that clearly contained only a few scholars; the rest, which numbered as many ladies as men, represented a humanity he had not considered at all. His palms grew damp as Baccio sang, 'Since my fate has been so cruel never more shall I wish for women's love. Henceforth I would cull new flowers, boys in their spring when all are fair and lithe.'

A gasp sounded throughout the hall. Angelo suffered all eyes turning his way, not least those of Giovanni Pico, who looked appalled.

Orpheus continued to denounce all womankind. 'How wretched the man who changes his purpose for a woman, or ever for her is happy or sad!' Baccio sang on, but now his voice seemed to lose its power of enchantment. His own doubts on these verses unsettled his confidence. 'Or who barters for her his liberty, or who puts faith in her pretences or her words. She is ever lighter than a leaf before the wind. A thousand times a day she will and will not.'

With mounting discomfiture Angelo listened to all his spite pouring from the hero's mouth. 'The married man,' Orpheus cried in conclusion, 'I urge to seek divorce, and all to flee the company of women.'

Angelo turned to the audience with an exaggerated shrug. 'A joke!' he said. 'Ha!'

'And this at a betrothal!' someone shouted above the growing hubbub.

'Oh, Oh, Oh, sisters!' cried a Bacchante, and she had to raise her voice high to be heard. ''Give him death! Let the villain die, let him die!'

Raucous sopranos, the Bacchantes ran on to the stage to fill the hall with their strident cries. Their hair was wild, their lips livid, their manner fiery. Their shrill voices chopped like axes. 'Cast the evildoer into damnation, tear from his breast his palsied heart, death to the scoundrel.' They pursued Orpheus, chasing him from the stage.

Angelo prayed that the wrath of his audience would be appeased by the death of the hero. As the Bacchantes roared back, holding aloft the dripping head of Orpheus, the audience sat in stunned silence. The play ended with satyrs and Bacchantes singing a drunken chorus, their lurching voices colliding with the music.

Such was the tumult in the hall that it was impossible to know whether it stemmed from approval or the opposite. Angelo was carried towards his patron on a surge of people, to have the Cardinal clip him on the ear, grin as a man of the world, and glance towards Giovanni Pico with raised eyebrows. 'Well…!'

Giovanni Pico, buffeted this way and that, made the most of the confusion; pulling Angelo with him, he tried to escape and at the same time contrive a collision with Isabella d' Este. This left Angelo standing face to face with the girl's mother, Eleanora of Aragon, the daughter of the King of Naples and the wife of the Duke of Ferrara. Swallowing nervously in the face of her penetrating stare, he asked her lamely if she had enjoyed the music.

'More than you appreciate women, Maestro,' she said. She was dressed in powder blue velvet. Her chestnut hair seemed weightless. She was not a beautiful woman in the usual sense, she was fleshy and her eyes were small, but at the same time she was made beautiful by some inner force shining out of her; and whatever the nature of that power, it was because of it that Duke Ercole d'Este lived and functioned. This was his secret; this woman was the power of the duke. Angelo felt his right knee buckling, as if kicked from behind. The next thing he knew, he was bowing, a courtier in the court of Venus.

✝

The following morning Baccio had difficulty in rousing his friend from a sleep that had been achieved through an excess of wine. Angelo was drawn back from oblivion by the horrible sensation of water being poured slowly over his face. 'Giovanni?' he asked.

'Giovanni Pico has gone.' Baccio put down the jug and settled himself on the bedside. 'He left at dawn for Paris. I am surprised that you live, that you were not hauled out during the night to be torn limb from limb, or to meet a more Christian end at the stake. For the love of God, what possessed you to tell husbands to divorce their wives?'

'Gone? Paris? For how long? Has he left no message?' Angelo struggled to rise against the iron band round his head that was being tightened by screws.

'He fled while he had some reputation left. Is it surprising if he no longer wishes to be associated with a decadent poet who pimps for boys?'

'For mercy's sake, my head!' Angelo fell back on his pillow, shielding his eyes from the light. 'He knows better than that. It is my patron who did not understand.'

'You should choose your patrons more carefully.'

'Would that I had the choice.'

Baccio regarded his friend affectionately. 'You did it deliberately to get yourself expelled. Not having the courage just to walk away, you put yourself into a catapult and persuaded others to fire it.'

Despite the pain, Angelo smiled at the image, seeing himself flying over the lakes of Mantua in the direction of Florence. His smile faded: Florence did not want him, or at least, one man in Florence did not. But then he remembered Ficino had written: *The others join me in showering you with innumerable good wishes.*

'Baccio, my friend,' he said, groaning and trying to retreat under the sheets. 'I do not know which is worse this morning, my headache or your company.'

'I shall leave you then. I only wanted to know how you are, to see how contented a Mantuan you have become.'

'It pleases me greatly to be thought a Mantuan, as Virgil before me.'

'O fickle soul.' Saying that he was to depart in an hour for Florence, Baccio rose. Angelo, who was due to attend the Cardinal in the chapel, bade him farewell.

'By the way,' said Baccio. 'Since you have not asked, I shall tell you – Lorenzo wishes to be remembered to you.'

Angelo sat up like Lazarus.

'It was not for my interest that I came to find out how you are.' Baccio drew a letter out from his jacket, fastened with the Medici seal, and threw it on to the bed. 'It arrived this morning, along with instructions for my departure. As I said, I leave on the hour...'

An hour later, with the letter and its Medici seal tucked inside his shirt and resting against his heart, Angelo Poliziano left Mantua for home without a word of farewell to the Gonzaga.

✛

Florence, August 6th, 1480

Today two momentous things: the Turks have invaded Italy at Otranto, and my brother has returned home. When Angelo entered the sala, I saw a grown man. The light in his eye was neutral, neither the puppy-dog look of the patronised, nor the arrogant gleam of the independent. It was neutral. He was who he was, and he had come home. I wanted to leap across the room and hug him but was caught in the nets of decorum and restraint. I stood with the Medici. He came forward a few paces and then, dear God, he went down on one knee before us.

'Rise up!' Lorenzo commanded him. 'Is this what they teach you in foreign courts? I am only a citizen as you are.'

Angelo stood.

'Welcome home, Maestro.'

'I thank you, my lord.'

Pride like a toad was squashing all natural speech. This was more formal than meeting ambassadors from hostile courts. I felt like a pushed spring and longed to leap between them and bang their heads together. Perhaps they should have met alone and not with the ladies present. Perhaps that would have been easier.

Lorenzo cleared his throat. 'We have much to discuss, but I have asked you here today since my wife has a favour to ask of you. How strong is your bond to the Gonzaga?'

'I believe it is broken forever and cannot be repaired.' Angelo smiled sheepishly.

'I am delighted to hear it,' said Lorenzo, hiding his own smile. He turned and invited Monna Clarice to step forward.

And so they stood face to face, Angelo and Clarice. She alone seemed not to find the occasion difficult but met him squarely and with dignity. Angelo, if he expected anything at all, thought she would speak about the education of the children. His composure fluttered when she spoke the name of his erstwhile tutor in Greek, 'Johannes Argyropoulos'. Was it the name itself or the fact that she could pronounce it? – either way, he gazed at her as at a wonder of nature.

'Johannes Argyropoulos,' she repeated, 'the professor of Greek studies at the Studio, has left Florence, and his departure creates a vacancy. My husband has put this gift in my hand to bestow. It has always been the habit in this city to have the Chair of Greek occupied by a Greek, but I understand that you speak the ancient Greek language better than the Greeks do. Also it has been decided to expand the office to include the study of Latin poetry, and I know of no Greek who speaks both languages with the facility of our own Angelo Poliziano. The letters of your name seem to have appeared miraculously on this chair, the chair of Professor of Latin and Greek, and, if you accept, you would be the first Italian to hold it. Well, what do you say?'

Angelo said nothing. He could not speak. He stared at her uncomprehending. Clarice continued. 'We have had our differences, Maestro, but they were resolved when you took Holy Orders. That said, I would have it be known that if you do not take your priestly function seriously, you should let it languish and not pretend to be what you are not. I leave it to you and make no demands.'

'Oh, but I do!' I said, astonishing everyone, not least myself. I rushed on while I still had the courage. 'I have a demand to make of you, my brother. You will honour this noble function of teacher, and know this honour to be a gift from God in reward for your devotion to your true love, Pallas Athene, the goddess of wisdom, to whom you were led by her sister Calliope. For the professor of poetry should be a teacher and a poet, and not a critical scholar. Therefore be the priest of your goddess, and her disciple, be received by her, serve her forever. And through her, serve God. And,' I added, with the boldness of Pallas herself, 'take your sister into your home and do not send her to the nunnery, for she desires to be a celibate outside the cloister, and not locked up for the sake of custom.'

Everyone stared at me, but the oracle had nothing further to add.

465

47

AFTER THE RETURN of Angelo, the entries in Maria's journal grow sparse and, for the period of the invasion, are entirely absent. She, like the rest of us, must have been too frantic about the Turks to continue in her daily pursuits. They landed on the Adriatic coast in the south of the country, laid waste the land and reduced its people to slavery. Running ahead of them like waves on a beach were fear and hopelessness, washing over the country and drowning all hope for the future. Marsilio Ficino, may his name be praised, kept working, determined that his Plato be finished before destruction overtook us. It was so finished, and hurried off to a printer for publication.

The Duke of Calabria, who had remained in Siena, calling our Tuscan city his own, was the devil on our doorstep. He was also our saviour. The only Italian commander capable of standing up to the Turkish forces, the duke led his armies south, against his will but in response to the need of Italy. Other territorial disputes among the Italian states were forgotten as the country moved together as one, behind the leadership of the Duke of Calabria, to expel the alien from its shores. With Italy rode the powers of Aragon, Portugal and Hungary. And so, there we were, our civic-national pride all stirred up and muddied like too many colours mixed together. Small wonder that each man looked to his own and did not worry about his neighbours except to feel peculiarly sentimental about them.

Oh, what do I say now about cause and effects? What will you believe? You will believe what you are predisposed to believe. Here, then, are two versions. The first is based on Plato's mathematical vision of the world as a unity of interrelated parts. In this version, prayer is effective and the concentration of good men gives power to the Good. The second is based on our usual perceptions, formed by minds that hold beliefs contrary to our faith, full of contradictions, inconstant and hypocritical.

The first version: Throughout the war Ficino had written powerful letters in the cause of peace to both Pope Sixtus and the King of Naples. Now, with the invasion, he convened meetings every night comprising members of the Platonic Academy and various brotherhoods such as the Company of the Magi. We met in several places: Santa Maria degli Angeli (the church of the Camaldolese Order), the Cathedral, San Marco monastery, the Badia at Fiesole, the Palazzo de' Medici. Depending on the company present, we either prayed in true Christian fashion or we performed hermetic and orphic rites. These last were, naturally, confined to the inner circle of the Platonic Academy. Between us, and in a singular concentration of will, we did not elicit the help of heaven but lent our power to heavenly work.

The second version: The battle against the Turks was won, not by the superior force of the Christians, but by the timely – one might say miraculous – death of Mahommet II. Robbed of their leader, the Turks fled back to their boats, leaving Italy in a more unified condition than they had found it. This, to the popular, muddled mind, was a result of good luck, coincidence and the grace of God.

It is your choice. But on the tenth day of September, 1481, the angels of the empyrean and the gods of Olympus sat back with a sigh, their labours done. Although it had taken a Turkish invasion finally to free Lorenzo, the work was now accomplished.

Lorenzo never did lay face down on the floor of St Peter's basilica in total submission to the Pope. Instead he sent twelve volunteers to apologise to the Throne of Peter. The Pope switched the backs of these loyal, representative Florentines with some vigour and thereafter was quiet.

✜

The land healed, the burnt stubble was ploughed in, seeds were sown which soon showed as green blades, new corn became a yellow crop which was scythed down, threshed and milled. The cycle of the seasons was back in motion, water wheels were turning again. Before setting Angelo free, Lorenzo gave him one last gift, a little villa of his own on Fiesole, above the Badia and on the shadowy, windy side of the hill. Though it was small and not well-appointed, Angelo loved it as if it were a palace. Everyone was welcome there, and everyone came. As his reputation grew – for who else among all the universities of Europe could lecture on Homer or Aristotle in verse? – so did admirers begin to come from further and further afield. He took in the students of his choice and filled his little home with Englishmen and Portuguese, tutoring them, tuning them to such a pitch that, when they returned to their native countries, they took the Orphic hymn of Florence with them in their souls.

✝

I am kept busy running the house for all these men, but Angelo has put me under discipline as if I were another of his students. It is his will that each day, for five hours, I must read. The study has a beautiful view over the garden and looks towards Florence. There stands my brother's desk, ink-stained, an old war horse that has seen many battles. And beside it a newly carved one, small and light. Yesterday he presented me with another gift, a heavy medallion sculpted by Bertoldo and cast in bronze. It was given, he said, in gratitude, for since I came into his life, his heart has found peace and his mind direction. On one side of the medallion is his portrait in profile, on the other, mine. This is my greatest treasure.

It seems to all that we are a model of familial harmony, but I confess that sometimes, in the privacy of our home, beyond the prying eyes of neighbours looking always for some new sensation, I argue with him hotly in the perennial debate of the Platonists against the Aristotelians, and will not let him win just because he is bigger and older than I, a professor and a man. He has to prove his arguments before I will agree with them. I am, he says fondly to his friends, the comb of his intellect, tugging on his knottier ideas and releasing them. 'For that which cannot be understood by a simple woman is not the truth, but merely a mental abstraction.'

I like this little adage too much to kick him on the ankle for calling me simple.

✢

Among the residents at the villa was Giovanni Pico, now the Count of Mirandola, returned from France to study Greek at the university under the new professor. Throughout his stay of two years he protested every day that the house was too small, its siting too grim, and that he would not be staying a day longer.

✢

I have given Giovanni Pico a room to himself, the best room, with windows that face the dawn. Angelo spends the evenings beguiling him with encyclopaedic conversations while I spend the days instructing the servants in recipes to please a Mirandolan palate, ordering wines from the north and doing everything I can to make our home irresistible to him. Advised by my correspondents among the ladies of Europe, I put sprays of blossom in vases and fill the air with the fragrance of crushed herbs. Whenever I can I play the lute in a distant room so that he hears it but softly, not as a distraction but as a measure that is a reassurance, like the heartbeat of the mother to the baby in the womb. By such means we cure the restlessness in our itinerant friend and give him a home. He complains that the hospitality of the Ambrogini family would cause pilgrims to stop their wanderings and shooting stars to pause in the sky. Sometimes he calls me Circe and himself the waylaid Odysseus. We open the doors and tell him to go. He stays.

✢

When Pico finally left, it was for a villa of his own fifty paces away on a path through the woods.

I visited Angelo sometimes, but the comfort and happiness of his house was gall to me in my prolonged bereavement. I preferred to live on my own in my house in Florence. My work with Ficino done, I sought employment where I could and learnt to live on little. On one visit Maria gave me a strip of lace. 'It has Elena as one of its threads,' she said. I have it with me now, and I wonder,

469

as I have wondered every time I have copied from her journal, what became of her. Women, neglected by the records, have a tendency to disappear like footprints on a beach. I have written to Florence and made enquiries but no one knows where she is, whether she lives or has died, unrecorded, the forgotten sister of the famous man.

✠

I have three more things to write about: two bereavements and one camelopard.

In 1482, Monna Lucrezia Tornabuoni-Medici, wife of Piero, mother of Lorenzo, died.

✠

Yesterday came news that Monna Lucrezia was nearing her hour. Angelo and I rode at once to Careggi. Despite the sadness of the occasion, it was a rare pleasure to be alone with him for, since the university appointment was made, Angelo is always in company, whether surrounded by students, or his own entourage, for now he has a servant, an assistant and a secretary, and moves through the world no longer alone but in a small group. He is recognized in the streets and hailed by well-wishers, pointed out by fathers to their sons as one to emulate, stopped by those who attended his last lecture and wish to display their own knowledge under the guise of 'questions.'

But we rode to Careggi, just the two of us, to pay our last respects to the one who has been our mother in the absence of our own. On the way, we stopped at Ficino's villa and found Tommaso de' Maffei was with him. We persuaded Tommaso to come with us to the Villa Medici. He came willingly enough, saying that it was his greatest wish to be reconciled with Monna Lucrezia, though he doubted she would want to see him at such an hour. We left him in the courtyard to wait while we went upstairs.

Lorenzo was at his mother's bedside, so struck down by grief that Angelo took him out of the room to comfort him. Lucrezia was conscious and summoned me with her eyes. Her lips were dry and cracked: Monna Clarice bathed them with a piece of moistened linen.

'My daughters,' she whispered. *'You two are my true daughters. I leave the care of my sons, my Lorenzo, my Angelo, to you. You know the secret.'*

Monna Clarice and I exchanged glances, not sure that we did.

'What is the secret, Mother?' Clarice asked.

'In St Paul. Love them, serve them, so that they may love God. Do not look for their love for yourself. That is the secret.' Her eyes suddenly blinked and filled with fear. *'I do not want to die!'* she said.

'But Mother, think of what awaits you in the next life.'

'Indeed! Intense heat and perpetual suffering!'

'No, no, no,' said Clarice soothingly. *But I understood, and sent a servant to fetch Tommaso. He has altered so much, become a lean instrument on which God plays a Spartan song. Monna Lucrezia gazed on him in horror as on the angel of judgement, but Tommaso touched her face tenderly.*

'Are you going to tell me it was not my fault?' she whispered.

'No. But I do not blame you. I never did. I trusted God, and God took her away. It is not for me to question that, or blame any human agency. We fear death too much. Go on your way, Madonna. We shall follow soon enough. All the joys you have known on this earth have been but shadows of the eternal bliss. Let go. God awaits you. And Giuliano.'

Monna Lucrezia gasped, and the gasp was followed by the sigh of her final breath. Her eyes were open as she died, and were gazing past me as if on the one she loved above all others, as if Giuliano himself were in the room. I turned: it was Lorenzo who was behind me.

✣

The corn was scythed down; the land ploughed, the seeds planted. As the new shoots emerged once more, Angelo received news that his brother Derio was seriously ill in Montepulciano. Angelo and Maria journeyed south at once.

✣

The propensity of nature to recover from man's destruction is truly wonderful. Everywhere the land is lush with blossom on the fruit trees and poppies in the new corn. We rode slowly up the long slope leading to our native city, for our horses were weary. When we came to the Gozzano fountain, we paused and slid from our saddles, and while the horses drank we went about collecting flowers to lay at this shrine to the memory of a dead father. Once our prayers were done, Angelo turned and looked out over the valley of paradise towards the lake shimmering on the horizon.

'According to Pico,' he said, 'there is nothing lasting in this world but the eternal verities: truth and beauty.'

'He is right.'

'So why does my heart pound with longing when I see this view?'

'Oh, you are confusing beauty with the object of sense. Nature is a great seductress.'

'And my sister is a philosopher,' he said, throwing his arm about me affectionately. We walked the rest of the way up the road to the gate where another family now makes ironware at the forge. Through the gate and up the lane, on the left was the fine brick house of Ser Benedetto. Angelo stared at it in wonder. The place had featured so often in his dreams that he was surprised he barely recognised it. How different it seemed in real life, how ordinary – just a house. Another boy ran out of its door as we stood there, another hound on his heels. The son of a neighbour, he ran past us unheeding as he would any strangers. Angelo's gaze, following him, stared into the past.

Cammilla is quite changed. All the jolly ampleness has been replaced by the sharp angles and hard edges of concern, threatened as she is not only by the imminent loss of her husband but by the loss of everything. Her thin sons cling to her skirts, as if they know, though they are so young, that the foundling hospital awaits them. She led the way to a room that was filled with women. Around the bed where Derio lay, sweating out his life in a fever, were cousins and sisters-in-law, as well as our sisters Lucrezina and Saracina.

I greeted my family with swift, warm embraces before turning to the bed. 'Oh, he is too young!' I cried. 'Too young to die. Dear God, do not let him die!' As I fell to my knees to pray at the bedside of this brother I have known so briefly, Lucrezina brought Saracina to meet Angelo, and he held out his hands to her, speaking to her softly. Gradually I became aware of another woman who watched at the bedside, one who in distress stared now at me and now at my brother. I knew who she was, even though I have no

472

memory of her face. I knew her at once, and so did Angelo. She is nearly fifty years old, her face lined and dry, her body bowed. He did not move, but stood there frozen.

'Mother?' I said, barely above a whisper. She nodded and took my hand in hers, but was looking past me to her immobile, frosty son.

'Angelo…' she said.

'I thought you were dead.'

'Would that I were, rather than see you now, and your hatred.'

'My hatred? It was you who threw me out.'

She turned her head slowly, side to side, like a beast tired of avoiding flies. 'No,' she said quietly, 'no, that is not true. And you know it. If I had kept you – and had it been possible, I would have done – what would you be now? A lawyer in Montepulciano. You think I did not want to keep you? Of course I did. For all your learning you understand nothing.'

Then the great poet, the Professor of Latin and Greek, collapsed to his knees and approached his mother on his knees, buried his head in her lap and wept. Monna Antonia stroked his hair, over and over. 'It is the custom, Angelo. The Salimbeni took me and my dowry back. I had to marry again. I had to part with the children. It is the custom, the custom.'

His weeping grew louder.

The custom that had destroyed our family was about to destroy Derio's.

'You thought I did not love you? How could you think that? You know nothing, nothing. My love for you has never wavered. All these years I have prayed for you every single day. I loved you even though you despised me; that is the nature of a mother's love – it is like a river's torrent, oblivious to anything in its way.'

Robbed of all his misconceptions, Angelo felt boneless. Loneliness, abandonment, all came up like filth from a drain and had to be washed away by tears. My attention was truly divided between my brothers, both of them dying, one physically, one in spirit. Angelo was inconsolable, the tears coming in a pulsing flow like mortal blood from a severed vein. In the bed, Derio's head kept lifting and falling back, lifting and falling back, his eyes witless and staring at his wife without recognition.

'Derio, Derio,' Cammilla cried. 'Please don't go, don't leave me. Please, Derio, please. Try to live. Try!'

Such were the forces running up inside me that I wanted to scream, to make it all end. I converted the passion of grief into prayer. Prayer not for results. Prayer for prayer's sake. My ignorance, my lack of understanding, my insignificance, my nothingness: I offered it all to the Lord in prayer. Thy will be done.

Suddenly the only sound in the room was Angelo's weeping, and that too stopped. We, the Ambrogini, the lost members of a tribe gathered together for this short time, all fell quiet at our brother Derio's passing. And then the keening began.

✠

I seek myself in my mother's face. Clearly Angelo and I take after our father, and Monna Antonia is forever holding our faces and seeing her beloved husband there. She is nobler in mien and closely resembles Saracina. But now and again I see myself as a spirit in her features, a small gesture of her hands, the way she sits, the sound of her voice. She is both myself and a complete stranger. We enjoy discovering each other. She is much disturbed by my fate and berates Angelo. 'Is it so difficult to find a husband for this lovely girl?'

'I am not looking. I want her for myself.'

Outrage! She is our mother no longer, but every woman of every small city, furious in the face of unconventional happiness.

'She lives with me, is my housekeeper,' said Angelo.

'No, no, no. This is a rupture of custom! You cannot bring such shame on our heads, Angelo, no!'

'Mother!' he said, suddenly angry. 'Do not speak to me of custom. It was custom that tore our family apart. This custom of tornata. *I have blamed you all these years for sending me away, but it was custom that wrenched us apart. Custom – the rigid, thoughtless application of law. It is the custom also that girls be not educated in letters, these girls who grow up to teach their children to read. Custom! May God help me to keep my brother's family from such a fate as ours suffered. My nephews shall not go to the foundling hospital, not while I live, nor shall they be parted from their mother. I have a fine house in Florence, recently renovated after a flood and about to be leased out. Camilla may have it, and live there with her children under*

474

my protection. This is not saintly generosity on my part, it is simple duty. Besides, the boys need educating. The men in this family have a tendency towards baseness, my father being the notable exception. If I adopt the boys it is to raise them as Benedetto raised me. Perhaps they will prove impervious to the lessons, but I think in Lattanzio I see some signs of bright intelligence.'

'Angelo!' our mother gasped.

'Will you come with us?'

'I cannot. Of course I cannot, not while my husband lives.'

'And when he dies?'

'I shall go to the convent and be content to spend what remains of my life preparing my soul for death.'

'Then we shall not meet again?'

'No.'

In a quiet time after the funeral, Angelo went alone to the Cathedral of Montepulciano to find a priest to take his confession. On his knees he asked absolution of his sin, which was to have blamed all women for the crime he thought his mother had done to him. The priest told him to ask forgiveness of the Holy Mother herself, and for a penance gave him a decade of Ave Marias to recite. This penance he performed with due sincerity and attention, enunciating the prayers with the full power of his beautiful voice. And the Holy Mother heard the voice of Poliziano and drew him back within the folds of her protection.

48

It is impossible for a man with an intellect like a winged horse, lauded on all sides, whose voice is a universal authority on language, words, poetry, whose friends include princes and Pico della Mirandola, not to fall victim to arrogance. It is impossible for those who love such a man not to wish to cure him. There were several of us in the conspiracy dreamt up by Piero de' Medici, including myself and Maria.

A herd of assorted African beasts, a gift from the Sultan of Egypt, were due to arrive in Florence to be presented to the Signoria. The Professor of Greek and Latin, engaged as he was in a work arguing that poetry is the mother of civilisation, was oblivious to this event of mere sensation. We saw him but rarely, so busy was he at the university, but on one day he had been drawn out to view a portrait of himself. At the church of Santa Trinità, in the recently completed Sassetti chapel was a small, private party consisting of all those portrayed upon the walls. The painter, Domenico Ghirlandaio, took much pleasure in introducing each man to his likeness. I stood among the real – Lorenzo de' Medici, Francesco Sassetti, Lorenzo's sons and various members of the Sassetti family – looking up at the likenesses and judging them against each other. Not one of us was anything but overwhelmed by Ghirlandaio's talent in *mimesis*, mimicry of nature.

Set against the story of Saint Francis receiving the Order from Pope Honorious was a very strange scene of contemporary life: Poliziano emerging from a crypt with his pupils and mounting the stairs towards Lorenzo de' Medici.

The real Angelo was giving a brief lecture on *mimesis* to anyone who would listen. Maria interrupted him. 'But what are you supposed to be doing, coming out of a hole in the floor?'

He, whose ready knowledge on all things knowable sat on his

face like a sheen, looked irritated at the interruption. 'Must you take everything literally? This entire chapel is a hieroglyph of the rebirth of ancient values, planned and programmed for Master Domenico with my help, but if this is your understanding, my own sister, what will the ignorant see?'

'They will see a holy scene dominated by your coming out of a hole in the ground!' Maria replied.

'Piero, explain it to this simple woman.'

Now a handsome youth nearly sixteen years old, and recently betrothed to a young cousin of his mother, Piero translated all the hidden messages of the walls that spoke of a new Augustan age dawning under the rule of his father. 'And here, in this scene,' he said, 'Poliziano is restoring Lorenzo's sons, bringing us back from the underworld to meet our father.'

'Oh,' Maria said.

Later, Piero drew Maria aside. 'Master Angelo,' he said, 'thinks that the meaning of a word is integral to the word, but I think it is not. I think the meaning of a word is integral to the object it denotes.'

Maria followed his argument. 'The Count of Mirandola would agree with you, I think.'

'I have conceived a way to demonstrate my thesis.'

'Will it rob my brother of his pomposity?'

'I think it may.'

'What may I do to help?'

'Bring the professor to Poggio a Caiano tomorrow. It must be at the third hour.'

'On what pretext?'

Piero nibbled a finger nail. Fair haired, silky-skinned, with the fine-toned body of an athlete, he seemed intent on disturbing his perfection by chewing at himself. He bit, pulled, swallowed and thought.

'We shall tell him that my father has discovered a most unusual word. I will have Lorenzo send him a note. Master Angelo will find such an invitation both mysterious and irresistible.'

And so he did. Accordingly the next day Angelo rode out to Poggio a Caiano in the company of his sister and with his nephew Lattanzio sitting behind him, hanging on to his back like a son. Drawn into the conspiracy by Maria, I went with them.

After a ride on the long, straight road through ploughed fields towards Pistoia, a low hill appeared and on it a large framework of scaffolding with men like ants filing up and down ladders. 'This new villa,' Angelo lectured Lattanzio (and anyone else who was listening), 'is not the renovation of an earlier structure but is being built by the architect Guiliano da Sangallo from Lorenzo's own plans.'

Petrarch had advocated the villa as a place of repose and contemplation but had not thought further than the villa as a farmhouse on a country estate. Lorenzo had conceived a house specially built for the purpose based on plans of geometrical perfection. The past – the genius of Rome – was to be drawn into the present. 'Once upon a time,' said Angelo, 'we had in Florence a most wonderful architect in Leon Battista Alberti, who studied the works of the ancients to discover their secrets in the art of building. These he wrote down for us in the Ten Books of Architecture. Now Lorenzo is building this villa based on Alberti's principles. Everyone is at work on it.'

'Are you at work on it?' Lattanzio asked.

'Furiously. I have specified the subjects for a frieze that will sit below the pediment – it will have a pediment, as in a Greek temple – and I am working with Botticelli on a new painting, one of a centaur being dragged up by the hair by Pallas Athene. It celebrates in symbols Lorenzo's triumph in Naples. It also represents what this house shall stand for: the triumph of civilisation over barbarism.'

'Are centaurs real, uncle?' Lattanzio asked.

'Opinions are divided.'

'What do you believe?'

'I believe they are real, but perhaps not in this reality.'

'That is the sort of thing Aunt Maria always says.'

'Well your aunt is a wise woman.' Angelo glanced at his sister, his eyes dancing with amusement at this sleight of self-praise. 'A Diotima of our own times,' he said, his eyes still resting on her affectionately. Lattanzio wanted to know who Diotima was, and I told him she was the woman who instructed Socrates in the wisdom of divine love.

'Yergh!' said Lattanzio, to whom any kind of love was, at this stage in his life, sickening. He wanted to know what we were going to see at Poggio a Caiano today.

'Oh, we shall see many strange things for sure,' said his uncle. With the land now at peace, Lorenzo had the leisure to pursue his delight in country life and farming. He was building an aqueduct to irrigate the land round Caiano, canalising the River Ombrone that embraced the site of his villa, and laying innovative plans for agriculture.

'He is planting mulberry trees from China, which are the food of the silk worm,' Angelo told us. 'That will cut down the price of silk. He intends to learn how to make cheese, using very productive cattle from Tarentum, so we no longer have to import extra supplies from Lombardy. He will bring hogs from Calabria and rabbits from Spain, chickens from Padua and geese from Rome. There are already quails and peacocks, pheasants and doves. But I suspect the surprise he has in store for us is the final design for the frieze. The scenes, which I have gathered from ancient myths and stories, celebrate the agricultural year but also relate to the transmigration of souls and allude to Plato's myth of Er...' Before Angelo's riverine mind could flow back through time to tell us everything about the afterlife from Plotinus to the ancient Egyptians, citing a multiplicity of references all the way, I interrupted.

'I thought you said the note you had from Lorenzo was mysterious.'

'Yes, it was. A very cipher of a message. He said I was to come to the villa to meet a word. That is what he said in his note. "Come at once. There is a word I want you to meet."'

Lattanzio laughed his boy's laugh, and swung his boy's legs, and I saw in Angelo the very bliss of fatherhood, teaching his nephew as he had been taught by Ser Benedetto, richly, peripatetically, enjoying a sense of completeness in his life he had never anticipated. Cammilla was in the house in the Via dei Fossi, and filling it with such a substance of love that the plaster would never fall off the walls again. Maria was doing the same in the villa on Fiesole. Both houses were now filled with lodgers, students from England, France and Hungary, who had come to study with Poliziano, grown men, not callow youths, who appreciated the comfort of the accommodation as much as the tuition. Rumour was rife, of course, about what these unattached women were doing with all these men, but under the protection of Lorenzo – the new Augustus – we were all free to challenge custom with intelligence.

As we approached the site of the villa, Angelo described how it was to look, that its style was being based on a temple to Jupiter south of Rome, but that the proportions were derived from the Etruscans. 'It will be a temple, yes, a temple to the seven liberal arts, to humanity at its finest, to civilisation.'

Lorenzo was standing at the site with the chief mason and the architect, Giuliano da Sangallo. He turned to greet us, looking happy and excited.

'Angelo, look!' he said. 'We have the plans for the frieze.' He had two of the labourers unravel a large scroll between them, to show the scenes that were to be made in glazed terracotta and mounted beneath the triangular pediment above the main door. Both he and Angelo tripped over each other in their enthusiasm to explain everything to the rest of us. Between them they spoke of the Golden Age, symbolised by farming, of warfare, of animal sacrifice. Angelo started talking about the god Janus, whose two-faced form was in the centre of the design, 'The god of doorways, of going in and coming out, the god of beginnings who gave us our name for the first month. See, in his hands the figures 300 and 65, for he is the god the year. Two ways…'

'Two ways,' Lorenzo interrupted him. 'For every soul that is born, there is the choice of two ways, whether to descend into the animal nature or to rise into the angelic nature. We all inhabit this world and think the reality of our senses is the only reality, but there is a door that opens into another realm, and my villa Ambra is just such a door…'

Angelo butted in to amplify this with a plethora of examples of this scheme from ancient authors. Lorenzo overrode him, keen to show us the two faces of Man: one gazing this way on the evil of warfare and greed; the other on the good of farming and honest work. 'This is *gentilezza*,' he said. 'The sweet new life of culture and art based on virtue and fair dealing.' The pediment was to be sculpted by Bertoldo, but the scheme of it, the elaborate programme of symbolic imagery, had been provided by Angelo Poliziano, '…who knows more about everything than any man alive,' said Lorenzo indulgently. Angelo glowed.

'*Gentilezza*,' Lorenzo murmured, gazing up at the space his new house would occupy as if upon a vision of beauty.

Presuming this was the word he had been brought here to meet, Angelo felt the swelling of the heart he had suffered at the sculpture garden by San Marco that night when Lorenzo left for Naples. Lorenzo's vision was coming to be. This was not the threshold to a house so much as a threshold to a new civilisation. Reflecting thus, and his mind transported by wonder, he was unaware of a creature being brought up behind him by his pupil Piero. Maria kept Angelo occupied with questions about the symbolism of the architecture until the creature was in place. Then she turned and said, 'Oh!'

Angelo turned. He found himself face-to-breast with a massive beast whose ochre-coloured hide was dappled like a leopard's with ginger patches. His eyes started. He yelped. He laughed in fright. It had a neck like a swan's, but when its head came down to meet him, he stared into the long-lashed eyes of a camel with two stubby horns between its ears. Four legs it had, with those at the front being longer than those at the back, a fly whisk for a tail, and feet like trenchers.

The keeper of the beast put some fruit into Angelo's hand; as the soft, whiskery mouth of the beast snuffled up the figs, the ticklish Professor of Latin and Greek laughed and shuddered like a little boy. Suddenly it was as if the rivets which held together the body and soul of Poliziano began to shake themselves loose and he began to tremble violently.

'We call it the *zarafa*,' said its Nubian keeper.

Poliziano could not reply. He was dumbfounded. The poet-grammarian was suffering a word on its anagogic level, meeting its fullness of meaning, a meaning that was eating figs from the palm of his hand. If he wanted to cry, it was because he was confronted by the mystery of God which is the essence of all creatures, a mystery that nothing written can reveal. Little sounds of a shaken heart came out of him as, in the person of a camelopard, a vision of Creation opened up, whole, entire, imbued by love. The creature looked down on him in gentle concern; being a mother, she knew distress even when displayed in a member of another species; she nudged the Professor of Greek and Latin with compassion. Poliziano's trembling ceased; as he stood staring at the camelopard the sheen of knowing became the radiance of understanding.

GOODNESS, PRAISE GOODNESS.
LIFE AND LIGHT, FROM YOU COMES
THE PRAISE AND TO YOU IT RETURNS.
I GIVE THANKS TO YOU, FATHER, THE STRENGTH OF
ALL MY POWERS. I GIVE THANKS TO YOU, GOD,
POWER OF ALL MY STRENGTH. YOUR WORD THROUGH
ME SINGS TO YOU. RECEIVE ALL BACK THROUGH ME
BY THE WORD, A SPOKEN SACRIFICE.

FROM THE SECRET HYMN OF HERMES TRISMEGISTUS

HISTORICAL NOTE

MOST HISTORIES of the Renaissance touch on the events of this period 1478-1480, but to my knowledge the best account of the war is that by E. Armstrong, *Lorenzo the Magnificent* (1895), while the fullest treatment of Poliziano in this period is G. Piccotti, *Umanistiche Ricerche*, (1955) which formed the basis of Alan Moorhead's *Villa Diana*. Isidore del Lungo's *Florentia* (1897) is equally full of vivid personal detail.

Apart from Tommaso, Elena and Iride, there are no fictional characters in this story. Every effort has been made to stick to historical fact but where there are gaps in our knowledge, invention has been given its head, most notably in the characters of Maria Poliziana and Maso Ambrogini. Sometimes the novelist's instincts are born out by subsequent research. Since writing this book I have discovered that a network of women such as described did actually occur in the Peace of Cambrai of 1527, in what is now called 'The Peace of the Ladies.'

The real name of Maso Ambrogini was Tommaso di Antonio di Cino, but I changed it to avoid confusion with Tommaso dei Maffei. Similarly Angelo's brother Desiderio has been shortened to Derio, to avoid confusion with a major character in the first volume of this trilogy, *A Tabernacle for the Sun*. I am indebted to Antonio Sigillo of the Commune of Montepulciano for his insistence that Maso was not the irredeemably bad man portrayed by history, also for showing me the actual site of Benedetto's murder, which is not where stated in the history books. His re-enactment of the scene, in full operatic manner, in the rain, by the side of a road now busy with traffic, is a memory I shall cherish forever. We do not know either the date or the manner of Maso's death. As for Maria, her character can only be a product of the imagination.

As with most women of the time, she is known only by her association with a man, in this case her brother. Her existence would have been forgotten but for two things: mention of her by Angelo in one letter, and her image on four medals. In his letter to Monna Lucrezia of May 25th 1479, written not long after his sister arrived from Montepulciano, Poliziano complains of being exhausted by Maria's exhortations for him to obtain the Provostship of Fiesole. Superficially the complaint suggests an unhappy relationship, but the medals, as well as the contemporary gossip, indicate that Maria was his companion in the house probably for the rest of his life. It is thought that the medals were made by Bertoldo, the master of Lorenzo's sculpture academy. Two of them pair an image of Maria with that of her brother; two of them pair her image with symbols. Three of them portray her as a young girl with her hair loose, and one as a mature woman with her hair worn in a bun. In the youthful image her hair parts over the ear. Since Angelo's hair is shown doing the same, both on the medal and in his portrait by Ghirlandaio in Sta Trinità one suspects a family trait of either thin hair or protruding ears; but it is more likely that the relevance of this feature is symbolic and means 'having the ear to hear', the naked ear denoting someone alive to inspiration and the voice of the Muse, or simply someone whose dominant sense is hearing.

Of the symbols on the reverse of two of the Maria medals, one is a mythological figure of Constancy, bearing the motto 'Constantia'; the other shows the Three Graces with the word 'Concordia.' Concordia is Italian for harmony; it is also the name of a territory between Mantua and Ferrara of which Giovanni Pico's family were the rulers – Counts of Mirandola and Concordia. Furthermore, not only does the obverse of at least one medal of Giovanni Pico show the Three Graces, but it is the same image, cast from the same mould as Maria's. Through the medals we may infer a strong and symbolic connection between Maria Poliziana, her brother and her brother's best friend. The nature of this friendship will be explored in the final volume of the trilogy.

That Maria was scholarly we have no evidence. If she wrote

anything, it does not survive. She seems to have been content to be linked with her brother, and more likely to have been his willing servant than a woman striving for personal recognition, such as Cassandra Fidelis for example. I have chosen to see her relationship with Poliziano as similar to that between Dorothy and William Wordsworth. If the qualities Maria chose to associate herself with – harmony and constancy – truly reflect her character, then she would have been a precious addition to the household of a poet who suffered so much in the realm of human affections.

Perhaps it is not strange that a man capable of devoted friendship also had a tendency to attract enemies. More than most, Angelo Poliziano had his detractors, both during his life and since. Historians over the ages have picked up certain stories planted by his enemies and have presented them as the truth. Some of the blame for this can be laid at Poliziano's own door. After all, his candid nature led him to confess faults which others would tend either to ignore in themselves or to deny. And then his brilliance, combined with a certain impatience with fools, was bound to make him many enemies.

In recent years there has begun a re-evaluation of his Italian literary work, and as it progresses so does his stature increase. Many of his poems have been reunited with the music with which they were, at the time of composition, inseparable, and can be found on recordings of Italian music of the fifteenth century, particularly those of composers such as Heinrich Isaacs and Josquin Desprez. *Il Favolo d'Orfeo,* reconstructed and recorded by the Huelgas Ensemble, is available on CD. This first secular and musical drama of the Renaissance is usually mentioned at the beginning of books dealing with the history of opera.

The true face of Poliziano will only fully emerge once his Latin works are translated into either Italian or English. Until such times, there remain the ghosts of ill-repute which some still love to perpetuate, especially in works of history (which are often more fictional than novels). It is hoped that this novel may help lay a few of those ghosts, for it is my conviction that Poliziano was neither ugly nor repulsive, neither homosexual nor a pederast, that he did not have an incestuous relationship with his sister, nor was Maria a concubine living in his house under his name. All these things are reflections of the men who have tried to murder his reputation, either for their own benefit or for the sake of a 'good' story. The truth of him lies in his own works, and those of Giovanni Pico. For example, in Pico's 'Commentary on a poem about love by Benivieni', love between men is described as being more pure than the love of man for woman, as being indeed the Heavenly Venus, *but only insofar as it is chaste*. It is details of this kind which are overlooked by those who do not want their more florid images disturbed.

Regarding the role of women at the time, and the customs of marriage, there is a growing body of literature, including J. Kiershner, 'Pursuing Honor while Avoiding Sin: the Monte delle Doti of Florence', *Quaderni di Studi Senesi, 41* (Milan 1978), Christiane Klapisch-Zuber, *Women, Family, and Ritual in Renaissance Italy* (Chicago 1985), *Women of the Medieval World,* edited by Julius Kirshner and Suzanne F. Wemple (Oxford 1985), and *Saints and She Devils* (Foundation Werplaats Wetenschap en Maatschappij 1987).

St Jerome made two translations of the Psalter. The first was his translation out of Greek into Latin, but the original language was Hebrew. Once he had sufficiently mastered Hebrew, St Jerome made another and better translation. The second version was adopted everywhere except in Italy, which continued to use the first. A philologist such as Poliziano would have known this, and his desire for purity in language and preciseness in translation would have formed part of his objection to its use. The battle between him and Clarice is usually portrayed more simply, that he objected to the use of scripture in the education of children, giving a colour to his character which is misleading.

The painting *Pallas and the Centaur* by Botticelli, in the Uffizi Gallery, Florence, was probably painted 1483-4. It shows Pallas Athene (Minerva to the Romans) armed for battle and pulling up a centaur by the hair. Its symbolism is rich and multi-layered. The scene behind is said to be Naples, and the little galley the one carrying Lorenzo to the King. The interlocked rings and the laurel leaves on the robe of the goddess are devices of Lorenzo. The battle-axe signifies the blade of reason, while the centaur represents the dual nature of the soul, as described by Plato in *The Republic*: 'The soul is like the eye: when resting upon that on which truth and being shine, the soul perceives and understands and is radiant with intelligence; but when turned toward the twilight of becoming and perishing, then she has opinion only, and goes blinking about, and is first of one opinion and then of another, and seems to have no intelligence.' The centaur, half beast, half man, has its feet in the mundane world and its eyes turned to the heavenly. It was the work of Lorenzo, Ficino and the Platonic Academy to lift men's eyes to the realisation of their own nobility (*gentilezza*) and divinity.

ACKNOWLEDGEMENTS

THE AUTHOR and publishers would like to acknowledge the following as the source of various quotations in the text:

Quotations from Hermes Trismegistus are taken from *The Way of Hermes*, translated by Clement Salaman, Dorine van Oyen and William D. Wharton, 1999.

Quotations from Ficino's correspondence are taken from *The Letters of Marsilio Ficino,* translated by the Language Department of the School of Economic Science. For Ficino's letters to the main protagonists of the war, including prophecies and angelic messages, see Volume 5 (1994).

Quotations from Epictetus are from the translation of Hastings Crossley, 1925.

The passage describing lace is derived from Thomas Wright, *The Romance of the Lace Pillow*, 1919, reprinted 1982.

The opening verse to Virgil's *Aeneid* is from the translation by John Dryden.

The lines from Poliziano's *L'Orfeo* are from the translation by John Addington Symonds.

LIST OF SUBSCRIBERS

WE ARE VERY GRATEFUL for the generous support of the following in the publication of this book:

John Allitt
Kay Aldous
Raymond and Christina Auerbach
Mrs Muriel Baillie
Mary Barnes
Graham Blackbourn
Rosemary Broadbent
Ann Cadman
Noel Cobb and Maria Totman
J Cook
Darby Costello
JK Davis
Lesley Davis
Eileen and Norman Daw
Elizabeth Edmunds
Elizabeth Fairbairn
Arthur Farndell
Therese FitzGerald
Bill and Ann Fox
Mrs D L Francis
Dr Alice Greene
Jethryn Hall
John Hemmings
Brian Hodgkinson
David and Catherine Hodgkinson
Ursula Holden
Peter and Jill Holland
Margaret Hollis
Belinda Hunt
Candida Hunt
Marigold Hutton
G Keepax
R Keepax
Ulrike Kohler

Jill Line
Michael Macmillan
Charlotte Mendes da Costa
Joanna Migdal
Arthur Morgan
Jocelyn Morris, FSA
Robin Mukherjee
Jeremy Naydler
Geoffrey Parkes
Shirley Passey
Joanna Payne
Valerie Petts
Sine Pickles
Louanne Richards
Janice Rowan
Roger and Jacqueline Russell
Juliet Salaman
BW and PM Scott
Michael Shepherd
Claudia Shiebek
Andrew Sisson
Mr and Mrs B Skeggs
Jenny Spencer
Donna Thynne
Doreen Troman
Pamela Tudor Craig
Hugh Venables
Dr Angela Voss
Sue Walsh
Katharine Watson
Nir Wegrzyn
Kate Wells
Allegra Wint
Mary Zajicek

A TABERNACLE FOR THE SUN

THE FIRST VOLUME in the Botticelli Trilogy, of which *Pallas and the Centaur* is the second, is narrated by Tommaso dei Maffei. Forced to leave his native Volterra after its destruction by the forces of his idol, Lorenzo de' Medici, Tommaso is taken to Florence and apprenticed as a scribe just as the printing press is coming into use. It is a time of political and social upheaval, the power of the Medici challenged by the Pazzi family, the Pope and Tommaso's own family. An uprising is imminent and Tommaso must choose. Does his loyalty lie with the cultural and spiritual values of the Platonic Academy, of which Lorenzo is patron, or with his own family and their desire for revenge for the sack of Volterra?

This brilliant and lyrical first novel portrays all the colour and vivacity of Renaissance Florence. Resonant of today's conflicts, it challenges ideas of democracy and freedom in our own violent age. A memorable and enthralling debut which will establish Linda Proud as one of the most thoughtful writers of the decade. ALLISON AND BUSBY, PUBLISHERS

A truly wonderful book operating on so many levels… There is much wisdom in it. TIM PEARS

This is historical fiction at its best.
TOWSE HARRISON, *HISTORICAL NOVELS REVIEW*, AUG. 1998

I have studied the Florentine Renaissance all my life – but nothing, not even walking in the streets, brings it to life as this book does.
PAMELA TUDOR CRAIG

The Etruscans, Volterra, Impruneta, etc. – [Linda Proud] knows these places better than anyone I know in Tuscany. GIOVANNI CASELLI

The research in art, history and philosophy is breathtakingly thorough, and a moral uplift reminiscent of Mary Stewart's Arthurian trilogy carries you through the densely woven tapestry of people, politics and teeming city-scapes. RUTH PADEL, *MAIL ON SUNDAY*, 23 NOV 1997

GODSTOW PRESS

Because philosophy arises from awe, a philosopher is bound in his way to be a lover of myths and poetic fables. Poets and philosophers are alike in being big with wonder. St Thomas Aquinas

THE SONG OF ORPHEUS, the music that charms stones, wild animals and even the King of Hades, is the song of poets who have a sense of the divine at heart. For the forces of greed and evil to succeed, that song must be drowned out by noise.

What is today if not noisy? Not only in our society but within ourselves there is the clamour of many distractions. Just living life we forget ourselves and the song that we heard as children is heard but rarely if at all.

The aim of Godstow Press is to sing the Orphic song, through books of fiction, poetry and non-fiction, as well as through CDs. Besides publishing first editions we shall include on our list works which have been privately produced by writers and musicians who have thought, perhaps, that they sing alone.

Together, artist and audience, we shall form a choir.

We have no plans at the moment to make our books available through the trade and we depend entirely on personal contact with readers. For more information and inclusion in our database, please get in touch with us.

Godstow Press
60 Godstow Road
Wolvercote
Oxford
OX2 8NY
UK

www.godstowpress.co.uk

info@godstowpress.co.uk

tel +44 (0)1865 556215
fax +44 (0)1865 552900